REMEMBER

*Also by Karen Kingsbury and
Gary Smalley in Large Print:*

Redemption

*Also by Karen Kingsbury
in Large Print:*

Oceans Apart
One Tuesday Morning
A Time to Embrace
A Treasury of Miracles for Women:
    True Stories of God's Presence Today

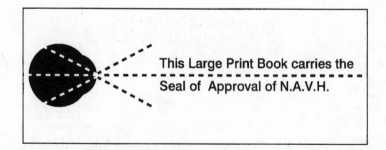

REMEMBER

Karen KINGSBURY
with Gary SMALLEY

Thorndike Press • Waterville, Maine

Redemption Series #2

Most Scripture used in this book, whether quoted or paraphrased by the characters, is taken from the *Holy Bible*, New International Version®. NIV®. Copyright © 1973, 1978, 1984 by International Bible Society. Used by permission of Zondervan Publishing House. All rights reserved.
Scripture quotation of Psalm 23 on p. 537 is taken from the *Holy Bible*, King James Version.

Published in 2005 by arrangement with
Tyndale House Publishers, Inc.

Thorndike Press® Large Print Christian Fiction.

The tree indicium is a trademark of Thorndike Press.

The text of this Large Print edition is unabridged.
Other aspects of the book may vary from the original edition.

Set in 16 pt. Plantin by Minnie B. Raven.

Printed in the United States on permanent paper.

Library of Congress Cataloging-in-Publication Data

Kingsbury, Karen.
    Remember / by Karen Kingsbury with Gary Smalley.
        p. cm. — (Thorndike press large print Christian fiction)
    ISBN 0-7862-7326-7 (lg. print : hc : alk. paper)
    1. Large type books. 2. Indiana — Fiction. 3. Young women — Fiction. 4. Alzheimer's disease — Patients — Fiction.
5. September 11 Terrorist Attacks, 2001 — Fiction. I. Smalley, Gary. II. Title. III. Thorndike Press large print Christian fiction series.
PS3561.I4873R46 2005
  813'.54—dc22   2004025475

TO OUR PRECIOUS FAMILIES,
who provide us with amazing memories
and countless seasons to remember.

AND TO THE AUTHOR OF LIFE,
who has, for now, blessed us with these.

As the Founder/CEO of NAVH, the only national health agency solely devoted to those who, although not totally blind, have an eye disease which could lead to serious visual impairment, I am pleased to recognize Thorndike Press* as one of the leading publishers in the large print field.

Founded in 1954 in San Francisco to prepare large print textbooks for partially seeing children, NAVH became the pioneer and standard setting agency in the preparation of large type.

Today, those publishers who meet our standards carry the prestigious "Seal of Approval" indicating high quality large print. We are delighted that Thorndike Press is one of the publishers whose titles meet these standards. We are also pleased to recognize the significant contribution Thorndike Press is making in this important and growing field.

Lorraine H. Marchi, L.H.D.
Founder/CEO
NAVH

* Thorndike Press encompasses the following imprints: Thorndike, Wheeler, Walker and Large Print Press.

Authors' Note

The Redemption series is set mostly in Bloomington, Indiana. Some of the land-marks — Indiana University, for example — are accurately placed in their true settings. Other buildings, parks, and establishments will be nothing more than figments of our imaginations. We hope those of you familiar with Bloomington and the surrounding area will have fun distinguishing between the two.

The New York City settings combine real observation with imaginative re-creation.

Acknowledgments

In addition to our families and wonderful support teams, we'd like to thank the good people at Tyndale House Publishers for sharing our dream and vision and helping make the Redemption series a reality. A special thanks to Ron Beers, Ken Petersen, and Lynn Vanderzalm for their determination to see this series be everything it could possibly be and to Anne Christian Buchanan for her freelance editorial contribution.

Also thanks to our agent, Greg Johnson, at Alive Communications. Greg, you are a builder of dreams, a talented man who allows yourself to be used of God at every turn. This series wouldn't have happened if you hadn't first introduced us. Thank you a million times over.

A special thanks to the brave men and women of the FDNY and the NYPD, as well as to the countless volunteers who answered questions at Ground Zero and helped lend credibility to this story. We hurt alongside you; we pray along with you. We always will.

Finally, thanks to Sherri Reed for allowing us dozens and dozens of hours with Alzheimer's patients and for opening to us a world of research and theories we once knew nothing about. The time spent with those people has left us forever changed. Thank you for your kind heart and your amazing gift with the forgotten ones among us. We pray this book sheds light on the struggles and issues facing the elderly — especially those with Alzheimer's disease.

Chapter One

Dr. John Baxter received news of the fire the moment he arrived at St. Anne's Hospital that afternoon. An emergency-room nurse flagged him down on his way back from rounds, her face stricken.

"Stay nearby; we might need you. An apartment complex is burning to the ground. A couple of families trapped inside. At least two fatalities. And we're already shorthanded."

John felt the familiar rush of adrenaline that came with working around disaster. He filled in only occasionally at the hospital emergency room — in the summers when he didn't have classes to teach, or when a disaster of some sort demanded extra personnel. But for him the excitement of ER medicine never lessened. It was as quick and consuming now as it had ever been.

He glanced at the others making preparations and then back to the nurse. "What happened?" Already sirens were blaring across Bloomington.

The nurse shook her head. "No one's sure. They're still working the blaze. They lost track of two men, firefighters." She paused. "Everyone's fearing the worst."

Firefighters? John's heart sank to his waist.

He followed her into the back, where a flurry of medical personnel were preparing for the first victims. "Did you get their names? The missing men?"

The nurse stopped and turned around. "It's Engine 211. That's all we've got so far."

John felt the blood drain from his face as he launched into silent, fervent prayer. He prayed for the people fighting the fire and the families trapped inside — and for the missing men of Engine 211.

He pictured them lost in an inferno, risking their lives to save mothers and fathers and children. He imagined them buried beneath burning rubble or cut off from all communications with their chief.

Then he prayed for one of Engine 211's men in particular. A strapping young man who had loved John Baxter's middle daughter, Ashley, since the two of them were teenagers.

The money was running out.

That was the main reason Ashley Baxter

was out looking for a job on that beautiful summer morning — the type of blue-skied, flower-bursting day perfect for creating art.

The settlement from her car accident four years ago was almost gone, and though she'd paid cash for her house, she and little Cole still needed money to live on — at least until her paintings began to sell.

Ashley sighed and ran her hand through her short-cropped, dark hair. She studied the ad in the paper once more:

Care worker for adult group home. Some medical training preferred. Salary and benefits.

As mundane as it sounded, it might be just the job she wanted. She'd checked with her father and found out that caregiver pay tended to be barely above minimum wage. She'd be working mostly with Alzheimer's patients — people with dementia or other age-related illnesses, folks unable to survive on their own. She would have wrinkled bodies to tend, hairy chins to wipe, and most likely diapers to change. The job wasn't glamorous.

But Ashley didn't mind. She had reasons for wanting the job. Since returning from her sojourn in Paris, everything about her life had changed. She was only twenty-five, but she felt years older, jaded and cynical. She rarely laughed, and she wasn't the kind of mother Cole needed. Despite the heads she turned, she felt old and used up — even ugly.

Paris was partly to blame for who she had become. But much of it was due to all the running she had done since then. Running from her parents' viewpoints, their tiresome religion, their attempts to mold her into a woman she could never be. And running from Landon Blake — from his subtle but persistent advances and the predictable lifestyle she'd be forced into if she ever fell in love with him.

Whatever the reason, she was aware that something tragic had happened to her heart in the four years since she had come home from Europe. It had grown cold — colder than the wind that whipped across Bloomington, Indiana, in mid-January. And that, in turn, was affecting her only true passion — her ability to paint. She still worked at it, still filled up canvases, but it had been years since she did anything truly remarkable.

Ashley turned off South Walnut and began searching for the address of the group home. In addition to bringing in a paycheck, working with old people might ward off the cold deep within her, might even melt the ice that had gathered around her soul over the years. She had always felt a kind of empathy for old folks, an understanding. Somehow they stirred a place in her heart that nothing else could touch.

She remembered driving through town a week ago and seeing two ancient women — hunched-over, gnarled old girls, probably in their nineties — walking arm in arm down the sidewalk. They had taken careful, measured steps, and when one started to slip, the other held her up.

Ashley had pulled over that afternoon and studied them from a distance, thinking they'd make a good subject for her next painting. Who were they, and what had they seen in their long lifetimes? Did they remember the tragedy of the *Titanic*? Had they lost sons in World War II — or had they themselves served somehow? Were the people they loved still alive or close enough to visit?

Had they been beautiful, flitting from one social event to another with a number of handsome boys calling after them? And did they grieve the way they'd become invisible — now that society no longer noticed them?

Ashley watched the women step carefully into an intersection and then freeze with fear when the light turned, catching them halfway across. An impatient driver laid on his horn, honking in sharp, staccato patterns. The expression on the women's faces became nervous and then frantic. They hurried their feet, shuffling in such a way that they nearly fell. When they reached the other side, they stopped to catch their breath, and again Ashley wondered.

Was this all that was left for these ladies — angry drivers impatient with their slow steps and physical challenges? Was that all the attention they'd receive on a given day?

The most striking thing about the memory was that as the questions came, Ashley's cheeks had grown wet. She popped down the visor and stared at her reflection. Something was happening to her that hadn't happened in months. Years, even.

She was crying.

And that was when she had realized the depth of her problem. The fact was, her experiences had made her cynical. And if she was ever going to create unforgettable artwork, she needed something more than a canvas and a brush. She needed a heart, tender and broken, able to feel in ways she'd long since forgotten.

That afternoon as she watched the two old women, a thought occurred to Ashley. Perhaps she had unwittingly stumbled upon a way to regain the softness that had long ago died. If she wanted a changed heart, perhaps she need only spend time with the aged.

That's why the ad in this morning's paper was so appealing.

She drove slowly, scanning the addresses on the houses until she found the one she was looking for. Her interview was in five minutes. She pulled into the driveway, taking time to study the outside of the building. "Sunset Hills Adult Care Home" a sign read. The building was mostly brick, with a few small sections of beige siding and a roof both worn and sagging. The patch of grass in front was neatly manicured, shaded at the side by a couple of adolescent maple trees. A gathering of rosebushes struggled to produce a few red and yellow blossoms in front of a full-sized picture window to the right of the door. A wiry, gray-haired woman with loose skin stared out at her through the dusty glass, her eyes nervous and empty.

Ashley drew a deep breath and surveyed the place once more. It seemed nice enough, the type of facility that drew little or no attention and served its purpose well. What was it her father called homes like this one? She thought for a moment, and it came to her.

Heaven's waiting rooms.

Sirens sounded in the distance, lots of them. Sirens usually meant one thing: it'd be a busy day for her father. And maybe Landon Blake. Ashley blocked out the sound and checked the mirror. Even she could see the twinlike resemblance between herself and Kari, her older sister. Other than Kari's eyes, which were as brown as Ashley's were blue, they were nearly identical.

But the resemblance stopped there.

Kari was good and pure and stoic, and even now — five months after the death of her husband, with a two-month-old baby to care for by herself — Kari could easily find a reason to smile, to believe the best about life and love.

And God, of course. Always God.

Ashley bit her lip and opened the car door. Determination mingled with the humid summer air as she grabbed her

18

purse and headed up the walkway. With each step, she thought again of those two old ladies, how she had cried at their condition — lonely, isolated, and forgotten.

As Ashley reached the front door, a thought dawned on her. The reason the women had been able to warm the cold places in her heart was suddenly clear.

In all ways that mattered, she was just like them.

There was no way out.

Landon Blake was trapped on the second floor somewhere in the middle of the burning apartment complex. Searing walls of flames raged on either side of him and, for the first time since becoming a firefighter, Landon had lost track of the exits. Every door and window was framed in fire.

His partner had to be somewhere nearby, but they'd separated to make the room checks more quickly. Now the fire had grown so intense, he wasn't sure they'd ever find each other in time. Landon grabbed his radio from its pocket on his upper jacket and positioned it near his air mask. Then he turned a valve so his words would be understood.

"Mayday . . . Mayday . . ."

He stuck the radio close to his ear and waited, but only a crackling static answered him. A few seconds passed, and the voice of his captain sounded on the radio.

"Lieutenant Blake, report your whereabouts."

Hope flashed in Landon's heart. He placed the radio near the valve in his mask once more. "Lieutenant Blake reporting Mayday, sir. I can't find my way out."

There was a pause. "Lieutenant Blake, report your whereabouts."

Landon's stomach tightened. "I'm on the second floor, sir. Can you hear me?"

"Lieutenant Blake, this is your captain. Report your whereabouts immediately." A brief hesitation followed; then the captain's tone grew urgent. "RIT enter the building now! Report to the second floor. I repeat, RIT report to the second floor."

RIT? Landon forced himself to breathe normally. RIT was the Rapid Intervention Team, the two firefighters who waited on alert at any job in case someone from the engine company became lost in the fire. The command could mean only one thing: Landon's radio wasn't working. His captain had no idea that he'd become separated from his partner or where to begin looking for him.

Landon made his way into the smoky hallway and heard his radio come to life again. He held it close to his ear.

"This is an alert. We have two men trapped on the second floor, and the radios aren't working for either of them. Backup units are on the way, but until then I need everyone in the building. Let's move it!"

So he was right. The radios weren't working. *Dear God, help us. . . .*

Landon fought off a wave of fear. In situations like this he'd been trained to scan the room for victims and then fight his way out of the building. Choose the most likely place for an exit and barge through burning beams and broken glass. Do whatever it took to be free of the building.

But Landon had gone back into the building for one reason: to find a five-year-old boy in one of the apartments. He would find the child — dead or alive — and bring him out. He had promised the boy's frantic mother, and he didn't intend to break the promise.

The smoke grew dense, dropping visibility to almost nothing. Landon fell to his knees and crawled along the floor. The flames roared on either side of him, filling his senses with intense heat and smoke. *Don't think about the broken radios. They'll find me any minute. Help is on the way. Please, God.*

He still had his personal accountability safety system, a box on his air pack that would send out a high-pitched sound the moment he stopped moving. If that signal worked, there was still a pretty good chance his engine company might locate him. But they'd have to get here fast. If they waited much longer, ceiling beams would begin to fall. And then . . .

Landon squinted through the smoke, his body heaving from the excruciating heat and the weight of his equipment. *God, help me.* He crept through a burning hallway door. *I need a miracle. Show me the boy.*

Just ahead of him he saw something fall to the ground — something small, the size of a ceiling tile or maybe a wall hanging. Or a small child. Landon lurched ahead and there, at the bottom of a linen closet, he found the boy and rolled him onto his back. He held a glove against the boy's chest and felt a faint rise and fall.

The child was alive!

Landon jerked the air mask from his own face and shoved it onto the boy's. He switched the mask from demand to positive pressure, forcing a burst of air onto the child's face. The boy must have hidden in the closet when the fire started, and now here they were — both trapped. Landon coughed hard and tried to breathe into his coat as the acrid smoke invaded his lungs.

Then he heard crashing sounds around him, and he glanced up. *No, God, not now.*

Flaming pieces of the ceiling were beginning to fall! He hovered over the child and used his body as a covering. Inches from the boy's face, he was struck by the resemblance. The boy looked like a slightly older version of Cole, Ashley's son.

"Hang in there, buddy!" Landon yelled above the roar of the fire. He removed the mask from the boy for just an instant and held the child's nose while he grabbed another precious lungful of air. Then he quickly replaced the mask over the boy's face. "They're coming for us."

He heard a cracking sound so loud and violent it shook the room. Before Landon could move, a ceiling beam fell from the roof and hit him across the back of his legs. He felt something snap deep inside his right thigh, and pain exploded through his body. *Move,* he ordered himself. He strained and pushed and tried to leverage the beam off his leg. But no matter how hard he tried he couldn't get free. His legs were pinned by the burning wood.

"God!" The pain intensified, and he reeled his head back, his jaw clenched. "Help us!"

He fought to stay conscious as he lowered himself over the boy once more. His training had taught him to limit his inhalations, but his lungs screamed for air, and he sucked in another deep breath. The smoke was choking him, filling his body with poisonous fumes and gasses that would kill him in a matter of minutes — if the falling debris didn't bury them first.

His air tank was still half full, so the boy should be breathing okay — as long as Landon stayed conscious enough to buddy-breathe with him.

The heat was oppressive. The visor on his helmet was designed to melt at 350 degrees — a warning that a firefighter was in a dangerous situation. Landon glanced up and saw a slow, steady drip of plastic coming from just above his forehead.

This is it. There's no way out.

He could feel himself slipping away, sense himself falling asleep. He borrowed the mask once more, gulped in one more breath of air, then firmly placed the mask back on the child's face. *Keep me awake, God . . . please.* He meant to say the words out loud, but his mouth wouldn't cooperate. Gradually, the pain and noise and heat around him began to dim.

I'm dying, he thought. *We're both going to die.*

And in the shadows of his mind he thought about the things he'd miss. Being a husband someday, and a father. Growing old beside a woman who loved him, standing beside her through the years, watching their children grow up.

A memory came to him, sweet and clear. His mother, frowning when she first learned of his intention to fight fires. "I worry about you, Landon. Be careful."

He had smiled and kissed her forehead. "God wants me to be a firefighter, Mom. He'll keep me safe. Besides, he knows the number of my days. Isn't that what you always say?"

The memory faded as smoke burned its way down his throat again. A dark numbness settled over Landon's mind, and he was struck by an overwhelming sadness. He held his breath, the smoke strangling what little life remained in him. He no longer had the strength to choke out even a single cough, to try for even one more breath of clean air. *So this is it, God. This is it.*

His impending death filled him not with

fear, but with bittersweet peace. He had always known the risks of being a firefighter. He accepted them gladly every day when he climbed into his uniform. If this fire meant that his days were up, then Landon had no regrets.

Except one.

He hadn't gotten to tell Ashley Baxter good-bye.

Chapter Two

The place smelled like urine and mothballs.

Ashley shut the door carefully behind her and looked around. The front door led directly into an oversized living room lined with four faded recliners, three of them occupied by shrunken, white-haired women. The house was warm — too warm — but each of the women was buried beneath at least one homemade afghan.

Ashley spotted an old television set in the corner of the room. *A relic, like everything else,* she thought. The tinny dialogue of a morning talk show rattled from its fabric-covered speakers. A cheap VCR sat on top of the TV, a few battered video boxes stacked beside it.

Only one of the residents was awake.

Footsteps sounded, and Ashley turned to see a slender woman with conservative gray hair bustle around the corner. "Ashley Baxter?"

Ashley stood a bit straighter and flashed a smile. "Yes."

"I'm Lu." The woman held out her hand. Perspiration dotted her upper lip and she was out of breath, as though she'd spent the morning running from one end of the house to the other. The corners of Lu's mouth rose but stopped short of a smile. "I own the place. We spoke on the phone." Her eyes gave Ashley a quick once-over, taking in her dark jeans, duster-length rayon jacket, and bright-colored shell. "You're on time. I like that." She turned and motioned for Ashley to follow her down a long hallway. "This is the third vacancy we've had this year." She sighed, and the sound of it trailed behind her like exhaust fumes.

Definitely overworked.

They entered an office at the back of the house. A stout woman in her early forties spilled over an orange vinyl chair.

"This is Belinda; she's the office manager." Lu didn't stop for the introduction but continued across the office to a small desk made of pressed wood. The surface was cluttered with documents, a dozen different sizes and colors.

Belinda wore aqua stretch pants and a T-shirt that read "Don't even go there!" She crossed her arms and glared at Lu. "Your ad should read 'No pretty girls.' "

Ashley took the only other chair and narrowed her eyes at Belinda. Maybe this wasn't such a good idea after all.

"Oh, quit." Lu clucked her tongue against the roof of her mouth. "Give her a chance."

"Pretty girls never last." Belinda sneered in Ashley's direction. "Too much lifting." A laugh devoid of any humor slipped from her throat. "Let's get this over with."

"Look." Ashley started to stand. "Maybe I should leave."

"Nonsense." Lu waved her hands in the air as though she were shooing away a swarm of bees. "Don't mind Belinda. She needs a vacation."

She needs more than that, Ashley thought. But she kept quiet and sat somewhat stiffly in the chair.

Lu snatched a pair of bifocals from the desk drawer and set them low on the bridge of her nose. Then she sifted through the papers until she found Ashley's application.

"Hmmm." Lu scanned the piece of paper. "No experience."

"No, ma'am." Ashley kept her eyes from Belinda. The interview was going from bad to worse. She couldn't imagine working for a miserable woman like Belinda. No wonder they had trouble keeping help.

"You understand the job duties?" Lu handed Ashley a printed list. "Alzheimer's patients are often delusional. At Sunset Hills it's our job to keep them grounded. In other words, we do everything we can to make them live in the here and now."

Ashley glanced at the list of tips and suggestions for working with Alzheimer's patients: *Use simple sentences. Remind them where they are and who they are. Ask them if they need to use the bathroom. Suggest daytime naps when they're —*

"You're a . . . ?" Lu lifted her eyes to Ashley's. ". . . a painter, is that it?"

The list fell to Ashley's lap. Her patience was wearing thinner than the plasterboard walls. "I'm an artist." She hesitated. "Actually, it's more of a hobby for now."

Belinda chuckled. "What she means is, painting don't pay the bills."

"Wait a minute." Ashley shot the heavy woman a hard look. There was no point being polite. If the job wasn't going to work out, they'd all be better off knowing up front. "You run the house here, right?"

"Ten years straight." Belinda lifted her chin.

Ashley looked at Lu. "She doesn't want to work with me. We're wasting our time."

"It's not her decision." Lu glared at Belinda. "I do the hiring around —"

"Look," Belinda cut in. She crossed her arms and raised her eyebrows an inch. "People come here thinking they'll spend all day baking cookies and watching soap operas with Grandma. It isn't like that." She cast a dismissive glance at Ashley. "Pretty Girl needs to know the facts; that's all."

Ashley locked eyes with Belinda and slowly rose from her chair. Then without blinking she dropped to the floor and peeled off thirty purposeful push-ups. From the corner of her eye she saw Lu wink at Belinda. The heavyset woman could do nothing but stare at Ashley, her lower jaw hanging from her face.

When Ashley finished she stood up, dusted her hands on her jeans, and took her chair again. It wasn't the first time her morning workout routine had paid off. "Some of us pretty girls" — she was barely breathing hard — "are stronger than we look."

Belinda said nothing, but Lu took Ashley's application and tapped it on the desk. "When can you start?"

Anger seared its way through Ashley's veins. She shifted her attention to Lu. "I

31

didn't say I'd take the job."

"Fine." Lu shot another look of disdain at her manager. "Think about it for a day, and let me know tomorrow. I'd like you five days a week, seven to three."

Lu shook Ashley's hand and excused herself.

Before Ashley could leave, Belinda cleared her throat. "Look, I'm . . . uh, sorry. We needed someone yesterday, and . . . well, I didn't think you could handle the job." She shrugged. "Maybe I was wrong."

Memories of every other time Ashley hadn't measured up shouted at her. She wanted to spit at the woman and tell her what she could do with her apology. *Calm, Ashley . . . be calm.* She pressed her lips together and breathed in through her nose. "Don't worry about it."

Ashley left the room without saying good-bye. She was halfway through the main room when a rusty voice called to her from one of the recliners.

"Dear? Are you leaving?"

Ashley stopped and turned. One of the white-haired women was sitting straighter in her chair, smiling at Ashley, bidding her to come close. Images of Belinda's mocking face came to mind, and Ashley hesitated. *I have to get out of here.* She crossed the room and stood before the old woman.

"Yes." A gentle smile lifted the corners of Ashley's mouth. "I'm leaving."

The woman reached up and took Ashley's hand. Gently, with a strength borrowed from yesterday, the woman pulled her close. The skin on her face was translucent, gathered in delicate bunches. Her eyes were foggy from the years, but her gaze was direct. "Thank you for stopping by, dear. We should visit again sometime."

The words did unexpected things to Ashley's heart. "Yes." She ran her thumb over the old woman's wrinkled hand. "Yes, we should."

"My name's Irvel."

"Hi, Irvel. I'm Ashley."

"My goodness." Irvel stared at Ashley and brought a shaky hand up toward her face. With a featherlight touch, she brushed her fingers through a lock of Ashley's hair. "You have the most beautiful hair. Has anyone ever told you that?"

Ashley smiled. "Not lately."

"Well, it's true." Irvel strained to see past Ashley and out the window. "Hank's out fishing. He'll be here anytime."

"Hank?"

"My husband." Irvel worked her tired

33

lips into a smile. "He brings me here for tea. Peppermint tea." She managed a wink. "He likes fishing with the boys. Has plenty of fish tales when he comes back."

Ashley dropped to her knees and tried not to look confused. "Is that right?"

"He's later than usual." Fear fell like a veil over Irvel's face. "You don't think he's run into trouble, do you?"

"No, it's still early. When does he usually —"

Belinda rounded the corner and planted her hands on her hips. "Telling stories again, Irvel?"

Ashley's blood ran cold. Belinda's tone wasn't cruel or even unkind. It was patronizing — as though she were the parent and Irvel the distracted child.

Before Ashley could defend the woman, Irvel smiled, and a nervous chuckle sounded from her throat. "We were just talking about Hank." The corners of her mouth fell back into place. "He's . . . he's later than usual."

Belinda lowered her chin and raised her eyebrows. She patted Irvel on the back. "It's time for your nap, old girl."

Ashley felt the muscles in her jaw tense. "She doesn't look tired." Ashley shifted her gaze from Belinda back to Irvel. "We were

34

having a nice talk, weren't we?"

"Yes." Irvel patted Ashley's hand. Her face relaxed some, and she looked grateful to have Ashley as an ally. "We were talking about Hank's fish tales, right?"

"Right." Ashley tilted her head and smiled at the older woman. Somehow in their few minutes together, Ashley felt a connection with Irvel, the kind she had hoped to find with each of the residents if she'd been willing to take the job. Ashley flashed a warning look at Belinda but kept her tone even. "I want to hear all about Hank."

"Yeah, well . . ." Belinda huffed and rolled her eyes in a way that wasn't altogether mean. Then she lowered her face so she was inches from Irvel. "Hank's been dead fifteen years, Irvel. Remember?"

Ashley's heart dropped to the floor.

Hank was dead? The realization set in. Of course. These were Alzheimer's patients. Ashley wanted to cry. She would have done anything to shield the precious woman beside her from Belinda's cruel reminder.

"No. No . . . that's not true." Terror filled Irvel's eyes, and she began to shake her head in small, jerky movements. "Hank's fishing. He told me so this morning. Before tea."

Belinda's eyes grew wide, her tone bored and gently sarcastic, as though she and Irvel had this conversation every morning. "There's no tea, Irvel. You live in an adult care home, and Hank's been dead fifteen years."

Panic joined the emotions wreaking havoc on Irvel's expression. "But . . ." She looked at Ashley, desperate for help. ". . . my friend and I just had tea together. Hank always takes me to tea with my friends when he fishes." Her eyes implored Ashley. "Isn't that right, dear?"

Ashley shifted her gaze to Belinda as Lu's words came back to her. *We do everything to keep them living in the here and now.* Belinda's eyes dared her to find an acceptable answer for the old woman. Ashley faced Irvel again. "Tea was wonderful. We must do it again sometime."

"Yes." Peace flooded Irvel's eyes, easing the wrinkles on her forehead. "That would be lovely."

"Whatever." Belinda uttered a humorless chuckle under her breath and walked off toward the kitchen.

Irvel touched Ashley's hair again. "Has anyone ever told you, dear, you have the most beautiful hair? Short, but so very pretty."

36

"Thank you, Irvel." Ashley gave the woman's hand a light squeeze. "Now, if you'll excuse me, I have some business to take care of."

Irvel settled back in her recliner and nodded, holding Ashley's gaze. A contented smile settled low on her face. The woman seemed to draw strength from Ashley. "Everything's going to be all right, isn't it?"

"Yes, Irvel." Ashley looked beyond the woman's cloudy white cataracts to the soul behind them. "Everything's going to be fine."

Completely at ease once more, Irvel returned her attention to the television set. Around her, the other women continued to sleep peacefully. The moment the situation seemed stable, Ashley stepped into the adjacent kitchen and found Belinda scrubbing a pan.

"I need to talk to you." Ashley pointed down the hallway.

Belinda rolled her eyes but dried her hands on a dish towel and followed Ashley to a place out of earshot from Irvel and the others.

"Where's Lu?" Ashley crossed her arms.

"She's busy." Belinda was matter-of-fact, just short of being rude.

"Tell her I want the job."

"Old Irvel got to you, huh?" Belinda's expression was just short of a sneer. "Fine. Take the job. But don't come in here all high-and-mighty, thinking you're going to rescue Irvel." Belinda lowered her chin, the sarcasm gone. "Sometimes life's hard. I found that out the day my husband walked out on me. So what, right? Get over it. Didn't get much education growing up, so I work here. Tough, right? Break my back every day to make a living. That's life."

She paused, her eyes hard. "Ever heard of Vicodin?"

Ashley shook her head. Why was Belinda telling her this? To make up for her attitude earlier?

"Vicodin kills pain. I take it every other day just to survive. That's what working with these dear, sweet, old folks has done for me. Lifting them into the bath, heaving them into a chair, picking them up off the floor. It'll kill you eventually." She grabbed a quick breath. "So don't think you're going to be some kind of savior. People like ol' Hank die. That's life. The more the patients here understand that, the better off we all are. And that's why Irvel and her friends need to be grounded in the present day. It's what their families want, and it's part of the job. If you don't like it, maybe you should think about another line of work."

Ashley could think of a dozen smart responses, but she didn't feel like fighting. "I'll keep that in mind."

Belinda took a step backward. "I'll tell Lu to call you with a schedule."

Ashley felt the muscles in her face relax. As Belinda turned and walked back toward the kitchen, Ashley realized she was no longer angry at the heavyset woman.

She pitied her.

And somewhere in the back alleys of her soul — though she didn't often pray — Ashley begged God that the patients at Sunset Hills would help her remember what was important in life. That they not harden her heart the way they had hardened Belinda's.

But rather that they might revive it.

Chapter Three

Landon Blake's chances for survival were almost nonexistent.

Just before noon, he was wheeled into the emergency room, his long, muscled body motionless on the stretcher. He was unconscious, suffering from severe smoke inhalation, a fractured leg, and a burned back. A thin line across his uniform pants had melted into the back side of his thigh.

John Baxter was waiting for him in the ER. "God, help us," he whispered when he saw Landon's blood oxygen level. "We're going to need a miracle."

Paramedics, friends of Landon's, wheeled him into a treatment room and carefully lifted him onto a bed. John rattled off orders as the medical team sprang into motion. "Get his uniform off, but be careful."

The oxygen treatment tank was ready, and John slipped a mask over Landon's face. "Hang in there, Landon. Come on." It was unusual for a firefighter these days to suffer from such severe smoke inhalation. After all, Landon should have had breathing apparatus. Unless — for some reason — he hadn't used it.

The treatment was administered through a ventilator that would breathe mechanically for Landon, forcing clean, damp air mixed with medication into his lungs in an attempt to clean out the smoke and chemicals. But damage done in a fire was often too severe for the treatment to do much good.

The first hour was critical.

Red numbers flashed on a monitor. Minutes after his rescue, Landon's blood oxygen level had been in the seventies — barely high enough to live. Paramedics had intubated him immediately, but even now his oxygen level was dangerously low. He had mild burns on his throat, but miraculously his blood tests didn't show severe carbon monoxide poisoning.

A strapping young paramedic came up alongside John and stared at Landon. "We . . . we can't lose him, Doc. He's the best there is."

John glanced up and saw fear on the paramedic's face. For a moment their eyes held; then John looked back at Landon's still form. He crossed his arms tightly in front of him. "I've known Landon Blake since he was a boy." John pinched his lips together, his chin quivering. "I'm not letting go of him yet."

There was silence for a moment, and the paramedic coughed. "How's the boy? The one who came in before Landon?"

"He's fine." John gazed at the oxygen monitor. Eighty-nine . . . eighty-eight. . . . *Come on, Landon, breathe!* "The child has some smoke damage, but not bad." John shot a look at the paramedic. "It's amazing, really. He was in the fire as long as Landon. Smoke like that usually kills children first."

"Then you don't know?"

John leaned against Landon's bed. "Know what?"

"It was Landon. He gave the boy his air mask. Saved his life." The paramedic drew a steadying breath. "When the firemen found them, Landon was unconscious, collapsed over the boy like a shield. He'd covered his own mouth with the neck of his coat. Probably saved his life. Somehow he managed to use the weight of his arm to keep the air mask over the boy's face."

Realization settled over John like a damp cloak. While the child breathed from Landon's air tank, Landon had breathed smoke — thick, poisonous, deadly smoke. John looked at the monitor again. Ninety . . . eighty-nine . . . it would take a miracle. "What about the other firefighter, the one trapped with Landon?"

"He got out unharmed."

"Good." John gave a slow nod. "The next hour will be crucial."

The paramedic nodded, too choked up to speak. He took Landon's hand and squeezed it. "Breathe, buddy." He swallowed hard, his chin quivering. "We need you."

Long after the paramedic left, John stayed by Landon's side, monitoring his oxygen level and making sure his burns were being tended to. They weren't as bad as John had originally thought — probably more steam burns than anything else. The fireproof material in Landon's uniform pants must not have melted until the last few seconds. The burns were on only a small section on the back of his thighs and a few spots near his lower spine. They might even heal without skin grafts. He would need surgery to set his broken leg, but it was a clean break. It could have been worse. Besides, it wasn't Landon's burns or the broken leg that worried John.

It was his damaged lungs.

At the end of the first hour, Landon's oxygen had reached the low nineties — not where John wanted it, but better than before. At least Landon was alive.

The moment John could break away, he called home and told his wife what had happened.

"Oh, John . . . no." The concern in Elizabeth's voice was the same as if the news had been about one of their own children. "He's going to make it, isn't he?"

"It's too soon to tell." John was anxious to get back to Landon. "Tell Ashley, will you? She needs to know."

By then Landon's parents, his extended family, and half a dozen firemen had arrived at the hospital. One by one they'd been in to visit him, pray for him, encourage him to hold on.

John hoped Ashley would get the news quickly. He had a feeling her presence might mean more to the young man than all the other visits combined.

Two hours passed, then three, with no sign of Ashley. John checked on Landon as often as he could, and by four o'clock his oxygen meter read ninety-three. Still not good, but an improvement. As John's shift ended, a reporter from the local paper called.

"We understand the injured firefighter gave his air mask to a child, is that right?"

"Yes. The child is fine, scheduled to go home in the morning." John steadied his voice. "The firefighter is in critical condition. We'll know more tomorrow."

"So the firefighter's a hero."

"Yes." John swallowed a lump in his throat. "No question about it. His selfless efforts saved the boy's life."

The moment the interview was finished, John headed toward his car. He had to find Ashley. Landon's oxygen level was too low for his brain to survive, too low to sustain consciousness, especially given the fact that he was on a respirator. With mechanical help, Landon's numbers should have been in the high nineties. If they didn't improve soon, Landon might not live through the night. And if he did . . .

John shuddered at the thought of Landon confined to a bed, living the rest of his days brain damaged, in a vegetative state.

Wherever Ashley was, she needed to get to the hospital. Needed to let Landon hear her voice, tell him she was pulling for him, caring for him.

Or at least tell him good-bye.

Before time ran out for both of them.

★ ★ ★

Kari Baxter Jacobs — John and Elizabeth's second daughter — sat in the corner of the Baxter living room, cradling her daughter, Jessie. She and the baby had been visiting a friend, and she hadn't received word about Landon Blake until an hour ago. By the time she arrived at her parents' home in Clear Creek, just south of Bloomington, the house had been full of people praying for his survival. Kari's youngest sister, Erin Hogan; their brother, Luke; and his girlfriend, Reagan Decker, sat around the room, quiet and somber.

All of them guessing at places where they might find Ashley.

Kari glanced up from her baby and met her mother's eyes. "She left Cole with you this morning. Didn't she say when she'd be back?"

A sigh slipped from Elizabeth's lips. "The interview was supposed to be over before noon. I thought she'd come straight home."

"Typical Ashley move." Luke shifted to the floor and rested his back against Reagan's knees. Kari had watched the two of them grow close these past months, and she'd talked to Luke about his intentions. There was no question about it — Luke was in love. And Kari was convinced Reagan felt the same way.

Luke was still carrying on about Ashley's absence. "Poor Cole upstairs playing by himself and you stuck baby-sitting all day. Again." He sputtered. "I mean, come on, Mom. She could've at least called."

"I'm sure she has a reason."

"Sure, Ashley always has a reason. Especially when it's —"

Kari tuned them out. It didn't matter where Ashley was or why she wasn't home by now. What mattered was Landon Blake — struggling for his life, every breath an uncertainty.

Kari ran her finger over Jessie's tiny forehead, her mind wandering back to another time when she had waited for news about someone lying injured in a hospital bed. The years melted away, and Kari could hear the football game playing from the television in this very room, hear her father's voice calling her.

"Kari, quick! Ryan's been hurt."

His words were as clear now as they'd been all those years ago when Ryan Taylor had been nearly paralyzed. She had been in love with him back then, and she could still picture him lying on the football field, still see his distraught mother at the hospital later that night.

The memory faded, and a more recent one took its place. A memory of her and Ryan last year at Lake Monroe, where for the first time she had understood the truth about what happened so long ago, in the aftermath of his injury.

Kari blinked.

Since her husband, Tim, had been murdered, she'd done everything possible to avoid thoughts of Ryan Taylor. It simply wasn't the time. She was still reeling from last year's incredible sequence of events. First, Tim's bombshell — his affair with a college student. Then finding out she and Tim were expecting a baby. After that came Tim's refusal to talk with Kari or get counseling, all of which led to her rekindled closeness with Ryan Taylor.

And ultimately her decision — and Tim's — to do what was necessary to make their marriage work.

She would forever remember Tim's face, his tenderness toward her on the last morning of his life. They really had been growing close again, after all the hurt. Who would have thought it would all end so tragically, so senselessly? A stalker. A fanatical college kid on steroids bent on marrying Tim's lover. How was it possible that he'd shot Tim outside her apartment — when the only reason Tim had stopped by was to tell her he couldn't see her again, to assure her that he was in love with Kari and always would be? There'd been no tense hours of hospital waiting with Tim. He'd never had a chance; he was dead on arrival.

Jessie stirred and flopped a small hand against Kari's arm.

"That's right, sweetie. Mommy's here." Kari stared at her daughter, awed at the way the tiny baby in her arms had helped her through the past months.

She knew better than to dwell on the awful memories of Tim's death — or to let her mind camp too long on the shores of all she once shared with Ryan Taylor. As always when it came to Ryan, the timing was wrong. Ryan was in New York coaching the Giants, fulfilling a longtime dream. And she was here in Bloomington, a grieving widow learning how to be a single mom.

But now, with Landon in the hospital, Kari couldn't help but remember. And maybe that was all right. If she never walked through the past, never allowed the painful areas in her heart to heal, she would never be able to move forward.

The front door creaked. Kari's father walked quickly into view. He scanned the room. "Where is she?"

"Ashley hasn't been home all day." Elizabeth stood, and Kari watched her parents embrace. "How is he?"

Her father's gaze fell to the ground. When he looked up, Kari could see the weariness in his soul. "He might not make it through the night. His oxygen level is —"

Before her father could go into any detail, they heard the front door open again. This time it was Ashley. Kari saw her sister's eyes grow wide as she stopped short and took in the full house.

She has no idea what's happened, Kari thought. Then, without hesitating, Kari felt a prayer wind its way through the alleys of her mind. *Whatever happens to Landon, use this, God, please. Use it to help Ashley believe again.*

Ashley slowly pulled off her jacket. "What's going on?" She looked around the room, and her eyes settled on their father's stricken face.

Luke shifted forward, balancing himself on the edge of the sofa. Even angry, he looked handsome. Like a young Robert Redford, only taller. But he'd had little good to say about Ashley since she'd come home from Paris. "Nice of you to check in."

Ashley spun around and stared at Luke, her expression more surprised than angry. "What's that supposed to mean?"

Elizabeth put a hand on Ashley's shoulder. "We expected you hours ago, dear. I was worried."

For a moment Ashley's mouth hung open. "I told you I wasn't sure when I'd be back."

"Yes," their mother nodded. "But you said the interview would be over by noon."

"Okay, so I took care of some errands." Ashley gestured at the others gathered around the living room. "Is that what this is? Some kind of search party for crazy, irresponsible Ashley?"

Their father cleared his throat and stepped forward, bracing Ashley's shoulders with his hands. "Landon's hurt. He was trapped in a fire this morning." His voice was thick with emotion. "He inhaled a lot of smoke. We're . . . we're not sure he's going to make it."

Since they were teenagers, Kari had wondered about Ashley's feelings for Landon Blake. The poor boy had sought after Ashley year after year, getting barely a

51

friendship for his efforts. When he returned home after college, nothing had changed. He was still determined to love her, and she was equally determined to stay clear of him. Whenever Kari would ask about Landon, Ashley would deny having feelings for him. He's too predictable, she'd say. Too much like Mom and Dad.

But now, after hearing the news that he'd been hurt, Ashley's true feelings were clearer than water. She loved him. The depth of fear and desperation in her eyes told Kari that much.

Ashley raked her fingers through her hair and shifted nervously. "I thought they wore air masks."

"He gave his to a little boy. Saved the child's life."

For a moment she looked paralyzed. Then, as though she'd been jump-started into reality, she jerked back. "I have to be there." Ashley yanked her jacket on again. "Can I see him?"

"He's in ICU; I'll call and make sure they let you in." Dad leaned over and held Ashley close for a moment. "He needs you, Ash."

Ashley's eyes glistened as she glanced around the room. "Pray for him, okay?"

She swallowed hard, her hands shaking. "He . . . he loves God a lot. God'll help him. I know he will.

"Tell Cole I'll see him later." She turned to their mother. "I'll stay as long as they let me."

Elizabeth nodded. "Call us."

"Ashley . . ." Their father's face was masked in heavy concern. "Hurry, sweetheart. Please hurry."

Chapter Four

Ashley's heart stayed lodged in her throat until she was in Landon's room. Then it seemed to sink somewhere beneath her kneecaps.

Tubing ran into his arms, and a mask nearly covered his face. His leg was braced and wrapped to almost twice its normal size, and he was propped up on one side to avoid pressure on his burned back and thighs. A machine made rhythmic breathing sounds, forcing air into his lungs. Ashley grimaced at the mechanical rise and fall of Landon's chest. Otherwise he lay motionless among the busy beeps and whirrs of machinery.

She took a chair already stationed by his bed and stared at him. How had this happened? Bloomington never had dangerous fires. Not once had Ashley considered the possibility that Landon's job might put him in any real harm, let alone cost him his life.

Come on, Landon. Wake up.

She stared at him, willing him to move. In all the time she had known Landon, she'd held his hand only twice. The last time had been ages ago, long before she went to Paris. But here, now, Ashley sensed he needed her touch as much as she needed his. Tentatively, she reached out and took Landon's lifeless right fingers in her own, careful not to disturb the IV line. Tears stung at her eyes, and the image of Landon blurred.

She rose out of the chair so her face was closer to his. When she spoke, her voice was barely louder than the gentle hum of machinery keeping him alive. "I always thought you were too safe." Ashley ran her thumb over the top of Landon's hand. "You crazy guy. Now look at you."

Something seemed to move near the end of the bed. Was it Landon's foot? Ashley stared at his toes poking up beneath the blanket. A minute passed, then two, but there was nothing. Her father was right; Landon was unconscious. If he didn't start breathing on his own, if his oxygen levels didn't improve, he might not make it.

What if he died? What if she never got to talk to him or laugh with him again? All her adult life she'd known that Landon was in love with her, waiting for her, even when she did her best to maintain the distance between them. She remembered when he'd come to her parents' house the week before she left for Paris. That night when he said good-bye, they had lingered for a while beneath the moonlit sky.

"I'll miss you." Landon had leaned against his Blazer and stuffed his hands in his pockets, gazing down at Ashley with a crooked grin.

Ashley hadn't planned on an emotional scene with Landon. After all, he was setting off for college in a few weeks. She wanted to leave without any romantic ties in Bloomington, nothing to keep her from experiencing life in a city that breathed creativity. Regardless of their shared high school days, they were about to chase separate dreams.

She had stared at the gravel, dragging the toe of her tennis shoe in small circles before answering him. "Hey, you'll be fine." His words had rattled around in her heart while she tried to ignore them. "Besides, you'll be busy with all those college girls."

For a long while Landon had simply looked at her, almost as though he was trying to memorize her eyes, her face. When he finally spoke, he'd said something

Ashley remembered clearly to this day. "Just once" — he had given her a sad smile — "just once, I wish you'd look at me like you love me."

Even then, Ashley had refused to let her heart be sucked in, refused to acknowledge the feelings she had always had for Landon. Feelings that weren't exactly love, but were certainly deeper than ordinary friendship. Feelings of, well, *connection*, which frightened her more than any crush ever could have. But instead of allowing her eyes to reflect her deepest emotions, instead of kissing him as she'd done just once, she had made a joke. Pushed him or tickled him or kicked his foot — Ashley couldn't quite remember what. But in a matter of seconds the mood had changed, and they were back on more comfortable ground, teasing and laughing and wishing each other the best before saying good-bye.

A nurse entered the room, and Ashley jumped. Self-consciously she let go of Landon's hand and sat back in her chair. The nurse nodded at her and checked the monitors set up around the head of Landon's bed.

Ashley followed her every move, trying to determine from the look on the nurse's face whether Landon was doing better. "How is he?"

The nurse glanced at the clipboard in her hands. "About the same. We need to see an improvement in his blood oxygen level before morning." Her eyes raised and met Ashley's. "Are you his girl-friend?"

"No." Ashley's answer was quick, and instantly she regretted it. What if Landon could hear them? She gave a quick laugh. "I've known Landon forever. We're . . . we've always been close."

"Take another ten minutes." The nurse was fiddling with the IV bag. "After that, his parents want to see him again."

"Okay." Ashley nodded. "May I stay in the waiting room? I want to be here . . . when he wakes up."

The nurse smiled. "Definitely."

When she was gone, Ashley leaned forward and took Landon's hand once more. She still didn't know what she felt for this strong, handsome man who somehow always made her feel suffocated. If he were awake, she'd have no more promises for him now than she'd had that summer night before she went to Paris.

But here, watching him fight for his life, not sure if she would ever get a chance to speak to him again, Ashley was certain of one thing.

She loved Landon Blake. Loved him with a strength that took her breath away. The odd thing about it was that admitting she loved him didn't change anything. Not really. Strange that you could care for someone so fiercely and still be sure he was all wrong for you. And yet, the thought of losing him . . .

Ashley held her breath. Maybe that would stave off the sobs building in her heart. All her life people had hurt her or looked past her or misunderstood her. But not Landon. He had loved her with a singleness of purpose, believed in her long after she'd stopped believing in herself. But for all his kindness — for every time he'd walked away when she needed space or smiled when she deserved a cold shoulder — all she'd ever given him was grief.

Tears slid down the sides of her face, and she let her head fall against the railing of the hospital bed. Her time was almost up, and Ashley knew she might not have another chance. She squeezed her eyes shut and lifted her head, hoping that when she opened them, Landon would be awake, smiling at her, promising her he was going to survive.

Instead, he lay stone still, his chest still rising in time to the rhythm of the machine.

She drew an unsteady breath and bent close to his ear. "Landon, it's me — Ashley." Three small sobs worked their way to the surface, and she hesitated, waiting until she had control once more. "I keep thinking of all the times you made me smile. When you brought me those silly comic strips in high school and took me sailing. When you showed up at Cole's baby dedication and when you kept seeing me everywhere — like at that café or at the grocery store."

Fresh tears burned her cheeks. She sucked in two quick breaths and tried to find her voice. "Remember when you told me you wished I'd look at you like I loved you?"

Ashley smothered another wave of sobs with the sleeve of her jacket. "I'm . . . I'm sorry I never said it before." She steadied her voice. He deserved to know the depth of her feelings. The words he wanted to hear had to be said. Now. In case he didn't make it. In case he never —

She couldn't finish the thought. "I love you, Landon. I've always loved you." She sucked in another breath. "I still don't —"

She wanted to add that she still didn't want anything romantic with him, but she stopped herself. What was the point? He was unconscious, anyway. But in case he could hear her, she wanted him to know she cared. "That's all." Another sob constricted her throat, and she waited for it to pass. "I wanted to tell you before another minute passed."

As soon as the words were out of her mouth, Ashley felt as though her heart had grown wings. No, she wasn't in love with Landon. But if love could be measured by how much a person cared, then indeed she loved Landon deeply, and having told him so lifted a mountain off her shoulders. Everything about who she was and how she appreciated this man was suddenly alive and bursting within her, as though she'd somehow been in a prison and now she was finally free.

It was a feeling as wonderful and delicious as Christmas morning. And in the bustle of the ICU, in the remaining moments she had left with Landon, she had the sudden assurance that he was going to survive. She thought about Irvel and the job at Sunset Hills. The way her heart felt softer already.

Yes, they were both going to survive.

"Everyone's praying for you, Landon." She sniffed twice. "The little boy you went in after — he's doing great. You saved his life." She brought his hand to her lips and kissed it. "You're going to make it, Landon. I know it." She squeezed his hand tenderly. "I'll be here when you do."

The head ICU nurse on duty that night was filling out a patient chart at the desk when a beautiful young woman approached her. As she drew closer, the nurse could see she'd been crying. "I'm Ashley Baxter. Dr. Baxter's daughter." The pretty woman pointed down the hall. "I've been visiting Landon Blake. His family can see him now. I think they're in a private room somewhere." She tapped her finger softly on the desktop. "Please . . . if anything changes, I'll be in the waiting room."

The nurse nodded. "I'll find you." She bit her lip. If this was the doctor's daughter, then she already knew her firefighter friend was in grave danger. "Your friend's got the best doctor in Bloomington."

The Baxter woman managed a brief smile. "Thank you."

When the visitor was gone, the nurse grabbed Landon's chart and walked quickly back to his room. Last time she'd checked, his blood oxygen level was still in the low nineties. The ventilator was helping, but clearly the man's lungs had been damaged. Maybe beyond repair.

The nurse stepped into the room and stopped short, her mouth open. The man was working the fingers of his right hand. He was coming out of the coma! That could mean only one thing.

She shot a look at the monitor near his bed. His oxygen level was at ninety-seven. Ninety-seven! Somehow his body had found the strength to suck in far more air than before. She stared at the number and watched it climb to ninety-eight.

She couldn't think of another time when she'd seen a patient turn around so quickly. What had the doctor's daughter said or done while she was in here? Without waiting any longer, the nurse ran to find his family and tell them the news. Then she looked for Ashley Baxter.

When the nurse found her, she saw raw fear in the young woman's eyes. "Is he . . . is he worse?"

The head nurse smiled. "No. His oxygen level is higher. He's waking up."

The fear vanished, and in its place she saw hope and joy and relief mingled against the backdrop of something sparkly and soft and undeniable. Something that spoke of honor and a lifetime of memories. Something she had seen often enough to recognize.

And in that instant the head nurse knew why this woman's presence had so profoundly affected the injured man. He obviously had feelings for her, feelings deep enough that her voice had beckoned him off death's doorstep. Whatever their relationship was, the woman's eyes told at least half the story.

Dr. Baxter's daughter was in love with Landon Blake.

Chapter Five

Ashley spread the final layer of frosting over Erin's birthday cake and tried to get a grip on her emotions. This was no time to break down. Her parents were throwing a party for Erin, and the entire family would be here. Ashley bit her lip and planted a row of candles on the cake.

The Baxter house was the last place she wanted to be.

If she had any sense, she would have stayed home tonight, sat by the window and sorted through her feelings, or done a little painting. In all her life, she couldn't remember a more emotionally draining forty-eight hours. But she'd promised her mother she'd help set up the party, and she wasn't about to back out now. She exhaled hard and set the cake in the center of the counter. Cole was still down for his nap, and the house was quiet. The others wouldn't arrive for an hour or so.

She would simply have to do her thinking here.

How had things between her and Landon gotten so strained? Ashley took a stack of plates from the cupboard and began setting the table. One minute there had been the stark possibility of losing him, the thought that she might never see him again. The next moment she had felt the amazing joy of standing beside his bed with his family gathered round, holding Landon's hand while his father thanked God that he'd survived.

And sometime since then, the walls that so long had guarded her heart from him had shot up higher and more impenetrable than ever. Sometimes she wanted nothing more than to sit with Landon, encourage him about his recovery, and catch up on old times. But other times she desperately wanted to run.

Since Landon had regained consciousness, Ashley had sensed an unspoken obligation. As though somehow, in the time it took him to open his eyes and begin to speak, she had become his undisputed girlfriend.

It had all been so simple that first night. She loved him, no questions asked. And she had no regrets about voicing her feelings for him that night in the hospital room. How terrible it would have been for him to die without knowing how she felt. But those feelings didn't change things between them.

Now that he was awake, the issues that had always loomed between them seemed bigger than ever. They were too different, their views on life and faith and family too far apart for them to ever be a couple. Besides, she had a new job. On Monday she would report for duty and begin working with Irvel and her friends at Sunset Hills. In the process Ashley intended to learn something about the human heart, about the emotions she'd sent into exile while in Paris. When she wasn't working, she needed to care for Cole — even if she sometimes thought he'd rather be with her parents. And then there was her painting. If she was ever going to make her mark as a serious artist — something she fully intended to do — she needed to spend time with her art.

All of which meant she had no room in her life for Landon Blake, even if everyone else seemed to think otherwise. Especially her sister Kari, who always believed in the power of love — even now, when her unfaithful husband lay dead in the grave these past five months.

But why shouldn't Kari believe in love?

Kari had lost a husband, but she had Ryan Taylor waiting in the wings, whether she wanted to believe that or not. He might live a thousand miles away, but he was waiting — Ashley had no doubt of that. Even after all that had happened to Kari, the knowledge that Ryan was there for her and that the two of them were perfect for each other was bound to make things easier. Bound to encourage her to get on with life. Because Ryan Taylor was definitely a man worth moving on for.

Ashley thought of the day she and Ryan had spent together last December. Their lunch date, the conversation they'd shared. The kiss. As good as that afternoon had seemed at the time, it had been wrong. Ryan didn't love her; he loved Kari.

That much was obvious from how the day ended.

Ashley sucked in a deep breath. Ryan's quick departure that evening had dropped the temperature of her heart another ten degrees, even when she knew he was right to walk away. She'd never told anyone about what happened. How could she? Kari was the only one of her three sisters who still cared anything for her.

The other Baxter girls — Brooke and Erin — might have been on another planet, for all the closeness they shared with Ashley. And Luke was worse. No matter how close they'd been as children, Ashley's time in Paris had changed everything between them. Now her brother was little more than a stranger — a mean-spirited, judgmental stranger.

Her world had once revolved around this sprawling country house, her parents, and the brother and sisters she'd grown up with, but Ashley now felt little connection to any of them. They all wanted her to be like Kari, even if they never said as much. They wanted her to give up painting and get on with life — the way *they* thought her life should go. Which of course meant church attendance, volunteering for the PTA, making bread like her mom, being a much better mother than she currently was. Plus, if she could swing it, going back to school and landing a prestigious, high-paying medical job like Brooke's or a glamorous one like Kari's modeling. The whole works — all on top of a satisfying marriage to someone like Landon Blake. The truth was, they wanted her to see Landon the way the rest of them did: a man with the deepest sense of integrity and commitment, a man who might be a father to little Cole if only she'd allow it, a man who was sought after by single women across Bloomington, but who had eyes only for Ashley.

They just couldn't see what Ashley saw — that Landon Blake wasn't right for her.

Despite his job, he was too safe, too predictable. Too good. Life with him couldn't bring either of them anything but misery. Besides, the very thought of spending her life with Landon — or any other man, for that matter — was enough to make her heart race with anxiety. Landon's injury had helped her voice her feelings for him, but it hadn't changed the facts. Though she loved Landon, she wasn't in love with him. Not really. Not the way he wanted her to be.

Ashley checked the freezer to be sure there were two gallons of ice cream for the party. The cartons were there, of course. Her mother wouldn't forget a single detail. Birthdays were a big deal in the Baxter family. Even Ashley's.

They might not have agreed with her choice of quitting school to work full-time, or with her lack of faith, or with the amount of time she spent away from her young son. But they still celebrated her birthday.

Ashley walked slowly back into the

kitchen and took a dozen glasses from the cupboard. A sense of dread filled her when she thought about visiting Landon later. The air between the two of them now felt stiff, charged with tension. Forced almost. The way it had felt when she was a senior in high school and Landon had asked her out. Back when the idea of having a steady boyfriend and a predictable future had first begun to suffocate her.

There was only one possible explanation for their sudden awkwardness around each other: Landon had heard her that night when he lay in intensive care.

If that was true, if he could easily recall every word she said, then maybe he was waiting for her to say it again now that he was awake. Maybe he hadn't understood the kind of love she meant. If not, her silence on the matter was bound to have confused him. Certainly if she could make a declaration of love to him while he was near death, she could make it now that he was recovering, right?

At least that's how Landon might be seeing it.

From the front of the house, Ashley heard voices and she let go of her thoughts about Landon. Besides, she wasn't the only Baxter daughter who seemed to be struggling. Kari had shed her share of tears in the last year. And Erin hadn't been herself lately either. She was quieter, more withdrawn.

Maybe Erin and Sam needed a vacation now that school was out. Erin was a kindergarten teacher. After an entire year, she was bound to be depressed about saying good-bye to her students. Especially since she hadn't been able to have children.

A vacation might give Erin a whole new perspective.

Whatever the trouble, Ashley wanted Erin's birthday celebration to be happy. And as the others arrived and began filling the house, Ashley determined to hide her concerns about Landon. This was no time for her to be sorting through the jigsaw puzzle of her emotions looking for pieces that belonged together.

She would go by the hospital after dinner. But this was Erin's night. Ashley's feelings for Landon — whatever they were — would have to wait until after the party.

Kari walked into the kitchen and tossed her purse on the desk.

"Hey, Ash." She rolled up her sleeves. "Need some help?"

"Sure." Ashley's arms were full, and she

pointed her chin toward the counter. "Grab those napkins, okay?"

Kari did as she was told and followed Ashley into the dining room. "Where's Mom?"

"She went up to check on Cole. I was going to do it, but he'd probably rather have her, anyway."

Kari ignored her sister's defensive tone. She set the napkins on the table. "Any sign of Erin and Sam?"

"Not yet."

"Hmmm." Kari followed Ashley around the table, laying napkins at each place. "I'm worried about her."

"Me, too." Ashley arranged glasses in front of the last two plates. "She hasn't been herself."

Once the table was set, Kari stole a quick look at the stove timer. Their mother had made roasted chicken and squash, and Kari had barely enough time to make Jessie a bottle before dinner. What was it about Erin? Was she pregnant? Was that the reason for her recent moodiness? Or were she and Sam struggling?

Whatever the problem, Kari hoped to find out more this evening.

She measured the formula and added warm water, shaking it as she made her way into the family room. A baseball game played on television, and her father had Jessie propped up on his lap. "Can I feed her?"

Kari smiled at the picture her father and daughter made together. John Baxter was an accomplished doctor, respected by his patients and peers, but sitting there with Jessie, he looked like a little boy begging quarters for the candy store.

"Yes, Dad." Kari handed him the bottle. "Her tummy's a little upset, though." Kari grinned. "Don't say I didn't warn you."

He held Jessie up and wiggled his nose against hers. "Papa's not scared of crummies in the tummy, is he?" He shot Kari a look. "Besides, if I could feed you, I can feed her. You still hold the record for baby mess-ups."

"Ah yes, the good old days." Her mother entered the room, holding a sleepy-eyed Cole by the hand. Cole pressed against his grandmother's side, clearly not up to conversation yet. Kari ruffled his hair, and he treated her to a little smile.

"Could you do the salad, Kari?" Her mother grinned as she sat down and pulled Cole onto her lap. "Since Grandma and Papa are busy with more important matters?"

A ripple of laughter tickled Kari's throat, and she reveled in how good it felt. Very gradually, in fits and starts, her sense of life and love and laughter was returning. She remembered a verse Pastor Mark had quoted in a sermon recently: "The joy of the Lord is your strength."

It was true; she was living proof. The greater the joy that stirred in her heart, the stronger she felt. And the more she was able to believe she would somehow survive despite everything that had happened. And despite the confusion and emotional numbness that still seemed to darken most of her days.

In a matter of minutes dinner was ready, and the entire Baxter family gathered around the old oak table. Over the years her parents had added two leaves so that it was long enough to accommodate their growing family. Brooke and her husband, Peter, sat at one end with their young daughters, four-year-old Maddie and two-year-old Hailey. Across the table were Luke and Reagan and, next to them, Erin and Sam. Ashley and Cole sat at the other end with Kari. And in the middle — together as always — were their parents.

When their father had finished praying, he turned to Ashley. "Landon's doing remarkably well. One of the nurses tells me you've been in to see him every day."

Ashley stared at the mound of squash on her plate and nodded.

John gave the others a quick update on Landon's condition. "Truthfully, I didn't think he'd survive that first night. I've never seen anyone pull through that kind of lung damage."

Kari watched Ashley and felt her sister's pain. Earlier that morning they'd talked about her feelings for Landon. Somehow in the mix of wanting him to survive, Ashley feared she might have unintentionally given him the impression she was in love with him.

"You poor girl," Kari had told her.

"What? It's not me I'm worried about; it's Landon. He needs to focus on getting better, not worrying about someone who's been hurting him since junior high."

"That's not what I mean." Kari had given her a gentle smile.

Ashley had blinked. "I don't understand."

"You don't see it."

"See what?" The conversation had taken place at Kari's house. Ashley had been sitting on the floor, her knees hugged close to her body.

"You gave Landon the impression you're

in love with him because you are."

Ashley had denied every bit of it. But Kari was convinced otherwise.

The timing was wrong — that much was certain. Ashley was still trying to figure out who she was. But Kari had no doubts that when Ashley was finished fighting her feelings, the truth would be obvious. And that one day Landon Blake would occupy another chair around the Baxter dinner table.

But now, with the others watching Ashley's reaction, waiting for her to share something about Landon, Kari felt sorry for her. She slipped an arm around her sister's shoulders and grinned. "Ashley has a new job. Does everyone know that?"

The conversation hopscotched from the old folks at Sunset Hills Adult Care Home to the escapades of Maddie, Hailey, and Cole to the frustrations shared by the doctors in the family that the blood bank was at an all-time low.

When dinner was nearly finished, Erin looked at Sam and flashed him a brief smile. As if on cue, he cleared his throat and pushed back from the table. Taking Erin's hand in his, he scanned the eyes of those around him. "Erin and I have an announcement to make."

Immediately Kari felt the excitement

build within her. An announcement from Erin and Sam could mean only one thing: They were going to have a baby! That would explain the recent changes in Erin's personality. She was probably suffering morning sickness. Yes, that had to be it. Kari studied her youngest sister. Another baby in the family! How wonderful would that be?

Sam was practically glowing, but . . . Kari shifted her attention to Erin. If she knew her sister at all, that wasn't gladness in Erin's eyes. It was pain and sorrow, the kind that could not possibly be associated with pregnancy. Kari held her breath.

With everyone waiting, Sam continued. "I've been offered a job in Texas." He could barely contain his enthusiasm. "It's in Round Rock, just outside of Austin. I'll be managing a division twice the size of the one where I work now. The money's amazing, and we'll be able to buy the house we've always wanted." He grinned briefly at Erin. His smile faded some when she didn't return his enthusiasm. "We . . . we wanted you to be the first to know."

For a moment no one said anything.

Sam must wonder what's wrong with us, Kari thought. A normal family would be bursting forth with congratulations. But

Erin's husband didn't know the Baxter family very well if he thought moving Erin across the country would excite them.

Tears filled Erin's eyes and she shrugged. "Well?" A sound that was more laugh than cry slipped from between her lips. "Aren't you going to say anything?"

Elizabeth was the first to recover. The corners of her mouth lifted halfway, and she set her napkin on her plate. "That's wonderful, Sam. Texas is a fine place to live."

"Yes." Their father rose to his feet and reached across the table to shake Sam's hand. "You have a very bright future ahead of you, Sam. We've always known that."

"Wow." Ashley slipped her hand into little Cole's. "When do you leave?"

"Not for a while." Sam was quick to answer. "Sometime this fall, probably." He grinned, something Erin hadn't done since the announcement. "We'll visit the area over the summer to check out housing, but the move won't happen until the end of October at least."

Kari glanced around discreetly at her siblings. Brooke was staring at her plate, pushing her fork at a piece of chicken. Luke leaned forward, his forearms anchored on the table as he studied Erin.

But Ashley's reaction was most telling.

For years, Ashley had pretended to be a fringe member of their family. She joked about being the black sheep, the Baxter child whose place among them was more tolerated than welcome. Every time Ashley talked that way, Kari corrected her. But Ashley seemed bent toward aloofness, determined to be less connected than the others.

Now, though, her eyes bore a sadness that was unmistakable. Ashley cared more about the rest of them than she ever dared admit. She might not always fit in, but she belonged all the same.

Kari imagined Erin and Sam's packing their things and setting off for Texas. No wonder everyone was having trouble being excited. The Baxters had never been apart, not really. There'd been the six months Kari had spent modeling in New York City, and Ashley's year in Paris. But none of them had actually relocated for good.

The phone rang, and Luke jumped from the table to answer it. "Hello?" His eyes lit up, and he motioned to Kari. "Yeah, she's here. . . . Uh-huh. . . . Lots better. He's still in the hospital but out of ICU, breathing on his own and all. . . . Yep, everyone's fine. . . . Okay, I'll get her for you."

Kari watched, puzzled. Who would call her here, at her parents' house? Someone from church? The conversation around the table stalled as Luke handed the phone to Kari and said the words that made her heart rate double.

"It's Ryan."

Chapter Six

Kari needed a quiet place to talk.

She thanked Luke, took the phone, and headed upstairs to her old bedroom, the place where she'd stayed so often in the past year. When she was alone, she exhaled and held the phone to her ear.

"Hello?"

"Hi." His voice worked its way across her heart, soothing out the wrinkles that had collected through the day. "Did I catch you at a bad time?"

"No." She sat down on the bed and closed her eyes. "We were just finishing dinner. It's Erin's birthday."

"I tried you at home first." He paused, and Kari could hear the concern in his voice. "My mom told me about Landon Blake. Luke said he's better."

"Much better, thank God." Kari leaned back on a stack of pillows. "Dad says it's a miracle. He won't even need skin grafts for the burns."

"Has Ashley seen him?"

Kari pictured Ryan sitting in a New York apartment, worrying about the people back in Bloomington. Landon's older brother had graduated from high school the same year as Ryan. And everyone who knew Landon knew of the torch he carried for Ashley. "She's practically set up housekeeping at the hospital. I think it's been good for her. Helped her take stock of her priorities, you know?"

"Yeah." Ryan's voice was quiet. "Nothing like a hospital to make you do that."

Something in his tone told Kari there was more on his mind than Landon Blake's injury. Was he missing her, wishing he hadn't taken the job in New York? Or did picturing Landon in the hospital have a way of drawing Ryan back to those days after his football injury? The same way it had drawn her back?

Whatever he was thinking, Kari wasn't willing to guess. There was no point in getting into a deep conversation with Ryan. He was too far away, and she was still sorting through the ashes of her life. Besides, every thought of Ryan made her sick with guilt, as though she were betraying Tim and their marriage and everything they'd shared together.

Whenever Ryan called, she was careful to keep things on an informational level. Updates about Jessie, talk about training camp, that kind of thing.

"So," she asked casually, "what's up?"

Ryan uttered a tired sigh. "Meetings, meetings, and more meetings."

Kari laughed. "Ready for camp, huh?"

"Two weeks and counting. We open July 26, and everyone should be there. No holdouts. Preseason begins a month later at New England." He chuckled. "Between managing the personalities on the team and juggling the depth chart, I'll barely have time to coach."

"You'll do great." The laughter remained in Kari's voice, but more because it was what Ryan expected. The truth was, she found his impending heavy schedule a little frightening. Though she wanted to be independent, to make a life for herself and Jessie, Kari had to admit she looked forward to Ryan's calls. She liked the way he asked about Jessie, checking on her milestones and celebrating when she smiled or slept through the night. Talking to him was different from talking to her family about those things.

But with the season starting, he wouldn't have time to call — or certainly not as often as before. It was another reason why she had tried not to depend on him since Tim's death. Ryan had his own life in New York. Anything could happen once he began traveling with the team and coaching games. He could lose track of her or meet someone else and fall in love.

Kari couldn't blame him if he did. She hadn't given him any reason to hang on.

Ryan broke the silence. "So how's Jessie?" Kari could hear the smile in his voice.

"Beautiful. Growing like a weed."

"Letting her mother get any sleep?"

"Of course not. We have diaper duty at midnight, hunger pangs at three in the morning, and meaningful discussions at five." Kari sank deeper into the pillows. She was more tired than she'd realized. "Sleep is a thing of the past."

"You know what I wish?" Ryan's voice grew softer. He paused for a moment. "I wish I were there to help. Take the midnight-to-five shift, just once in a while."

Ryan's tone was so clear, so real, he might as well have been sitting beside her. "That's nice. But we're okay."

"Really, Kari?" His tone was velvet. "Are you?"

"Yes." She sat up. "Jessie and I need this

85

time together. Figuring out where we go from here, you know? Working through the memories."

"Are you modeling much?"

"A few days a month." Kari stood, cradling the phone on her shoulder as she walked over to the window. The evening summer sunshine washed over her face. She'd modeled since graduating from high school, and in the past few years she'd done a lot of catalog work, but when her marriage fell apart, she'd taken time off. Now that Jessie was sleeping through the night, she was gradually getting back into it. Tim's insurance money wouldn't last forever, and she needed the income. But it wasn't fun like before, and Kari understood why. Tim's death had created a void in her life that modeling jobs didn't fill. "I don't know how much longer I'll do it."

"How come?"

"Life's too short. I want my time away from Jessie to count for more than pretty pictures."

They were quiet for a moment. She leaned on the windowsill and gazed at the old farms in the distance. She never tired of this view, the trees behind her parents' house bursting with summertime.

Kari bit her lip. She wanted to ask Ryan

what he was doing, how he was spending his free time. But she couldn't. It would hurt too much to hear he was dating, to know he'd moved on since their time together last fall.

Of course, it would also hurt to know he was waiting for her, as he'd done so often before. Because a part of her heart — the part that was capable of love and relationship and togetherness — had been numb since Tim was killed. There was no telling when it might thaw — or if it ever would.

Kari watched two bluebirds dancing in midair outside the window. "So, you're about to be crazy busy."

"I'm crazy busy now."

"True. Meetings and, you know, whatever else." Again Kari resisted the urge to ask questions.

When she was silent, Ryan spoke, reading her heart as easily as he had always been able to do. "What's that supposed to mean?"

"Nothing." She knew her answer was too quick. "I'm glad you're busy. That's all."

"Kari . . ." He released a quiet laugh. "Just come out and ask me."

She tried to sound indignant. "Ask you what?"

"Okay, fine. Don't ask." Once more she

could feel his smile, see the sparkle in his eyes despite their distance. "I'm not seeing anyone, okay? Is that what you're thinking?"

Kari whirled around and flopped down on the bed once more. "Ryan Taylor, that is not what I was thinking."

The teasing faded from his voice. "Really?"

"Really." She closed her eyes briefly. Lying never was easy for her, but she had no choice now. Wherever her wandering thoughts had taken her, she had not been a willing passenger. It wasn't fair to let Ryan know she wondered what he was doing in his spare moments. Not when she was still grieving Tim's death, still thinking her heart was permanently broken.

"Okay." His tone was tinged with disappointment. "But just for the record, I'm not dating anyone."

Kari stared at the pockmarked bulletin board near the door, the one where teenage pictures of her and Ryan once hung so many years ago. "You don't have to tell me."

"I know." He drew a slow breath. "I wanted to."

They were moving into dangerous territory, and Kari fought back a wave of anxiety. Now was not the time to fan the fires of all she'd ever felt for Ryan Taylor. Hers was a life taken up completely with mothering and learning to live without her husband. She could not possibly see what lay beyond this lonely season. Not yet, anyway.

Hearing the emotion in Ryan's voice only confused her, made her desperate for his presence, his arms around her.

His kiss.

And that made her feel like a wicked, unfaithful woman who would cheat on a husband dead not even six months.

"Hey." She massaged her eyebrows with her thumb and forefinger. "Thanks for calling." She hesitated. "I'll understand if I don't hear from you for a while. Once camp starts, you'll be too busy to eat." Kari ached from missing him, hating herself for betraying the memory of Tim.

"I might be too busy to eat." He waited a moment. "But as long as I'm breathing, I'll find time to call."

A sense of relief filled her soul before she could stop it. "Okay." She let loose a soft bit of laughter. "You know where to find me."

When they hung up, Kari stood and gripped the windowsill again, staring out at the clear blue sky. Was she crazy? Her conversation with Ryan had been seeped in deeper meaning and innuendo. Here she was, trapped in the pain of losing Tim and convinced that grieving his loss was something she needed to do alone. Yet she couldn't go a day without thinking of Ryan Taylor.

She drew a slow breath and narrowed her eyes, willing herself to focus on God's presence, to hear his voice above the roar of emotions battling for position in her heart. *Lord, all of this confusion could have been avoided if only you had let Tim live.* Sadness came over her like a bad cold. Jessie would never know him, never hold his hand, never run into his arms. *It's so unfair, God.*

Her knees grew weak, but almost at the same time she felt herself standing straighter, being held up by invisible hands.

I am with you, daughter. Even now. I know the plans I have for you.

The voice was quiet, a mere whispering in her soul. But the words were familiar; they had sustained her throughout the past year. And Kari was sure they were true. God was with her; he had great plans for her. But what about Tim? Why hadn't God been with him when he went to that woman's apartment? If God had kept Tim safe, she wouldn't be here wondering about Ryan, dreaming of when she might see him again and feeling guilty for every moment of it.

Kari opened her mouth. The near silent words that came out were soaked in pain. "You could have saved him, Lord." She squeezed her eyes shut. "We were . . . we were supposed to be a family."

A Scripture verse came back to her, one that had been on a dozen sympathy cards she'd received after Tim's death, one that seemed to appear in sermons and devotions at least once a week since then.

And we know that in all things God works for the good of those who love him, who have been called according to his purpose.

They were words she had heard all her life, but they had seemed empty and trite after Tim's murder. What good could come from losing her husband — and just months after the two of them had survived the greatest test of their marriage? What good was there in watching a little girl grow up without her father?

As hard as the past five months had been, she had recovered at least enough to believe that things would get better. Somehow . . . someday. What was it her mother had said? Beauty from ashes. Yes, that was it. God would honor the truths laid out in the Bible, truths that Kari believed completely, even if they didn't seem to make sense. But still, her belief didn't ease the pain of daily living, the uncertainty of what tomorrow held.

No, she didn't struggle with *whether* God would deliver on his promise to make something beautiful out of the shattered remains of her life.

She struggled with *when*.

Chapter Seven

Ashley was never nervous.

But as she made her way through the hospital lobby and up the elevator to the third floor, she could barely keep her hands from shaking. It was time to talk to Landon, time to find out what was eating at him and why weeds of tension had shot up between them these past few days. Time to find out if what she guessed was true.

The dinner party at her parents' house had been hard to leave. Conversations about Erin's move had blended into talk about Luke and Reagan, which had led to more discussion about the blood bank at St. Anne's Hospital. Apparently it was lower than it had been in a decade, and Brooke, the oldest of the five of them, was willing to take up the cause.

Ashley leaned hard against the elevator wall. Of course Brooke was willing. She was a doctor, after all — she and Peter both. By spearheading a blood drive, they would make the mighty John Baxter happy. They would be in tight, following in his footsteps, deserving his praise. Even if they didn't go to church or believe in God.

Normally at a family gathering, Ashley would have been anxious to leave. But tonight she had taken it all in, studying the people who made up her family, wondering why she didn't fit in, why she wasn't like them. Before she left, the conversation had turned to Alzheimer's. She told them Lu's advice about keeping the patients in the here and now.

But Brooke had disagreed. "That works sometimes, but doctors today are talking more about distraction. That's the preferred treatment now."

"Distraction?" Ashley had been ready to leave, but if Brooke knew something that could help her at work, she was interested.

"Yes." Brooke nodded, then added in her official doctor voice, "The moment an Alzheimer's patient veers off the course of reasonable normalcy, distract them. Change the subject, introduce an idea or an activity, anything to deter them from their delusion."

The idea sounded better than arguing with the old folks. "Why can't I just agree with them, let them think their husbands

94

are alive or that they're visiting for a few hours instead of confined to a home for sick people?"

"That would never work." Brooke's laugh made Ashley feel stupid. "It'd be like pouring gasoline on the flames of dementia."

The memory faded, and Ashley crossed her arms.

If anyone should be leaving town, she should. Certainly no one would be broken up about that the way they were by Erin and Sam's leaving. That was something else. Ashley had actually felt sad at her sister's announcement. She would miss seeing Erin once a week at the family dinners. Erin had always been the quietest Baxter, the simplest and the plainest. But Erin was genuine as a summer sunset, her smile enough to light the room. Ashley had visited her kindergarten classroom a few times and been amazed at the handmade decorations on every wall, the attention to detail in the learning environment her sweet sister had created for her students.

Erin was a stabilizing force, really. She looked like their mother, acted like her, and had the same calm demeanor. Erin's life — even when she was younger — had never been anything but normal and good. At least it had always seemed that way.

Erin's presence in their lives was something Ashley had always taken for granted.

The same way she'd taken Landon Blake for granted.

Ashley closed her eyes for a moment. Maybe she was wrong about him. Maybe he wasn't upset by her lack of emotion. Maybe he'd fallen in love with someone else or had plans he wasn't willing to share — that could be the reason he was acting so stiffly toward her. Whatever it was, Ashley knew she couldn't wait any longer to find out.

She exited the elevator and nodded to the nurse on duty. They all knew her by now — Dr. Baxter's daughter, the one who couldn't stay away from the injured firefighter. Ashley was sure the nurses had created a marvelous love story in their minds, marrying the two of them off before Christmas.

That was fine. People could believe what they wanted to. She and Landon knew the truth. Despite their history, and despite the attraction they felt for each other, a romance between them would never work. It couldn't. They were simply too different. Regardless of how things looked to her family and friends or even to the nurses at St. Anne's Hospital.

Ashley walked down the hall and turned into room 312. Landon was sitting gingerly in bed, keeping his weight off the bandages that covered his burns, staring at the television monitor anchored near the ceiling. A baseball game played silently on the screen.

"Hi." She smiled at him, clutching her crocheted bag to her waist. She sat in the chair beside his bed.

"Hey, I didn't think you were coming." His eyes met and held hers. What was it she could see there? Regret? Anger? Uncertainty? Ashley wasn't sure, but something was definitely wrong.

"It's Erin's birthday." Ashley leaned back in the chair and set her bag on the floor. "Baxter dinner parties can run pretty late."

Landon's smile did not erase the distance in his eyes. "I'm sure."

Ashley studied him. "You look good." There was more color in his face. "How long before they let you go?"

"Not sure. No skin grafts, so that's good news. They want my lungs to function better." He grinned. "I have a strict doctor."

"You're telling me." Ashley rolled her eyes, a smile tugging on her lips. "I grew up with him."

They were quiet, and Ashley looked at the television again. This was the moment, her chance to ask him what he was thinking. But before she could find the words, Landon broke the silence.

"Why, Ash?"

Her eyes returned to his. "Why, what?"

"Why are you here?"

She shifted positions, her heart thudding against the wall of her chest. She couldn't back out now. "I'm worried about you."

"I get that." He motioned toward his monitors. "But I'm not in danger now. I haven't been for twenty-four hours." He looked at her, his gaze working its way deep into her soul. "So why are you here?"

What should she tell him? Had he heard the words she'd spoken when he was near death the other day? Was he waiting for her to say them now, to his face? She bit the inside of her lip and searched desperately for the answers. "I'm your friend, Landon. I care. That's why."

Landon let his head fall back against his pillow. For a moment he watched the ball game again, staring at the screen while a burly batter missed two pitches and hit the third out of the park. Ashley watched, too, not sure what to say.

When the game broke for a commercial,

Landon used his remote control and clicked the Off button. The screen went black.

Once more Landon turned his attention to her. "I heard you."

Ashley felt the blood drain from her face. "What?"

"The first night, when I was unconscious." Landon peered at her through eyes laden with emotion. "I heard everything."

"You . . . you couldn't even breathe. What do you mean you heard everything?"

"Look, Ashley, as far back as I can remember I've tried to figure you out." He tossed out his hands, his eyes darting about the room, looking for answers that had long since eluded him. "What would Ashley want? What would Ashley think? Why doesn't Ashley want me?" His gaze met hers again. "God's given me everything I've set my mind on, Ashley. Everything . . . except you."

The heat in Ashley's cheeks felt strong enough to warm the entire room. He had heard her, just as she'd feared. And now they were both too confused to know how to act, what to say, how to move ahead from here. Her tone was soft. "What did you hear, Landon?"

"No, Ashley." He worked the muscles in his jaw. "You tell me. Tell me the same thing you told me that night. Then tell me what you meant by it, so I can have some form of sanity here."

"Please, Landon." Ashley wanted to shout, but instead she pleaded with him, begging him to understand. "I thought you were dying."

A single exasperated laugh came from Landon's lips. "As long as I live, I don't think I'll ever understand you, Ashley Baxter. Why I let you get under my skin all those years ago, I'll never know." His face grew softer, more serious. "Tell me, Ashley. Tell me what you told me when you thought I was dying."

No! She couldn't tell him!

A hundred thoughts ricocheted off the walls of Ashley's mind, vying for position. Love between her and Landon could never work, never amount to anything more than heartache for both of them. He needed a sweet, Christian wife — someone who would sit at home waiting for him to return from the firehouse, someone who would pray for him every time sirens rang out across Bloomington. Someone quaint and cute and conservative.

Ashley was none of those things. Especially after Paris. She could never love a man unless she had the freedom to tell him what happened that year in France. And if there was one person she could never tell, it was Landon Blake. No way. He was moral and righteous, a man of the highest standards — a hero, no less. She couldn't stand having him think of her as dirty and cheap.

What point was there in loving him now?

Ashley blinked. Yet, that's what she'd told him, wasn't it? That she loved him.

Landon coughed twice and took a sip of water. Then he looked at her again. "I already know, Ashley. Tell me."

Like an avalanche, Ashley felt the walls of her pride give way. Her shoulder slumped forward, and when she spoke, there was none of the fierce independence that usually rang in her voice. She locked eyes with Landon and told him the truth, the way she felt still, even if it was the craziest feeling in all the world.

"I . . . I told you I love you." She leaned forward, her voice barely audible over the ticking of the clock. "I didn't want you to die without knowing."

"That's what I thought you said." Landon's eyes welled up, and his face twisted into a mask of confusion. "But I couldn't believe it. Not until now. Not until I heard it from your own lips." He searched her face. "Why is it so hard for you, Ashley? To tell me how you feel? When you know how I've always felt about you?"

"Because . . ." Ashley felt like a person falling from a cliff. ". . . I didn't want you to get the wrong idea."

Landon leaned forward, stiff, as though someone had dropped an ice cube down the back of his hospital gown.

"I . . ." Ashley crossed her arms and dug her fists into the knots in her stomach. ". . . I didn't want you to get the wrong idea, Landon. You know, like I wanted something between us. A relationship or something."

The pain that flashed in Landon's eyes sliced straight through her. But it was gone almost instantly, gathered back into a closet of his heart where she clearly wasn't allowed.

He chuckled quietly and shook his head. "Of course not, Ash." Gone was the intimacy of a moment ago, and in its place was the protective veneer, the casual friendship she'd grown accustomed to. The one she was more comfortable with. "I would *never* think that. Not of the mysterious Ashley Baxter."

"Landon . . ." Ashley wanted to kick herself. This was going all wrong. Yes, she had feelings for Landon. But where could they possibly lead? "I didn't mean it like that; it's just . . ."

Landon held up his hand. "It's okay." Resignation was written across his face. "I understand." He drew in a deep breath and held out his hand to her. She reached up and took it, allowing him to weave his fingers between hers. "I have something to tell you."

Ashley wanted to think straight, but the feel of Landon's hand in hers was almost more than she could bear. She forced herself to focus. "What?"

"I'm moving." He worked his thumb over the back of her hand. "I was looking for a chance to tell you before I got hurt."

Ashley was unable to breathe for a moment. Landon was kidding, lying. Trying to get back at her for not loving him the way he loved her. She felt suddenly awkward holding his hand. Her fingers eased free, and she crossed her arms again. "Moving where?"

"New York." Peace came over Landon, and he settled back against his pillow once more. "Jalen's there. I told you about him, right?"

Jalen? The name was vaguely familiar. Ashley's mind raced. She was struck by how little she'd really listened to Landon since she'd been home from Paris. She'd been so determined not to fall in love with him that she'd barely heard him. "Vaguely."

Landon smiled. "Jalen and I met at the University of Texas as freshmen. He's the one who convinced me to get on the volunteer fire department in this little town outside Austin. When we left school he went to New York City. I came home to Bloomington to train and get in the department here."

Ashley felt sick to her stomach. "But New York, Landon? Isn't this kind of . . . I don't know . . . sudden?"

"Not really. I've been thinking about it for a while." He shrugged. "Jalen and I talk once a month or so, and he's always in the thick of things. Saving people, rushing into burning high-rises, that kind of thing. In New York City, fighting fires is a passion. Here in Bloomington it's more of a pastime."

"So you're moving to New York to fight fires with Jalen because there's not enough excitement here? Is that it?" Ashley gestured at the cast on Landon's leg, the bandages on his back and thighs. "Haven't you had enough excitement for a while?"

"It isn't the excitement, really. It's making my life count." He stared at her and, for an instant, he allowed his emotions to surface as they had before. "After hearing your voice when they brought me in here, I actually had doubts about going. That's why . . . I don't know . . ."

"Why you've been so quiet?" It all made sense finally — the awkwardness she'd been feeling, the strange uneasiness between them. Landon was moving. He had been looking for a way to tell her, but then he'd been hurt. And as he lay near death, her words of love had made him wonder if he was making a mistake by going.

He nodded. "Exactly."

"I'm sorry, Landon." She reached for his hand again. "I had no idea."

"I know. It's okay. I shouldn't have read so much into what you said. It's just . . . when you told me you loved me, I had to know what you meant. Because if you meant it — well, if you meant it the way I'd hoped, I could never leave."

There it was again. Landon's true feelings laid out before her like an open gift. If only she could love him the way he loved her. "Sometimes I wish I were normal. Like other girls."

Landon laughed and leaned over, gently

brushing his fingers across her brow. "You could never be like other girls, Ashley. It would be wrong to try."

"You have a job there? In New York, I mean?"

"I flew out for an interview a month ago. They ran me through a week of tests and drills." He shrugged. "I made the cut. I was supposed to start the first of August."

Ashley looked again at the cast and the bandages. "That's three weeks from now."

"I know. I called them this morning." He grimaced. "They've rescheduled my start date for November. That way I'll have my cast off and time to get my leg back in shape."

A wave of acceptance washed across the shore of Ashley's heart. "So you're really moving to New York?"

"Yep. It'll be Jalen and me, fighting fires and saving lives right there in the heart of the Big Apple. Action and more action every day we're on duty."

Ashley nodded, suddenly concerned. "How long will you stay?" She had no right to ask. But still, she wanted to know.

"Maybe a year, maybe forever." Landon gave her a crooked grin. "Jalen says fighting fires in New York gets into your blood. Makes you never want to leave."

A thread of fear sewed its way through her, leaving her in knots. She remembered back when Landon had left for the University of Texas. Somehow she had always known he'd come back to Bloomington. But this time . . . this time he might not. Maybe never.

She blinked back the tears. "I know I'm weird. About relationships and stuff. But don't forget something while you're out there fighting fires with Jalen."

"What's that?" Landon took hold of her hand again and brought it to his lips, kissing her fingers, his smile light and easy, the seriousness long gone from his expression.

Ashley slid to the edge of her chair and spoke words she hoped would take root squarely in his heart. "I do love you, Landon. Maybe not the way you want me to. Maybe not the way I should. But I love you. I always have."

Ashley stood and leaned partially over him. She hugged him close, clinging to him, dimly aware of a new, curiously intoxicating effect his body had on hers. "Can you remember that when you're far away in New York City?"

"Always, Ashley." Landon nuzzled his face against hers and whispered into her ear. "Always."

Chapter Eight

The idea hit just before midnight.

After talking to Ryan at her parents' house, Kari had gone home with Jessie and spent the night praying, begging God to show her some small bit of good that might come from the sadness in her life.

And now, suddenly, her course of action was clear.

For years she'd dreamed of helping married couples — praying with them, counseling them, working with them so they might not become another statistic. But when Tim moved out with his girlfriend, Kari figured any dreams of her helping married people had been destroyed right along with her wedding vows.

True, in the end she and Tim had trusted God and found a way to make their marriage work. But their story wasn't really much of a success. In the end, Tim's affair had still cost him every chance at a happy ending. It had cost him his life, after all.

108

But as Kari sat in the darkness staring out the window at the streetlight, she realized something she hadn't before. With God's help, she had survived first Tim's affair, then his death. How many women at Clear Creek Community Church were battling similar situations? Maybe their husbands hadn't moved in with a girlfriend — or been murdered. But if God had brought her through those trials, he could bring other hurting women through their trials, whatever they were. Even better, maybe Kari could be part of that healing process.

A picture began to develop in Kari's mind. The longer she sat there, the clearer it got. She could start a ministry for the walking wounded, for women who thought their marriages were over, who had no idea what to do next in order to save their relationships or their sanity. Women just like her.

Pastor Mark Atteberry had been telling her for weeks that God had something special planned for her. All the time, Kari had wondered in the back of her mind if that something might be a relationship with Ryan Taylor. She felt terrible for thinking it, but she'd thought it all the same. Not that Pastor Mark would have meant that. He was merely sharing his impression with her. When he prayed for her, he'd been given the strong sense that God was up to something big.

How shortsighted she'd been to think it would involve Ryan!

The big plan Pastor Mark must have sensed was this vision she had now, the one that seemed real enough to touch. A ministry for other hurting women, women who would meet with Kari one-on-one for Bible study and comfort. The setting would be private, protecting the identity of the women who came. Kari could meet with a different woman each day of the week if necessary.

Excitement began to build until it overflowed from her heart. Back before she'd known about Tim's affair, she had pictured the two of them working such a ministry together. Meeting with couples, mentoring them, helping them reach a higher place in their marriage. But clearly that was not to be.

This ministry, the one God had placed on her heart now, was one that would give her life new purpose and direction. The lifeline that would lift her from this season of grief and loss, and vault her into a time of grace and hope for women whose relationships still had a chance.

Kari opened her Bible and studied the words she'd read earlier that morning. They came from Romans 12:

Love must be sincere. Hate what is evil; cling to what is good. Be devoted to one another in brotherly love. Honor one another above yourselves. Never be lacking in zeal, but keep your spiritual fervor, serving the Lord. Be joyful in hope, patient in affliction, faithful in prayer. Share with God's people who are in need. Practice hospitality.

When she'd read the words before, they had seemed rather obvious. A list of directions on how to treat people. Certainly nothing remarkable or life-changing. But now, in light of the vision God had given her, they seemed vibrantly alive.

A new kind of love resonated within Kari, a love for women suffering in marriage. It was a love as sincere as anything she'd ever felt. She hated the evil of adultery, hated it enough to pray with women who'd fallen victim to it, enough to pray with those determined to cling to the good in their marriage and trust God for renewal.

Then there was the joy part. *Be joyful in*

hope. . . . Wasn't that the feeling rattling the windows of her heart even now? Joy? After months without feeling any whatsoever, Kari had no doubt that it was. The idea of helping other women mend their marriages filled her with more joy than she'd thought possible. Obviously the only way she could answer this call of God was by being patient, by praying, by sharing and practicing hospitality among the women who needed her support — just as these verses instructed.

But the thing that seemed handwritten in the text for her alone was the part about honor.

That's what it came down to, really. Tim had honored her by leaving his girlfriend, repenting, and promising to work on their marriage. Ryan had honored her by moving away, letting her love Tim the way she knew she should.

Now it was her turn to honor the women at their church who needed her support — by using the memories of all that had happened in her own life as a way of giving others hope.

Jessie's faint cry sounded from the other room, and Kari shut her Bible. As she did, she realized there were tears on her cheeks. Tears that had sprung from a place in her heart that had felt numb and dry before tonight.

A place that had somehow, in the past few hours, been brought back to life.

Chapter Nine

Ashley wondered if she'd ever get used to the smell.

It was her first day on the job, and even after an hour with Irvel and her friends that morning, the pungent odor that clung to the walls and furniture was still enough to gag her.

Lu had said there was nothing anyone could do to make the house smell better. "It's clean," Lu told her when they talked by phone after Ashley's interview. "Just tinged with the smell of death."

Ashley would have to get used to it if she wanted to work there for long. She sat at the breakfast table and smiled at the faces around her.

At the head of the table sat Irvel, the self-appointed social coordinator. Next to her on the right was Edith, a quiet woman who picked at her food and said little. Across from Edith was Helen, without a doubt the loudest in the threesome. Laura Jo lay down the hall, confined to a bed and probably weeks away from death. And then there was Bert, the only man in the mix.

Lu had warned Ashley about him. "Take his meals to his room." Lu had clucked her tongue. "Bert's a doozie. Gets up in the morning and circles his bed. All day."

"Circles it?" Ashley hadn't understood.

"After he's up, you'll make his bed and lay out his bathrobe. The minute he's done eating, he starts circling. Starts at the top of the bed, making circles with his hands along the comforter — slow, careful circles. He works his way down to the foot of the bed and back around to the other side. Then he starts again. Every day, same thing."

So far Lu was right on.

Before feeding the three more mobile residents, Ashley had brought a liquid breakfast to Laura Jo, who'd never even opened her eyes. Next she took a tray to Bert. He sat in his rocker and ate while she laid out his clothes and made his bed. Like clockwork, the minute she took his tray, he eased into the robe, shuffled to the top of the bed, and began making circles on the comforter.

Poor crazy guy, Ashley thought.

These women, the ones around the table, were more fun. They were the reason she'd taken the job. Irvel and Edith and Helen — the girls, Irvel called them.

"Well, girls . . ." Irvel slid back from the table. She'd eaten half a piece of toast and an egg. "Hank's fishing, so I've got all day."

Helen scowled at her plate. "I thought we were having lasagna. Where's the lasagna?" She banged her fork against her plate three times. "Where's the lasagna?"

"You know" — Irvel shook a finger in Ashley's direction — "that girl has the most beautiful hair." She cocked her head. "Has anyone ever told you that, dear?"

"Thank you, Irvel. I appreciate that."

"I said . . . !" Helen banged the table. Lu had warned her about that too. Helen was always banging something, hitting a wall, or smashing her fist against the table to make a point. "Where's the lasagna?"

"Umm, Helen . . ." Ashley cleared her throat. "We're having eggs and toast this morning."

Helen glared at her. "I was having lasagna."

Irvel nodded in Ashley's direction, trying to keep control of the situation. "Yes, dear, I think she was having lasagna. That's what she says."

"Eggs and toast." Edith's voice was quiet

116

amidst Irvel's chirping and Helen's thunder. Still, Helen heard it and slammed her fork against her plate again.

"Lasagna. My mother makes me lasagna every Sunday, and this is Sunday."

Irvel placed a gentle hand on Helen's arm. "Dear, I believe it's Wednesday."

"Oooh, boy." Ashley muttered the words and blew out a short, hard breath. Were Monday mornings always like this? She stood and planted her hands on her hips, remembering Brooke's advice about distraction. "How would you like a cinnamon roll, Helen?" Ashley smiled at the stocky woman. "They're cool enough to eat."

"Cinnamon rolls with lasagna?" Helen spat something from her mouth onto her plate. Ashley couldn't bring herself to look at it. "I want more lasagna."

Irvel looked at Ashley, her eyes wide. Then she smiled and shrugged her shoulders in as dainty a manner as Ashley had ever seen. "The girl wants lasagna."

"Well." Ashley brought the tray of cinnamon rolls from the kitchen and held them out for the three older women. "The lasagna's gone. All we have now are cinnamon rolls."

"What?" Helen sat back slowly in her chair, her face a twisted mass of sorrow and disappointment.

"It's gone, Helen."

"Really?" Angry tears appeared to well up in Helen's eyes. "The lasagna's gone?"

"Yes." Ashley forced an adamant tone. "Completely gone."

Helen thought for a moment. "Fine." A huff slid from her weathered mouth. "I'll have a cinnamon roll." She went to take one from the tray but stopped her hand in midair. "Wait a minute." As quickly as she could, she turned and stared at Ashley. "Have you been checked?"

Ashley glanced at the skin on her arms, her hands. *What in the world?* "Checked?"

"They have to check everyone. Very carefully."

"Good." Edith painstakingly lifted a forkful of eggs to her lips. "Good, good eggs."

"Yes." Irvel folded her hands delicately on the table. A serious look came over her face as she glanced about. "We've all been checked. Right, Ingrid?"

Helen fired an impatient glare at Irvel. "The name's Helen!"

"That's what I said, dear." Irvel gave a light roll of her eyes toward Ashley, as if to say that Helen was quite possibly a few drawers shy of a file cabinet.

118

Ashley smiled and shifted the tray to Irvel. "A cinnamon roll?"

"Why, yes, dear." Irvel used the tips of her fingers to take a single roll.

Edith hesitated for a moment, looking from her plate full of eggs to the roll and back again. "I like the eggs."

For the moment Helen was forgotten. "Would you like a cinnamon roll, Edith? You can have both if you want."

"She's already been checked," Helen barked. "Give it to her."

"I like the eggs." Edith lowered her brow. She began to tremble, nervous and perplexed by the daunting task of deciding whether or not to take a cinnamon roll.

Poor woman. Ashley tilted her head and gave Edith an understanding smile. "You eat your eggs, Edith. That's okay. You can have a roll later."

Ashley set the tray down on the middle of the table, inches from Helen's plate. "Help yourself."

"That's it!" Helen looked at her friends and threw her hands in the air. "Has anyone checked her? She shouldn't be here if she hasn't been checked." Helen lowered her head as though this next part wasn't for Ashley's ears. "What if she's a spy?"

Edith's hand shook so badly her fork rattled against the plate. Ashley shot a concerned look in her direction. The mound of scrambled eggs was only slightly smaller than before. "Are there . . . are there more eggs?"

"Of course." Ashley patted Edith's hand. "As soon as you finish those, I'll get you some."

Edith studied her plate. The skin around her eyes bunched curiously. "I did finish them." She lifted her eyes to Ashley, fear and confusion slow-dancing across her face. "Someone gave me more. Is it okay to eat them?"

There had to be a better way. Ashley lowered her chin. "Yes, Edith. Go right ahead."

"Dear . . ." Irvel cupped her fingers around her mouth and lobbed a quiet note of concern toward Ashley. "Edith is becoming a bit forgetful."

"Right," Ashley whispered. "That's okay."

"Yes." Irvel wrinkled her nose politely and nodded. "I thought so." Irvel stopped suddenly and stared at Ashley. "My goodness, dear, you have beautiful hair. Has anyone ever told you how beautiful your hair is?"

Ashley cast Irvel a patient smile. "Yes,

that's very nice. Thank you for —"

"This is ridiculous." Helen brought her fist down on her thigh and winced at the contact. "Is anyone going to answer me?" She pushed her chair back and gestured toward Ashley. "The girl needs to be checked. We can't have spies running the place."

"Helen" — Ashley nodded with conviction — "I've been thoroughly checked." She held up her hands in surrender. "It's okay. I'm not a spy."

"Well!" Helen slapped her knee for emphasis. "It's about time."

The sound of a door opening stopped the conversation. Ashley checked her watch. It was nine. Time for Belinda's shift to begin. Belinda worked nine to five and, according to Lu, she spent most of the day in the back office handling paperwork, ordering medication, and dealing with suppliers who kept the house stocked. Belinda would help give baths after breakfast, but otherwise Ashley would be on her own.

"Uh-oh." Irvel dropped her voice to a whisper. "It's that woman."

Helen nodded, suddenly on Ashley's side. "Is she a spy?"

Irvel sank down in her chair and looked at Helen. "I think so."

Edith picked at her plate. Her fingers shook more than before. "I like the eggs."

Ashley's heart rate quickened. What was this sudden tension over Belinda's arrival? What had the supervisor said or done to make them so nervous?

Belinda tramped into the kitchen, set her purse down, and glared at Ashley. "It's nine o'clock."

"Yes." Ashley settled back in her chair. "Some of us pretty girls can tell time."

"We start baths at nine o'clock." She waved her hand at the older women. "Why are they still eating?"

"Well . . ." Ashley raised an eyebrow, careful to keep her tone calm and gentle. She put her hand on Edith's. "Edith isn't finished with her eggs." Ashley pointed to Irvel and Helen. "And the others are working on cinnamon rolls."

Belinda scowled. "What took so long?"

"Madam . . ." Irvel cleared her throat. "If I might explain . . ."

Gone was the social coordinator bubbling with enthusiasm over how she and the girls were going to spend the day. Instead, Irvel's voice trembled with uncertainty. Ashley stared at the white-haired woman in awe. The poor dear was scared to death, but still she cared enough about

Ashley to take a stand. The gesture touched Ashley's heart more than she could grasp.

Belinda rolled her eyes in Irvel's direction. "Make it quick."

"Well" — Irvel smoothed out the wrinkles in her dress — "we were chatting. Getting to know each other."

"Look, Irvel." A chortle worked its way up Belinda's throat, and she gave that old woman a sardonic smile. "If you girls don't know each other by now, you might as well stop trying."

"Yes, but . . ." Irvel swallowed, looking to Ashley for help. "Hank dropped me off an hour ago, and the girls and I were going to visit. Maybe have some peppermint tea."

"That's right." Ashley stood and began clearing dishes from the table. From her spot by the kitchen sink — out of view from Irvel — Ashley shot a look at Belinda. "No harm in taking a few minutes to visit." Her voice remained kind, but she made sure her eyes got the point across. "Is there?"

"Yes." Irvel's voice regained some of her earlier confidence. Ashley returned to the dining room and anchored herself protectively near Irvel. The woman reached up and took hold of Ashley's hand. "Visiting is nice. At least until Hank comes to get me." Irvel smiled at Belinda. "Isn't this girl's hair beautiful? I've never seen such beautiful hair."

"That's it." Belinda marched toward them and forced Irvel's chair back from the table. Then she lowered her face so it was inches from Irvel's. "Hank's dead, Irvel. Fifteen years now. You live with these other old folks in an adult care home for people with Alzheimer's disease." Her tone was loud and rude, as though she were talking to a troublesome five-year-old.

Ashley was too shocked to do anything but watch.

Belinda grabbed a quick breath. "There's not a tea bag in the house, and there never has been. There'll be no getting to know each other, and Hank will never come back for you. He's dead. It's bath time, so don't say another word. Get your cane and follow me."

"Y-y-yes, madam." Irvel's shoulders began to shake as Belinda turned and slouched down the hallway.

"Oh, Irvel." Ashley came alongside her and saw tears on the old woman's soft, wrinkled cheeks. "I'm sorry."

"I n-n-need a bath." Irvel struggled to

her feet with Ashley's help.

Around the table there was silence. Edith had set down her fork and leaned against the back of her chair. Her eyes were closed, but her head made a subtle nodding motion, and her lips moved in a repetitive pattern. When Ashley bent closer, she could hear Edith's voice, the quietest whisper, saying, "No . . . no . . . no . . . no . . ."

"Edith, are you okay?" Ashley took a few steps toward the quiet woman.

"Bath." She pushed herself back from the table, struggled to her feet, and inched her way toward the bathroom. "I need a bath . . . need a bath. . . ."

Ashley, Irvel, and Helen watched her go.

"The madam always upsets Edith." Irvel clucked her tongue. "Poor Edith."

"I told you." Helen gripped her elbows, her brow marked by deep rivers of concern. "That woman's a spy. She's always been a spy."

Suddenly the air was pierced by the loudest, shrillest scream Ashley had ever heard. It came from the bathroom where Edith was supposed to be waiting for someone to help her with her bath.

Ashley raced around the corner as another of Lu's warnings came back. *Edith's*

125

a screamer. No one knows why."

Rounding another wall, Ashley ran into the bathroom, where Edith was standing frozen in place, eyes wide, mouth locked open, screaming as though she'd witnessed a murder.

"Edith . . . Edith, it's okay."

The woman's arms and legs were as rigid as steel beams. Before Ashley could make any further attempts to calm the woman, Belinda shoved her way into the bathroom and shouted at Ashley, "Edith's not to take a bath alone. Didn't Lu tell you?"

It was impossible to talk above the sounds of Edith's screams. Before Ashley could think what to do next, Belinda positioned herself behind Edith and forcibly guided her down a hallway into a bedroom.

Ashley watched them go, horrified. Was this how people died — afraid and alone? humiliated? She made her way back to the dining room, barely aware of her steps. Irvel and Helen hadn't moved, and now they were both silent, their eyes filled with terror. Within three minutes, Edith's screaming stopped, and Belinda pounded her way past them toward the other bathroom, mumbling something about incompetence, her face a twist of angry knots.

"She's a spy," Helen hissed.

Ashley had no idea what to do or where to start. She wanted to check on Edith, but Irvel and Helen needed her too. Was this how Belinda always treated these people? With angry hostility and no respect? Shouting at the poor dears and ordering them about? If so, Ashley would have to do something about it.

"Irvel!" Belinda's voice boomed from down the hallway. "Get in here. Your bath's ready."

Irvel slid her feet forward, first one, then the other, while Ashley walked helplessly at her side. She was too new to change the routine. Besides, Belinda was in charge, and she'd already made it plain that if Ashley didn't follow protocol she'd get fired. Now, after spending time with Irvel and Edith and Helen, Ashley was more certain than ever that she wanted to stay and help, wanted to let them work on her heart and make it tender again.

Halfway up the hallway, Irvel stopped. "Hank's . . . not really gone." She made a slow turn and faced Ashley. "Is he?"

Irvel's eyes begged for the answer she wanted to hear. For a moment Ashley said nothing, not wanting to make things worse. Then an image came to mind of

Landon lying in the hospital bed, telling her he was moving to New York City. She wouldn't see him again — not for a year at least, and maybe not forever. But that didn't change the way she loved him.

"No, Irvel." The image of Landon faded, and Ashley used gentle hands to take hold of Irvel's shoulders. "As long as you love him, he's never really gone."

"I love Hank." Irvel's words were slow, deliberate, the emotion in her eyes so raw it almost hurt to look at. "You don't know how much I love him."

"Well, then . . ." Ashley's voice was thick, and she felt the sting of tears. ". . . he isn't gone, is he?"

"No." Irvel straightened a bit and shook her head. A smile steeped in gratitude forged its way up her sagging cheeks. "He isn't gone at all. He's fishing . . . just like always."

They heard a sharp sound. "Irvel?" Belinda's voice echoed off the plasterboard walls, and the fragile old woman jumped.

Ashley winked at Irvel and yelled ahead in a pleasant voice, "She's coming." It would be pointless to argue with Belinda now. It would only make Irvel and her friends more upset.

Irvel brought her head close to Ashley's,

her voice a whisper. "You're very kind, dear. I truly hope we can have tea sometime." Irvel took a few more steps and stopped. She raised a single finger and pointed at Ashley. "You know something? You have the most beautiful hair. . . ."

Ashley spent the rest of the day with various other tasks. She oversaw lunch and helped the women to their chairs for an afternoon nap. She checked on Laura Jo and Edith, but they were both sleeping. On Belinda's desk in the office, next to Edith's file, Ashley noticed a bottle of medication. Sedatives — obviously Belinda's way of getting Edith to stop screaming.

Several times she looked in on Bert. Lu was right. When he wasn't eating or napping, he was circling — round and round and round the bed, rubbing out the wrinkles in the comforter with meticulous care.

"Bert?" Ashley came to him and touched his arm. "Bert, my name is Ashley. I'm new."

Bert said nothing. He neither stopped nor looked up. Instead, he maneuvered himself awkwardly past Ashley, his hands moving in constant circles all the while.

"Okay then, Bert. I'll be in the next room if you need anything."

On her way out, Ashley noticed a framed

black-and-white photo on Bert's dresser. It was a picture of a handsome, strapping man and a striking young woman, side by side on horseback.

Ashley glanced over her shoulder at Bert, still making his way around the bed. "I'm here for you, Bert. Call if you need me."

Late that afternoon, Irvel's niece came by. Lu had explained about the regular visitors, and Irvel's niece was one of them. She came every Monday afternoon and read the Bible out loud to her aunt. When she was finished, they would recite the Twenty-third Psalm together and then sing Irvel's favorite hymn.

Ashley peeked in and watched the scene from the hallway. The two women were arm in arm, singing in a way that was far from perfect but much more beautiful. "Great is Thy faithfulness, great is Thy faithfulness. . . ."

The song built and then came to a close. Irvel was polite and enjoyed the company, but clearly she didn't recognize her niece. She remembered almost nothing about her life except a few choice things: her name, her Hank, her favorite hymn.

And every single word of the Twenty-third Psalm.

When her niece left, Irvel hugged her

and smiled. "I'm Irvel, dear. So nice to meet you. We should have tea sometime. Peppermint tea."

"I love you, Aunt Irvel," the woman told her. "Jesus loves you too."

"Yes, dear." Irvel's eyes twinkled as if she were twenty years old again. "The Lord is my shepherd. Isn't that wonderful?"

On the way home from work, Ashley couldn't stop thinking about the old woman and her sweet way of welcoming those around her. Before picking up Cole from her parents' house, where he stayed while she worked, she stopped and bought the one thing Sunset Hills Adult Care Home absolutely could not do another day without.

A box of peppermint tea bags.

Chapter Ten

You reap what you sow.

That was the only way Luke Baxter could make sense of how good his life had become recently. Not just at school and at church, but with Reagan — with her most of all.

They were thirty thousand feet up in the air and headed for New York City. The trip had been Reagan's idea — a chance to spend a week together before school started and to meet her parents at the same time. Luke cast a glance at his girlfriend, sleeping with her head against the window, and silently sent a prayer of thanks to God for her. Reagan was everything he'd ever wanted in a girl. Everything.

She had legs that went on forever and long, golden hair. More than once, people had commented that she looked like a taller, longer-legged Anna Kournikova, the beautiful tennis pro. Luke thought they were wrong. Reagan was far more beautiful than Kournikova. He was six feet two, and Reagan was six feet with heels. She attracted attention everywhere she went. And on top of that she was funny and sweet, and she loved a good softball game. Most important, she was committed to God, just like Luke. Everyone agreed she was perfect for him. He thought so too.

Reagan stirred and sat up straighter in the seat. "What time is it?"

"Almost one. Another half hour and we'll be there."

"Good." She snuggled against his shoulder, her voice sleepy. "I can't wait for them to meet you."

"You're sure they'll like me?"

"Silly." She gave him a grin and tapped the end of his nose with her finger. "What's not to like?"

She drifted off again, and Luke thought about what she'd said. That was it, wasn't it? He'd tried to live his entire life in a way that honored God. And as a result, his life was turning out just the way it should.

Not like Ashley, who'd run off to Paris and gotten pregnant — and who knew what else? — before dragging herself back home. She'd been raised with the same morals, the same beliefs that he had. But she'd thrown them all away, and her life had been a mess ever since. Even worse, her choices had shamed the family.

And what about Tim, Kari's husband, who'd not only cheated on her but actually moved in with one of his students? He had not only disgraced the family; he'd been killed in the process! Before then, of course, Tim had come home and tried to make things work with Kari, and Luke supposed that was a good thing. But why hadn't Kari avoided Tim in the first place? The guy had been all wrong for her, too old and academic. Especially when a guy as wonderful as Ryan Taylor had loved her all her life.

Luke leaned back in the seat. He still wasn't sure what he thought about Tim's murder. It had been tragic, of course. But in the end Tim had reaped what he sowed too. Luke couldn't help but think that Kari was better off now, no matter how hard it had been.

Luke yawned.

Sometimes when he thought about things this way, he wondered if he was being heartless or judgmental. Ashley certainly thought he was. But that wasn't it, not really. It was just that he cared about obeying God and doing the right thing. Upholding the honor of his family. And it bugged him when people in his own family just didn't bother.

Not that he was perfect. He knew he was a sinner — everyone was. But he'd tried hard to live the way he should, the way he'd been raised. He prayed. He went to church. He'd always made a point of not drinking or partying and had done his best to avoid situations with girls who were too tempting. He felt he owed it to God and to his family. To himself, for that matter.

And now all his efforts were paying off — that was clear. He was reaping what he had sown.

This trip to New York was just one more bit of evidence.

Luke felt as if he were flying — the view from the eighty-ninth floor of the north tower of the World Trade Center was that amazing.

Reagan's father, Tom Decker, was giving the tour, with Luke and Reagan trailing a few feet behind him.

"I can't believe this," Luke whispered to Reagan.

She giggled, her own voice barely audible. "Wait till you see his office."

Reagan was right. Her father led the way into a wood-paneled room, and Luke had to catch himself to keep from gasping out loud. The view was beyond anything Luke could have imagined. But he didn't want Mr. Decker thinking he was out of his element. After all, one day soon he'd have a degree of his own and an office much like this one. At least he figured he would.

"This is something else, sir." Luke moved to the window and stared down. Viewing the city from eighty-nine floors up was surreal, almost like looking down from an airplane.

"I like it." Mr. Decker grinned. "Most people are pretty shocked when they come up for the first time."

"I know I was." Reagan looped her arm through her father's. "The elevator ride alone is enough to make me queasy."

The phone on Mr. Decker's desk rang, and for a moment he was caught in a conversation. Luke glanced at Reagan and raised his eyebrows. "Nice." He mouthed the word, and she released her father's arm and joined Luke near the window.

She stared down, her forehead against the glass. "Looks like a postcard."

"I always thought I'd stay in Indiana." He slid his hand a few inches down the windowsill so it was against hers. "But being here in New York — I don't know.

There's something addicting about it. An excitement, an energy." He caught her eye. "Like I won't really have conquered the business world until I conquer it here."

Reagan grinned. "You're kinda young to be conquering anything yet."

"Hey." Luke nudged her with his elbow. "Give a guy a chance."

Behind them, Mr. Decker hung up the phone. "They need me down the hall for a quick meeting. Shouldn't be more than ten minutes if you can wait." He tapped his watch. "I'd like to take you to the top for lunch if you have time."

"Sure." Reagan lifted one shoulder. "We have all day, right?" She looked at Luke.

"Right."

"And we're seeing *Riverdance* tonight — is that what's on the schedule?"

"It is." Reagan lowered her chin and gave Luke a warning look. "And no complaints from you guys, okay?"

Luke stifled a grin and held his hands up. "Not me."

"Luke likes men in tights." Mr. Decker gave him a light punch in the arm as he rounded his desk.

"Especially Irish tights."

They could still hear Reagan's father laughing as he closed his office door and headed down the hallway.

Luke stared at Reagan. "Can you see it?"

"What?" Her eyes danced. She leaned against the window, facing him.

"Me. In an office like this." He gestured to the oversized leather chair behind the desk. "Working right next to your dad."

"I guess." A quiet ripple of laughter sounded on her lips. Luke closed the gap between them. She was so beautiful, and she seemed so happy spending this past week with her parents. In fact, these last few days with Reagan and her family had been enough to convince him.

One day — maybe one day soon — he would ask Reagan to marry him. They could have such a wonderful life together, maybe right here in New York. And no matter what hard times might come, the life of faith they would share together would feel like nothing but blue skies and sunsets. Day after day, year after year.

He wanted to kiss her, to take her in his arms and pull her close the way he'd longed to since they'd left Bloomington together. But her constant nearness was getting to him. If he wanted to keep his thoughts pure, they needed space between them — as often as possible, anyway. He backed up a few steps and fell into her father's chair. Kicking his heels up on the corner of the desk, he linked his fingers behind his head and grinned at her. "Know what I want?"

She rested her back against the window and angled her head. "A pair of Irish tights?"

"After that."

This time she let her head fall back, gentle laughter spilling from her like a song. "Okay." She caught her breath. "Tell me what."

"I want a position at the firm here . . . and an office down the hall from your father. That way" — he gave his voice a haughty sound — "I can support his daughter in the manner to which she has become accustomed."

Reagan batted her eyes. "Oh, yeah?"

"It's that or the glass slipper." Luke grinned at her. They'd been dating for less than a year, and their discussions about forever were never very serious. But he was close to crossing the line here. "You know the score, Reagan. One way or another, I want you in my life."

"Really?" She was teasing him, feeling him out.

"Really." He held out his hand, and she came willingly. When she was close enough, he pulled her onto his lap and brought his nose up against hers. "You like New York, right?"

"I like glass slippers too."

Suddenly the moment changed, and Luke's words got stuck in his throat. He wove his fingers through her hair and kissed her until they heard footsteps in the hallway outside.

"He's coming!" Reagan breathed the warning against Luke's face and jumped back to her place by the window.

At the same time, Luke flew out of the chair and tried to strike a casual pose a few feet away. They were both out of breath when the door opened.

"Meetings!" Mr. Decker gave them each a quick glance and circled back behind his desk again. He set down a portfolio and clapped his hands together. "Okay . . . you two hungry?"

Luke glanced at Reagan. The man had no idea. He turned back to Mr. Decker and shrugged. "Sure."

"All right, then. Windows on the World it is."

When they passed by the office next to Mr. Decker's, Luke pointed to the name-plate, shot a glance at Reagan, and mouthed, "Luke Baxter."

And in that moment, he had no doubt that one day it would be true. Not just the nameplate, but everything — the job, the wedding, the place in New York City.

Even the glass slipper.

Chapter Eleven

God was honoring her.

As Kari walked to Pastor Mark Atteberry's office that Tuesday afternoon, she had no other way to explain her feelings. Days had passed since she'd stayed up late into the night, dreaming of how to use her painful experience to help other women. And her heart had felt lighter every day since.

In the weeks after Jessie's birth, there had been times when Kari cried with joy — and other times when fear and loneliness loomed large. Her husband was dead, after all, and somehow she would have to survive. Even with her faith, even with her family nearby, there were entire days when the task felt daunting — or worse.

And her feelings for Ryan Taylor complicated matters. It was a good thing he lived in New York. At this season in her life it would have been unbearable to see him on a regular basis, to shoulder the constant reminder of all she and Ryan had once shared. Just thinking about him made her feel unfaithful, like she was cheating on Tim's memory.

But now that God had planted new purpose in the soil of her life, Kari could talk to Ryan and enjoy herself. She no longer depended on a phone call from him to ease the burden of grief at the end of a day of caring for her fatherless child. Indeed, God had taken her to a separate place, a place away from the pain and anguish. Away, even, from the brief flashes of pleasure she felt when she spoke with Ryan.

Her place now was clear and close and constant, as though God had drawn her into his very being. She'd read in the Scriptures about the Lord being a mighty fortress, a tower, a hiding place. But only now was she realizing those truths in her own life. She was there now, safe in a place she had longed to find since she was a young girl.

But she never would have guessed the ticket there would cost so very much.

Kari rounded a corner in the church hallway and held Jessie's infant carrier against her body, careful not to disturb her tiny sleeping daughter. Jessie was nearly three months old now, and Kari could see a routine developing in her sleep patterns. If the routine held, Jessie wouldn't wake for another hour.

Pastor Mark's door was open.

"Kari, come in." He stood and gave her a side hug as he positioned himself behind Jessie's carrier. "Let's take a look."

Kari beamed, letting her gaze follow that of the pastor's. "She's pretty, isn't she?"

"Oh my." A soft breath came from Mark's lips. "She's beautiful. No question she has her mother's face."

The corners of Kari's smile softened some. "And her father's eyes."

"Yes." Pastor Mark nodded, squeezing Kari's shoulders once more. "I was going to say that." He gave her a glance. "You doing okay?"

"That's why I'm here." Kari moved to a small sofa a few feet away and sat down. She set Jessie's carrier on the floor nearby, rocking it gently.

"So . . ." Pastor Mark returned to his desk chair and leaned forward, his elbows on his knees. "How's your family?"

"Good." Kari smiled, reminding herself to be patient. She had known this wouldn't be a short discussion. "Mom got a good report from her doctor last week. Still no cancer. It's been nearly ten years now."

"That's wonderful. I hadn't talked to your father yet. He was worried."

"He was?" Her father hadn't said anything about being troubled by her mother's test.

Pastor Mark shrugged. "He's always worried when your mom goes in for tests. Anytime people battle cancer, there's a chance they'll have to battle it again."

"Well . . ." Kari pushed the thought from her mind. "Her doctors say she looks great."

"Good." The pastor crossed his legs. "How about the others? Brooke, Erin, Ashley, Luke?"

"They're fine. Brooke's little girl is still sick a lot, and Erin and Sam are moving this fall. Ashley took a job at Sunset Hills — that small adult care home off South Walnut."

"Yes, we've had church members wind up there on occasion."

"Heaven's waiting room, Dad calls it." Kari tilted her head. "Sweet people, from what Ashley says."

"She must be glad Landon's okay."

"Yes," Kari sighed. "I think God has something special planned for those two."

The pastor cast her a curious look. "So she's finally decided to let him catch her?"

"Ashley?" Kari laughed quietly. She stopped rocking Jessie and leaned back. "Not my sister Ashley. She'll do everything the hard way, including falling in love. She cares for Landon, but she'd be the last to admit there's any kind of romance."

"What about Luke?" Pastor Mark stroked his chin. "I haven't seen him around for a few weeks."

"He's in New York City visiting Reagan's family."

"Reagan?" The pastor raised a single eyebrow. "So it's serious, huh?"

Kari grinned, picturing her brother and Reagan. "They're beautiful together. They study and laugh and pray. The two of them remind everyone watching that love is still a good thing." She nodded. "I'd say it's serious."

"Is she from New York, then?" Conversations with Pastor Mark were always like this — several minutes of Baxter news before anything serious could be discussed. It wasn't small talk to the pastor. It was news the man actually cared about, as though he, too, were part of the Baxter family.

"Her parents lived there a long time ago; then they moved to North Carolina. Last year her father was hired by a big accounting firm in the city. He works in the clouds, from what Luke says. Near the top of the World Trade Center."

"Must be an amazing view." Pastor Mark smiled. "Nothing quite like it in Bloomington, I'm afraid."

"Luke's getting the full tour this week." She smiled. "The other night my sisters and I figured out the whole scenario. Luke will graduate, marry Reagan, and the two of them will move to New York. Then Luke can have an office right up there in the sky beside Reagan's father."

"Could happen." The pastor winked and drew a slow breath. "But I don't think that's what you came to tell me." His eyes grew deeper, more intent. "It sounded important when you called the other day."

"It is." Kari could feel her eyes come to life. She'd been wanting to talk about this since that night. "Okay." She held out both hands. "I know what God wants me to do with the rest of my life."

"Well" — the pastor's kind chuckle filled the room — "that's more than most of us can say." His eyes narrowed in a thoughtful way. "Tell me about it."

Kari tried to sit on her enthusiasm. She would need to be calm and concise in order to give Pastor Mark a clear picture of her vision. "I'm thinking there are other people like me in the church. I mean, people who are hurting. The walking wounded. Am I right? I'm not the only one?"

A sad smile punctuated the pastor's expression. "You've been bugging my phones." He leaned back in his chair a few inches and raised his brow a notch. "There are more wounded people than most care to guess."

Kari bit her lip. "That's what I thought." She drew a steady breath. "Before Tim died . . . before he told me he was having an affair . . . I pictured the two of us working with married couples, people struggling to make it work." She uttered a rueful laugh. "People like Tim and me, I guess. Obviously, that didn't work out."

Jessie cooed lightly and stretched a tiny fist. Kari leaned over and set the carrier gently in motion once more. "Anyway, last week I practically felt God tap me on the shoulder and tell me there's still something he wants me to do. Women who are hurting — I mean *really* hurting — won't necessarily seek help from a weekly Bible study." She locked eyes with Pastor Mark. "What they need is, well, sort of a mentor. Someone who will meet with them one-on-one, study the Scriptures with them, cry with them, and listen when they bare their soul. Sort of an anonymous friend who can keep their secrets. Someone who can look them straight in the eye and say, 'I made it through the fire, and you can too.' You know, to bridge the gap between pain and progress."

Kari spread her fingers across her chest, her voice soft but filled with holy passion. "Someone like me."

Pastor Mark nodded. "Hmmm." His eyes filled with understanding. "People trapped in their pain, you mean? Sort of an anonymous way to find help and support."

"Yes." Kari's heartbeat quickened. "From someone who's already walked that road. At least in one form or another."

The pastor snagged a pen and paper from his desk and began jotting something down. "I can think of a woman right now who would jump at the chance to meet with you. Her husband's on the verge of an affair. He's already talking divorce. She's a very private person. Doesn't want anyone at church to know." He tapped the pen on his knee, staring at his notes. "Meanwhile, she's wasting away spiritually. If I called her and told her about your offer, I'm sure she'd be interested." Then he put down the pen and turned toward Kari. "But something tells me it's a bit soon."

"Soon?" She gave a polite sniff. "My feelings are fresh enough to make a difference."

"But they could be *too* fresh. I think you might need a little more time to heal before you start counseling someone else."

The excitement leaked from Kari's heart like air from a punctured tire. She fell back against the sofa.

"Healing takes time, Kari. It takes remembering — sorting through the pieces of your past and savoring what was good, learning from what wasn't. In that way you honor your yesterdays. After that" — he smiled — "I have a feeling God will use you to help more people than you can imagine."

"You really think so?" Hope stirred within her.

"Definitely. But it's crucial you don't rush this, Kari. You and God have a lot to work through before you can take on a ministry."

At the end of the hour, Pastor Mark wrote a list of books Kari could read, studies on healing and learning from the memories of a painful time or difficult loss. They prayed together, committing Kari's dream to God and asking for his guidance in the coming months.

Kari left the pastor's office with a renewed peace and a purpose that filled her from her ankles up. Maybe this wasn't the time to start helping other women. But that time would come. How glad Tim would've been to see where God was taking her — first through the memories that made up her past and then into a future where all her remembering would help in the lives of other women.

If only you knew, Tim. God is so good; he's giving me another chance at life.

On the way home she turned left instead of right and wound up at the cemetery.

The day was decked in bright blues and vibrant greens. Sunshine streamed through the clusters of trees and splashed light over the quiet sea of death. Kari gazed across the field. On a summer day like this, the rows of gray cement tombstones appeared almost warm.

She grabbed a bottle for Jessie, took the sleeping infant from her car seat, and cradled her close. "Come on, little girl." She nuzzled her face against her daughter's. "Let's go talk to Daddy."

Kari had come here a handful of other times since Tim died. For the most part she did her grieving at home, a Bible in one hand and a box of tissues in the other. But sometimes she just needed to remember, needed to connect once more with all that would never be again.

She drew a deep breath and crossed the parking lot. *Give me strength, God.*

Carefully she maneuvered past stones of varying shapes and sizes until she found one that looked newer than the rest. Around its base, fresh grass poked up through the dirt — a sign that life was pressing on. The stone was simple, traditional, but it expressed the way Kari had felt about Tim. The way she still felt: *Timothy Allen Jacobs. Loving husband and father.*

It was true, no matter what people said. Tim had made some awful mistakes, and yes, she'd been angry at him — angry enough to hate him at times. But he had also come to his senses. He had moved back home and committed himself to a full course of counseling sessions with Kari. In the months before his murder the two of them had grown closer than Kari had ever dreamed possible.

And during those precious months, she'd caught a glimpse of the type of father Tim would have been. He would hold his head near her abdomen and make up songs for their unborn child. Just before he was killed, he'd brought home a tiny stuffed eagle, white and downy soft. Jessie's first toy — the one Kari set at the foot of her daughter's crib each night.

Kari stared at the stone. *How can you be gone?* She glanced at the two dates engraved beneath his name, not nearly enough years spread between them. He had been so young — only thirty-four years old. It was still hard to believe. He lay deep in the ground while his killer sat behind bars in the local jail, winning one delay after another in the trial proceedings. The district attorney had said it could be spring or later before Tim's killer would finally face a jury.

Little Jessie began to stir, and Kari leaned against a tree. She slipped the bottle into her daughter's mouth, as a breeze picked up and played through the leaves in a nearby tree. *You're here, aren't you, God?* Kari lifted her chin and closed her eyes, letting the cool air move across her face.

The rustling leaves seemed to answer in response. *Always . . . always . . . always.*

A Scripture passage from a recent sermon filtered into Kari's mind like so many more rays of sunshine: *"His compassions never fail. They are new every morning."*

Kari opened her eyes and gazed at Jessie. *Yes, Lord, they are. Every single morning.*

Her eyes moved once more toward Tim's gravestone. "It's happening, Tim." She uttered a quiet laugh. "Just when I thought it never would." She paused. "I'm learning to live."

Jessie was more awake now, the sound of her sucking more pronounced. Kari swallowed, searching for her voice. "I'm praying that God will let you know something." Tears nipped at the corners of her eyes, and a small, happy sob welled up from someplace in her soul. "He's given me a way to help — a . . . a way to share what I learned with you." A single tear slid down her nose. Kari wiped it on her sleeve before it could fall on Jessie. She sniffed twice. "I'm going to be okay, Tim."

Jessie drew back from her bottle, cooed sweetly, and gave Kari a dreamy smile. Kari smiled back, kissing her daughter's forehead. "We're both going to be okay, aren't we, Jess?"

The breeze stilled, and a silence hovered over the place where Tim was buried. "Well . . ." Kari looked back at the stone. "We have to go now. Jessie needs to get home." She felt a sudden catch in her throat. "I . . . I wish you could see her,

Tim. She's so pretty. You would have been the proudest father."

Again Kari sniffed, and this time she stood, staring into the blue. *Lord, lead me forward. Please.*

Then, with a strength that was not her own, Kari clutched more tightly to Jessie and set off toward the car. One step after another, away from the sadness and sorrow that had gripped her for many months.

And into a future she hadn't believed in until that week.

Chapter Twelve

Landon was no longer the enemy.

Now that Ashley had been honest and explained how her love for him had nothing to do with commitment or marriage or even dating, suddenly everything about Landon wasn't bad at all.

It was almost fun.

He was still off work, waiting for his leg and burns to heal, and Ashley had started bringing Cole over to his house on Saturdays to help him pass the time. They would spend the afternoon watching TV or playing games.

Always, on these visits, the mood between Ashley and Landon was light and upbeat — playful even. None of the deep eyes or serious tones that had colored that memorable night at the hospital. Not even the uncomfortable game of pursuit that marked their encounters before that.

Landon was wonderful with Cole, letting the little boy draw with markers on his cast, partnering with him for Uno or Go

Fish, and teaching him the difference between a ball and a strike if the Cubs were on TV.

Later, when Cole was busy coloring or playing by himself, Ashley would tell Landon everything about Irvel's longing for her husband and Edith's screaming and Helen's insistence that everyone who entered Sunset Hills was a potential spy.

Landon was a patient listener. He seemed interested in everything she said, and not just because he was a captive audience. In fact, he was the perfect sounding board, and talking with him gave her a way to process her experience at Sunset Hills.

At times Ashley would catch herself watching Landon a bit longer than necessary, enjoying herself more than she'd intended. But in the end she always kept her focus. All the reasons for their not being together were still valid, after all — and besides, Landon was moving to New York. These were possibly their last times together, the final days of a friendship that had taken root back when they were barely more than kids. They were on safe ground. Landon spoke nothing of the feelings he'd admitted to in the hospital. Ashley chose to believe that he'd finally let go, that he had taught himself not to think of her that way.

One Friday afternoon four weeks after Landon's injury, he called Ashley at work, desperate for a diversion. "Can Cole come over and play?"

"Don't do that to me!" Ashley laughed. "I need to know the world outside these walls is still sane."

"Sorry." Landon let out a half-chuckle, half-moan. "I'm so bored, sitting here in this body armor, and my leg is itching like crazy. Tell me you're bringing my favorite little boy over tomorrow."

"Well . . ." Ashley carried the portable phone into the living room. Edith, Irvel, and Helen were snoring peacefully while *Matlock* played out on the old television set. "I have to clean my garage. And later, let me think . . . oh, yes. I'm supposed to straighten my bookshelf."

"That busy, huh?"

"You know it." She stifled a giggle and leaned against the living-room wall. "Never a dull moment."

"How's the screamer?" Landon's mood was still light, but his tone was softer. He cared about the people at Sunset Hills. The more Ashley talked about them, the more connected he seemed to get.

"She screamed right on target, poor thing. The minute she hit the bathroom."

"Did Belinda dope her up again?"

"No." Ashley let her eyes settle on Edith. "Belinda was out running errands."

"So, what'd you do?"

"Talked to her, sat with her." Ashley gazed out the window. It was another beautiful summer day, the kind that made her feel like painting. "Took about half an hour, but eventually she calmed down. She said the strangest thing."

"What?"

"She said she'd seen a witch. A witch that wanted to kill her."

Landon whistled low. "No wonder she screams."

"Yeah, that's what I was thinking." Ashley looked back at Edith again. The woman was completely at peace now, with no memory of whatever she'd seen earlier.

"Maybe it's spiritual, Ashley. Maybe she really is seeing something."

"Come on, Landon." Ashley resisted the urge to laugh out loud. "You don't believe that, do you?"

"Well . . ." Landon's tone was even. When it came to matters of faith, he never preached at her. He knew her position and didn't try to change her way of thinking. "I do, actually. Tell you what. I'll make you a promise."

"What's that?" Ashley looked down and made invisible flower patterns on the table with the tip of her finger. Why was she so uncomfortable whenever he talked about God things?

"From this day on I'll pray about Edith's screaming. Until something happens, okay?"

"Okay." Ashley kept her voice light. "Whatever makes you happy."

There was a pause and Ashley wondered if he was frustrated with her. After a moment she heard a munching sound. "Mom brought me homemade caramel corn." He chomped a bit more. "Cole would love it."

She grinned. Good. He wasn't mad. "You think my bookshelf can wait — is that what you're saying?"

"I'm saying, what time can you bring that boy over to play?"

She laughed. "Okay. Fine. We'll come over after naptime. About three o'clock, okay?"

"In the morning?" Landon sounded hopeful, more like her four-year-old son than the strong, stoic firefighter.

"In your dreams." Ashley let loose another quiet laugh. It was refreshing to know both sides of the man. Refreshing and just a little dangerous. *He's not your type*, Ashley reminded herself. *He'd have you cooking casseroles for the church potluck in no time. Besides, he's moving to New York. Keep it simple.*

"Well, Miss Ashley, you flatter yourself." Landon's tone was teasing. She could almost see the sparkle in his eyes. "I was talking about Cole. He could come for a sleepover. We could build a tent and play cops and robbers and have guy talks. You know, eat caramel corn all night and not sweep up the crumbs — that kind of thing. It'd be a blast. Come on, Mom."

Ashley's smile faded some. A wistful wind blew against her conscience. Sleeping in a living-room tent, playing cops and robbers, guy talks — all the things Cole was missing out on by not having a father.

She swallowed, keeping a lid firmly on her simmering heart. "Very funny. We'll be there at three . . . in the afternoon." She glanced at the clock. She had chores to do, and she needed to check on Bert and Laura Jo before her shift was over. "See you then."

Ashley let Cole oversleep on Saturday afternoon.

While he napped, she started work on a

new painting — a portrait of Irvel with a teapot. Ashley had captured the image with a snapshot taken the week before. Deeply involved in sketching out the piece and laying down a background, she lost track of time. It was four-thirty when they finally picked up two pizzas and drove the short distance to Landon's house.

He met them at the door, crutches under both arms, his fully casted leg stretched out in front of him.

"Hey, pizza and my favorite boy all in one afternoon!" His grin shot a burst of adrenaline straight to Ashley's heart. He said nothing about her being late. "Come in, guys."

"Guess what?" Cole skipped over to Landon's side and looked up, his eyes wide. "We got the cheese kind!"

"No!" Landon bent at the waist. He couldn't have looked more surprised if Ed McMahon had stopped by to tell him he'd won a million dollars. "The cheese kind?"

"Yep." Cole worked his head up and down. "Wanna eat it now?"

Landon shifted his gaze to Ashley. "Do we?"

"No, we do not." Ashley sent Cole a pointed look. "You just had an apple on the way here."

"Okay." Cole looked past Landon into the house. "Wanna play a game?"

"Sure. Definitely." In a graceful motion, Landon spun around on his crutches and headed toward the living room. His house was small and simple, in an older neighborhood not far from the university. Something about it made Ashley feel safe. Or maybe it was Landon who made her feel that way.

Landon grabbed a deck of Uno cards, eased himself onto the sofa, and patted his knee. "Be my partner, okay?"

"Yippee!" Cole ran toward Landon.

"Watch it, buddy." Ashley winced. "He's got a hurt leg, remember?"

"I know." Cole climbed onto Landon's lap and settled against his chest. "I was careful."

The card game got under way, but Ashley had trouble concentrating. She kept sneaking glances over the top of her cards, watching the way Landon brought his face alongside Cole's as they discussed which card to play. He was the most patient man she knew. She wanted to set up her easel and re-create on canvas the image they made together. Man and boy — her son in the arms of a young man who loved him. The type of moment that had happened only a handful of times in Cole's life — and most of them in the past month.

Watching Cole and Landon together did unfamiliar things to Ashley's heart, things she didn't understand. There were moments when she wanted to join them on the sofa and beg Landon to stay, to promise him that her heart would figure out a way to care for him as more than a friend. But there were also flashes of relief in the knowledge that this intimate family scene couldn't possibly become anything more serious. Not when Landon was leaving in a few months.

Ashley tried to focus on her cards. But no matter how hard she tried to steer them, her thoughts wouldn't sail a straight course. Was it wrong to be here, unfair to Cole and Landon? Maybe it wasn't wrong; maybe she should talk Landon into never leaving Bloomington.

Maybe she needed professional help.

The afternoon moved quickly from Uno to cheese pizza to the tail end of a ball game on television. At seven-thirty, Cole began to yawn.

"Time to get you home, buddy." Ashley stood and stretched. Then she caught Landon's gaze and held it. "Thanks. We had a good time."

Landon held out his hand and Ashley took hold of it, helping him to his feet. She passed him his crutches, and he balanced himself, resting his hands on Cole's shoulders. "Come back next week, okay, little guy?"

Cole beamed. "Next time I'll bring my baseball cards."

"Great." Landon high-fived Cole. "Maybe we can trade."

"Really?"

"Sure. I've got great cards."

"Cool." He hugged Landon's long legs and darted toward the front door. He dropped to the floor and began working his sandals back on his feet.

Ashley looked at Landon and shrugged. "It's all I can do to keep up."

"Tell me about it." Landon grinned. "Hey . . ." He checked his watch. "Do you think your parents would take Cole tonight?"

Ashley's resolve flapped in the wind. Her times with Landon had been safely platonic in the company of Cole. But this invitation to come back without him was something new. "Tonight?"

"Yeah." Landon's voice was careful, casual. It kept Ashley at ease. "We could watch a video or play another round of

165

Uno." He pointed his shoulder toward the kitchen and gave her a crooked smile. "I have leftover pizza."

"True." Ashley laughed. She searched her list of reasons and couldn't find a single one that would justify saying no, especially when the idea sounded so appealing. "Actually, my parents are home tonight. They'd probably be happy to watch him." She gazed at her son, still struggling with his second shoe, and gave a small smirk. "Why not? He practically lives there anyway. Sometimes I think that's his real home and I'm just the baby-sitter."

He chose not to respond to the hurt in her voice. "So you'll come?"

"Okay. But no cops and robbers, all right?"

"All right." Landon grinned as he hobbled along next to her toward the front door.

"Okay." She took hold of Cole's hand and waved. "See you in a bit."

"Yeah. See ya."

An hour later she was back in Landon's driveway. She had been right about her parents. They loved spending time with Cole. In some ways they were the family her son didn't have. Of course, Ashley's brother would never see it that way. Luke thought Ashley took advantage of their parents. Sometimes Ashley wondered if he was right. She had never been sure she loved Cole the way she should. And some days Ashley could feel Cole's distance, as though the child could sense her uncertainty, her ambivalence at being a mother. Her uncertainty about love of any kind.

She put those dark thoughts out of her mind and stared at Landon's front door. Was his invitation as innocent as it seemed? For a moment she closed her eyes and heard his voice as it had sounded in the hospital that night, days after he'd been hurt. *"I'm moving, Ashley . . . It'll be Jalen and me, fighting fires and saving lives right there in the heart of New York City."*

No, she was sure Landon had no ulterior motives tonight. They were simply two old friends who'd rather pass the time together than alone. She glanced at the rearview mirror and ran her fingers through the roots of her hair.

When she climbed out of the car, she left a hint of jasmine behind her.

Despite his broken leg, Landon wasted no time moving his crutches across the living-room floor at the sound of Ashley's car in the driveway. For an hour, he'd been doubting the wisdom of asking her over. What was he hoping to achieve, really? They were enjoying their time together these past weeks, but Ashley was his friend. Nothing more.

That night in the hospital she'd made her feelings painfully clear.

Since then he'd worked to accept the way she felt about him. Ashley was right. The two of them could never love each other the way Landon had wanted. She wasn't someone he could marry or spend his life with.

He wanted a woman who shared his faith, his feelings. His future. Someone who would be his other half — not perfect, but perfectly in love with him. And that was more than Ashley could give. More than she was capable of giving. After so many years, Landon finally understood that. Somehow, someday, God would bring the right woman into his life, and these years of loving Ashley would fade into boyhood memories.

Wouldn't they?

After all, he was on the brink of a whole new season in his life, a change that might take him away from Bloomington forever. A change Landon embraced fully.

But then why had he invited Ashley back tonight?

Landon opened the door and took in the sight of her, beautiful and breathless on his front step. The smile in her eyes was as familiar as his own name.

Why, indeed.

"You made it."

"Grandma and Papa were thrilled." Ashley stepped inside and tossed a grin over her shoulder. "Besides, my bookcase doesn't need cleaning till next week."

He hobbled across the living room while she detoured into the kitchen. "Want some water?"

"That'd be great." Landon maneuvered to the sofa, laid his crutches on the floor, and eased himself down, mindful of the bandages on his back. "I should be waiting on you."

"Well . . ." Ashley rounded the corner, carrying two tall glasses of ice water. "When the cast's off, you can make it up to me." She set the drinks down on a magazine and flopped down beside him. "Deal?"

"Deal." The corners of his lips stopped short of a full smile. Once his cast was off, he'd be working and getting ready for the move. There'd be little if any time for Ashley and him to share moments like this.

"Hey." Ashley tilted her face. Her deep

blue eyes shone with sincerity. "Thanks for playing with Cole." She leaned her head back against the sofa cushion and stared at the ceiling. "He loves coming here."

For a moment Landon wanted to shout at her, *Can't you see it, Ashley? You and me and Cole — we belong together.* Instead, he worked his face into a smile and chuckled. *Play it straight, Landon. Play it straight.* "The feeling's mutual."

Suddenly he understood why he'd invited Ashley back tonight, why the words had spilled from his heart. A Scripture verse he'd learned as a boy came back to him: *Out of the overflow of the heart the mouth speaks.*

His mouth had uttered the words of invitation for one reason alone: No matter how hard he tried to convince himself otherwise, and despite his best intentions to move on with life, his heart still overflowed with feelings for a wide-eyed dreamer who danced to her own music. A girl who stirred his emotions and made him feel whole and alive.

A girl named Ashley Baxter.

Chapter Thirteen

The evening passed in a blur.

Ashley and Landon were talking about Sunset Hills again, about Irvel and Edith and Helen and the others. Country videos played on TV, but they hadn't gotten around to watching a movie since Ashley arrived. She was glad. It was more fun talking.

"So he circles the bed all day?" Landon leaned against the arm of the sofa so he could face her and take some of the pressure off the burns on his back. "I don't get it."

"That's the problem." Ashley anchored her elbows on her knees. She laced her fingers together and let her chin rest on top. "No one gets it. Poor Bert stays up there in his room rubbing circles into his comforter all day, and meanwhile his family is too upset to visit."

"I can see why." Landon cocked his head. His eyes shone like sunbeams in a watercolor. He raised his hand and began

171

making small circles in the air. "Course, if I make circles all day when I'm older, you'll come and visit *me*, right, Ash?"

She laughed. "Right, Bert."

"I'll bet the old guy has his reasons."

"I know." Ashley sat back again. "If only I could find out what they are."

"Maybe if he looked up for a minute and saw you, he'd stop circling."

Ashley dropped her chin. "I don't get it."

"You know, if he actually *looked* at you." Landon stifled a grin.

"How would that make him —"

"Stop!" Landon's eyes were suddenly wide, his tone awestruck.

"What?" Ashley glanced over her shoulder. "Don't do that to me, Landon. You scared me."

"I'm sorry." He moved an inch closer, reaching his hand out toward her face. "But my goodness, dear. You have the most beautiful hair." He fanned his fingers through her short-cropped bangs. Then his eyes found hers. "Has anyone ever told you that?"

Realization dawned, and Ashley could feel the grin break across her face. "Very funny." She grabbed the sofa pillow beside her and in one swift motion whacked Landon over the head with it.

"Hey, not fair." Landon waved his arms

to defend himself. "I'm crippled, re-member?"

Ashley leaned forward, pillow in hand, poised for another attack. "All Bert needs is a look at my hair, is that it?"

"Well" — again Landon threw his hands up in surrender — "Irvel seems to think so."

"That's it." Ashley got up on her knees and closed the distance between them. She held the pillow over him and hit his flailing arms three times before he caught both her wrists with one hand.

"Okay, you asked for it." They were facing each other, and he began tickling her, poking her in the ribs while she fought to break free.

"Help!" She laughed so hard her words were impossible to understand. "I . . . I can't . . . breathe."

It was true. But it wasn't merely Landon's tickling that made breathing dif-ficult. There was something else, a feeling she'd never had before around Landon Blake. Something about his nearness, the touch of his hands, his body brushing against hers as they played. She could feel her cheeks growing hot. *Why am I here? Why are we doing this? What's going on?*

Ashley dismissed her questions. There

was no point asking them. Whatever the answers, she wouldn't pull herself away. Not so much because she couldn't, but because she didn't want to.

"Let me go!" She pulled one hand free and poked her finger into his side. His muscles tightened in response. "So . . . I'm not the only ticklish one!"

"No." In one move he trapped her hands again, this time behind her back. "But you're the only one being tickled."

He had the most wonderful laugh. The sound of it did mysterious things to her heart. Ashley was breathing hard, her body shaking. The battle was wild and exhilarating, but she needed a break. She let her body go limp. "Okay, I give up." She laughed again. "Truce."

Landon still had her hands pinned, but now he gently let go of them. As he did, she lost her balance and sat back on the knee of his good leg. Suddenly awkward, Ashley started to move off him.

But Landon put his arms around her waist and linked his fingers. His eyes were bright, but Ashley couldn't tell if he was teasing her or drawing out the moment. He tightened his grip on her and grinned. "Can I trust you?"

"Landon!" Ashley was still breathing

hard. She turned partway, still balanced on his knee but ready to spring off the moment he released her. She tried to act serious, but it was impossible. She was enjoying herself too much. "Let me go!"

The teasing in Landon's face dissolved, and slowly he loosened his arms from around her. Their eyes found each other, and everything about the moment changed. Gone was the teasing, the tickling, the battling for position. Instead a quiet came between them, a quiet charged with emotions neither of them was ready to talk about.

After an eternity, Landon looked straight to her soul and spoke in a voice Ashley could barely hear. "I let go."

"I know." There was a pull between them, a pull that couldn't have been stronger if she were magnet and he were steel. Slowly, imperceptibly, Ashley shifted so they were face-to-face again. Their eyes met, and Ashley's heart began to speak before her head could interfere. "Hold me again, Landon. Please."

"Ashley . . ." It was more of a question than anything. But her name sounded like silk on his lips. They were poised at a line they hadn't crossed since they were kids. If they crossed it now, everything would change.

"Hold me." Her voice was barely a whisper. She slipped her arms around his neck and let her forehead fall against his. Her eyes closed as finally his arms came around her once more.

Her heartbeat was strong, steady against his chest. She felt his sweet breath on her face, breathed in the musky smell of his day-old cologne. He eased his hands up along the small of her back and let go again. Before Ashley could wonder what he was doing, she felt his fingers against her cheeks, her jaw. "Ashley, look at me."

She blinked her eyes and pulled back far enough to look into his eyes. In them she could see his heart — a heart deeper than she'd ever wanted to explore. She traced a single finger across his forehead and down along his lower lip. "Landon . . ."

In a way neither of them could have stopped, they came together. Their kiss made time stand still, made Ashley question every belief she'd ever held, every presumption she'd ever made about the tender man before her. Ashley pulled back first, her lips open. This was not some lighthearted game that had gotten out of hand. It was something entirely different — something she had wanted since that night in the hospital.

"I love you, Ashley." He kissed a feathery trail along her brow and down her temple toward her ear. "No matter how hard I try, I can't stop loving you."

Common sense had something to say, but Ashley refused to listen. She brushed the tip of her nose against his. "I've wanted to kiss you since . . . since I saw you in the hospital, unconscious." She rested her hands on his shoulders. "When you told me you were moving, I didn't know if I'd ever get the chance."

She slipped off his knee and snuggled up beside him, angling herself so his face was just above hers. "Did you ever feel that way? I mean, who'd have thought we'd have this chance —"

"Shhh." He brought his finger to her lips. Ashley would remember the look on his face forever, no matter where life took the two of them after this. Part desire, part contentment, as though he'd never felt this right in all his life. As though he never would again. "You talk a lot for a girl who keeps her distance."

Ashley felt the beginning of a smile, and she bit her lip. Before she could say another word, Landon cradled his arm around her neck and drew her close. This time their kiss was longer, more intense.

The feelings coursing through Ashley were so new they took her breath away.

Paris was one thing, but this . . . this was something Ashley had never felt before in her life.

Was it love, the kind of love Landon had always wanted her to feel for him? They paused, and then their lips came together again, saying things neither of them was ready to voice.

It was Landon who pulled away first.

He nuzzled his face against hers, holding her close, letting her feel his heartbeat against her chest. "Tell me, Ashley."

"Hmmm." She brought her lips to his cheek, felt the day's growth of beard tickle her face. "Tell you what?"

"About Paris."

A splash of cold water couldn't have wrenched her more quickly from the magic of the moment. She sat back a foot and looked at him, puzzled. "What about it?"

His expression was unchanged. The reckless emotion that had been there seconds earlier still played across his features. He ran a finger lightly along her jaw. When it was clear to him that her answer wouldn't come easily, he leaned back and took her hand in his. "When you left for Paris, you were young and beautiful." He gave a sideways nod of his head. "Somewhat wild, somewhat rebellious. Determined to see life through the jaded lenses of your own imagination. But with a heart as transparent as the air between us."

Ashley listened, reminding herself to breathe. The jaded lenses of her own imagination? When did Landon Blake become a poet? And what did he know about Paris? Her heart skipped a beat and settled into an unfamiliar rhythm.

She waited for him to continue.

"When you came back, you were every bit as wild and rebellious." A sad smile simmered on the corners of his mouth. Again he looked straight into her soul. "Every bit as beautiful. But something terribly wrong had happened, something that showed in your eyes. It was there every time we met after that."

Ashley shook her head. No, he had no right to talk about this. Not now, not when they were finding something they'd never shared before. Landon would never find out about Paris. He couldn't. And certainly he didn't already know; that was impossible. "I . . . I don't know what you mean."

"Yes, you do." He gave her shoulders a gentle squeeze, his eyes never leaving hers.

"Someone captured your heart in Paris, but whoever it was locked it up and put it in a cell, a dungeon of darkness." His words were slow and quiet, soaked in kindness. "A dungeon with walls so high and thick that even now you'd rather let your heart stay there than find the painful way of escape."

Ashley's head was spinning. How could he know this? How could he have spent so little time with her these past four years and still know the exact condition of her heart? She opened her mouth, but nothing came out. Instead, tears filled her eyes, and she shook her head, unable to talk.

Landon leaned down and kissed her forehead. "Don't cry, Ash." He dusted his thumb beneath one of her eyes and caught her tear as it fell. "You don't have to tell me."

Two quick sobs came from her throat and she sniffed, shaking her head in short bursts. "I . . . I can't, Landon." She lowered her face so that only her eyes were raised in his direction. "I can't."

Landon brought his lips first to one of her eyes, then the other. "I love you, Ashley. Do you know that?"

She nodded, swallowing another series of sobs.

He inhaled long and slow. "I'm moving away, and you'll get on with your life. You don't want a relationship; you've made that clear. But whether or not this is the last time we're together . . ." He kissed her again. "Together like this, that is . . . I want you to know something." Another kiss. "Nothing — *nothing* you could have done in Paris would change the way I feel about you. Not ever."

A dam that had held secure for years broke, and tears cascaded down her cheeks. "I'm . . . I'm such an idiot."

"Hey, come on now." He caught another of her tears with his finger. "Don't say that."

She sniffed. "I am, though." He still had his arm around her shoulders, still held tight to her hand. "Why couldn't I just fall in love with you after high school like any normal girl?" She twisted her face, desperate for an answer. "I should never have gone to Paris."

"I don't know exactly what happened there." Landon's tone was softer than before, his gaze more direct. "But I know you came home with Cole. And because of that" — he hesitated, too choked up to finish until he had control again — "because of that, I believe God worked things out for the good, Ashley. Whatever happened."

She closed her eyes again. Not only did Landon love her in ways that defied reason; he also loved her son. So why couldn't she return that love, beg him not to move away, promise to stay by his side forever?

The reason was so close it terrified her.

He only *thought* he could understand about Paris. Once he knew the truth, he would never see her the same way, couldn't possibly cherish her the way he did now. He'd never again look at her the way he'd looked at her tonight — not if he knew about Paris.

"You can tell me, Ashley." The resolve in his eyes was unyielding. "Whatever it is, it'll only make me love you more." He leaned in and kissed her for a long while before pulling back again.

"Why . . . why would you love me more?" As hard as she tried, she would never understand him, never be clear on why a man who looked and acted like Landon Blake would waste his time on someone so difficult.

He wove his fingers between hers. "For trusting me enough to tell me."

There was nothing she could say, no

promises she could make. She believed Landon, but the idea of telling him about Paris was as impossible as moving a mountain with her bare hands.

When she was quiet, he turned his attention to the television. "Maybe we should watch that movie, huh?" He pulled her closer. "It's getting late."

They watched a comedy, something that allowed Ashley to enjoy Landon's nearness without having to dwell on the conversation they didn't have — the one about her past. When the movie was over, Landon struggled to his feet and helped her up as well. "It's after midnight."

She yawned, desperate to hide her disappointment. How could she leave when all she wanted was to kiss him again? She stretched, releasing his hand for the first time in hours.

Reality barged in, leaving the door open and allowing the winds of uncertainty to cool the closeness between them. The night was over, and Ashley doubted there'd ever be another like it. After all, they were going their separate ways. In all likelihood, this strangely marvelous night would be the last time they'd be together this way — kissing, touching, admitting feelings they normally hid so well.

He walked her across the living room. When they reached the door, he leaned his crutches against the wall and took her in his arms. Their lips met again, and the passion that had been there earlier ignited in an instant. When Landon pulled back, Ashley felt flames of desire hotter than anything she'd ever known. She knew he was feeling the same way because he was shaking. They both were.

"I'll never forget this." Landon grabbed a quick breath and exhaled hard. "Not ever."

"Me either."

As Ashley made her way out to the car, Landon called after her one more time. "Hey, Ash."

Fresh tears welled in her eyes, and she turned around, hoping he couldn't see them. "Yeah?"

"You have the most beautiful hair! Has anyone ever told you that?"

She drove away laughing, wanting nothing more than to turn around and go to him again. Stay through the night, through the weekend. Forever. But that wasn't the kind of love Landon would want. He would hold out for the real deal — marriage, family, a lifelong commitment.

Ashley drew a deep breath and held it. She could think of a million reasons why it wouldn't work. She wondered whether Landon could see through the cracks in her armor to the place where her heart was in turmoil. Because it was. As she drove across Bloomington, the tears streaming down her face underlined the fact.

Despite her conviction to remain aloof and lighthearted with her friend Landon Blake, she'd spent the evening kissing him. He was deep and wonderful and charming and connected to her soul like no other man. Certainly he could see that her feelings for him were changing — that she was finally falling for him.

But she couldn't let that happen — not when she knew he would stop loving her the moment he knew the truth about her past. Ashley gripped the steering wheel. Maybe she should tell him anyway. Then he could move to New York with a clear conscience, knowing there could never have been anything lasting between them.

The tears came harder as she pictured herself voicing the words, telling a story she'd never told to anyone, let alone to the only man who'd ever truly loved her. She pictured his face, imagined what he would say. He would be kind, of course, listen patiently, hold her when she cried. Say all the right things. But in the end he would know that she could never be the kind of wife he wanted and deserved. Not ever. And when that was clear in his mind, he would move away and never look back.

The image tore at Ashley's heart and made her breath catch in her throat. There was only one thing more frightening than the idea of falling for Landon, and that was this:

The thought of watching him walk away once he knew the truth.

Chapter Fourteen

Work was the antidote.

Ashley's feelings were far too jumbled to unravel in a day or two, so when Monday came, she merely wadded them up, stuffed them into the back pocket of her heart, and set about doing the work she'd come to love: making life more bearable for Irvel and her friends.

The women were at their places around the table having lunch when the doorbell rang.

Irvel's face lit up. "I wonder if it's Hank!"

Ashley headed for the door as Helen called after her, "Whoever it is, don't forget to do the check. We don't need more spies around the place."

"Yes, Helen," Ashley called back over her shoulder. "I'll do the check." A smile lifted the corners of Ashley's mouth as she opened the door.

A woman stood on the porch, clutching her purse with both hands. She looked to be in her late fifties. When she saw Ashley, she hesitated, the lines and furrows in her face deepening. "Hello. You must be new."

"Yes." Ashley was curious. "And you are . . . ?"

"I'm Sue Brown. Helen Wells's daughter."

Helen had a daughter? No one had mentioned it. "I'm sorry." Ashley stepped aside and opened the front door. "Come in."

When the door was closed behind them, the woman let her eyes fall to the floor. "I'm afraid I . . . I don't come very often." She glanced up, and Ashley saw pain in her eyes. "Mama doesn't remember me."

The revelation hit Ashley like a blow to the gut. This poor woman was Helen's daughter, but Helen no longer remembered her. How horrible would that feel? Ashley thought of her own mother, healthy and vibrantly alive. Would there come a time when their eyes would meet without the spark of love and recognition?

Ashley refused to dwell on the possibility. "No one told me about you."

The woman shrugged. She looked barely able to stand under the weight of dread. "As I said, I don't come often."

"I'm sorry." Ashley led the way back toward the dining room.

Sue stayed close behind her. "It's okay. It's been this way for years."

The moment they rounded the corner, Helen looked up and spotted her daughter. "She's back!" Helen motioned at Sue and then shot a look toward Irvel. "She's a spy too."

Ashley was horrified. No wonder Sue didn't come very often. "Helen." Ashley made her way around the table and placed a gentle hand on the woman's shoulder. "She's not a spy. This is your daughter, Sue. Remember her?"

"No." Helen's eyes grew wide and she shook her head, slowly at first and then with greater speed. She stared at Ashley. "Is that what she told you?"

Sue entered the room quietly and took a chair. Clearly she didn't want to make a scene. "It's okay, Mama." Sue's voice was calm, defeated. "I've been checked."

"What?" Helen looked appalled. "I am not your mother. My daughter is . . . is someone else. I haven't seen her in years." Helen waved her hand toward Sue. "What did you do with her? You're a spy! You kidnapped my daughter!"

Edith closed her eyes and began rocking. Next to her, for the first time since Ashley started working at Sunset Hills, Irvel had nothing to say. She merely watched the exchange, her eyes wide and confused.

"Helen . . ." Ashley was desperate to help Sue. "You're almost finished eating. Let's go into the other room and visit."

Helen brought her fist down hard against the table. "Not if you haven't checked her." She motioned toward Sue again. "That woman stole my daughter!"

"That woman is your daughter, Helen." Ashley worked to keep her tone even.

Helen hesitated, a scowl planted low across her brow. "No, she isn't!"

"She is, Helen. Really."

Helen hesitated for a long time, her frown finally fading some. "Fine."

Ashley helped Helen into the other room while Sue followed silently behind. When they were situated, Ashley cast Sue a helpless look. "Is there anything I can do?"

"No." Sue smiled in a way that fell far short of her eyes. "It's like this every time."

Helen settled into her recliner and stared at Sue. "What'd you do with my daughter?"

There was a rocking chair nearby. Sue pulled it up and sat beside her mother. "I *am* your daughter, Mama. I'm here because I love you."

"You're not my daughter!" The anger

was gone from Helen's face. In its place was a pure, raw terror. "Where's my daughter?" Helen flashed a look at Ashley. "Help me, please! I want my daughter. I . . . I miss her so much."

Sue stood up and swallowed hard, her eyes damp and distant. Across the room Ashley could feel her heart breaking for this woman, this daughter.

Without waiting another moment, Sue patted her mother's hand and smiled through her tears. "I'll see you again sometime, okay? I love you, Mama."

Helen's breathing was fast and hard, her eyes wild as they darted about the room. "Make her leave! I'm not her mother. Please . . . make her go!"

Sue wiped at her tears and nodded in Ashley's direction. "Thank you."

Before Ashley could think of any way to salvage the moment, Sue left through the front door and quietly shut it behind her.

"Help me!" Helen began groping for something. Ashley stared at the space in front of the old woman. There was nothing there. "Help me! Help me! Help me!"

Helen's screams grew louder with each request for help. From the next room Irvel called out, her voice laced with panic.

"Will someone help her, please. She needs help!"

Ashley was at Helen's side just as Belinda rounded the corner. "What's going on?" She stared at Ashley, her hands anchored on her hips.

"Helen's dau—" There was no point upsetting Helen further. "Sue Brown came for a visit."

"Help me! Help me! Help me!" Helen began flailing her arms over her head.

Belinda took hold of Helen's shoulder and gave her a firm shake. "Stop screaming!"

"Help me!" Helen pummeled her fists at the place where Belinda held her.

"Fine." Belinda stormed out of the room. The entire time she was gone, Ashley tried to think of something to do. Helen often said delusional things, but she'd never done this — never flipped into a bout of hysteria, screaming the same words over and over.

When Belinda came back she had a pill in the palm of one hand and a glass of water in the other. "Open your mouth, old girl."

"Help me!" Helen fired a desperate look at Ashley. "Help me!"

Belinda squeezed the sides of Helen's

mouth together and forced the pill onto her tongue. Then she held the water up to her lips and tipped it until finally, mercifully, the screaming stopped and Helen drank. When she had swallowed the last mouthful, she waved her arms again. "Help me! Help me!"

"Next time her daughter comes, tell me first, will you?" Belinda shouted above the noise and glanced at her watch. "She'll be out in a minute or so."

Belinda turned and disappeared back down the hallway toward the office. Ashley took nervous steps toward Helen, and when she was close enough, she laid her hand on the old woman's shoulder.

Helen's eyes began to droop, and gradually her screaming softened and then stopped altogether as she slipped into a heavy sleep.

Ashley returned to Irvel and Edith and helped them to the bathroom and then into their recliners on either side of Helen. When they were all asleep, Ashley found her notebook and sat in the rocking chair. Poor old Helen — terrified by the sight of her own daughter!

Would she feel that way about Cole one day?

The thought sent shivers down Ashley's

spine and made her feel nauseous. If only there was something she could do, some way she could bridge the gap for the people at Sunset Hills.

A way to help them remember.

Ashley opened her notebook and stared at the pages of scribbled information inside. A week ago she'd attended a one-day seminar at the university for workers in adult care homes. The course was sponsored by a medical group, and Lu required all new Sunset Hills workers to take it.

"State-of-the-art information," Lu had told her. "You'll have a lot better idea of how to handle our residents after the course."

Ashley had actually been looking forward to it. But instead of offering new information, the instructor had merely reemphasized the old. Ashley ran her eyes over her notes:

- Never argue with Alzheimer's patients, but always remind them of the reality of their situation.
- Keep them living in the present-day world.
- Correct them gently when they speak things that don't make sense.

Ashley understood the reasoning behind this philosophy. If the brain could be reminded of what was real and right, then perhaps the knowledge would slow the inevitable wearing away of the memory. But she'd seen firsthand how poorly those pieces of advice worked on the people at Sunset Hills. She'd watched Irvel fall apart again and again when forced to consider the idea that her beloved Hank was dead. She glanced at Helen. Reminding her of reality had nearly shot her through the roof.

Ashley stared out the front window at the trees in the yard. Maple trees, much like the big one that shaded Landon's window. For a moment she allowed herself to drift back forty-eight hours, to the way she had felt in Landon's arms.

She savored the wonder of the memory and the goodness of how it felt to live it again in the quiet of the afternoon. Even if she and Landon were all wrong for each other . . . even if they never again shared another moment like that, the memory would always be a good one.

How would she feel if she'd voiced her thoughts aloud and someone had yelled at her to be quiet or informed her that Landon was gone, that she was no longer in his arms but at an adult care home?

Ashley looked back at her notes, and suddenly she saw a connection. If a single memory had caused such a bright light on her day, why weren't the people at Sunset Hills allowed the same luxury? What was wrong with living in the past, anyway? It felt good to remember, as long as the memory was a happy one. What was the harm in letting people stay there?

A loud snore sounded from Helen, and her hands shook for a moment before she settled back to sleep. Ashley tried to imagine being confined to a house like this one, locked away to bide her time until death would mercifully take her.

Of course it would be more enjoyable to live in the past!

She turned the page in her notebook and saw an Internet address. The instructor had given them several Web sites to explore, places where further research could be done on caring for Alzheimer's patients.

Quietly, so she wouldn't wake Helen and the others, Ashley checked on Bert and Laura Jo. Then she stationed herself at the computer. It was in a small alcove off the living room, intended for the residents' use. Of course, not one of them had any idea how to use a computer or even

196

that the Internet existed.

Ashley signed on and typed in the Web address. Images of elderly people began to appear on the screen.

"Caring for Alzheimer's Patients — An Alternate View," the home page read. She scrolled down a list of links until she saw one that caught her eye: "Past-Present — A Christian Perspective."

She hesitated. The "past-present" idea intrigued her, but the "Christian" part made her nervous. She tended to think religious people were biased — brainwashed, really. It was hard to imagine that they might have anything worthwhile to say about something that was clearly not a matter of faith.

Still, she clicked on the link, and an article appeared on the screen. She read the opening:

If you've ever cared for an Alzheimer's patient, you've asked, "Why can't we let them live in the past — where they're comfortable?" The answer is usually predictable: Doctors believe encouraging such fantasies about the past is dangerous for victims of Alzheimer's disease. Indeed, studies have proven that Alzheimer's patients who are allowed to live in the past die more quickly than those who are continually reminded about current-day reality.

Ashley kept reading. A pastor in Michigan was quoted as saying:

Distant memory is God's merciful way of helping us survive a disease like Alzheimer's. Regardless of whether living in the past speeds up the disease process, those of us who care for the elderly ought not rob them of the chance to remember.

The chance to remember.
That last line played in Ashley's mind again. What better use of time could there possibly be for people like Irvel and Edith and Helen but to remember — their childhoods, their families, their married days? This was the time when they could remember every moment, live it again, walk through it, reread every page in the book of their lives. Even if the entire experience was a delusion — what was the harm?

Ashley scrolled down the page and was reading another section of the article when she heard footsteps. She spun around and found Belinda scowling at her, staring at the computer screen. "You're supposed to be mopping."

"I'm studying." Ashley raised the notebook in her hand. "Lu had me take a course last week."

Belinda laughed. "It never helps."

"Of course it helps." Anger stirred in Ashley's gut. She pointed to the computer. "There are other ways, you know. Besides treating them like children."

Belinda's face hardened. "Don't tell me about different ways." She reached past Ashley and clicked off the monitor. "I make the decisions around here."

"All I'm saying is that maybe there's another —"

"Listen." Belinda's tone was low and threatening. "You do your job and don't make waves. Otherwise, you're gone."

She turned and left Ashley fuming. Was it so difficult to think out of the box, to try new methods that might help the people at Sunset Hills be happy and more peaceful? She sighed. There was no reaching someone like Belinda, someone so bottled up and angry that her misery spilled over onto everyone she came in contact with.

Ashley finished cleaning and was setting out a snack when Helen approached her. Helen got around better than the others at

Sunset Hills, but each step was still slow, deliberate.

She was clutching something to her chest, and as she came closer, Ashley saw it was a picture frame.

"Hi, Helen. What do you have?"

"You've been checked, right?" Helen's voice sounded scratchy, no doubt because of her earlier screaming episode.

"Yes, Helen. I've been checked."

Helen nodded, satisfied. "I want to show you something." Moving with the greatest care, Helen lowered the picture frame so Ashley could see a colored photograph of a striking teenage girl. Even with the sixties-style hair and the fading colors, there was no question that the girl in the photo was a younger version of Sue Brown, the woman who had been by to visit earlier. "Oh, Helen, she's beautiful."

"That's Sue." The lines eased around Helen's mouth. "My daughter."

The pastor's words from the Internet article came back: *Those of us who care for the elderly ought not rob them of the chance to remember.* Ashley cleared her throat. "You must be very proud of her."

"I am." Helen angled her head and stared longingly at the girl in the photo. The corners of her mouth found a way up through the folds of facial skin. It was the first time Ashley had seen Helen smile.

"Do you have other children, Helen?" Ashley wasn't sure whether this was the time to ask — or even whether Helen would remember other children if she had them. But she wanted to make the moment last as long as possible.

"No." Helen furrowed her brow and thought for several seconds. "I don't think so." She looked at the photo again and touched the image of Sue's face with her fingertips. "Just Sue."

"Well, she's very pretty."

Helen's eyes lifted to Ashley's. "Have you seen her?"

"Not lately." Ashley thought quickly. "Have you?"

Tears pooled in Helen's tired eyes, and she cradled the photograph close to her heart. "Sue's missing. Someone took her from me."

"I'm sorry, Helen." Ashley felt her throat grow thick. "I didn't know."

Helen nodded, tightening her grip on the photo frame until her knuckles were white. Tears spilled down her face and trickled to the floor. "I . . . I don't think she's ever coming back."

Ashley remembered Sue Brown's tormented face. *She probably feels the same way about her mother.* Carefully, Ashley put an arm around Helen's shoulders. "If there's anything I can do to help you find Sue, I'll do it." Ashley blinked back tears. "I promise you that, Helen."

"Thank you. No one's ever wanted to help me find her before. And . . . I miss her so much." With that, Helen's shoulders hunched forward, and she began to weep. Desperate sobs shook her body, and she fell against Ashley, too broken to move. Gone were the loud screams from earlier that afternoon. In their place were the soft, quiet sobs of a mother aching for her only child, a child who would never, ever be found again.

Holding Helen, Ashley suddenly found herself desperate to soak up everything she could from her life. These, after all, were the days she would remember when she was old, and what did she have to show for them? Cole, yes — certainly him. But the boy was closer to her parents than to her.

Her relationship with Cole had never been ideal, not for either of them. And the reason was obvious. After her year in Paris, Ashley's heart had all but died to love. Certainly, to the love of a man who had shown her nothing but respect and compassion every time they were together. And even to the love of her only child. No matter what either of them did, she couldn't respond freely. She would always, eventually, pull away.

Now, with Helen crying on her shoulder, Ashley knew only one way to move beyond the terrible secrets that had held her captive these past four years. She needed to take Landon at his word and trust him, tell him the things she was terrified to say, the things that would stand between them until she found the courage to lay them out in the open.

Ashley drew a slow breath.

Then and there she made up her mind. The next time she was alone with Landon, she would tell him the truth. Whatever happened after that, at least she wouldn't spend the best years of her life keeping her heart hidden behind walls of fear.

Only then, Ashley thought, could she have what Helen had. Something to remember. Something worth remembering.

Something so beautiful and real that one day, if she was very lucky, it might even make her weep.

Chapter Fifteen

The picnic took place on one of those beautiful days, the kind whose memory would warm a winter morning years from now.

John Baxter took his wife's hand and stared out across Lake Monroe. Sunshine glistened off the water and bathed the shoreline where John and Elizabeth's entire family was gathered.

"Another successful picnic," John gazed at the little ones playing tag at the water's edge.

"Yes," Elizabeth sighed. "Another summer behind us."

John ran his thumb along the back of his wife's hand. "You always loved summer."

"Always." She smiled and shaded her eyes. "Schedules and school and even time stands still for summer."

Every year since Brooke was born, John and Elizabeth had spent Labor Day here at Lake Monroe. Some years they had a fish fry. On others they barbecued. But always they spent part of the day on the water, soaking up enough sunshine to get them through the winter.

Over time, the summer's-end gathering of the Baxter family had grown. John scanned the beach and smiled as he took in each of his loved ones. Brooke and Peter played on the shore near the children, Maddie, Hailey, and Cole. Ashley and Kari sat nearby in beach chairs, with baby Jessie cradled in Kari's lap. Erin and Sam tossed a Frisbee with Luke and his girlfriend, Reagan.

John watched as little Maddie separated herself from the group and climbed the sloped beach toward them. "Grandma," she called. Her small voice was nearly lost on the breeze.

"Yes, sweetie, what's wrong?" Elizabeth was on her feet, meeting their small blonde granddaughter halfway. The two of them turned and finished the rest of the walk hand in hand until they reached the picnic tables where John's and Elizabeth's chairs were set up.

"I don't feel good." Maddie's cheeks were flushed.

"Come here, darling; let Papa feel your head." John touched her brow. "Hmmm. Not too hot." He patted a towel beside his chair. "Why don't you come lie down for a while? A little rest will help you feel better."

Maddie did as she was told and spread out beside him. Elizabeth covered her with a clean towel from a stack on the table. "There, sweetheart. Get some rest before dinner. Papa's making his famous hamburgers, okay?"

"Okay." Maddie smiled, and it led to a yawn.

She was out before Elizabeth was back in her chair. "Poor darling." She smiled at the child's sleeping form. "Must be exhausted."

A soothing quiet fell between them, and John reached once more for his wife's hand. "We have so much to be thankful for."

Elizabeth smiled. "Especially this week." She gave John a half-smile. "I was more worried about the tests than I let on."

"Me too." John squeezed her fingers. It was something they lived with, the fact that Elizabeth had survived cancer years ago. Back then her doctors had been straight with them: They hadn't gotten all the bad cells from her lymph nodes. It wasn't a matter of whether the cancer would return. It was a matter of when. So each time she went in for tests, there was always a chance the news would be bad.

Lately Elizabeth had felt more tired than usual, and John had been particularly concerned. But the good news had come back Friday afternoon.

"Look at them." John narrowed his eyes, watching the way his family played and loved and laughed together. "You'd never know they had a problem in the world."

"Kari's doing well with Jessie." Elizabeth's expression was wistful. "I always knew she'd make a good mother."

"She misses Tim."

"And Ryan." Elizabeth angled her head and gave John a knowing look. "She doesn't fool me with all that talk about 'learning to be on her own.' "

"It's an important part of the grieving process, don't you think?" John shifted his jaw. "She's got to come to terms with losing Tim."

"I know." Elizabeth smiled. "But there's still a place in her heart that beats for Ryan Taylor. Even if he's a thousand miles away."

John studied his middle daughters. From the back they looked almost like twins. Ashley's hair was shorter, of course, and even darker than Kari's, but they had the same delicate features. And now that they were both single moms they had more in common than ever. "Wonder what she and Ashley are talking about."

"Landon Blake."

John chuckled. "You act as though you know."

Elizabeth grinned. "I do."

"Well . . ." John cocked his head for a moment. "Ashley and Landon have been together a lot lately."

"He's back to work now, moving to New York — did Ashley tell you?" Elizabeth leaned forward in her seat and rested her elbows on her knees. "He wants to fight fires with a friend of his there."

John pursed his lips. "That's too bad. I always thought he and Ashley might wind up together someday."

"He'll be back." Elizabeth stood and crossed in front of him.

She stooped down and felt Maddie's forehead. "She feels cooler. Poor dear probably just needed to rest."

John folded his arms. "What do you mean he'll be back?"

"My sweet love . . ." Elizabeth flashed him a knowing smile. "The boy's been crazy about Ashley since the first day they met in middle school. Nothing could keep him away from her — certainly not a few

New York City fires."

"Ashley said he might come by later." John looked behind him at the parking lot. "They took off his cast last week."

"So I heard."

John shook his head. "The burns have healed well, too — much faster than I would have expected. It's a miracle the boy's alive."

"It's all part of God's plan." Elizabeth shifted so she was facing John.

"Plan?" John leaned on one elbow. He cherished times like this, afternoons when everyone he loved was well and happy and together in one place. Times when he and Elizabeth could take stock of all they had to be grateful for.

"The one I pray for every night." Elizabeth's gaze rested on Ashley. "That someday Ashley will remember the truth she believed as a child. That Jesus loves her."

"Oh, you mean the one we *both* pray for." He smiled. "And you think Landon's part of the plan, huh?"

"I think he might be." Elizabeth tilted her head. "God has something up those mighty sleeves of his."

"He always does."

"Same thing for Luke and Reagan."

John let his eyes drift down the beach to the place where his son was swinging Reagan near the water, threatening to toss her in. "They seem pretty friendly."

Elizabeth was quiet. He turned to her, seeing the uncertainty in her eyes. Their hearts were so connected, he had always been able to feel her smile before her mouth had time to act it out. This was no different. "What?"

"She won't stay in Bloomington forever."

"She's close to her family."

"Soon as she has her degree, she'll move to New York City." Elizabeth's eyes narrowed. "And it won't surprise me if she takes Luke with her."

John gazed at their son. "He's still talking about Reagan's father."

"And his office in the World Trade Center."

John stared at the sky. What must it be like working nearly ninety floors off the ground, looking eye level at the clouds? Seeing all of New York City and the harbor from an office window. "Reagan says Luke and her dad hit it off pretty well." John smiled. "You think he could get Luke a job?"

Elizabeth uttered a light huff. "From the

sound of it, he practically hired him on the spot."

"That worries you?" John studied his wife, struck as always by her delicate features and still-dark hair. Every year he was more in love with her.

"I'd like to keep him closer." Elizabeth gave him a sad smile. "But Erin's moving away soon, and one day we're bound to be spread out. That's the way of life."

"Ah, honey, listen to you." John ran his fingers up her arm. "You'd think God had given you a blueprint for the next decade. Luke and Reagan aren't moving out next week."

"He's our only son, John." She narrowed her eyes, her gaze fixed on the sight of Luke playing near the water. "Wherever he goes, I'll miss him." She looked back at him again, her smile wistful. "Life is so uncertain."

"With one exception, my love."

"What's that?" She waited. There was no fear or worry in this conversation, just a parent's desire to keep close those children they'd spent a lifetime loving.

"Wherever Luke goes, he'll take God with him." John moved his fingers gently along the base of his wife's neck.

"Yes." Elizabeth's smile spread further up her face, as though the thought brought her deep comfort. "He does love the Lord, doesn't he?"

"With all his heart. I don't think anything could shake that boy's faith." John stood and stretched. "Not even a job overlooking New York City."

Kari leaned back in her beach chair and laid Jessie along her legs. The air was still warm, but it was cooling some, and she didn't want her daughter getting chilled. "Grab me a blanket from the diaper bag, will you, Ash?"

"Sure." Ashley reached for the pink-and-white blanket and handed it to Kari. As she did, they spotted Landon Blake walking toward them from the parking lot. Cole shouted his name and ran to him.

Silently, Kari and Ashley watched the boy jump into Landon's arms. Landon tossed him into the air and hugged him close. Then he set the boy down, grabbed his hand, and started toward Ashley.

"Cole's crazy about Landon." Kari kept her tone free of innuendo. The statement was merely an observation anyone could have made.

"I know it." Ashley looked away. She picked a rock up from near her feet and tossed it toward the water.

"Don't get mad at me for saying this . . ."

Ashley met her gaze. "Saying what?"

"I don't think Cole's the only one."

Landon and Cole were only a few feet away, and Ashley waved, ignoring Kari's comment. "You're not limping."

"I feel great." He waved to Kari and then came to stand next to Ashley. "Like I've been set free."

"Landon wants to take a walk." Cole bounced up and down a few times. "Come with us, Mommy. Please!"

Ashley pulled Cole onto her lap and kissed his cheek. "How could I tell my two best guys no?" She laughed and stood up, setting Cole down beside her and dusting the dirt from her shorts. "Let's see who can find the prettiest rock."

"Okay!" Cole's eyes lit up. He slipped one hand in Landon's, the other in Ashley's. "Let's go before Papa's burgers are ready."

Kari watched them set off, walking toward the setting sun. She smoothed a finger over Jessie's silky forehead. Ashley was out of her mind if she let Landon go now, after the two of them had clearly found something other people waited a lifetime for.

A heavy sigh made its way between Kari's lips as she stared out at the lake. This was the first time she'd been back since that fall day when she and Ryan came here. Had it really been almost a year ago? Kari let her mind wander aimlessly down the dusty roads of yesterday to that November afternoon when time had stood still.

Despite the cold, they'd fished for hours and built a campfire. Then they'd done something they should have done years earlier. They talked about why — after a lifetime of caring for each other — they had let their relationship fall away. The answer felt as painful and unbelievable now as it had that November day.

A series of misunderstandings had caused her to believe that Ryan was in love with someone else. As a result, Kari had done everything she could to get on with her life — even marrying Tim Jacobs.

Jessie stirred, and Kari adjusted the blanket so it sheltered her daughter's face. Her whole life, it seemed, had been a series of badly timed events.

That November night, she'd felt lonelier than she'd ever been. Tim had admitted his affair and moved in with his student lover. And though Kari had been determined to fight for her marriage, being alone with Ryan on this very beach had tested her resolve. She'd needed every ounce of her strength not to run off with him and never speak to her husband again.

But it had taken just one kiss, one moment of longing for what might have been, to snap Kari back to reality. She could still see the understanding in Ryan's eyes when she told him she couldn't — couldn't kiss him, couldn't fall in love with him — no matter how much she wanted to. Not when her marriage hung in the balance.

That day together had led to a time of soul-searching for Ryan. In the end, he had decided that if she wanted to make things work with Tim, he would not stand in the way; his love for her wouldn't allow it. In fact, his decision to love her had led him to take the coaching job in New York.

Who'd have thought that three months later Tim would be dead?

And now here she was, alone again — she and Jessie. She looked down the beach at the faces of her family. It could be worse. How would she have survived without her parents and the others, especially Ashley? Her younger sister had been the family member most frustrated with Kari's determination to remain married to

Tim. But now that he was gone, Ashley was the most supportive, the most sympathetic.

Maybe it was because Ashley, too, understood loneliness.

"Come and get 'em!" Her father's voice carried down the beach, and Kari smiled. How many Labor Days had they gathered at this same spot, played on this same beach, and heard their father make that same announcement?

No, she wasn't alone at all.

Besides, she had God, his presence, his Word alive within her. That was more than she could say for poor Ashley.

"Save some for me, Papa!" Cole came darting into view from behind a band of trees. Kari was making her way toward the picnic tables as Landon and Ashley appeared, hand in hand and laughing.

Landon's part of your plan, isn't he, Lord? Kari waved in their direction. From across the beach, the others headed for the barbecue pit. Luke was careful to steer Reagan away from Ashley. His differences with his sister hadn't eased with time, that much was sure.

Kari was the last to reach the tables. As she made her way up the shore, holding Jessie against her shoulder, she watched

Ashley and Landon — the way Ashley's eyes sparkled when he spoke, the way he seemed in tune to everything she said, every move she made. It was finally happening. Landon had figured out how to squeeze his way into Ashley's heart.

Yes, Landon was part of God's plan for Ashley — Kari was certain of it. And if things went the way she hoped they would for her sister, one of these days very soon Ashley would welcome more than Landon Blake into her heart.

She'd welcome God himself.

Chapter Sixteen

It was the time.

Ashley knew it the moment she saw Landon walk toward her that afternoon. She had made a decision to tell him the truth, to share with him the secrets she'd planned to keep forever. And if he never again looked at her with longing and love after tonight, so be it. At least she wouldn't be resigned to living in fear the rest of her life.

During the barbecue, with a dozen conversations in full swing, Ashley slipped next to her mother and squeezed in beside her.

"Can you take Cole with you when we're done?" She kept her voice low. The last thing she needed was for Luke to hear her. He'd probably make some comment about how often Ashley pawned Cole off on their parents.

"Sure." Her mom dabbed a napkin to her mouth and turned so she could see Ashley. "What's up?"

"Nothing." Ashley's answer was quick. She didn't want her mother to get the wrong idea. There was nothing serious between her and Landon, and after tonight — well, after tonight there might not be anything between them at all. "Landon and I are going to stay a little later. That's all."

"That's all?" A grin played on the corners of her mother's mouth.

"Yes, Mother, that's all." Ashley uttered a short laugh. "He's not proposing to me or anything. We're just friends, remember?"

Elizabeth raised an eyebrow and discreetly directed her gaze toward Landon. Ashley did the same. He sat tall and strong at the next table, talking to Cole and helping the boy spread ketchup across his hamburger bun. "Good friends, I'd say."

"Fine." Ashley sighed. No matter how far she and Landon had come, she still hated this part, this Baxter magnifying glass, this chance for everyone to see them together and guess what might be happening. "The point is, we need to talk. Without Cole."

Her mother moved back from the table a few inches and put her hand on Ashley's knee. "I didn't mean to upset you." She gave Ashley an apologetic smile. "I like Landon very much."

"I know." Resignation sounded in Ashley's tone. "Me too."

"Of course I'll take Cole." Her mother slid back into position at the table.

Ashley returned to her seat and told Landon about her parents' offer. "Can you stay awhile? Here at the lake, I mean?"

"Sure." Landon's brow rose just enough to show his surprise. "You sound serious."

"I . . . I have something to tell you."

"Uh-oh." Landon tossed her a grin that didn't quite hide the concern in his eyes. "That can't be good."

"No." Ashley pulled away from his gaze and picked at the watermelon chunks on her plate. "Probably not."

The hour passed quickly, with more conversations and, after dinner, a marshmallow roast around the barbecue pit. Luke had brought his guitar, and the group sang along as he played a series of their family's favorite songs by artists such as Garth Brooks, the Eagles, George Strait, and Skip Ewing.

Ashley and Landon sat away from the others, their chairs side by side. Cole was at Luke's knee, singing along as much as he could, his off-key voice punctuating

Luke's clear, strong one.

Partway through the brief concert, Landon leaned closer. "What's with you and Luke?"

"He doesn't like me." Ashley's whispered answer was the first thing she could think of. Usually she'd make some remark about how the two of them didn't see eye to eye or how he'd become a judgmental, self-righteous conservative. But maybe those statements were only cover-ups, ways to hide the pain. Because the rift between them hurt more than she cared to admit.

Luke played on as Landon knit his brows. He kept his voice low so none of the others closer to the firepit could hear him. "Of course he likes you. The two of you were best buddies as kids."

Ashley felt the beginning of tears, and she blinked them back. "Not after Paris."

Landon said nothing. Instead, he settled back in his chair and returned his attention to Luke. But this time — in a way that soothed the painful cracks in her heart — he reached out and quietly took her hand in his.

She savored the feel of his fingers against hers. His touch felt so good she wanted to cry. Even when no one else understood, Landon did. Why was she realizing that only now, when it was too late? When he was ready to move on with life and leave her behind? And why was she holding his hand, anyway — letting him get to her the way she'd always vowed he never would?

There was no point, no matter what Landon felt for her now. After tonight there'd be no holding hands, no shared closeness. Once he knew who she really was, he'd pack his bags for New York City and never look back.

When Luke finished playing, the group gradually headed for their cars. Ashley and Landon joined in, making promises to get together with Erin and Sam sometime soon and bidding good-bye to Cole and Kari and the others.

Finally they were alone. As the last of her family's cars drove away, Landon turned and eased her to him. They hugged for a long moment. "All night you've been in knots, Ashley." He drew back enough to see her face. "What is it? What's eating you?"

The sun had set, and only a few faint streaks of light remained in the sky. Except for the glow from the fire and the light of the moon, the beach was dark. Ashley bit the inside of her lip. "Let's sit."

The night felt cool after the day of solid sunshine, and the breeze off the lake had picked up a little. They left their chairs off to the side, and Landon spread a blanket out near the barbecue pit. There they sat together, their shoulders touching. After a minute of silence, Ashley drew a deep breath. There was no easy way to begin. She pulled her knees up to her chest and tilted her face so she could see him. "I want to tell you about Paris."

"Is that what this is about?" Compassion flooded his tone, and he slipped an arm around her shoulders. "No, Ashley." She could feel him shaking his head. "You don't have to tell me."

"I want to." She stared straight ahead, her eyes fixed on the dying embers. "I thought I could bury the past. Just move on like it never happened." She paused. "But I can't."

"No." His voice mixed with the breeze and played softly in her mind. "Life doesn't work that way."

"You were right the other night." She was quiet, desperate to avoid what was ahead but still determined to go on. "The only way to bring down the walls is to talk about what happened."

With gentle hands he framed her face. "But you're so afraid, Ashley. I can see it in your eyes."

"Yes." She mouthed the word but no sound came out.

"I don't know what your feelings are for me, Ash — whether they've grown stronger lately." He searched her face and tenderly kissed her brow. "But nothing you could tell me would change the way I feel about you."

Ashley nodded. *He thinks that now.* "I wanted to do only one thing in Paris —"

Landon was quiet, giving her the space to talk. He kept his arm around her but shifted some, drawing up his good leg.

"Paint." She gazed up at the sky. "I wanted to live life on my own and paint." With that, the story began to tumble from her heart. "Before I left, I made arrangements to work at an art gallery. . . ."

The gallery had been located in the heart of Montmartre, a part of Paris known for its artists. One of Ashley's instructors in Indiana had worked out the details.

As her departure for Paris neared, Ashley packed more than her clothes. She brought a second suitcase full of her four best paintings.

The day after she arrived in Montmartre, she dressed in a simple black skirt and jacket, wrapped up some art pieces, and reported for duty. "When the gallery director saw my work, she patted my arm and told me to keep my projects off the premises." Ashley rolled her eyes. "Like they were trash or something! Like they'd bring down the quality of the gallery if she so much as looked at them."

Landon winced.

"Yeah." A single sad laugh came from Ashley. "That's how I felt."

Ashley continued the story. She'd been told that most galleries allowed aspiring artists to work in one of their back rooms or studios. But clearly they wanted Ashley answering phones and greeting the English-speaking tourists rather than painting. When she wasn't working, the manager wanted her off the property.

But that changed the first weekend, when the gallery opened an art show featuring one of the area's most exciting new artists, Jean-Claude Pierre. The man was a modern-day Impressionist with a ground-swell of interest in his work. People were already talking about him as though he were a legend.

Ashley had seen his work and his photograph. Both left her breathless. She was thrilled just for the chance to meet him.

Of course she was able to attend only because she was on the clock. Her job was to walk the floor looking for English-speaking customers and answering whatever questions she could. Someone else would handle the local clientele.

She didn't mind. She would have walked on the ceiling for a chance to meet Jean-Claude Pierre.

The gallery had hired a classical ensemble and catered in champagne and *foie gras* for the event. The evening was about to get under way when a man in his late thirties breezed through the door. Ashley took one look at him and felt the force of his presence like a physical blow. In that moment, he seemed everything she'd ever wanted in a man — dark looks, mystery, and an unbelievable gift of placing on canvas that which grew within him.

There was only one problem. On his left hand he wore a wedding ring. And attached to his arm was a petite blonde, about his age. Even from across the room, Ashley could see that Jean-Claude was bored with the woman, but there was no question, she was his wife. Her diamond ring lit up the gallery.

Jean-Claude had been there only a few moments when he spotted Ashley. He was chatting with his companion, gesturing to the manager about the display, when suddenly his eyes met Ashley's from across the room. For the briefest instant, he paused in midsentence and simply stared at her. Then the corners of his lips rose slightly, and he gave her a polite nod.

Ashley did the same and turned away. Her cheeks burned from the fact that he'd caught her staring, watching him with a look that could not possibly have hidden the attraction she felt for him.

The rest of the evening passed without the two of them speaking. Jean-Claude and his wife made their rounds, visiting with all the right people and graciously speaking with buyers who had written checks and were taking home pieces of his work that night. At ten o'clock the guests began to leave, and from the corner of her eye Ashley watched Jean-Claude kiss his wife on the cheek. Then he motioned to a driver outside and bid his wife good night.

Ten minutes later, Ashley was adding the evening's receipts when he came up beside her. "You are new, yes?"

She spun around and found herself trapped in his gaze. *Stop, Ashley. Walk away. He's married.* Everything her parents had taught her screamed at her to be polite but distant. Nothing good could come from falling for a married man. Instead, she locked eyes with him and smiled. "Yes. From the States."

"I knew it." His voice was soft, sensual, with a touch of humor. "I like American girls," he said. "So bold, yet so . . . unspoiled. I hope you are happy here." He took her hand with a grace and elegance Ashley had only dreamed of and lifted it to his lips. The tips of his fingers played lightly on her palm as he left a velvet kiss near her wrist.

The gallery manager was in the back office, and they were alone on the floor. Ashley didn't know what to say. Jean-Claude's English wasn't perfect, and neither was her French. But there was no mistaking his intentions when he brought his face near hers, his voice a whisper. "You must come with me, *chérie*. I want to show you my city."

Ashley leaned back, staring at the blanket of stars that had spread across the sky. "If only I'd told him no."

"You went out with him?" Landon's tone was curious, nothing more.

"Yes." She glanced at Landon and saw he was listening intently, but with open eyes. If the story was making him jealous or angry, he wasn't showing it.

Give him time, Ashley thought. *This is only the beginning.*

She drew a calming breath and narrowed her eyes as the memories returned once more. "I didn't get home until two in the morning. . . ."

Jean-Claude had taken her to a dozen famous spots that night, places where they shared coffee and conversation and finally cognac. Ashley and her art friends drank on occasion back in Bloomington. But the effect had been nothing like French cognac warming her insides in the presence of a man as exciting as Jean-Claude Pierre.

When he took her back to her small rented flat, he walked her to the door and kissed her — first slowly, then with more passion, until she was crazy with desire. She was about to invite him inside when he kissed her ear and whispered, "Tomorrow, *chérie?*"

Ashley was helpless to say anything but what he wanted to hear. "Yes . . . tomorrow."

And so began a routine. After spending the days apart, they would meet at the gallery and share the evening. On their fifth night, Ashley studied Jean-Claude over a glass of wine. "You're married."

It wasn't a question or an accusation, merely an observation. A fact Ashley wanted him to know she was aware of.

"Yes." He raised one shoulder. "My Gabrielle, she does not like the nightlife so much."

Ashley wanted to ask Jean-Claude if his wife liked his spending time with another woman — a woman half her age. When the words wouldn't come, Jean-Claude reached across the table and lifted her chin. "France is different from the States."

"Different?"

"Men" — he painted invisible strokes in the air, searching for the right words — "men are allowed to . . . how do you say it? . . . express themselves." He took her hands in his. "Passion is not a bad thing." He smiled, and Ashley was struck by the toll it took on her heart. "How else could I paint if I could not express myself? My wife, she understands this. She wants me to do good work."

Ashley felt dazed the rest of that evening, her body physically assaulted by his nearness, by the spell he'd cast on her. What was she doing? She asked herself the question again and again as the hours wore on. But when he walked her up the stairs that night, she had no doubt what would happen.

Or that she wanted it to.

She opened the door and let him in. And there, on her foldout futon, in the arms of a married artist twice her age, Ashley put to death a lifetime of conviction.

Even as a rebellious teenager, she had somehow managed to hold on to what her parents had taught her about waiting until marriage. But this was Paris, and she was smitten. She didn't *want* to wait.

That night, Jean-Claude touched her in a way that completely silenced her conscience and left her hungry for more.

When they said good-bye, the sun was coming up.

Ashley paused. She hadn't voiced all the details to Landon. They would only hurt him, hurt them both. She rested her forehead on her knees. "This is harder than I thought."

"You were young, Ashley. All alone in a foreign country." Landon eased his grip on her shoulders and ran a finger down the side of her face.

"Wait." Ashley shook her head. "There's more."

She'd gone this far with the story, she might as well finish. Then it would all be laid out in the open. Whatever happened after this, at least they would have no more secrets between them.

Ashley lifted her head and let it fall against Landon's shoulder. No matter what he thought of her when she was finished, she needed his support. Needed to know he wouldn't jump up and run off, leaving her in the mucky mire of her own memories. She closed her eyes briefly and continued.

After her first night with Jean-Claude Pierre, Ashley had known there would be others. It wasn't something they talked about. It was something that simply was. She had found a connection so physically addicting that there was no turning back. For nearly a month they were together every night.

Then one evening he showed up at her flat with a friend.

"Angelo is an artist also," Jean-Claude explained. "He wants you to sit for him."

Even now, Ashley remembered the butterflies that swarmed in her belly as the men stood there, staring at her.

"Now?" Ashley stepped back, puzzled.

Jean-Claude and his friend laughed. "No, *chérie*, not now. Tomorrow."

"Why . . . why's he here now?"

"He wants to see you."

"See me?" Something in Jean-Claude's smile turned Ashley's stomach.

"Yes, *chérie*. All of you."

Ashley took another step back. "No!" She searched Jean-Claude's face, desperate for any sign of humor. There was none. And she felt every inch the provincial, unsophisticated American she was desperate not to be.

Disappointed, Jean-Claude and the man left. After that, the visits from Jean-Claude came less often.

Then one night he showed up at her gallery around closing time. He barely spoke to her, merely assumed she would go with him. And she did. They walked the streets of Paris for an hour or so. And afterward he took her someplace he'd never taken her before — to his private art studio.

It was a beautiful place, with high ceilings and skylights from one end to the other. Jean-Claude's paintings hung on the walls and leaned in the corners. Ashley could hardly believe he'd brought her there.

"I thought he might ask me to paint with him, maybe share some technique with me." Ashley shrugged, and her eyes met Landon's. "I should've known better."

Instead, Jean-Claude pointed to an area near the window where an easel stood a few feet from a leather sofa. "Take off your clothes."

Ashley blinked. Was he joking? "What?"

"Take off your clothes, and lie on my sofa." Jean-Claude touched her chin, but his eyes were far from gentle. "I want to paint you."

Ashley didn't move. "I'm an artist." She managed a smile. "Not a model, Jean-Claude."

Tears pooled in Ashley's eyes at the memory of what happened next. She shifted her gaze, unable to look at Landon for this next part. "And then he . . . he laughed at me. He . . . he told me he'd seen my work and it was . . . worthless. Worthless . . . American . . . trash."

Beside her, Landon moaned. "Oh, Ashley, he's wrong. You didn't believe him, did you?"

She lifted her eyes to his once more, her voice tinged with a rejection that had never quite died. "What was I supposed to think? He was the expert." She sniffed, and her voice fell quiet again. "He told me the only thing artistic about me was . . . my body." Her voice dropped a notch. "He told me that's why I needed to . . . to sit for him. Because my flesh was the most beautiful form of art."

Anger flashed in Landon's eyes. "He never saw your heart . . . or the way you involve it in your work." Landon reached behind him and grabbed a corner of the blanket. He used it to wipe the tears from Ashley's cheeks.

"Thanks." Shame all but suffocated her. She sniffed again, wrapped her arms around her knees, and somehow found the strength to go on. "I wanted to run, leave him there with his easel. But I was like a helpless schoolgirl."

She met Landon's eyes. "I even asked him if he loved me." A sad chuckle mingled with her sobs. "Isn't that crazy?"

Landon said nothing, just made circles along the small of her back. His silent support gave her the strength to go on.

"He laughed at me and told me no, of course he didn't love me. He said I was a diversion, a way for him to 'explore his passions.' So there I was. Humiliated as an artist, as a woman. And I stayed. I could've walked away and never looked back, but I didn't."

Again Landon was quiet, encouraging her with his presence.

She drew a shaky breath. "He had me . . . take off my clothes and pose on that sofa. He took some photos — said they were prep work. He got out a new canvas and sketched for a while. Then he came over to me and . . ."

Ashley couldn't finish. Years of pent-up anguish broke free and shook her until her teeth rattled. "I felt . . . so dirty, Landon. He didn't care about me at all. But I still couldn't walk away."

The sobs were slowing now. She sniffed and shook her head.

"He didn't even take me home that night. I had to take the Metro. And all I could think of, all the way back, was my family . . . and you . . . and God." She struggled to catch her breath. "How . . . I'd let you all down. And how" — her voice took on a bitter tinge — "I'd still go back to his studio if he asked me."

"Ashley." Landon circled his arms around her and held her close, stroking her back.

Minutes passed while she tried to get hold of her emotions. She didn't deserve Landon's understanding, but he was giving it anyway. Why wasn't he running? How could he sit here with her now that he knew the truth?

When her sobs eased some, she finished the story. "And I did go back. Whenever Jean-Claude asked, I was there — no matter what he wanted. And then . . ." Her voice settled into a monotone. ". . . I found out I was pregnant."

The next time Jean-Claude came into the art gallery, Ashley told him they needed to talk. Jean-Claude seemed irritated. He had plans for the night, he said. But he led her to a private studio in the back of the gallery.

"What is it you wish to say?" Gone was the sweet-talking romantic.

Ashley fidgeted with her fingers. Where was the attraction she'd felt for him before? Now she felt cheap, dirty, used. "I'm . . ." She couldn't meet his impatient gaze.

"Don't act as a child." Jean-Claude glanced at his watch. "I am here now. Say it."

Panic choked out her ability to think. Without waiting another moment, she drew a quick breath and closed her eyes. "I took a test. I'm . . . pregnant."

The minute Ashley opened her eyes, she knew it was over. The look on Jean-Claude's face told her that would be the last conversation she'd ever have with him.

She still remembered his reaction. The news worked its way across his features in a matter of seconds. Then Jean-Claude backed up a step and shook his finger at her. "This is your trouble, *chérie*. Not mine." A bitter chuckle eased from his throat. "When you play, you must use caution."

He turned to leave, and Ashley shouted, "Wait!" She lurched toward him, grabbing his sleeve. "I'll sit for you again. I'll do anything, Jean-Claude. Just stay with me. Help me. . . ."

With a jerk of his arm he pulled away. "Get back. Your child is not mine." He lifted his chin and cast her a haughty look, a look that made her feel like last week's leftovers. "I am a married man." Before he left, he tossed her one last barb. "There is a clinic down the street. Maybe they will know the answer."

Two nights later, Ashley was leaving the art gallery when she spotted Jean-Claude arm in arm with a slender young man. Stunned, Ashley watched them cross the street and head into a café — the same place he'd taken her back when their relationship first began.

That's when it hit Ashley.

She hadn't had a relationship with Jean-Claude. She hadn't even had an affair. He was a married man with enough charm to get whatever woman — or man — he wanted. Girls like Ashley were merely entertainment for Jean-Claude, a form of entertainment even his wife found acceptable.

Ashley had been devastated by the realization. She went back to her small flat and vomited throughout the night. In the morning she went to the clinic Jean-Claude had mentioned.

A kind woman at the front desk assured her that abortions were confidential and quick. A fifteen-minute wait at the most.

Good, Ashley had thought. *In an hour I'll be rid of everything that could ever remind me of Jean-Claude Pierre.*

Ashley hung her head again and began to shake.

"Hey, it's all right." Landon tightened his embrace, sheltering her the way he might if she were a little girl. "Everything's okay."

She still shook, but the warmth of his body permeated her soul. What was this feeling, this longing for a man she'd worked so hard to avoid? And how could she fall for him now, when the truth was bound to change his feelings for her?

"Obviously, you didn't go through with it." Landon's voice was gentle against her cheek.

"No." She dabbed at an errant tear. "The whole time I was waiting, I thought about my parents and everything they'd taught me. If I went ahead with the abortion, there'd be no turning back. And . . . and . . ."

Her voice broke, and she shuddered. How close she'd come to losing Cole. "I kept thinking, even though I wouldn't be a very good mother . . . it wasn't the baby's fault."

Landon stroked her back again. Once more, his touch gave her the strength to go on.

"When they called my name, I turned around and ran. As fast and hard and far away as I could get." A few quiet sobs shook her shoulders again. "I came home a few months later and . . . and I couldn't tell anyone what happened. It was too awful."

Ashley pulled back some, searching Landon's face. "Want to know the worst part?"

Clearly, Landon knew what she was going to say, but he waited.

"Coming home." Fresh tears filled her eyes. "I was always a little different before. You know?"

Landon gave her a crooked smile. "I know."

Ashley held his gaze. "But when I came home, everything was worse. I wasn't just the girl who gave my parents more trouble than the rest. I was the black sheep. No one knew what to do with me. 'Poor Ashley.'" Her tone became quietly sarcastic. "'Runs off to Paris and comes home pregnant. What'll we do with her?'"

Ashley spread her fingers across her chest. "Everything they said only made me feel worse. Like none of them could ever accept me or love me or care about me again. Especially Luke." She bit her lip. "He was the worst."

"I'm sorry, Ashley." Landon cupped her face with his hand.

"In here" — she made a fist and pressed it to her heart — "I was still just a girl, Landon. A girl who'd had her dream of painting ripped apart by one of the most popular new artists in Paris. But when I got home and realized what everyone thought of me — what I thought of myself — I knew my life would never be good again. Because . . ." She covered her face with her hands as a new wave of tears came.

Once more Landon circled her with his arms. "Because what?"

"Because . . ." She looked up at the

blurred image of his face. ". . . I wasn't worth anything. Not as an artist *or* as a person. I wasn't . . . worth loving anymore." She used the blanket to wipe her tears again. "There." She sat up straighter. "Now you know."

"Ah, Ashley." Landon reached for her hands and held them in his own. "You don't even know what you're worth."

"And Landon . . ." She had something else to say, and the pain of it tore at her heart. She'd told him the truth. Now it was time to let him go, to dismiss him from any obligation he might think he owed her. "You can let go of your silly dreams about me because I'm none of the things you thought I was."

She swallowed a lump in her throat. There was no point crying. The two of them would never have worked out anyway. Landon was pure and upright and good, and she was. . . . She sniffed again. "You deserve someone better than me."

"Ashley, no . . ."

She squeezed his hands and let go, crossing her arms tightly against her body. "Don't worry about it, Landon. I don't expect you to call or come see me. Just make your plans and move to New York. Make a life for yourself, the kind of life you deserve." Ashley blinked so she could see more clearly. "But when you remember me . . . remember the person you thought I was, okay, Landon? Not this." She motioned to herself. "Not the truth."

Landon's eyes grew wide, and he shook his head. "Don't say that." His voice was intense, filled with conviction. "I'm *here*, Ashley. I know the truth about you, and I'm not running. I'll never run."

She hung her head, and with tender fingers he lifted her chin. "No." She closed her eyes and turned her head away. "Don't."

"Come on, Ashley." He brushed his thumb against her jaw. "Look at me."

"I can't." Ashley's heart raced within her. Why wouldn't he leave her alone? Everything about her was wrong for him. She was about to jump up and run away when suddenly she realized what he'd just said.

"I'm here, Ashley. I'm here."

Realization dawned in her heart. It was true, wasn't it? He had cared enough to ask her about Paris the other night. And he cared enough to be here now while she told him the truth. How easy it would have been for him to pat her on the back and apologize, then bid her good-bye and go his own way.

Instead he was here. Even though he knew the ugliest things about her, he was here.

Slowly she turned her face toward him and opened her eyes.

He gave her a lopsided grin. "Thank you." His expression relaxed, and he sounded calmer than before. "What happened to you in Paris could have happened to anyone. You were young. You had a dream. Maybe you didn't make the best choices, but I believe God redeems even the —"

"That's another thing." She studied him. "I was told that God loved me, God had a plan for me." Ashley had never voiced these thoughts before. "But God's plans are supposed to be good. And there was nothing good that came from that time in my life. Nothing."

"That's not true, Ashley." Landon lifted his other hand so that her face was cradled in his warm fingers. "God does love you. He does have plans for your life. And even out of the darkest days of all, he gave you something wonderful."

"What?" Ashley gripped Landon's hands. "What good did God give me?"

Landon's voice was barely loud enough to hear. "He gave you Cole."

His answer was like a physical jolt, as though her perspective had in a moment's time been altered forever.

Of course. Cole was the good that had come from Paris. Her beautiful, kind-hearted little boy.

All these years, she'd thought of him as an embarrassment to her family, a consequence. She loved him, sure. But she also pitied him — the boy with no father, the boy with a mother who was often gone, often too preoccupied with her own guilt and shame to see that right there, sleeping one bedroom down the hall, was a child who loved her more than life. He was more than a painful reminder of all that had happened to her in Paris. He was a precious child, a treasure from God himself.

"Oh, Landon," Ashley cried out loud. She stood and took three steps down the beach. Then she hung her head as a million memories came to mind of times when she had failed to see Cole as the gift he truly was.

He would bring her a rock or a feather or some other prize and hand it to her. "Here, Mommy, it's for you." His smile would light the room. But she wouldn't be thinking about her love for Cole and how fortunate she was to be his mother. She'd be thinking that one day he'd know the truth about how he came to be. And then he'd hate her, like Luke did.

Of course, no one hated her as much as she hated herself. And that's really why she hadn't been able to receive Cole's love. Hadn't been able to receive anyone's love — not even Landon's.

Especially not Landon's.

Ashley gritted her teeth. How many years had she wasted, refusing to allow herself to be close to Cole? or to anybody? Tears spilled from her eyes to the beach below.

Landon waited, giving her time to grieve. After several minutes she felt him come up behind her. He eased his arms around her waist and pulled her against him. "You thought I wouldn't love you if I knew about Paris? Is that it?"

"Who would blame you?" She let her head fall back against his chest. They were both facing the lake, staring straight ahead. "You thought I was like Kari or Erin or Brooke. A Baxter girl. But that's not me; it never has been." She sighed, tired of crying. It was too late for tears. Everything that had shaped her life had already happened. "I'm not the person you thought I was, Landon."

With care, he turned her so she faced him. He kept his arms linked around her waist. "Yes, you are."

Ashley's hands fell loose to her sides. She lowered her brow. What was he saying? She wiped the wetness from beneath her eyes. "I . . . I don't understand."

"Ever since I met you I've known who you are, Ashley — independent and daring, passionate and emotional. A girl with the guts to go to Paris alone and follow her dream. No, you're not like your sisters. I never thought you were. Inside you beats a heart with more depth than any woman I know." He searched her eyes. "Paris didn't change that."

Ashley's head began to spin. Why was he telling her this now? How could he say such kind things after all she'd just told him? This was the part where he was supposed to say good-bye and be rid of her. "You don't have to say that."

"Look" — Landon exhaled hard — "I'm telling you the truth. It kills me, the things that man did to you. But your past doesn't matter to me. All I care about is that you're here now, safe and well and ready to let me see your heart." His features softened. "Even just a little."

Ashley looked deep into Landon's eyes.

Did he really love her that much? There, in the most secret places of his heart? So much that not even the truth about her past could sway his feelings for her?

"Landon, I . . . I don't know what to say."

His eyes danced. "Don't you see, Ashley?"

"See what?"

"For years I've prayed for this moment. You've already told me exactly what I wanted to hear."

"I have?" Her tone was softer than before.

"Yes." Landon leaned down and kissed her. Not the slow, tentative kiss of attraction like the ones they shared the other night at his house, but a kiss of longing that swept away a mountain of doubts and left nothing unsaid. When he came up for air, he was breathless. "Ashley, sweet Ashley . . . you trusted me with your past." He dusted his lips along her cheekbone toward her ear, his voice a whisper. "And trust is the only way we'll ever find out what tomorrow holds."

They came together once more, their kiss longer, almost desperate. The feeling was more wonderful than anything Ashley could imagine — being wrapped in

Landon's arms, believing he loved her. Not just the outside part of her or some imaginary inside, but all of her. Every tainted back alley of her heart.

They were both trembling when Landon finally pulled away. "Okay." He took her hand. "I need a break." He pursed his lips and exhaled hard. "Let's take a walk."

Ashley laughed, and the sound of it danced across her mind. Never had she guessed this night would end with her and Landon kissing, laughing, holding hands as they walked along the shore. Even if Landon changed his mind about her after tonight, she would never regret telling him the truth. Not after what it had taught her about him, about herself.

And about Cole.

They were only partway down the beach when they saw a star shoot across the Indiana sky. The sight of it made them both stop in their tracks.

"Make a wish." Landon squeezed her hand.

"Okay." Ashley closed her eyes. She dreamed that someday, when Landon was finished fighting fires in New York City, they might have another night like this. Just one more night. She blinked her eyes open and shifted her gaze from the stars to the rugged outline of his face in the moonlight. "Your turn."

Landon looked at her a long while, his eyes shining with sincerity. "I already made mine."

They walked a little more, collected their beach chairs, and made their way back to the parking lot.

That night Ashley let Cole stay in her bed. Long after he was asleep, Landon's words about her son stayed in her mind. Just before midnight, she leaned up on one elbow and stared at Cole, his small features and wispy blond bangs.

Then she did something she hadn't done — not once since the day she'd found out she was pregnant.

She thanked God for her child and prayed that she would never again think of him as anything other than what he was: The most precious, prized gift God had ever given her.

Chapter Seventeen

The discussion was going nowhere.

It was the tenth of September, minutes before eight o'clock, and anyone knew what that meant: Football season was about to begin. The first Monday Night Football game of the season was on television that night, and Luke had no intention of missing it. The problem was he'd agreed to play a late softball game with Reagan and her friends.

"Football, Luke?" They were standing outside her apartment. Reagan grinned at him and leaned against her car. She had a duffel bag of equipment slung over her shoulder. "The team needs you. We never have enough guys."

Luke ran his fingers through his hair. The game was set to start in a few minutes. "Look, Reagan. You don't understand. This is Ryan Taylor's coaching debut. The Giants' first regular game of the season. They're at Denver, and anything could happen." He hesitated and bent his leg, lifting it slightly off the ground. "Did I mention my ankle's hurt?"

"Luke!" Reagan threw her hat at him. "Be serious."

"No, really. I turned it playing hoops."

"Luke . . ."

"Okay, tell you what." Luke searched for a compromise. "I'll play in the next five games. Just stay back tonight, and watch the game with me. Besides, it's dark. No one plays softball this late." He shot her his best smile. "Please?"

"The Giants?"

"Yes!" Luke took two steps back toward the building. There was no way he could miss this game. "New York's finest!"

"Well . . ." Reagan was teasing, playing with him, and suddenly Luke was certain he'd won. "The Giants *are* my dad's favorite team. Ever since my folks moved back to New York, he calls me after every game."

"Exactly." Luke waved one hand. "How can you have a meaningful father-daughter talk about your team if you miss the game?"

"Okay." Reagan laughed. She let her sports bag slip off her shoulder, then tossed it to Luke. Reagan was an athlete in every sense of the word. She'd come to Indiana University from North Carolina on a volleyball scholarship. But she could just have easily done so on her softball talent. "The next five games? You promise?"

"Absolutely."

He hefted her bag, grabbed Reagan's hand, and pulled her at a jog up the stairs, down the hallway, and into her apartment. Suddenly he froze as he remembered Reagan's roommate. "Is Wendy home?"

Reagan shook her head. "Not until Wednesday. She's at a family reunion in California."

"Good." Luke dropped the bag and flipped on the television. "She doesn't like me."

"Yes, she does." Reagan shoved him, her voice light and playful. "She just doesn't like guys in the apartment."

The announcers were just giving the starting lineup.

"Yes!" Luke dropped onto Reagan's old sofa. "It hasn't started."

"Sometimes it's scary" — Reagan tossed her baseball cap on the counter and sat down beside him — "how much you and my dad have in common."

"He's a good man." Luke kept his eyes on the screen. "Hey, look!" He was on his feet, pointing at the picture. "There's

Ryan. See . . . right behind that guy with the clipboard!"

"With the dark hair?" Reagan had only heard about Ryan. She'd never seen him until now.

"That's him." Luke sat back down. "He's so cool. Strong Christian, really loves God. Before he got hurt, he had the best set of hands in the NFL."

"Hmmm." Reagan grinned. "Not bad-looking, either."

"He's taken." Luke elbowed her in the ribs. "Ryan Taylor will never love anyone but my sister Kari. Too bad for you."

"Hey . . ." Reagan crooked her arm around Luke's neck and kissed him on the cheek. "I'm just kidding. Besides, why would I be interested in some football coach when I've got you?"

Luke turned his head in her direction and brought his lips to hers. For a moment, the football game was forgotten. Then Luke pulled free of her embrace and pointed to the screen. "Come on, Reagan." He elbowed her again. "Don't distract me."

"Fine." A sigh slipped from her lips. "I'll make sandwiches." She stood and turned the corner into the kitchen.

When she was gone, Luke realized something. They were breaking their own rule. As a way of avoiding temptation, he and Reagan had decided never to be alone in her apartment for more than a few minutes at a time — and definitely not at night. Normally, Reagan's roommate made the rule easy to keep.

But tonight . . . well, tonight he'd have to be very careful. Her kiss was a strong reminder of the reasons why.

He settled back against the sofa and thought for a moment. Why was he worried? This was different, wasn't it? They weren't here to be alone together. In fact, he would have gone home to watch the game if it hadn't been so late. But by the time he made it out to Clear Creek, where he lived with his parents, the first quarter would have been half over.

No, nothing would happen between them tonight. He'd just watch the game and be on his way. God was faithful. He wouldn't let them be tempted on a night like this, a night when both their intentions were completely innocent.

The first half went quickly, with the Giants trailing fourteen to seven at halftime. By then they'd eaten their sandwiches. Luke sat at one end of the sofa while Reagan stretched out along the length of it, watching the game. She wore sweats and a T-shirt, her hair pulled back in a ponytail. Luke glanced at her occasionally, admiring her long legs and narrow waist.

There was something so real about her. Athletic, but at the same time better looking in a dress than a girl had a right to be. The combination drove him crazy, and though Luke had dated several girls before her, he hadn't been joking that day in her father's office. He could definitely see this relationship lasting. They shared the same viewpoint on every issue that mattered — including their faith. Every day Luke spent with Reagan, he fell more in love.

When the network broke away for a commercial, Reagan shifted and rested her feet across Luke's lap. "I'm tired."

"I can see that." He cast her a wry glance and tapped her feet. "Are you comfortable?"

"Mmm, yes." A smile made its way up Reagan's cheeks, and she closed her eyes. "Good thing we didn't play ball tonight. I wouldn't have lasted three innings."

"I guess not." He tickled her feet. "But that doesn't mean you can take up the whole couch and leave me squished at the end."

"Hey!" She kicked him, giggling hard.

Sitting up, she reached over and pulled him down beside her. "We can share."

"Finally!" He laughed as she slid toward the front edge of the sofa, leaving room for him to stretch out behind her. The announcers were back, breaking down the game and analyzing how the Giants could tie the score.

Lying there behind her, it was all Luke could do to concentrate. *This is okay, isn't it, Lord?*

The words that flashed in Luke's mind were less than comforting. ***Flee! Scram! Get home fast!***

Luke let them go. He couldn't think of one reason why he and Reagan couldn't spend an hour stretched out on the sofa watching a football game. *Come on, Baxter.* A stifled sigh worked its way between his clenched teeth. *Focus on the game.* He lowered his brow and tried to make sense of the halftime report. But all he could think about was the way his feet felt wrapped around hers, the way her body gently rose and fell with every breath. He wondered if she was feeling the same thing.

When the game started again, Luke knew he couldn't lie there another minute. Easing Reagan forward, he bounced up off the sofa, grabbed a cup of water from the kitchen, and returned to his original spot.

Reagan flashed him a grin. "Don't say I didn't offer."

"It's okay." He lifted her feet back to his lap. "I can handle being squished."

The Giants tied the game at fourteen early in the third quarter. "I knew this was their year! I'm telling you, it's Ryan! He's the difference!" Luke hooted out loud, jumping to his feet and nearly knocking Reagan on the floor. "Go, Giants!" Luke pumped his fist in the air. "Look out, Super Bowl!"

"It's a tie game." Reagan glanced at the television. "I wouldn't celebrate yet."

Reagan proved to be right. The Broncos scored seventeen unanswered points, and midway through the fourth quarter a Giants' win looked out of reach.

By then, Reagan had dozed off and Luke was sitting on the floor, his back against the sofa. He looked at his watch. It was later than he thought. *I should go home.* He turned around and faced Reagan, brushing a lock of hair off her face. *Just turn off the television, kiss Reagan good night, and leave.*

But then what about the Giants? They still had time to pull ahead, didn't they? Luke stood and stretched. The floor was a lot harder than the sofa. Besides, Reagan wouldn't mind if he joined her. She was asleep, after all. What could happen?

Careful not to wake her, he crawled over her sleeping form and stretched out behind her again on the sofa. The movement was enough to make Reagan stir. She uttered something that didn't quite make sense; then in one graceful motion she rolled onto her other side, face-to-face with Luke.

His heart pounded out a strange rhythm. "Reagan," he whispered, "maybe you should go to bed. The Giants are losing, anyway."

"Hmmm." Reagan did a few slow blinks and then squinted at him. "You still watching the game?"

"Umm." Still watching the game? He could barely remember to breathe. "Trying to."

"Know what?" Her voice was sleepy. Luke had never seen her like this, in that not-quite-awake, dreamy state. Something about it made her unbelievably attractive.

"What?" He traced a finger along her chin.

"You're cute."

"Oh, yeah." Luke felt like he was being torn in two. Part of him wanted to bolt off the sofa, grab his keys, and head home before he did something stupid. The other half wanted only to erase the few inches that separated them and kiss her the way he was dying to do. "You're not bad yourself."

"I kinda like this. You know, lying here with you."

That was it. Luke couldn't speak, couldn't think. Couldn't come up with a single reason why he shouldn't kiss her. They were in love with each other, after all. What harm could one kiss do?

He slipped an arm around her waist and with little effort pulled her closer. She eased onto her back, leaving his face hovering above hers. When their lips met, the feeling shot fire the length of Luke's body.

"Luke . . ." She pushed back into the sofa, separating them for a moment. Her eyes searched his, frightened, unsure. "We can't."

"It's okay, Reagan." He glanced at the television. "The game's almost over. I'll go home then."

Luke knew it was a lie as soon as it came from his mouth. But still they kept kissing, crossing one line after another until neither of them noticed when the game ended. They barely noticed five minutes later when the phone rang. By then things were way out of control. Luke couldn't have stopped if he wanted to.

And he certainly didn't want to.

The answering machine picked up, and Tom Decker's voice came on the line. "Reagan? Honey, you home?" There was a pause.

"Tomorrow . . ." Reagan kissed Luke again. She was breathless, trapped in the moment. "I'll call him tomorrow."

The voice on the machine continued. "Oh, well. Just called to commiserate with you over the sad loss tonight. But hey, don't count the Giants out. You know, I was thinking — one of these weekends Mom and I should fly out and visit. The three of us could rent bikes or check out the shops. Let's plan it, okay?" He chuckled. "Anyway, call me tomorrow. Love you, honey."

There was a beeping sound, and the machine turned off.

"Reagan." Luke's voice was a whisper. He thought about standing up, getting away before they did something they'd both regret. The phone call had pulled him back to his senses. He had no doubt where they were headed. If they didn't stop, there would be no turning back. "I have to go."

But before he could even try, she kissed

261

him again, moving her face alongside his, drawing him closer.

"Not yet. Just a little while longer."

Luke closed his eyes. He felt as if he were falling from a cliff.

Help me here, God!

Now's your chance, son. Run! Flee!

Luke heard the quiet voice echo in the corridors of his soul. "Okay." He uttered the word as he kissed the side of Reagan's face, her neck, her throat. "Just a few more minutes."

But a few minutes became ten, and ten became thirty. It was nearly midnight when Luke got dressed and left the apartment. He was numb from what had happened, shocked. But as he pulled out of the parking lot, he wasn't thinking about Reagan or the consequences of their night together.

He was thinking about his sister Ashley.

The two of them had shared so much as kids. But everything had changed when Ashley came home from Paris, pregnant and defiant. She had made a mockery of all their parents had taught them, everything God's Word taught. And as a result, Luke had lost all respect for her.

But now, as he drove home, tears spilling onto his cheeks, Luke understood his sister. Once more they had everything in common, just like when they were kids. Because in one reckless hour he'd done the same thing Ashley had done.

In fact, he'd become just like her.

Chapter Eighteen

Ashley rarely worked the night shift.

But that Monday she'd agreed to fill in, and now that Irvel and the others were asleep, Ashley was glad she had. The quiet hours alone would give her time to work on her files.

Over the past few weeks, Ashley had put together a special file on each of the residents at Sunset Hills. Her goal was simple: to learn the stories of their lives — people they'd loved, activities they'd enjoyed, jobs they'd held. Maybe if she knew more about them, she'd find something that would shine a light of understanding on their behavior.

She'd already spent hours interviewing family members and friends. Anyone who visited was fair game, and she had made a number of phone calls as well. Ashley would question them, prod them, encourage them to remember. Each detail she learned was added to the appropriate person's file. And scrap by colorful scrap

Ashley had collected enough to piece together a patchwork picture of each resident's life.

So far, the files were fascinating. Ashley
studied them one at a time, looking for
themes and trying to understand what had
happened in decades gone by.

Edith's file told the story of a young girl,
lonely and isolated. Raised in a wealthy
family, Edith had been known for her
gentle spirit and her beauty. Last week one
of Edith's granddaughters had even provided Ashley with a photograph taken on
Edith's eighteenth birthday — the same
year she had been crowned queen of the
Ohio State Fair.

Ashley studied the photograph. There
was no question about it — young Edith
was one of the most gorgeous girls Ashley
had ever seen. Sadly, Edith's later life had
been less beautiful. She had married a
high-profile modeling agent and given him
two sons. Ten years later, he had run off
with a younger woman, leaving her to raise
the boys by herself.

Even then, Edith's looks were her
greatest asset. She graced the covers of a
dozen magazines and starred in several
print ads to pay the bills. There was no
shortage of men over the years — men

looking to rescue her, sweep her off her feet, and give her the life they felt she longed for. But after her first husband's betrayal, Edith apparently had no desire to marry again. Her heart had already been broken. It was in no condition to give to another man.

Years passed, and Edith's sons had grown. They'd married lovely girls and moved away, one to California and the other to Washington. Every few years they'd visited, but otherwise Edith had lived alone. Alzheimer's had set in early for Edith, not long after her sixtieth birthday. At age sixty-four, she was by far the youngest resident at Sunset Hills.

Ashley had called Edith's sons long distance for most of the information. A granddaughter who lived in the area visited on occasion. But none of them could figure out why Edith screamed.

Ashley studied the file again, trying to make sense of the mystery. The answer had to lie somewhere in Edith's past. But where? Had she been hurt or abused by one of her male friends? Had she witnessed some terrible crime or suffered a dramatic bit of bad news? Whatever it was, she seemed to remember it only in the bathroom. And what about her claim to have seen a witch? How did that fit in?

Ashley flipped to the next file. Helen's was fairly straightforward. She'd been plain and square-looking, with a functional marriage to Sue's father, a gruff, noncommunicative man. But without question, Helen's world had revolved around her only daughter. The two of them shared their deepest dreams, stayed up late reading or playing cards, and several times a year they had taken trips together — all the things Helen's husband wasn't interested in doing.

The hardest day of Helen's life was when Sue accepted a marriage proposal from a Navy man. In less than a year, Sue married and moved to Hawaii. At loose ends without her daughter, Helen went back to school and became a librarian. She looked forward to Sue's occasional visits and worked at her job in the library until she retired twenty years later.

By then, Sue and her husband had moved back to Indiana. But it was too late. Helen was already forgetting how to get home after a day out shopping, already drawing a blank when Sue would call about a lunch they'd planned.

The disease moved quickly for Helen. A

year after Sue moved home, Helen was placed in Sunset Hills.

Ashley looked back over her notes on Helen once more. There was still no explanation for the woman's angry outbursts, the way she slammed doors and pounded her fists. And no way to understand why Helen recognized an old *picture* of her daughter, but not the woman Sue had become.

Bert's file held only the bare details from his life. His only living child was a son who ran a dairy farm in Wisconsin and apparently had no trouble paying the monthly cost of keeping Bert at Sunset Hills. Ashley had called the son, but the man had been too busy to get into a deep conversation.

"Does your father remember you?" Ashley had asked the man.

She'd written his answer in the back of Bert's file: "I have no idea if Dad remembers me or not. When I visit, he doesn't say a word, doesn't look at me, doesn't notice I'm even in the room. To tell you the truth, ma'am, I've considered him dead for years."

The facts on Bert's past life were sketchy. He had grown up on a farm, married a girl he'd known all his life, and spent his adult years working with horses. Until ten years ago, Bert's son had been his right-hand man.

After Bert developed Alzheimer's disease, his son moved him to a nursing home in Wisconsin. Then Bert's sister, who lived in Bloomington, recommended Sunset Hills. She promised to visit him several times a week — a promise she kept until three years ago, when she died suddenly in her sleep.

Not long after that, Bert began circling.

Ashley opened the file on Laura Jo. It contained the least information of all. The comment that Ashley felt best about was one spoken by her granddaughter: "Grandma is resting now, finished with all that God's given her in this life. She has loved much and lost much. But she is at peace with her Savior; she's ready to go home."

Laura Jo was the one resident at Sunset Hills who wasn't a mystery. Her granddaughter's words said it all.

Ashley had saved Irvel's file for last. It told the story of a happy young girl who was the darling of her parents' life.

Always surrounded by friends, Irvel had been social from the moment she started school in Ann Arbor, Michigan. Though she dated other boys, she was knocked off her feet her junior year by Hank Heidenreich.

A blond, blue-eyed senior, Hank had moved to their area that year and immediately become popular with the girls. But that didn't matter much to Hank. From the moment he met her, he had eyes for Irvel alone.

The two of them quickly became an "item" and remained inseparable until World War II put them on different continents. He came home on crutches, a bullet lodged in his knee. The following spring, he and Irvel married.

As far as Ashley could tell, Irvel and Hank's life together was as full as any could get. Decade after decade their love grew stronger, until it seemed they might go on that way forever. Then, three children and forty-five years after their wedding, doctors noticed a dark spot on an X ray of Hank's lung.

Nine months later he was dead.

Ashley didn't need relatives or a file to understand what motivated Irvel. Hank was everything to her, just as he always had been. No matter that time had marched on. Irvel was stuck somewhere back in the days when her beloved husband was young and vibrant, back when he fished with the boys and spent evenings telling her about his adventures. With Alzheimer's, every hour found Irvel lost in the past, reliving the happy times.

And why not? Was it really better, healthier, for Irvel to be constantly mindful of her true place and position? Would waking each day to the reality of Hank's absence make her happier in these, her last days? Ashley was certain it would not. In this, at least, she had to agree with the pastor quoted in the Internet article. Distant memories were God's way of being merciful to those afflicted with Alzheimer's disease.

Yet Belinda was still determined to follow protocol, still bent on staring Irvel down and pounding the truth into her head. *"Hank's dead, Irvel — fifteen years now. Get over it."* Ashley cringed at the memory. Each time Belinda reminded her, Irvel reacted as though she were hearing the news for the first time.

The poor dear.

Ashley's favorite part of Irvel's file was the comment section in the back, the place where she wrote observations rather than facts — special things visitors had noted. Ashley read over Irvel's list slowly:

- Irvel and Hank were like two hands on the same person. The bond between them was such that you simply knew they were connected.
- Hank and Irvel's love was rare even in their day. They were a walking definition of how marriage is supposed to be.
- Everyone envied that special something Irvel and Hank shared. When one breathed in, the other drew life.
- Most everyone I know grieved for Irvel the day Hank died. When his heart quit, most of us were surprised hers kept beating. They were that close.

Ashley sighed.

What would it be like to know that kind of love — to live it every day the rest of her life? She stood and returned the files to their place in the hall closet. It was hard to believe that one day she'd be old like Irvel and her friends, maybe unable to remember whole decades of her past. Would she scream like Edith or pound her fist like Helen? Would she waste away in an adult care facility, waiting to die, or take up some strange habit like Bert?

Ashley hoped she'd be like Irvel — easing through her final years on the fuel of a love whose power knew no limits. Pleasant and social and happy with life — at least, the parts she could remember.

Was it possible that somewhere down the river of time, someone would put together a file on Ashley's life? If so, it would include Cole and her parents and her paintings. And maybe, just maybe, the name of a firefighter whose depth of love she was only beginning to understand. A man who honored her in a way that made Paris seem like a million years ago.

A man named Landon Blake.

Chapter Nineteen

On the morning of September 11, Kari woke to her usual routine. She fed Jessie, laid her out on a blanket, and did her Bible study. The Scripture passage that morning was a familiar one from 1 John: "The Spirit who lives in you is greater than the spirit who lives in the world."

Kari thought of all the times when that verse had applied to her — whenever she struggled with choosing God's ways over her own, and certainly when she felt discouraged. But this verse had become particularly precious over the past year, when evil seemed to surround her — first Tim's affair, then his murder, and even the temptation of being with Ryan back then.

There was no question that at times evil appeared to be winning the battle in Kari's life. How good it was, then, to fall back on God's promise that he was greater than the greatest evil. To realize, as Pastor Mark often said, that God wins. Period.

At times when Kari's grief felt over-whelming, the message of the verse from 1 John was an anchor that wouldn't budge. God was greater, no matter how bad things got, no matter how awful or evil or fright-ening.

God wins. It was that simple.

Kari worked through the questions in the study. Finally, at 8:50 she closed her Bible and stared down at Jessie, who had fallen asleep on the floor. Kari wasn't sur-prised; her morning naps usually began about this time.

"Okay, little one." Kari set her Bible down and stretched. "Let's get you to bed." She cradled Jessie to her chest, qui-etly carried her down the hall, and laid her in her crib. "Jesus loves you, Jessie," she whispered over her sleeping daughter. "Don't ever forget."

Normally, Kari would have set about doing laundry and tidying the house. But CNN's sports was about to come on, and she was dying to see reports on last night's Giants game. She'd watched it at her par-ents' house and several times caught glimpses of Ryan on the sidelines. It was the first time she'd seen him since Jessie was born, and now, despite her chores, she couldn't stop thinking of him.

Will there ever be a time when we're to-gether again?

Kari pondered the thought as she returned to the living room and flipped on the television. It was a few minutes before nine, and a talk show was wrapping up. A quick look at current news would come next, and then the sports. Once in a while reporters interviewed the assistant coaches, so chances were good that Ryan might be on this morning. Either way, Kari wanted to hear their assessment of the Giants' loss.

Kari grabbed a glass of water and nestled into the overstuffed leather sofa she and Tim had purchased three years ago. It felt good to relax. She leveled her gaze at the TV.

Suddenly the screen went blank and a banner appeared across the picture with the words *Special Report*.

What was this? Kari sat a bit straighter, waiting. Instantly the image switched to a frazzled reporter standing on a rooftop in New York City. Kari's breath caught in her throat, and she gasped. Behind the reporter in the distance stood the famous twin towers of the World Trade Center — and one of them was on fire.

She turned up the volume. "We have unconfirmed reports that approximately ten minutes ago an American Airlines jet crashed into the World Trade Center north tower." The reporter's eyes were wide, his voice strained with fear. "This is a building where thousands of people work and visit every day. We have no reports yet as to how many floors are involved or what the possible number of casualties might be."

Kari stared at the screen, her mouth open. Reagan's father worked in one of those towers. Somewhere near the top, from what Luke had said. "Dear God," Kari whispered, "help them. Please."

The reporter was still spouting details, revealing them as quickly as they came through his earphone. The jet had taken off from Boston's Logan International Airport with more than a hundred people aboard. There had been no reports of engine trouble by the pilot. Dozens of fire units were responding to the scene.

Kari could barely breathe. Flames engulfed several floors near the upper part of the building.

What could have caused a plane to swoop down from the sky and fly into a building? It was the most horrific accident Kari had ever seen. And she could do nothing but watch.

No, God. It's too awful.

Thick billows of black smoke curled up along the side of the tower, contrasting sharply with the city's brilliant blue sky. The blaze wasn't merely tongues of flames, but a glowing red furnace that grew larger by the second.

Kari was about to call her parents' house and see if they were watching when from the right side of the screen another jet entered the picture and flew straight into the second tower. A tremendous explosion shook the building as a fireball erupted into the sky.

"A second plane!" the reporter shouted, his voice frantic. "A second plane has hit the World Trade Center, this time the south tower." He paused and pressed on his left ear. "Reports now say it might not be an accident but an attack of some kind."

The entire scene was surreal, like something from a movie riddled with high-energy special effects. It wasn't possible. Two jets loaded with people couldn't have accidentally crashed into the twin towers minutes apart. And if this was an attack, who was behind it and what might happen next? Kari continued to stare at the screen, her mouth still open.

Lord, please . . . don't let this be happening.

The camera panned in closer, capturing the sight of debris and windowpanes and pieces of the building raining down on the streets of New York.

"Oh no!" The reporter shouted in alarm. Kari watched as several people fell or jumped from the burning floors and plummeted to the ground.

The reporter was as shocked as everyone else watching. His words were choppy and panic-stricken. "This is . . . this has to be the worst disaster New York City has ever seen. Hundreds of firefighters are flooding the scene, but the flames are eighty, ninety floors up. People are obviously desperate. It's difficult . . . difficult to believe that anyone in either of those jets could have survived."

Either of the jets? Kari's heartbeat hesitated.

Ryan would have been flying this morning from Denver to New York. What if he'd been on the second plane? Her heart began beating again with a double thud and then raced along at twice its normal rate. She ran to the kitchen for the phone.

Her mother answered on the first ring. "Hello?"

"It's Kari. Are you watching TV? Can you believe this is happening?"

"I turned it on a few minutes ago. Your father called from the hospital. Everyone's saying it's terrorists." Her mother's voice was shrill, desperate. "Reagan's father must be right in the middle of this."

"I'm . . . I'm . . ." Kari was so frightened she could barely find the words. Her hands and arms shook. She moved back near the television, too terrified to sit down. "Ryan was flying home this morning."

"Oh, Kari . . . no. There are hundreds of planes in the sky." Her mother tried to sound reassuring, but Kari could hear the tremble in her voice. The reporter had said nearly three hundred people were believed to be on those planes. What if one of them was Ryan?

"I've gotta go, Mom. I have to find him."

"What can I do?"

Kari closed her eyes and forced herself to think. "Pray." Her voice broke and she blinked, fixing her gaze on the terrible images playing out across the screen. "Pray, and don't stop."

The moment Kari hung up, she dialed Ryan's number. Maybe they'd arrived home earlier that morning, caught a red-eye to beat the rush hour. If so, he might already be back at his apartment. With each ring, Kari's fear doubled. Where was he?

Come on, Ryan . . . answer!

On the fourth ring, someone picked up. "Hello?"

It was Ryan's voice, and the flood of relief was strong enough to send Kari to her knees.

"You're there!" He was alive. Of the countless people who would be grieving a personal loss today, she would not be among them. Tears stung at her eyes. *Thank you, Lord . . . thank you . . . thank you.* "Ryan, thank God you're okay."

"Kari, what? You sound awful."

"You don't know?"

"Know what? I just got out of the shower."

"The World Trade Center's been hit. Both buildings." Then she remembered. Ryan had told her he could see the towers from his apartment window. "Look outside. I'm serious."

She heard the sound of his pulling up his blinds. And then his soft gasp. "What . . . what happened?"

"Turn on the news. Two jets crashed into the towers a few minutes apart." She was grateful he was alive, but the horror of the moment was still more than she could believe. Her television now showed streams of fire trucks rushing to the base of the buildings. "I thought . . . I was afraid you were on one of the planes."

"No . . . oh, sweetie, I'm sorry." He groaned as though he finally understood her concern. "We chartered an earlier plane. I got in half an hour ago and went straight to the shower."

Kari drew a deep breath. "I was so afraid, Ryan."

"Wait a minute. I'm turning on my TV." He was quiet. "I can see the whole thing out my window, Kari. It's worse than the pictures. It takes up the whole sky."

"Remember Reagan — Luke's girlfriend?" Kari stared at the screen. Ryan was right; the fire was tearing through the towers. She looked down at her hands. Her fingers were shaking again.

"Yeah, I think so. You've talked about her."

"Her . . . her father works on one of the top floors."

Ryan moaned. "Is anyone getting out? Have they said anything about the rescue?"

"It's a madhouse. People are using the stairs, but they're saying thousands are still inside." Kari gripped the phone more tightly. "Pray for Reagan, will you? For her father?"

"What about Landon Blake? Didn't he take a job with the New York City Fire Department?"

"His start date isn't until November first. But his best friend's there — probably at the scene by now."

She needed to call her family and see if anyone knew anything about Reagan's father. "Listen, I've gotta go, Ryan. Call me later."

"Okay. I'll be praying."

Kari hung up the phone. *Dear God, help us . . . help us. So many people are in the middle of that fire, Lord. Please . . .*

Almost in response, her Scripture verse from that morning came to mind: *The Spirit who lives in you is greater than the spirit who lives in the world.*

Kari clenched her teeth. *Let it be true, God. Even on a day like this . . . please.*

Her next call was to Ashley.

They had just finished baths at Sunset Hills when the phone rang.

"Sunset Hills Adult Care Home." Ashley cradled the phone against her shoulder.

"Are you watching the news?" It was Kari. Her tone was strained.

"No. Why — what's up?" Ashley enjoyed the sound of her own voice these days — light and upbeat, the way Kari's used to sound.

"Turn it on, Ashley. We're being attacked by terrorists. Two planes have crashed into the World Trade Center."

Ashley sucked in a quick breath. "What do you mean?" She had just helped Irvel settle into her recliner. All three women were tucked into their chairs, snuggled beneath blankets, and ready for their morning programs. Ashley flipped on the television, and immediately images of the flaming twin towers filled the screen. "How in the world . . . ?"

Kari sounded like she was crying. "I'm worried about Reagan."

Then Ashley remembered. "Her father works at the top of one of those buildings, doesn't he?"

"Yes. I'm gonna call Mom and see if she's heard anything. I'll call you back."

"Okay."

"Pray, Ashley. This is awful."

"I will." Ashley's answer came before she had time to think. She hung up the phone and pulled an empty rocking chair up next to Irvel, a few feet from the television.

"Is this a movie, dear?" Irvel gestured toward the screen. "Hank doesn't like me watching violent movies. Gives me nightmares."

"No, Irvel." Ashley turned and patted the old woman's hand. "It's not a movie."

"Looks like *King Kong*," Helen barked. She pointed to the television. "King Kong was on that building last time."

"King Kong," Edith muttered. She fixed her eyes on the screen.

"Yes, I think you're right." Irvel pointed at Helen and smiled. "King Kong did that in one of those violent movies. That's what it is."

The camera switched to a reporter standing on a New York City street. "We have word now that the Port Authority of New York and New Jersey has closed access to all bridges and tunnels leading into and out of the city. Triage centers are being set up in various locations around the twin towers. Fire officials say they estimate hundreds of people may be injured. There's no word yet about casualties."

From the corner of her eye, Ashley could see Irvel staring at her. "You know, dear, you have the most beautiful . . ."

Ashley tuned out the rest and patted Irvel's hand again. It was all she could do to hear the report, but she was afraid to turn up the volume. The women were already on edge.

"Hundreds of firefighters have responded to the scene, but reports say the heat is too intense to reach the top floors. Thousands of people may be trapped inside and —"

Firefighters? Ashley held her breath. It was September 11. If Landon hadn't been hurt, he would be there now. Right in the middle of the madness, rushing into a burning building more than a hundred stories high.

She caught her breath and stared hard at the screen. Landon was safe, but what about his friend? Hadn't Landon told her Jalen's company was stationed in lower Manhattan — near the World Trade Center? Certainly he would have responded by now.

Irvel leaned forward in her chair and glanced at the other women. "Does anyone know when Hank'll be back? I don't like him gone this long."

"Spies." Helen slapped her hand against the arm of her recliner.

"Hank's not a spy, dear." Irvel sent Helen a simple smile. "He's been checked."

Helen pointed to the television screen.

"Spies. King Kong has a whole army of spies. None of them have been checked."

A sound began to come from Edith. Her chair was situated at the far end of the room because she didn't often participate in the conversations between Irvel and Helen. "No . . . no . . . no . . . no . . . no . . ." The words were mumbled together in a fluid stream, but they were loud enough to understand.

Ashley stood and crossed the room. "It's okay, Edith. Everything's okay."

Edith moved her head back and forth in small, short shakes. She raised a trembling hand and pointed to the television. "No . . . no . . . no . . ."

"Would you like a nap, Edith?"

The woman froze and then nodded. She had the eyes of a frightened child as she took hold of Ashley's hand and followed her down the hall to her bedroom. "Everything's okay, Edith. You get some sleep."

Ashley returned to the living room as quickly as possible. Helen and Irvel were still debating whether King Kong had set the fires, and if so, whether spies were involved.

Meanwhile, the news continued to pour in. A different reporter was updating the public, saying that President Bush had announced the country was under an apparent terrorist attack. All airports in the United States had been shut down.

The country? Did that mean something else was about to happen? Something worse? Ashley folded her arms tightly in front of her and clutched her sides. Her stomach hurt. What if Reagan's father was still in one of those buildings?

Ashley felt a tap on her arm. "Excuse me, dear. My name's Irvel. My husband's fishing with his friends. Can you tell me when he'll be home?"

Ashley sighed. "It won't be long, Irvel. Everything's fine."

"What about King Kong?" Helen gripped the edges of her chair and slid forward. She waved an angry hand toward the television. "Look at that mess. Who's going to check those people?"

Ashley ignored the question. She fixed her attention on the pieces of news she could hear: ". . . reports that the fires are out of control in both buildings . . . hundreds of firefighters racing to the scene . . . command posts set up on the seventieth floor . . ."

"Excuse me again." Irvel took gentle hold of Ashley's hand. "Hank shouldn't be fishing today. I'm worried about him."

"He's okay, Irvel. Everything's okay." Ashley was desperate to talk to Landon, but she wasn't his wife, and she wouldn't call him at work.

The reporter's voice changed tone and grew louder. "We've just learned that another plane has crashed into the Pentagon. Officials are evacuating the White House. We'll take you live to a reporter on the scene."

Ashley's eyes grew wide as the image changed. The massive Pentagon complex in Washington, D.C., was masked in thick clouds of black smoke. An entire section of the building was missing, and balls of fire erupted into the sky.

The Sunset Hills women were silent for a moment, staring at the screen.

"It looks violent to me, dear." Irvel shook her head.

"You see!" Helen pounded her fist against her thigh. "It's King Kong! I knew it. My mother told me to look out for King Kong."

"Hank doesn't want me watching violent movies." Irvel made a polite coughing sound and tapped Ashley's arm once more. "Is this a movie, dear?"

Ashley covered Irvel's hand with her own. "No, Irvel. It's not."

"Oh." Irvel managed a weak smile. "Well, then . . ." She hesitated. "You know, I don't believe we've met. I'm Irvel."

Today was not a day for business as usual.

That was rapidly becoming clear in Dr. John Baxter's medical office, where patients and staff alike sat glued to the lobby television set and very little clinical work was getting done.

John Baxter had decided to simply finish with the patients who were there and cancel the rest of his appointments for the day. He was giving instructions to the office manager when Brooke burst through the glass doors of the office.

"Dad, have you seen it?" Brooke was rarely emotional. Intelligent and self-sufficient, she usually handled her feelings with the same precise care as she had once handled studies. But here, in light of what was happening in New York and Washington, D.C., she took his hands, her face frozen with fear. "They've hit the Pentagon too."

"I know." He wrapped his arms around her and stroked her back. "We need to pray."

"I have been praying — like crazy."

John resisted the urge to act surprised.

Brooke and her husband, Peter, were doctors. Though both were from families where faith was a mainstay, neither clung to those beliefs now.

At least not until today.

John led Brooke to the staff lounge, where two of his partners and several nurses were gathered around the television screen. In all his life John had never seen such horror. Hundreds of people were dead. Thousands more were probably injured. America was under attack.

But even now, John was certain God hadn't abandoned them. The Lord was there in those burning buildings, just as he was here beside them. God reigned even at a moment like this, and he would work all things out for the good of those who loved him. In the process he would cause the entire nation to remember what mattered in life — what really mattered.

Brooke jerked her head in his direction. "Have you heard about the switchboards at the hospital?"

"No. What's happening?"

"The phones are ringing off the hook."

John shifted his weight, confused. "Why are they calling the hospital?"

Brooke met his gaze straight on. "They're looking for a place to give blood."

★ ★ ★

Bloomington Fire Station #2 was thick with tension. Landon and five other firefighters sat in a tight circle around a small television in the lunchroom. They'd been there for nearly fifty minutes, ever since one of their wives had called with the news. Landon was the quietest of all — not because he had nothing to say but because he couldn't stop praying for Jalen.

He had no doubt that somewhere in one of those towering infernos, his best friend was trying to save lives.

"How many firefighters you figure are in those buildings?" one of the men in the circle asked.

"Gotta be hundreds."

"Hey, Landon, don't you have a buddy at FDNY?"

"Yeah." Landon's mouth was dry. There was nothing else he could say. He stared at the screen, unblinking. He'd talked to Jalen a few days ago. This was his shift, Landon was certain, and his station was in the vicinity. *Hurry, Jalen.*

The conversation around him continued.

"You have any idea how hot jet fuel burns? That place is a furnace by now."

"The whole building must be feeling it."

Their voices grew, filled with a knowing

292

fear for their fellow firefighters.

Come on, Jalen . . . get out. A building that hot wasn't safe. Landon had been thinking about that since the first plane hit. At a certain temperature the integrity of steel would be compromised, and if that happened. . . . *Get out of there, Jalen. Come on, buddy . . . get out!*

"Look at 'em." One of the guys rose to his feet. "Firemen are still pouring into the building. Must be fifty companies by now."

"What're they doing?" One of the others pounded his fist on the table. He motioned to the screen. "Someone get those men out of there!"

A reporter's voice cut through their dialogue. "We're getting reports that the south tower is shaking. Windows on the lower level are breaking out from the movement."

"Come on, people!" The fireman next to Landon shoved back his chair and swore out loud at the television set. "The whole thing's gonna come down! Get out! Go! Leave!"

Adrenaline shot through Landon's veins. Jalen was somewhere in one of those buildings. He could feel it. But there wasn't a thing he could do to help. *Leave, Jalen! God, make him get out of there.*

At that moment there was a strange shuddering sound, and in a matter of seconds, the south tower disappeared in a volcano-size cloud of smoke and dust and debris.

Landon could feel the blood draining from his face as he watched in disbelief. A hundred floors of steel and glass, tons of office equipment and people — all gone. Completely gone.

"The south tower just collapsed!" The reporter shouted the news against a backdrop of screaming people, all of them scrambling for their lives, trying to outrun the blast. "I repeat, the south tower of the World Trade Center has collapsed to the ground. There's nothing left standing."

"Jalen!" Landon was on his feet. He raised his arms and dug his fingers into his hair. The scene was complete madness. A wave of nausea gripped his belly. What had they just witnessed? Hundreds of people — maybe thousands — killed right before their eyes. How many of them had been firefighters, racing up the stairs while everyone else raced down?

The building wouldn't contain a single survivor after the force of the collapse.

No, it isn't possible. If Jalen was in the building when it collapsed . . . Landon closed his eyes and uttered the only prayer he could think of: *God, take care of my friend. And whatever happens, please . . . don't let him suffer.*

Luke had been in the middle of a ninety-minute economics lecture when a student tore into the classroom and shouted something about a terrorist attack. Immediately the professor had flipped on the television.

Every moment since then, Luke and his classmates had been glued to the screen.

All around him students were whispering, talking about the tragedy, commenting on the situation. But Luke was utterly silent, caught in a moment of prayer so deep and intense he could barely concentrate on the steady flow of news reports.

For thirty straight minutes, he'd been begging God to let Reagan's father live. He worked on the eighty-ninth floor of the north tower. By the looks of it, the plane had hit lower than that. Could Tom Decker make it down past the burning wreckage? And what about Reagan? Wherever she was, she had to know by now.

Luke remembered the phone call her father had made last night, and the knots in his stomach tightened. She hadn't answered it because they were . . .

Please, God. I've never asked you for anything like this before. Please let him live . . . please.

The harder he prayed, the worse the fire seemed to get.

There were reports of the buildings shaking, giving way. And then, in a single surreal motion, the south tower collapsed, plummeting to the ground. The students gasped, and an eerie silence came over the room. At first, Luke wasn't sure which building had fallen.

He held his breath while the reporters shouted the news. The south tower had collapsed. Some people were trapped; others were fleeing the scene. All federal office buildings in Washington, D.C., were being evacuated. The news was terrible. But Luke couldn't help the sense of relief flooding his body. The building Reagan's father worked in was standing. He still had a chance.

I beg you, God — not the north tower too. Please, God. Get Reagan's father out. She didn't get a chance to talk to him yesterday because . . . I'm sorry, God. It was my fault. Please don't punish her for my mistake.

Luke had felt awful since he left Reagan's apartment a dozen hours ago. Long before the news of the attacks, he'd been sick to his stomach over what had happened between them. How had things gotten so out of hand? And what would she think of him now? They'd both been determined to wait, sure that they would never fall to temptation the way others did. They were just watching a football game, after all.

But now how would Reagan feel if something happened to her father — if she'd missed out on her last chance to talk to him because she and Luke were breaking the most important guideline God ever set about relationships? What then? Luke couldn't imagine how she must be feeling.

A shaken Dan Rather appeared on the screen. He glanced at a stack of notes. "We have reports now that the north tower of the World Trade Center is unstable. There's concern it might collapse as well. Police are evacuating everyone except medical and fire personnel from the scene, and . . ."

The north tower? *No! God, you wouldn't let it fall.*

Without waiting another moment, Luke grabbed his things and raced from the classroom. Whatever happened next, he needed to reach Reagan — even if he had to search the whole campus to find her.

Landon and his colleagues hadn't moved. They remained fixated on the television, listening as reporters spoke of dozens of firefighters trapped in the collapsed building. A feeling of futility hung over them, and for the most part they no longer spoke.

The only sound around the table was an occasional grunt of disbelief or shock.

What could they say? There was nothing any of them could do to help, and the disaster grew worse by the minute. Landon tried to believe that Jalen was in the north tower, that somehow he'd avoided the ill-fated south tower and might still have time to get out.

But just as those thoughts flashed in his mind, the top part of the north tower peeled away, sending the entire massive structure down to the ground. One minute it was standing among the buildings of the city; the next it was reduced to a massive pile of rubble, shrouded in a black fog of debris even denser than before.

Landon could barely breathe. He glanced at the lunchroom clock: 10:28 a.m. The fire had been burning in the north tower for ninety minutes — enough time for firefighters to get in, make a rescue, and get out. Certainly some firefighters had gotten out. But was Jalen one of them?

God be with him. Be merciful. If there's a chance he can get out of there, help him. Please, God . . .

Fifteen minutes later the report came that another plane had gone down, this one in rural Pennsylvania. Reporters speculated that the crash must have been linked to the attacks. The flight pattern indicated the jet was headed for the Washington, D.C., area. Maybe even the White House.

Over the next hour, several of Landon's buddies took breaks from the unfolding horror. Only Landon couldn't leave his seat. He was desperate to hear about the New York firefighters. Had any of them gotten out in time, or were most of them trapped beneath the rubble? How many were missing? He was watching when the news he feared most was first reported. As many as a hundred firefighters were missing, maybe more. Whole engine companies, fire trucks and all, had vanished when the towers collapsed.

Landon listened to the news and clenched his jaw, working it first one way then the other. He wanted to cry, wanted to punch something or run until he couldn't breathe anymore. The idea of idly watching while Jalen might be suffocating under tons of rubble was more than he could take.

There was only one thing he could do, one way he could help his best friend now. He pushed his chair back and looked at the two other firemen at the table. It wasn't like he even had a choice.

"Guys . . ." He grabbed his hat and headed out the door. "I'm going to New York."

Chapter Twenty

Luke raced across campus like a madman.

Why couldn't he remember Reagan's schedule? Was she in physics this morning or journalism? He checked three classrooms, ran a hundred yards to another building, and checked two more before he remembered. It was Tuesday. Her first class didn't start until eleven on Tuesdays.

He raced to the student parking lot, found his car, and sped toward Reagan's apartment. Was it only twelve hours ago that he'd been with her, trying to decide whether he should stay, trying to ignore the way God practically shouted at him to go home?

How had everything changed in so little time?

He darted up the steps and pounded on her door. When no one answered, he tried the handle. It was unlocked. He opened it with a quiet push, careful not to frighten her.

"Reagan?" He heard a distant beeping.

"Reagan, are you here?"

No answer. Luke moved through the entryway and stopped short as he reached the living room. There she was, sitting on the same sofa where they'd lost control the night before. Her eyes were wide, her face frozen in a look of shock and horror that cut Luke to the core. She stared at the television screen, oblivious to the fact that the phone was off the hook beside her.

Luke followed her gaze. The TV showed smoke and soot and utter chaos. But as thick and dark as the cloud of debris was, the truth was plain for all to see. The north tower was gone. Where the World Trade Center once stood, there was now nothing at all.

"Did it . . . ?" Luke couldn't finish his question.

Reagan looked at him, her movements slow and unnatural. "It's gone. Dad's building fell."

"No. Reagan, it didn't." Luke was at her side instantly. "Tell me it's not true." He sat down beside her. But when he tried to put his arm around her, she held up her hand.

"Don't!" Her tone was loud and sharp. She slid over on the sofa, tightening her grip on the phone. "I need to call my mother."

Luke felt like he'd been slapped. Reagan was in shock; that had to be it. She'd never spoken to him that way before. He looked at the receiver, then at Reagan. "It's off the hook."

"Don't talk to me!" She stared at the phone as if she were seeing it for the first time. Then she pushed a series of buttons, held it to her ear, and waited.

Luke watched. There was nothing he could do to help. When the call didn't go through, Reagan dropped the phone to her side. It was still beeping. Luke kept his distance but held out his hand. "Let me try, okay?"

The small bit of fight in Reagan fizzled. She handed him the receiver without the slightest change in her expression. Luke held the phone to his ear, found a dial tone, and hit the Redial button.

A recording came on. "All circuits are busy. Please try again. All circuits are busy. Please try a—"

Luke hung up and set the phone on the coffee table in front of him. "We'll try in a few minutes."

Reagan hugged her arms to her chest. "You think he got out, right? My dad, I mean?" She swallowed twice. "He's coming to Bloomington with my mom.

We're going to see the town together." Her face was completely void of emotion. "Are they coming today?"

Reagan didn't blink. Luke studied her, his heart racing. What if she wasn't okay? What if she passed out or did something crazy? He'd never seen anyone act like this. She was waiting for an answer, frantically searching his face for something she could hold on to. "I don't know, Reagan."

She glanced at the television. "But he got out, right?"

"Yes." The word stuck in Luke's mouth. He was desperate for a glass of water. "I think he could be okay."

Her head bobbed up and down in a jerky fashion. "Right. Everything's okay. He's probably home sick today, or . . ." She blinked hard, her eyes darting about the room as though she were looking for an escape. "Or . . . he was away on business . . . or out on assignment or . . . or down the street getting coffee." She looked hard at him again. "Right, Luke. That could be it, couldn't it?"

"I'm trying your mom again." He picked up the phone and punched the Redial button once more. This time it rang, and Reagan's mother picked up almost immediately.

"Reagan?" Mrs. Decker sounded as anxious as her daughter. "I've been trying to call for the last half hour. Your line's been busy."

"This is Luke. Reagan's here beside me." He pinched the bridge of his nose. "Have you heard from your husband?"

"I'm . . . I'm all by myself here, Luke. I don't know what to do."

Luke wanted to scream. He didn't know what to do either. He was just a college kid, too far away to help even if he could. Instead he stared at his girlfriend, still sitting motionless across from him, and forced himself to be calm. "Reagan's pretty upset. Have you . . . has he called?"

Reagan's mother exhaled, and Luke could tell she was crying. "He called me after the first plane hit. It . . . it was his building. His office is just below the fire."

Luke could picture Mr. Decker's office, the way he had looked in his leather chair with all of New York City spread out behind him. How terrible it must have been to watch that plane fly into the building, to know an inferno was raging a few stories above.

Luke shuddered and tried to think of what to say next. "Maybe he got out." He shot a glance at Reagan. She didn't seem to be hearing his conversation. "There were reports of people escaping from that high up. If he made it to the stairwell in time, maybe he's at the hospital or looking for a way to call home. The circuits were busy when I tried a few minutes ago, so maybe —"

"Luke, stop." The woman was crying harder now. "He called me again. He . . . he said he was helping the firemen rescue people who couldn't move very fast. He wanted me to know they'd done all they could, and he was about to go down the stairs. He said he . . . he loved me and Reagan and that he was going to be fine. He'd see me in a few hours."

Luke didn't dare breathe.

"Five minutes after we hung up . . . the building fell." She sobbed out loud, a wailing, gut-wrenching cry like none he'd ever heard before. "Luke, he's gone. There's no way he could have survived that."

Reagan still hadn't moved, hadn't blinked as far as Luke could tell. *God, let there be a miracle here, please. This can't be happening. I don't know what to do.* He drew a slow breath. "You don't know for sure, though. Maybe he was able to —"

"Luke." The way she said his name

stopped him in mid-sentence. "I need to talk to my daughter. Please."

"Yes, ma'am." Luke winced. He held the phone out to Reagan. "She wants to talk to you."

Reagan took the phone, her movements even slower than before. "Hello?"

For a long while there was silence. Finally Reagan nodded. "I'll be there as soon as I can."

This time she replaced the receiver on the hook and sat there staring at the answering machine. Then she pushed the Playback button. On came her father's voice.

"Reagan? Honey, you home? . . . Oh, well. Just called to commiserate with you over the sad loss tonight. But hey, don't count the Giants out. You know, I was thinking — one of these weekends Mom and I should fly out and visit. The three of us could rent bikes or check out the shops. Let's plan it, okay?" His laugh sounded through the machine's speaker just as it had done last night. "Anyway, call me tomorrow. Love you, honey."

She waited a brief moment; then she hit the button again.

"Reagan? Honey, you home? . . ."

Luke slowly made his way toward her as

the message played out. He was afraid to touch her, afraid to show her any comfort at all. What could he say? Because of him, she had missed her last conversation with her father.

The phone rang before Reagan could play the message again. She jerked back as if the machine had come to life. Then she handed the receiver to Luke. "I . . . I can't talk."

"Hello?"

"It's Reagan's mom again." Mrs. Decker sounded calmer. She explained that Reagan's brother, Bryan, was getting a ride home from college. It was important that Reagan come too. "I've made her a reservation on the four o'clock bus out of Bloomington. Can you see that she gets there?"

"Definitely." Luke finished the conversation and hung up the phone once more.

The moment he did, Reagan moved her finger toward the Playback button. This time Luke held up a gentle hand and stopped her. "Reagan, don't."

She jerked his hand off and glared at him, her blonde eyebrows knit in a fury that took Luke by surprise. "Leave me alone. I'll listen to it as much as I want."

"It's not going to help." He kept his tone

patient, kind. The brush of his fingers against her elbow was the only support he felt free to give. Wasn't there anything he could do? His heart ached for a way to help her, but clearly she wanted nothing to do with him.

Small wonder after what happened last night.

He cleared his throat. "Your mother wants you to pack your things. She made you a bus reservation." He raised his hands a few inches and let them fall to his sides again. "You leave this afternoon at four."

Reagan moved away from the machine, her shoulders slumped forward, defeated. "I . . . I didn't take his call." She slid off the sofa, fell slowly to her knees, and sat back on her heels, her body bent. "Luke!" She cried out his name, and something in him snapped. It didn't matter if she pushed him away. He dropped to the floor beside her and put his arm around her, hugging her close.

"I'm sorry, Reagan. I'm so sorry."

"Why?" She looked at him, her face twisted in sorrow. "What did we do?"

"We didn't mean to, Reagan. It just happened."

Reagan cried out again and gave way to a battering series of sobs that shook her body until she could barely draw a breath. "It's my . . . my fault, Luke. If I would have taken his call . . ."

It was the same thing Luke was thinking. *If only she'd taken his call.*

Reagan and her dad would have chatted about the Giants, and her father would have caught her up on the latest family news. They would have talked about a visit to Bloomington and how Reagan's new classes were coming along. She would have told him she loved him. And by the time she hung up, the moment of passion he and Reagan were caught in would have been over. They would have called it a night, maybe joked about the close call and promised to never again let themselves be alone together like that. Not for any reason, even a Giants game.

If only she'd taken his call.

Luke wiped the palm of his free hand against his jeans. "You didn't know."

"God!" She wailed out the name, letting her grief have its way. Her head dropped back, and she stared at the ceiling. The word was barely understandable through her weeping. "Why?"

She turned to Luke and held out her hands like a broken child. "Help me!"

He put both his arms around her this

time, holding her as she collapsed against him. "I'm here, Reagan. I'm here."

"What kind of Christian am I?" Her voice was broken, beaten. Luke couldn't tell which hurt her worse — her father's death or that she'd intentionally missed having a final conversation with him. "My dad always told me . . . he knew I'd wait for marriage." She squeezed her eyes shut, the tears coming in torrents. "He . . . he told me I was one in a million."

Luke felt miserable, like his guts were being ripped out. Not only had Reagan lost her father. She'd lost him hours after doing something that would have broken his heart.

And it was all Luke's fault.

He rubbed his hand awkwardly along her lower back. "We didn't plan it, Reagan. It was an accident."

Reagan's shoulders shook again. "It . . . it doesn't matter if it was an accident." She gulped back a series of small sobs. Her eyes showed equal parts pain and guilt. "Don't you see, Luke? I didn't get to say good-bye."

"You can't think like that."

Her eyes were vacant. *She isn't hearing me.* He searched his mind, desperate for something to say, something to do. He should pray. That's what Christians did at a time like this. But what good would praying do now? It wouldn't bring Reagan's father back or restore the twin towers.

The reality of that left Luke dry and desperate and trapped. He had nowhere to turn, and absolutely no one to turn to.

He worked the muscles in his jaw. No, for the first time in his life he didn't feel like praying. He had nothing to say to God.

Nothing at all.

The line of blood donors wound down the sidewalk and out to the street.

After leaving his office, John Baxter worked alongside Brooke and Peter at the hospital for most of the day, helping supervise the drive. The Red Cross had too many volunteers to deal with, and their officials had made a quick arrangement with the staff at St. Anne's, naming the hospital as an alternate site for people wishing to give blood.

As busy as he'd been that day, every now and then John caught a news report.

At one o'clock that afternoon, President Bush came on TV and promised that the United States would "hunt down and punish those responsible for these cowardly acts." Several major airports had been evacuated for precautionary reasons, he said. In all, a total of four planes had gone down in what appeared to be a major terrorist attack.

John moved from table to table in the hospital cafeteria, where the temporary blood bank had been set up. He'd never seen anything like it. The people in the line were from all walks of life — college kids, old men, clergy, young women. The university's entire football team showed up in uniform to give. Several of them held American flags.

"Have you seen the line out there?" Brooke found him at one of the tables. Her straight dark hair was damp, her forehead glistening from the effort of getting people through the line.

John's heart lifted as he looked out the window. The river of donors was even longer than before. God was up to something amazing even now, in an hour cloaked in darkness.

His throat felt suddenly thick, and he worked to find his voice. "Those terrorists wanted to tear this country apart today." John swallowed hard and shook his head. "But you know something?"

"Yeah." Brooke gave him a sad smile tinged with hope. "It's made us remember everything important in life. In all our days, we've never been more together."

Ashley was in the Sunset Hills kitchen, ten minutes away from being done for the day, when the doorbell rang.

Laura Jo and Bert were napping in their rooms, Edith was asleep in her chair, and Helen and Irvel were watching *The Sound of Music* on video. Ashley had set up a small television in the kitchen to catch news updates on the attacks. She saw no point in upsetting the residents. Old movies were part of their routine. So even on a day that might change the course of history, the girls would watch Julie Andrews and be none the wiser.

None of the residents was expecting visitors, but then nothing about the day had been normal. She'd been tempted to call Landon, but the idea made her too uncomfortable. She'd never called him at work before. And today, especially, he was bound to be caught up in the tragedy at hand. He had to be worried sick about Jalen. From the reports coming in that afternoon, most of the firefighters who'd responded early were buried under the rubble of the twin towers.

Unless Jalen was off today — or unless his station hadn't been called to the disaster scene — the news couldn't be good.

The bell rang again. Ashley dried her hands and headed for the door.

"Dear . . ." Irvel waved at her from the recliner and motioned toward the door. "I think it's Hank."

"Wait!" Helen stared hard at the door, her brow lowered. "Hank's been checked, right?"

Ashley flashed a smile in Irvel's direction as she unlocked the door. "Let's see who it is first."

She opened the door and saw Landon, still in standard-issue, black firefighter pants and a white buttoned-down shirt. The rims of his eyes were red and swollen, despair written across his face. He neither moved nor spoke a word as Ashley went to him, taking him in her arms.

"I wanted to call you." She spoke in a whisper. "Have you heard anything?"

He brushed his cheek against hers. "I talked to his mother." He cleared his throat, his tone flat, broken. "Jalen was working today. His company was one of the first to respond."

Ashley felt the blow. "No, Landon."

He lifted his head and placed his hands on her shoulders. "I need you to take me to the bus stop."

"The bus stop?"

"I'm going, Ashley. I can't leave him buried beneath those buildings."

"What . . . what about your job?"

"I was nearly finished, anyway. The sooner I get to New York the better."

Ashley could think of a dozen quick reasons why Landon should wait. There would be enough people helping with the rescue effort. It was still too soon after the attacks. What if the enormous pile of debris wasn't stable? Landon could be hurt or killed if he put himself in the middle of the mayhem in New York.

But the most pressing reason was this: She wasn't ready for him to leave yet. They would have no long good-bye, no last week or last day or last time together, the way she had pictured it.

From inside the house, Irvel called out, "Dear, is it Hank?"

"No, Irvel." Ashley blinked. "It's not Hank."

Landon motioned inside. "Can I wait here until you're done?"

"Sure." She stepped back into the house, and he followed.

Once inside, he dug his hands into his pants pockets. "I have my stuff in the front seat. You could follow me home so I can drop off my car, then give me a ride to the station. The bus leaves at four."

"Of course."

"I already said good-bye to my parents." He met her gaze and held it. "I told them I wanted you to take me."

Irvel was waving her hand again. "Hello, dear. I'm Irvel." Her smile drifted from Ashley to Landon. "And hello to you too. Aren't you a handsome young man!"

Despite the tragedy of the day, the uncertainty of Jalen's welfare, and the staggering losses that were still being reported, both Ashley and Landon smiled. It lasted only a second or two, but the break in the sorrow felt wonderful.

Landon nodded in Irvel's direction. "Thank you, ma'am."

He had been to Sunset Hills one other time. After hearing about Irvel and her friends, he'd wanted to meet them. Now, just a few weeks later, it was clear by the looks on their faces that neither Irvel nor Helen remembered his visit.

"I've seen you somewhere before." Irvel held up a single finger as she studied Landon's face. "You're one of Hank's fishing friends, right?"

"No, ma'am. I've never fished with Hank."

Irvel shook her head. "I guess not. Hank's friends are a bit older than you."

"He's okay." Helen barked the statement from her chair a few feet away. "He's not a spy."

Ashley smiled and took Landon's hand. "No, Helen, he's not a spy."

She wove her fingers between his. Could he feel the way her hand trembled? Everything was happening too fast. In one hour Landon would be on a bus to New York City. Who knew when she might see him again? Or if she would?

Her stomach ached from the uncertainty. She forced herself to focus. Helen was talking about the people at Sunset Hills who'd been checked.

She glanced at Landon. "Did you hear about King Kong?"

Landon looked at Ashley, his expression blank. "King Kong?"

"It's a long story." Ashley gave him a crooked grin. "I'll tell you later."

"By the way, dear" — Irvel switched her attention to Ashley — "you have the most beautiful hair. Has anyone ever told you that?"

A sad smile lifted the corners of Landon's face as he elbowed Ashley.

"Yes." Ashley nodded. "Thank you, Irvel. That's nice of you to notice."

The door opened, and Krista, the care worker for the next shift, walked in. "Sorry I'm late. It's been a long day." She shut the door behind her and leaned against the wall. Her face wore a haunted expression. "My best friend's cousin was on one of the planes. I met her last year." Krista hung her head for a minute before looking up. "She was twenty-four."

Ashley let go of Landon's hand, crossed the living room, and hugged Krista. "I'm sorry."

Krista was a soft-spoken, heavyset college girl who was nothing but kind to the residents at Sunset Hills. She and Ashley hadn't had many opportunities to talk, but in their brief conversations they'd agreed that Belinda's harsh treatment of Irvel and the others was uncalled for.

Krista gave a quick glance at Landon and noticed his wet eyes. "I guess we've all been touched in one way or another."

Landon nodded.

"Well." Irvel folded her hands sweetly on her lap. "It looks like everyone's here. Time for peppermint tea."

Ashley gestured to Krista that she and Landon had to leave. Krista nodded and moved to Irvel's side. Tea had become a regular part of the afternoon since Ashley's arrival. She and Irvel and Helen had peppermint tea after lunch and sometimes again before her shift was over. Krista had begun including tea as part of her evening routine as well.

Belinda thought the tea was a waste of time, but she didn't forbid it. And today she was out of the office, so it wouldn't matter.

Krista patted Irvel's hands. "I think it'll just be us today, Irvel."

Ashley grabbed her purse and keys. She waved to Helen and Edith and kissed Irvel's cheek. "See you tomorrow, Irvel."

Uncertainty flashed in Irvel's eyes as she studied Ashley. "No violent movies tomorrow, okay, dear?"

"King Kong's loose," Helen interjected. She slapped the arm of her recliner. "Someone needs to catch him."

"Okay, Irvel." Ashley swallowed a lump of sadness. "Just the happy ones tomorrow."

"Yes." Irvel's features relaxed. "Just the happy ones."

Five minutes later, Ashley pulled up behind Landon in front of his house. He grabbed his things — two oversized duffel bags — and climbed in beside her. One of his friends at the Bloomington Fire Department was planning to rent Landon's house while he was gone. Originally he had planned to stay with Jalen once he moved to New York.

Landon said nothing of those plans or anything else as they drove. He merely reached over and held Ashley's hand, working his fingers gently between hers. By the time they reached the bus depot, it was three-forty.

Ashley parked, and for a minute they sat there, unmoving. "When do you get to New York?"

"Seven tomorrow morning."

She leaned against the steering wheel and studied him. The fear that was building within her was so real she could hear it in her voice. "Get some sleep if you can."

Landon nodded. "Ashley . . ." His lips parted, and a sigh escaped. He turned to her. "This summer . . ."

His words trailed off, and she bit her lip. "I know. It was great."

"It was more than that. It was . . ." He narrowed his eyes and stared straight ahead. She watched the muscles in his jaw flex; then he turned his attention back to her. "I'll never forget a minute of it."

"Neither will I." She took his hand, her voice choked with feelings.

Landon glanced at his watch. "Walk me in?"

Ashley nodded, her throat too thick to speak.

Hand in hand they made their way to the ticket counter and then to the gate. For a while they stood there, lost in an embrace that said more than words ever could. Finally he stepped back. "I better go."

She wanted to thank him for being honest with her back when he was lying injured in the hospital bed last July, thank him for loving Cole, thank him for taking the time to listen about Paris. Thank him for loving her even when she'd given him no promises, nothing to hang on to in return.

But there wasn't time. So she slipped her arms around his neck and brought her lips to his. It was a single kiss, one she hoped would tell him everything her words could not. When she drew back, she studied his face, his eyes. She saw the goodness there. She opened her mouth, but it took a moment before her choked voice worked. "Be safe."

"Will you do something for me?" His fingers came up along the sides of her face.

"Anything, Landon. You know that."

"Pray for me. Pray I find Jalen." His eyes welled up. "Pray I'm still the same person after all this."

Ashley tried to hide her relief. For a moment she had wondered whether he'd ask her to wait for him. It was the one thing she couldn't promise. It wouldn't be fair to him. He needed to go to New York with no strings attached, remembering her and the summer they shared as the coda to a wonderful friendship. What more could it ever be?

No, Ashley couldn't offer to wait for him, but she could agree to pray. She felt a smile inch partway up her face. "Yes, Landon. I'll pray for you. I promise."

A peaceful smile filled his face. "That means a lot to me, Ashley." He ran his thumb beneath her lip, his touch so light she barely felt it. "Thank you."

She gave a quick nod, blinking back her tears.

Praying wasn't something she thought about much. Not since Paris. She no longer believed there was anything helpful about talking to God. But she would keep her promise to Landon. It was the least she could do. In a matter of hours their lives had been riddled with sorrow and uncertainty. With Landon traveling to the heart of the battlefield, she could manage to say a prayer or two. Even if all it did was make Landon happy.

"Good-bye, Ash." His eyes found hers again.

"Good-bye."

"I'll call you."

Don't tell me that. Don't make me promises — not when I have none to make in return. She hugged him once more. "Go find Jalen."

He nodded and stepped away, heaving a duffel bag over each shoulder. Their eyes held a moment longer; then he turned and walked through the double doors.

Good-bye, Landon. God be with you.

Tears filled her eyes when she turned to leave. As she did, her breath caught in her throat. There in a small, semiprivate alcove stood her brother, Luke. He was talking in hushed tones to Reagan, and both of them looked upset. What were they doing here?

Then it hit her.

Reagan must be taking the same bus as Landon, going to be with her family in New York. Ashley had talked to Kari midway through the day, but neither of them had heard from Luke about Reagan's father.

Ashley dried her tears, found a seat just out of sight of the alcove area, and waited. After a while she saw Reagan board the bus. Then it pulled away, and a minute later Luke rounded the corner. He was crying. The little brother who had been her closest friend when they were kids was walking aimlessly toward the exit, tears streaming down his face.

At first he didn't see her, but when he was a few feet away, Ashley stood. The moment their eyes met, Luke froze. The walls shot up between them instantly.

Warily she looked at him, at the pain in his eyes, the devastation in his face. Whatever the news about Reagan's father, it wasn't good. They stared at each other for an interminable minute longer, stunned by what was happening.

For all their differences, here they were at the same bus depot, saying good-bye to people they loved in the wake of one of the most horrific days the United States had ever faced. As the realization dawned for both of them, the walls began to fall, crashing to the ground with as much force as the twin towers.

Only this collapse didn't leave a mountain of debris. It left brother and sister, their hearts raw and wide-open, needing each other in a way that made their differences seem petty and insignificant.

Ashley took the first step, and he matched it. In an instant they were in each other's arms, hugging, crying.

"How . . . how could it happen?" His words were a strained whisper, uttered from the deepest place in his soul.

Ashley hadn't realized just how much he'd grown in the last few years. But now, even as his sobs gently shook her body, she felt small and safe in his embrace. He said nothing else, but that was okay. Yesterday Ashley might have needed apologies or explanations before feeling love for Luke. But not today. Not after the losses they'd both been dealt. Not after all that had happened.

Here, now, Ashley needed no words.

The feel of her brother's arms around her was apology enough.

Chapter Twenty-One

They met at the Baxter house. The place where the family came together to celebrate and mark the passing of seasons. The place where they came to grieve. And the evening of September 11 was no exception.

Though John Baxter was tired from a full day, he was grateful for his family's presence. Too many people that night would be missing someone, waiting for a phone call, desperate for word from rescue workers that their son or daughter or parent or spouse had been found.

The heartache across the nation that night was too huge to comprehend.

It was after nine o'clock, and still they remained gathered around the television set, talking in muted tones about the latest reports and what President Bush was going to do. Already the president had declared the terrorist attacks an act of war. The death toll was thought to be in the thousands, with hundreds of firefighters and police officers buried beneath the rubble.

New York City's Mayor Rudy Giuliani had already coined a term for the desolate spot where the World Trade Center had once stood: Ground Zero.

Rescue efforts were in full swing, but so far no one had been pulled out alive.

"I don't see how we can move to Texas at a time like this." Erin crossed her legs and leaned hard against the arm of the family's old sofa.

Kari and Brooke and Peter sat on the floor, their backs against the same sofa. The grandchildren were upstairs sleeping, and Brooke was still talking about the blood drive at St. Anne's that day.

Across from them on the other sofa sat Luke and Ashley. John glanced at them, amazed. It was the first time in years they had sat on the same side of the room together, let alone next to each other.

Ashley had mentioned that they'd accidentally met up at the bus station. But it was obvious she and Luke had experienced more than a chance encounter. They'd had a meeting of the heart — the meeting John and Elizabeth had spent many hours praying for.

"Anything new?" Elizabeth sounded tired like the rest of them as she entered the room and sat down next to John. She slipped her hand in his, shot a look toward Ashley and Luke, and squeezed his fingers.

"Still no survivors." John returned her squeeze. "They said people are making cell calls from somewhere in the debris."

"That's awful." Kari pulled her knees to her chest, her eyes wide as the screen showed hundreds of workers atop a mountain of rubble.

"I can't believe they'll find anyone alive in that." Brooke shook her head. "The jet fuel's still burning down there. If the temperatures don't kill them, the fumes will."

"You're right," Peter sighed. "But they've got to try."

Elizabeth looked at Luke, and John followed her gaze. How was he handling this conversation? Reagan's father was one of those buried in the massive twist of cement and steel. Certainly Luke didn't want to hear his family dashing all hope that the man would be found alive.

"Luke, are you okay?" Elizabeth's voice was calm, gentle. It was one of the things John loved about her. Whenever life was in turmoil, her words and tone seemed to minister healing to their hearts, even if she was dying inside. She would show her own pain later, when the two of them were alone. But here, in front of their children, she was the picture of calm, the personification of God's truth that somehow everything would work out. That he was still in control.

"I'm fine." Luke's answer was curt, his eyes still fixed on the TV.

"Have you heard more from Reagan's mother?"

Luke shook his head. Then he glanced over his shoulder at Brooke. "They'll find survivors." He looked back at the screen. "Reagan's dad won't go down without a fight."

Brooke raised her eyebrows in Peter's direction and gave him a look that acknowledged she'd forgotten how personal the rescue was to Luke. She cleared her throat. "You're right, Luke. I wasn't trying to say there *won't* be survivors. Just that —"

"Never mind." Luke stood up and headed toward the stairs. "I'm going to bed." He avoided their eyes as he left the room.

Brooke cast her parents a helpless frown and mouthed the word *Sorry.*

"It's okay." John kept his voice a whisper. "You weren't thinking about Reagan's father. Neither was I. And I'm the one who brought it up."

"I hope he can sleep." Elizabeth met

Brooke's eyes and held them. "It's going to be a tough week." She turned to Kari. "Have you heard more from Ryan?"

"He and a bunch of the guys from the team are going down tomorrow to serve food and hand out water — whatever they can do for the rescue workers." Kari looked at Ashley. "When did Landon think he'd get there?"

"He talked to someone at FDNY headquarters." Fear covered Ashley's face like a veil. John understood. Working atop a hundred stories of collapsed building was bound to be dangerous, perhaps even deadly. Ashley bit the corner of her lip. "They're expecting him by noon tomorrow."

"I wonder if he'll run into Ryan." Kari turned back to the television.

The conversation stalled, replaced with a stream of reports and updates. By eleven o'clock, everyone had gathered their children and gone home for the night. Everyone but Luke, of course.

Throughout the evening, uneasiness about his son had nibbled at the foundations of John's confidence. Luke was rarely moody, rarely noncommunicative. Most family gatherings were marked by his silly antics or relentless teasing. Only around

331

Ashley was he usually anything less than joyful. But today it wasn't about Ashley. And John had that father's sense that it wasn't about Reagan, either.

Something was wrong with his only son, something that went beyond grief and fear and uncertainty. Whatever it was, John intended to find out.

He quietly climbed the stairs to Luke's room. From out in the hallway, he could hear the news playing on Luke's small television. John knocked softly before opening the door. "Can we talk?"

Luke was stretched out on the bed, his legs crossed at the ankles. He glanced up for a brief moment and slid over. "Sure."

There it was again — that strange coldness in Luke's tone. John entered the room and sat on the edge of the bed. "You okay?"

Luke leaned up on his elbows and shifted his gaze so their eyes met. "Not really."

"That's what I thought." John was struck by the ice in Luke's expression. "You seem mad."

"Well." A huff of air pushed its way past Luke's lips. "I *am* kinda mad."

"We all are." John gripped the top of Luke's foot. "Nothing's the same tonight as it was this morning."

"It's not just that." Luke shrugged and gave a hard laugh.

"Okay." John took a breath. Luke wasn't making this easy. "So why are you angry?"

"I was with Reagan . . . Monday night." Luke's eyes fell, and he studied the pattern of his bedspread. When he looked up, guilt was obviously among the emotions playing on his face. His next words came quickly. "We were watching the Giants, you know, caught up in the game." He crossed his arms. "Her father called, and Reagan ignored it. He left a message, but Reagan . . . she told me she'd call him the next night."

John closed his eyes and groaned. No wonder Luke felt guilty. He and Reagan had been having too much fun watching football for her to break away and take her father's call. And now it was too late. He blinked his eyes open. "I'm sorry, son."

"As soon as I saw the news at school this morning, I started praying, begging God to save her dad." Luke cocked his head. "And you know what? Until I talked to Reagan's mother, I actually thought God would answer my prayer."

God always answers our prayers. The words were almost out of John's mouth when he stopped them. Luke didn't need a theology lesson. He needed to be heard.

Luke sat straighter, pushing himself up against his headboard so that their eyes were level. "All my life, God's answered my prayers, Dad. If I prayed it, I believed it, and sooner or later it happened. God and me were like this." He crossed his fingers and held them up. "But when I found out Mr. Decker didn't make it out of the building . . ."

Luke's voice broke, and his head hung for a moment. John slid closer and placed his hand on Luke's shoulder. It was time for the theology lesson. "Son, God hears your prayers. Every one of them. If Reagan's father didn't make it out, then today was his time. That's the way life is. We never know when it might be our last day."

After a while Luke sniffed and looked up. Angry tears still welled in his eyes. "Fine. But here's what I want to know . . ."

John waited. The rage simmering in Luke's expression was frightening.

"What's the point in praying? If God's got it all figured out, then why bother talking to him? What difference does it make?"

John swallowed his surprise. "It makes all the difference. God isn't a genie, Luke. You know that. He doesn't do tricks at our command. But he does answer our prayers, one way or another. He healed your mother, didn't he?"

"I used to think so." Luke's eyes narrowed. "I prayed for her cancer to go away, and it did. But maybe it would have gone away by itself. Or maybe it *hasn't* really gone away. Maybe prayer had nothing to do with it."

"Prayer had everything to do with it." John kept his voice even.

"Okay, then, what about America? Land of the free, home of the brave. God's supposed to be our great protector, right? In God we trust." He pointed to the television. "Not true today. So maybe God got fed up with the United States. Maybe he washed his hands of us." Luke narrowed his eyes. "But don't tell me prayer made a difference today. Not for those people in the World Trade Center."

"Bad things happen, Luke. That's been true since the beginning of time." He squeezed Luke's shoulder. "The United States is no exception."

"But why wasn't God there for those people, Dad?" Luke's tone was loud, his anger filling the room.

John took his time formulating an answer. He waited until Luke seemed to have control again. "Son, God was there for every one of those people." John let his hand fall from Luke's shoulder. "When life doesn't go the way we want, he's still there for us, even on a day like this. Comforting us, giving us the peace we need — peace that the world knows nothing about."

"Yeah, well . . ." Luke looked back at the images on the television. "Today I needed Reagan's father to be alive, not buried beneath a hundred-story building."

There was a tension between them, something John had never felt before. Not with Luke, anyway. Should he bid his son good night, let him sleep off his doubts? Or should he keep talking, try to adjust Luke's faith to what it had been just twenty-four hours ago?

He decided on neither. "Let's pray. That's the only way we'll survive."

Luke turned away from the TV, but John could see his actions were more out of obedience and respect than any desire to pray. "Whatever."

Whatever? Again fear rippled through John's veins. *God, help my son. Don't let this awful day drive a wedge between him and you. Between him and me.*

The verse Kari had read earlier that day, the one she'd shared when he got home from work, flashed in his mind: *The Spirit who lives in you is greater than the spirit who lives in the world.* It was a promise John intended to cling to in the days to come.

He closed his eyes, returned his hand to Luke's shoulder, and prayed aloud. "God, so often we don't understand. And truthfully, Lord, this is one of those times." John drew a slow breath. "All we can do is stand on your truth and believe it. You are a good God, the author of life. The evil that happened today grieves your heart too. So many lives, Father. So many. Lord, if Reagan's father is among those who came home to you today, help us accept that. Help us be grateful that if he is gone from this earth, he is even now rejoicing with you."

John paused. "And please help Luke. Help him take hold of his faith and hang on no matter what the storms of tomorrow bring. Let him know that you do hear his prayers, that you love him and care about him. Be with Reagan and her family, and comfort them with the reality of your promises. In Jesus' name, amen."

Countless times while Luke was growing up, John had met him here, and the two had prayed together. Always Luke had been at peace afterward, his eyes filled with the certainty that God was in control of whatever the issue at hand.

This time, though, Luke's face was as angry and hard as it had been before. The moment the prayer was over, Luke's eyes found the TV screen again. There was none of the usual "Thanks for praying, Dad," no encouraging words or reassuring signs that Luke had even been listening during the prayer.

I can't force it, God. I'm giving him to you. John patted Luke on the back and stood to leave.

"Don't let go of your faith, son. You need it now more than ever."

Silence.

"Fine. Well . . . good night, Luke. I love you."

John turned to go, and not until he was halfway out the door did Luke respond. "Good night."

As John made his way down the hallway toward the room he shared with Elizabeth, he ached over the scene that had just taken place. And the fact that for the first time as far back as he could remember, his son hadn't told him he loved him.

The morning of September 12 dawned bright and sunny, the weather having no clue that the nation was in mourning. When John awoke, his wife was already sitting in the chair near their bed, reading her Bible.

The moment he sat up and rubbed his eyes, she gave him a knowing look. "Something's wrong with Luke."

It was more a statement than a question, but John knew she wanted an answer all the same. He stretched and leaned back against their headboard. He didn't want to worry her now, not when Luke was likely to wake up that morning and kick himself for ever doubting God. "He's upset."

Elizabeth lowered her chin. "He's more than upset."

"He's mad." John climbed out of bed and slipped on his terry cloth robe. "He asked God to spare Reagan's father." John headed for their bedroom door. "It's the first time God's answered the boy's prayers with such a powerful no."

"Are you worried?" Elizabeth's Bible was still open on her lap.

John stopped in the doorway. He hoped his wife could feel his confidence across the room. "Yes. But I've given it to God. I'm sure Luke will have a better attitude today."

"Where are you going?"

"I have to do something." He gave her a partial smile. "I'll be right back."

The whole way through the house, down the stairs, and into the garage, John couldn't help but think about what Luke had said the night before. Maybe God *was* finished with the United States, fed up with America.

John found the box he was looking for and opened it. Carefully he removed the family's heavy, hand-stitched American flag. He carried it outside to the pole in front of the house, attached it to a heavy nylon cord, and raised it ten feet above the ground.

Then he took three steps back and stared at it. The red, white, and blue flowed majestically in the morning breeze.

John stood there awhile, studying the flag and remembering the freedom it represented. Raising it today was a small gesture, but somehow it made him feel stronger, more hopeful.

No matter how bad the situation looked, no matter what people might think, regardless of the uncertainty of this moment in the history of their nation, John was convinced of two things.

God wasn't finished with America yet.

And he wasn't finished with Luke, either.

Chapter Twenty-Two

Two days had passed since the terrorist attacks, and the National Football League had made its decision. For the first time in its history, there would be no football that Sunday. The games were canceled as a way of honoring the thousands of people dead and missing.

Ryan Taylor was grateful.

Other teams might have been capable of playing football five days after the tragedy of September 11, but the teams in New York and Washington, D.C., certainly were not. It was all Ryan and the other coaches could do to keep the Giants focused on a light practice.

For the most part, none of the team members wanted to play football. They wanted to be out on the streets handing water bottles to firemen, passing out sandwiches, moving debris — whatever they could do to help.

The rescue effort was beyond anything Ryan had ever seen. A thick, pungent smoke hung across the city, and ash covered every exposed inch. But the area around Ground Zero had quickly become the scene of a massive coordinated effort as the wrenching process of removing, sorting, and disposing of layer upon layer of rubble got under way. As they searched for survivors, firefighters and volunteers faced the grim task of finding the remains of victims, some of whom had been their friends or coworkers.

Ryan and a handful of players had been allowed past security to a food-and-water station fifty yards from Ground Zero. What he saw from even that far away was unbelievable.

Off to the side of the main disaster site, in the midst of the rubble stood a perfect cross, formed by a section of steel beams that had fallen away from the rest of the structure. The cross towered fifteen feet high and stood strangely secure amidst the unstable ruins. That afternoon, as Ryan handed out water bottles and swapped somber conversation with weary rescue workers, he noticed the cross again. It had become something of a shrine. Flowers had been placed near its base, and small notes were tacked along the upright beam.

Dozens of chaplains made the rounds of

volunteers. At any given time that after-noon when Ryan looked up he saw people praying together, hugging each other, stopped in the middle of the rescue effort to comfort and convince each other that life would go on.

Often he caught himself staring up at the gaping hole in the sky, the place where the twin towers had stood. He'd lived in New York only a short time, but he'd quickly come to use the World Trade Center as a navigating landmark; his destinations within the city had been either on one side of the towers or the other. Now, though, nothing but deep blue sky marked the spot. So intrinsic were the buildings to the New York skyline that it was impossible for him to look up and not see the towers still standing, if only in his memory.

He would call Kari tonight and tell her what it was like down here. Since the at-tacks, she'd been on his mind even more, if that were possible. Life was short, and death too often quick and senseless. Tim's murder had taught them that much, and now this. . . . News shows were talking about further attacks, biological warfare, chemical weapons, nuclear threats. There were no guarantees any of them would live to see the morning.

Yet here he was in New York City, devoting his life to a game — a game that had done nothing but stand in the way of the life he might have shared with Kari. What was he doing here when the only woman he'd ever loved was alone in Bloomington? What sense was there in that?

Ryan had no answers for himself, except for the fact that he'd made a commitment to the Giants and needed to see it through. He stooped and brushed a layer of ash off an unopened crate of water bottles. As he did, he remembered his father's words, advice he'd spoken back when Ryan was a senior in high school, looking for a part-time job.

"Honor your commitments, son. If you take a job, give them your best. A man who honors God in the small things will honor him throughout life."

There was no question Ryan would honor the commitment he'd made to the Giants. Not just because it was the right thing to do. He loved his work, after all. Coaching in the NFL had been his dream ever since he hung up his jersey. But somehow the events of the past week had changed his dreams, made them seem shallow and unimportant. In fact, they'd made it painfully clear that his heart wasn't in New York at all.

It was a thousand miles away in Bloom-ington, Indiana.

Ryan slid his thumb beneath a layer of plastic and pulled the bottles from the crate. He coughed hard and looked up. The smoke was thicker than before.

"Hey, stranger." Ryan felt a tap on his shoulder, and he turned around to see Landon Blake.

"Landon . . ." Ryan wasn't sure what to say. The man was covered in ash, sweat dripping from his forehead. The pain in his eyes was stark. It told Ryan that however bad Ground Zero looked from this dis-tance, the view from up close was unspeak-ably worse.

Ryan reached out and shook Landon's hand. "Kari told me you'd be here. I sort of doubted we'd run into each other."

Landon gestured toward the makeshift station where Ryan was working. "Everyone knows this is where the Giants are helping out." He wiped his brow, smearing ash along his forehead. "I figured you'd be here."

Ryan handed him a water bottle. "You and I are both praying men." He gazed across the disaster scene, then back at Landon. "But right now it's hard to know where to begin."

"I know." Landon set his work boot on a nearby chair and leaned on his knee. "The smell of death and sulfur — it's awful. Suffocating. Like hell itself."

There was a pause, and Landon lifted the water bottle, tipped it straight back, and drained it. Ryan grabbed a wrapped sandwich from the table and handed it to him. "I'm sorry about your friend."

Landon nodded. "Thanks." He took the sandwich, pulled off the wrapper, and ate nearly half of it in a single bite. Despite the smoke, the sun was bright at that hour of the afternoon, and Landon squinted toward the rescue effort. "There's still a chance, you know. Jalen's strong." He clenched his jaw. "If anyone can survive this, he can."

Ryan stared at the ashes beneath their feet. What could he say to that? And how long would it be before the firefighters working at Ground Zero were resigned to the probability that they were looking for remains and not survivors? Ryan breathed in sharply through his nose and met Landon's eyes. "Is there anything I can do?"

Landon tossed his empty bottle and sandwich wrapper into the trash and took a step back toward the rescue effort. "Pray for a miracle." He waved and started to leave.

"Wait." Ryan jogged the few steps that separated them. "Was Jalen a believer?"

Landon hesitated. "I'm not sure. He knew about the Lord."

"Let's pray now. Is that okay?"

"Yeah." Landon removed his helmet. "Thanks."

Ryan put his hand on Landon's shoulder, and both men bowed their heads. There, with rescue workers scrambling to and from support stations, with cranes and dump trucks making their way down the ash-covered caverns of Manhattan, with the stench of ash and smoke a moment by moment reminder of the devastation around them, they prayed for Jalen.

They prayed for a miracle — one way or another. That the rescue crews would find him safe amidst the rubble. And if not, that Jesus would find him.

Safe amidst the streets of heaven.

For the first time that fall, Professor Hicks was making sense.

Since the semester began, Luke had dreaded his advanced communications class. The professor often used the time to express his opinions about a number of his

347

pet subjects — anything from the evils of commerce to the dangers of "religious fanaticism."

At first, Luke had actually agreed with some of what the professor said. Commerce could at times be the cause of a troubled society. And religious extremism had certainly caused heartache and misunderstanding throughout history.

But as the semester got under way, Luke quickly began to understand that to the professor, *commerce* meant any kind of corporate business, and *religious fanatic* primarily referred to any conservative Christian.

Professor Hicks had never said as much. In fact, he had made a point not to tell students exactly where he stood — he said it was important to maintain "objectivity." But he revealed his opinions through offhand remarks and sly digs — even through snide comments he'd written in the margins of the first project Luke had prepared for the class. In fact, the professor seemed so obviously biased — and his views so different from Luke's — that Luke had expected every class period to be a struggle.

Until now. Now, as Luke sat listening, the professor's words seemed to line up with thoughts Luke didn't even know he had.

In light of what happened September 11, Professor Hicks had introduced a semester-long assignment: Pair up with someone in the class, and create a class presentation arguing for or against the existence of God.

It was Monday, nearly a week after the attacks, and the professor was pacing along the front of the classroom, explaining his reasons for the assignment.

"You may have noticed how popular the American flag has become in the past week." He reached the far end of the class-room, paused, and smiled in their direction. "Many people want to say God is bringing our country together, uniting us in our greatest hour of need."

He chuckled and gave a sad shake of his head. "Okay, fine. This is a communications class, which means we will be learning methods of gathering information and presenting ideas in a persuasive manner. Let's use these skills to figure out what's actually going on."

He stopped pacing and clasped his hands behind his back, leaning slightly forward. "Now I realize this isn't a philosophy class, so I'm not requiring you to use formal logic. And this isn't a science class, so I'm not worried about strict scientific method. What I'm talking about is ideas, motivation, thinking clearly and persuasively about something that makes a difference in our world.

"This is important stuff, people!" His voice rose, and he stabbed his finger into the air for emphasis. "Is God really the one at work around the nation today? Or can the positive responses we're witnessing be attributed to something else?"

Luke sat poised with his pen over a blank piece of paper.

The professor ambled in the opposite direction, waving his hand above his head as though he were grabbing thoughts from an invisible storage unit. "Record numbers of people line up to give blood. Thousands sign up with the armed services. Countless more send in millions of dollars for the victims. Volunteers are streaming in from every city in America.

"God? Maybe." He stopped pacing and faced them head-on. "Maybe not."

Luke shifted in his seat. Before September 11, a discussion like this would have made him furious, ready to load up his backpack and stalk out of class. But now . . . now at least it seemed worth listening to. At the top of his notepad he doodled the word *God,* and beside it he penciled in an oversized question mark.

The professor shrugged and continued pacing. "I believe this assignment will push you to think about your worldview and communicate it coherently. It will require research — you need the facts to be an effective communicator. It will also require persuasive argument — another vital skill. And it will require a commitment to reality — because with reality staring us in the face these days, we don't have a foundation to stand on."

He paused. "I want you to think . . . really think." He smiled at them over his shoulder. "Is there a worldview that adequately explains the way society actually works, good and bad? Does it orbit around belief in some invisible higher being named God — what we call a 'theistic worldview'?" Here he made a fist to punctuate the phrase. "Or are there other factors at work, ideas that adequately explain human existence without resorting to belief in a higher power? In short, is there a God or isn't there?"

Luke had scribbled the words *theistic worldview.*

"However you choose to answer the question," the professor continued, "you must use facts and logic to support your argument." The professor ambled toward the whiteboard, grabbed a marker, and wrote in large letters the word *humanism*. He stepped back from the board. "If you choose to argue against the theistic view, you may do so by siding with an alternative view." He smiled. "Say, for instance, the worldview of humanism."

He pointed to the word. "Humanism, ladies and gentlemen, is the philosophy of the day for many people. Whereas theism is based on the assumption that all goodness originates from a higher being, humanism places trust in the power of human intelligence and the human spirit to conquer evil with acts of goodness."

Luke hid his grin. So much for objectivity. The man's tone made it clear he hadn't picked humanism as a random alternative view.

"You, of course, will form your own opinions in the course of this assignment," the professor was saying. He paced a few slow steps, then paused to look at them once more. "But I caution you — examine both sides. And base your arguments not on your own bias or upbringing but on the preponderance of evidence."

A dark-haired girl next to Luke leaned over and whispered, "Sounds interesting."

Luke cast her a quick glance and nodded. She'd sat next to him since the semester began, but he hadn't really noticed her before.

Two rows from the front a boy raised his hand. "What if our evidence leads us to conclude there is a God?"

Professor Hicks raised his eyebrows in a way that was mildly humorous. "More power to you — as long as you have adequate support for that conclusion." He directed his attention to the rest of the class. "I'm not telling you how to think here, people. I'm simply suggesting that we've never had a better opportunity to become part of what's happening around us — and in the process to learn valuable lessons about communicating."

His gaze shifted back to the student in the second row. "Be careful. Your paper mustn't be based on wishful thinking or parental propaganda. You must avoid stale or emotion-based arguments." He went on about the assignment specifics — the documentation required, the timing of the oral presentation, the importance of working with a partner. "We should finish up sometime after Thanksgiving."

Luke jotted down most of what the professor had said and stared at his notes. Was it possible? Had his own faith been nothing more than parental propaganda? Had he merely bought into a myth that had no bearing on reality?

He wouldn't have considered such a thing before the terrorist attacks. But now . . .

Every night since Reagan left, he had tried to call her at her parents' house. Most of the time no one answered. When someone did pick up, it was always a friend or relative. And every one of them said the same thing: Reagan wasn't available. Reagan wasn't taking calls. Reagan couldn't come to the phone.

Didn't she know he was dying without her — that the memory of that Monday night was enough to make him hate himself for what had happened? His family was no help at all. They were caught in a frenzy of patriotism and blind faith that in view of the terrorist attacks seemed completely unfounded.

In fact, the whole city seemed caught up.

Attendance at church yesterday was easily twice what it had been before the tragedy. Normally Luke and Mom and Dad would have sat near Erin, Sam, and Kari. But yesterday Brooke and Peter and even Ashley had been there — the first time they'd been together at a church service since Erin's wedding. Mom and Dad had both dabbed at tears as Pastor Mark reminded them that good can come from evil and that God had plans for America.

But what good plans could God possibly have?

Reagan's father was dead. She wouldn't come to the phone. And together they'd done something they'd promised never to do.

Luke thought back to that evening in the parking lot — back when his greatest concern was whether they'd play softball or watch a football game.

Good from evil?

The only good thing God could do at this point was turn back the clock to September 10 and give them a chance to do it all over again. Luke would watch the football game at home, and Reagan would talk to her father and warn him not to go to work the next day no matter what.

Short of that, Luke couldn't imagine any good coming from the attacks.

Professor Hicks had moved on to another topic, but Luke couldn't get his mind off Reagan and her father. Whenever Luke called her house, he asked about Mr. Decker. The news was never good. There'd been no sign of Reagan's father — no sign of any survivors in the enormous pile of debris. The last two victims found alive had been plucked from the rubble days ago.

By now the entire nation was beginning to grasp the enormity of the loss of life from the disaster. Even before the buildings collapsed, the heat inside the twin towers had been figured at nearly twice that of most crematoriums. Not only were rescue workers not going to find the missing people; they probably wouldn't find their bodies, either. No matter what hope Reagan's family held on to, the truth was obvious: Tom Decker wasn't coming home.

Luke drew squiggly lines along the sides of his notes and thought about the professor's theory. No God, only the power of the human spirit. People who were good, people who were bad. But as the outpouring of support after the terrorist attacks showed, a handful of bad people would always be defeated by a nation of good ones.

Was that all there was, then? The human spirit — nothing more?

It was hard to imagine existing outside the reality of God. What would the humanist theory say about death? That there was nothing after that? That people should be as good as possible, only to spend eternity rotting away in a casket?

Luke pulled himself from the cloud of his random thoughts and focused on God, what he knew of God. What he remembered. All the evidence gathering in the world wouldn't prove or disprove an invisible, omniscient God. Only one thing could do that.

Lord, I've never been more confused in my life. He stared at his paper and tapped his pen quietly. *How come everything's so crazy? Why . . . why did you let it happen?* He doodled the word *why* across the top of his paper. *If you're there, if you can hear me, make things right between Reagan and me. Please, God. That's all the proof I need.*

He looked up and saw the class filing out. The lecture was over. Luke slipped his notebook into his backpack and was heading for the door when the dark-haired girl fell in beside him.

"Hi." She threw him a confident smile. "We've never really met. My name's Lori Callahan."

He held out his hand. "Luke Baxter."

"Nice to meet you." She looked up at him and gave his hand a quick, friendly shake. Something about her was cultured and attractive in a brainy sort of way. "Listen," she said, "I have an idea."

"Okay." Luke wasn't completely listening. He wanted to get through his classes and go home so he could try Reagan again.

"Let's do the assignment together. You know, the one where we argue for or against God." She grinned. "My dad's a civil-liberties attorney. His peers think he's a little one-sided." She winked. "But he has more proof against God than anyone I know."

They were outside now, and Luke stopped in the middle of a stream of people. He stared at her. Proof against God? Who was this girl? And why was she suddenly interested in him? He blinked. She was practically reading his mind.

"Umm . . ." He started walking again and shrugged. "Why not?"

"Good." She tucked a small piece of paper into the pocket of his backpack. "Here's my phone number. Give me a call so we can get together."

"Okay."

"Hey, Luke . . ."

"Yeah?"

"I've wanted to talk to you since the first day of class."

"Really?"

She nodded. "I wanted to invite you to one of our meetings."

Luke blinked. What was he doing here? He didn't even know the girl. "What meeting?"

"Indiana Freethinking Alliance." She shrugged, and something shy flashed in her green eyes. It made her more attractive than before. "You know, dedicated to the promotion of free thought, skepticism, secularism, nontheism, and humanism." She rolled her eyes and grinned, "That's our mantra, anyway."

"Right." What in the world was she talking about? Luke gave a shallow laugh. "Sure."

"So, do you want to?"

"What?"

"Come to a meeting." She gave a playful kick against the toe of his tennis shoe.

"Uh, maybe sometime. Not this week, okay?"

"Okay." She hesitated. "Call me about the assignment."

"Right." He took a few steps backward. "See ya."

She waved and headed in the opposite direction. Luke made his way across campus to his next class, wondering the whole while about the girl and her certainty that between her and her father they could come up with enough evidence to disprove the existence of God.

Why had she chosen him, of all people?

There he was, praying for things to work out with Reagan, begging God for proof he was even there at all. And not two seconds later, he'd been approached by a girl who clearly was everything Reagan was not.

Luke huffed as he strode into his next class. Figures. The girl was just the type of answer his prayers had been reaping these days. The kind that would work well as evidence in his communications assignment.

Not the evidence everyone who knew Luke would expect him to find — in support of God.

But rather evidence against him.

Hope was getting harder to hold on to.

Six days had passed since the terrorist attacks, and Landon's existence had become almost mechanical: eat, sleep, work at Ground Zero. Occasionally he thought about Ashley. But somehow everything that had happened before his arrival in New York felt like something from a dream — as if debris and soot and death were the only reality anymore.

Twice he had picked up the hotel phone to call her, but what would he say? His emotions were buried as deep as the twin towers victims.

By now, the rescue workers had settled into a numbing routine, an assembly line of sorts, in which a truck-size shovel of dirt would be dumped at the feet of the supervising workers and then sifted, one bucketful at a time. As long as no victim remains were found, the bucket would be passed down the line to a waiting dump truck, emptied, and passed back to the top of the line. Bucket after bucket after bucket. When the truck was full, it would move off toward the appropriate waste station, and another truck would take its place.

If victims or partial victims were found, however . . . .

"We've got a body!" a voice shouted from the front of the line.

Landon looked up, weary. His throat was coated with a silty, strange-tasting ash, ash that all of them knew was more than crushed cement and debris. It was also human remains. He coughed and stared at the place where the action had stopped.

Two of the morgue workers approached with a body bag and a handheld stretcher. Landon watched as a small part — a hand or a foot — was placed inside the bag. A chaplain stepped in and placed his fingers on the stretcher. All the way down the line, hats were removed, heads bowed.

Landon was too far away to hear the prayer. But when it was over, the bag was placed on the stretcher and carried to a makeshift morgue set up in the back of a refrigerated truck.

The moment the body part was properly removed, the digging and sifting and bucket-passing began again. The same way it had for days now, hour after hour after hour.

Rarely did they find an entire body. When they did, it was usually a firefighter. The men had talked about this over coffee and sandwiches and agreed that the protective gear had helped preserve their bodies from the heat. Also, many of them had been in the stairwells, which meant they'd had less chance of being crushed between floors.

So far, however, there was no sign of Jalen.

Regardless of the time that had passed, not one of the workers or volunteers was willing to call this anything less than a rescue effort. They talked of the possibility of people's being trapped alive, of air pockets and cavities where victims could live for weeks. Especially since it had rained. Water might have trickled into areas where people were waiting for rescue. The moisture could have filled up small crevices and pockets and provided the victims with something to drink, a way to survive.

But privately Landon found such speculations hard to believe. How could any of them think there would be survivors in the smoldering ruins? The truth was something none of them wanted to admit: They were no longer working a rescue.

They were working a recovery.

Oh, the pace was still quick and frenzied — as though every minute counted and somewhere, somehow, they would find people alive. But with each passing hour the reality set in until now, nearly a week after the attacks, Landon had given up all hope of finding anyone alive, even Jalen.

Not that it mattered.

Dead or alive, Jalen and the others deserved to be found. In fact, when a firefighter's or police officer's body was found, the ceremony atop the rubble changed slightly. The body bag was placed on a stretcher as always, but then it would be draped with an American flag — a fitting tribute.

"Hey." The worker next to Landon elbowed him. "How long you think a man could live trapped down there? Say, if he had air and water?"

Landon glanced over his shoulder. The man beside him was a retired firefighter with thirty years' experience. Landon had chatted with him earlier that day. His name was Chuck and, like most of them, he'd watched the attacks and the collapse of the towers on television. But Chuck's two sons, young fathers in their twenties, had both been with FDNY. Both were buried in the pile somewhere.

Landon stared at the mountain of rubble in front of them. The man's sons were dead, like every one of the other four hundred missing firefighters.

"Two weeks." Landon bit his lip, his tone confident. "Three maybe."

Chuck sniffed and lowered his brow. He gave a quick nod of his head. "That's what I'm thinking. Three weeks."

Landon had worked alongside Chuck for six hours straight, and he had no doubt the droplets running down the man's face were more than sweat.

God give him strength. Give us all strength.

I will never leave you, never forsake you.

The words reminded him of a Scripture

passage, one he'd clung to before — one God had brought to mind in the days since he'd been trapped in the burning apartment complex in Bloomington. Now it whispered to a place deep in his soul, a place that was sheltered from the horror of the task at hand. Landon was grateful.

Remembering God here, in the midst of utter death and despair, was like grabbing a mouthful of sweet, fresh air.

But it was something that happened less often with each passing day.

"Wait a minute. Hold up!" A voice from the front barked the command, and the rescue workers froze, giving him their complete attention.

"We've got a flag." The man took three steps up the pile of debris and motioned to the men behind him in line. "I need some help."

Four uniformed firefighters joined him, and together they began freeing the American flag from the rubble. It was on a pole, probably one of those that had stood in the indoor courtyard area near the top of the World Trade Center. Several flags had been found since the rescue effort began, and each one had spurred the men to work harder, faster than before.

Using great care, the firefighters tossed

chunks of cement and broken beams off the flag until they were able to raise it from the debris. Then, without saying a word, the men carried it up a side of the towering pile of twisted steel and cement slabs and anchored it deep in the ash. A hush fell over the crowd as the tattered flag unfurled over the wreckage of the twin towers. People as far as a hundred yards away removed their hats and stood to watch.

Then, above the sound of heavy equipment and diesel trucks, a song broke out along the line of rescue workers.

"God bless America . . ."

It started low and grew as more voices joined in. Landon felt the sting of tears as they reached the last line — ". . . my home, sweet home!" — and then began it again. Still singing, they resumed the bucket brigade. Despite the weariness of working so many days straight, despite the enormous losses they all had suffered, despite throats raw from breathing soot and smoke and ash all day — despite everything, they sang. And in that quiet place in Landon's soul, the place he prayed would keep him sane, Landon begged God to do just that. To bless America and those who loved her.

Even if nothing would ever be what it had been before September 11.

Chapter Twenty-Three

For the first time in years, Ashley felt urgent about life.

In light of the attacks on America, she had no time to waste fearing what people thought of her, worrying about how she'd disappointed them. She had a son to love, a family to care for, a brother who no longer hated her. A God who maybe, just maybe, wasn't finished with her yet.

And a houseful of residents at Sunset Hills who were desperate for someone to care about them.

The files Ashley had compiled on Irvel and the others were almost complete. Ashley had read more Internet articles on the Past-Present approach to helping Alzheimer's patients, and what she read made sense to her.

The idea was to find that place in time and memory where each Alzheimer's patient was most comfortable, then to allow as much interaction as possible to be keyed around that time period. This might mean redecorating a room, avoiding certain topics or allowing others — whatever helped the patients feel happier, more at peace. According to some of the most recent research, when patients felt at ease, they were more likely to remember the important things they'd forgotten — the people and places and pictures that had once meant the world to them.

Ashley was convinced that at least some of the residents at Sunset Hills could benefit from the Past-Present ideas. The first step toward implementing them was to learn as much as possible about the patients' pasts. Ashley had done that. Now it was time to put some of her information into action.

She started with Edith, who still screamed every morning when she reached the bathroom. For some time, Ashley had taken special note of Edith's demeanor, her attitude as she made her way from the kitchen table to the bathroom. The woman was distant and sometimes confused, depending on whether or not she'd struggled over breakfast. But there was nothing fearful in her expression, no sign that Edith was being pursued by a witch — not until she reached the bathroom.

On the mornings that Belinda was there,

she would take a break from the office work, give Edith a sedative, bathe her, and set her in her chair. That way the poor old woman sleepwalked through the mornings and avoided screaming altogether.

But Ashley hated the idea of medicating Edith. There had to be another way. So when Belinda announced she'd be gone all week for a workshop, Ashley knew the time had come to do some experimenting.

The first two mornings, she watched as Edith meandered to the bathroom. The minute the screaming began, Ashley was at her side.

Each time, Edith looked the same — ramrod straight, hands balled into tight fists, eyes squeezed shut, her mouth a perfect circle. "A witch! It's a witch! Help me. Someone help!" Then she would scream as loud and shrill and terrifying a scream as Ashley had ever heard. It would take her thirty minutes or more to coax Edith out of the bathroom and into her chair, to convince her the witch wasn't after her, and to stop the screams.

It was an exercise in frustration, and Ashley read Edith's file several times through, searching for an explanation for her behavior and a clue to stopping it.

On the third day, Ashley tried something

else. After breakfast, when Irvel was enjoying her peppermint tea and Helen was convinced everyone in the room had been checked, Edith stood and began shuffling toward the bathroom. This time Ashley stayed close behind her, near the old woman's elbow. They rounded the corner into the bathroom together just as Edith caught sight of the mirrored medicine cabinet over the sink. For a split second, Edith stared at her own image in horrified silence. Then she shut her eyes and began to scream.

Ashley stared at Edith and then at the mirror. Realization dawned immediately. The woman was afraid of her own reflection!

Of course! It all made sense. Edith had been a beauty queen, a woman whose only certainty in life had been her own image. Alzheimer's must have caused her brain to activate a safety mechanism, just as the Internet articles claimed.

In Edith's case, the safety mechanism was the belief that somehow she still had her beauty. In her mind, she was not an aging Alzheimer's patient waiting to die in an adult care home. She was young and vibrant, living out her days in an imaginary place where she was still beautiful — a place where the ravages of time had not taken their toll on her fair skin and chestnut hair, back when her eyes didn't sag and her chin was still firm.

Dear sweet Edith. She wasn't seeing a witch in the bathroom. She was seeing her own reflection, the person she had become.

Ashley helped the woman through the routine of taking fearful small steps toward her recliner, helped her calm down and get comfortable. Then, without hesitating, she went to the linen closet and found an old sheet.

"Dear," Irvel called from the dining room, "are we having tea?"

"Just a minute, Irvel. I'll be right there."

It was bath time, but Ashley had something to do first. She carried the sheet to Edith's bathroom and covered the mirror, tucking the edges of the sheet around the edges of the cabinet so it wouldn't fall off.

The next morning when Edith headed toward the shower, Ashley again fell in quietly behind her.

"She's already been checked." Helen waved a hand at Ashley.

Without saying a word, Ashley turned and nodded at Helen. Then she held up a single finger and whispered, "I'll be right back."

Edith rounded the corner as usual, entered the bathroom, and stared at the covered mirror. Then she turned to Ashley and lowered her brow. "Did I eat my eggs today?"

Ashley wanted to raise a fist in the air and shout for joy. She'd done it! She'd solved the mystery! As long as Edith wasn't forced to look at her own image, she could go on believing age had never happened to her, go on existing in the remembered comfort of her beauty — without ever again being afraid of a witch.

After lunch Ashley scribbled details about the incident in Edith's folder, along with this bit of advice: Keep Edith away from mirrors.

Belinda wouldn't be returning for half a week, and Ashley intended to make the most of it. Early that afternoon Helen's daughter, Sue Brown, appeared at the front door. Ashley was fairly certain that Helen was living in the 1960s, back when Sue was a teenager and the two of them had spent most of their free time together, before Sue had married and moved away and everything about Helen's life had slid slowly downhill.

Ashley met Sue in the entryway and

whisked her off to a quiet spot in the dining room. They sat down and turned their chairs toward each other.

"I have an idea." Ashley opened Helen's file and spread it on the table. "I've been thinking about your mother's past, the things you've told me, the pictures she keeps in her dresser drawer."

"Yes, I wanted to thank you for that." Sue looked at the file. "No one's ever asked about Mom's past."

"Well . . ." Ashley motioned to the file. "New research says if you find out about a patient's history, it may be possible to figure out where they're stuck — what time period in their life." She looked at Sue again. "Does that make sense?"

"I guess." The woman settled back in her chair and set her purse on the floor.

"Apparently some Alzheimer's patients actually do better if you deal with them as though they're right." Ashley felt her body tense, certain of the angry response that was coming. "In other words, go along with what they're thinking. React as if it really were, say, 1965, or whatever time frame they feel comfortable with."

"That sounds wonderful." Relief made some of the lines on Sue's face disappear. "How can I help?"

Ashley stared at her. How could she help? That wasn't the response Ashley was expecting. Belinda had said the family members wanted their loved ones kept in the here and now. But if this was Sue's reaction . . .

It struck her then that maybe the family members didn't *know* what they wanted. Maybe they were simply going along with Belinda and Lu's philosophy. What could the relatives do, after all? Belinda and Lu were the specialists. If they said Alzheimer's patients should be reminded of reality, then the family members would almost have to agree.

Ashley's voice grew quiet. "I thought . . . you'd be mad at me."

"Mad?" Sue gave Ashley a puzzled look. "I want whatever will make Mama feel better. The way she acts now, I barely recognize her."

"Right." Ashley swallowed hard and stared at Helen's file. "Well, here's my idea."

Ashley explained that Helen seemed to be stuck in the 1960s. "She can't imagine she could have anything but a teenage daughter."

Sue nodded.

"So . . ." Excitement coursed through

Ashley. "You might have a better conversation with your mother if you don't even mention that you're her daughter."

"You think so?"

"I do." Ashley gave Sue a tender smile. "Tell her you've come for two reasons. To visit . . . and to talk about Sue."

"About me?" Sue leaned forward, her expression curious.

"Right." Ashley pointed to the file. "I think if you tell her you've been checked, assure her you're not a spy, but don't insist on being her daughter, then maybe she'd be willing to talk to you. You could even tell her you know Sue, find that common ground only the two of you share. You know, stories about your life growing up, funny memories, songs you used to sing together, things you used to do. Talk about all of it."

"As though I only *know* Sue?"

"Right." Ashley could feel her enthusiasm growing. Other than painting, her time with the people at Sunset Hills was the most exciting work she'd ever done. "Then she won't be afraid of you. See" — Ashley drew a steady breath — "your mom gets very frightened when you show up and tell her you're Sue. She still thinks of you as a teenager — eighteen, nineteen.

She doesn't want to see a woman in her fifties walk through the door and call herself Sue."

A light of understanding ignited in Sue's eyes. "I get it. But if we talk *about* Sue, we might begin to be friends."

"Exactly."

"Okay." Sue ran her tongue along her lower lip. "I'm nervous. But I'm ready. Bring her in."

Ashley practically jumped from her chair, and a minute later she led Helen into the room. "Helen, there's someone to see you. She wants to visit."

Helen wrinkled her nose and stared at Sue. "I've seen her before." She looked at Ashley. "She's a spy."

A shadow of pain fell across Sue's face, but it lasted only a moment. "No, Helen, I'm not a spy. I've been checked."

Helen cast a wary eye at Sue. "You have?" Her eyes lifted to Ashley's again. "She has?"

"Yes, Helen. I checked her before she came in. She's not a spy."

"Okay, then." Suspicion settled in around Helen's eyes. "Why are you here?"

Sue smiled and reached for Helen's hand. "I want to talk about Sue."

Neither of them spoke for a moment.

Helen blinked once, then again. "Sue?" Her tone was suddenly gentle, filled with longing and sorrow. "You know my Sue?"

As discreetly as she could, Ashley pulled out the chair beside Sue and helped Helen sit down. Then she stepped back and leaned against the wall. So far so good. It was the first time Helen had been willing to sit and talk with her daughter since Ashley had worked at Sunset Hills.

Probably much longer.

Sue still had hold of her mother's hand. "I know Sue very well. She's doing fine. She . . . she talks about you a lot."

Helen's expression was almost childlike. "She does?"

"Yes."

"What does she say?"

"She remembers when the two of you would go to the library and pick out books." Sue brought her other hand up and laid it gently across her mother's fingers. "Do you remember that?"

"Yes. We read The Chronicles of Narnia."

"Right." Sue blinked back tears. Ashley wanted to jump around the room shouting. It was working! Helen and her daughter were actually finding common ground, sharing a conversation.

Helen stared into space and then shifted her eyes back to Sue's. "The two of us would read by the fireplace, and when we finished, we'd switch books. Then we'd talk about the stories. Sometimes we had hot milk in blue mugs."

"Yes." Sue wiped at a tear on her cheek. "Sue tells me the two of you had quite a good time together."

Helen nodded. Then in an instant her expression changed. Worry and fear and suspicion were back, robbing Helen of even the joy of the memory. She studied Sue, her lips pursed, eyes narrowed in anger. "Someone stole her from me. My Sue."

"No . . ."

Ashley held her breath. *Come on, Sue. Don't give yourself away.* She pressed back another step, not wanting to interrupt.

Sue consciously raised the corners of her mouth. "Sue's fine, Helen. She told me so. She's happy and well, and she wants you to know."

Helen jerked back and slapped the table, causing Sue to jump. "Then where is she? How come no one will tell me where she is?"

"Well . . ." Sue looked nervous. "She lives far away. But she's making plans to visit."

The cloud of anxiety and anger lifted. "She is?"

"Yes." Tears shone in Sue's eyes again. "Until then, she wants me to visit you. That way I can talk about her with you."

Ashley angled her head, touched by the effort Sue was giving. It had to be terribly painful to sit hand in hand with her mother yet feel a million miles away from her.

"What else do you know about her?" Helen settled into the chair and looked intently at Sue. It was the most normal the woman had looked since Ashley had known her.

The conversation between mother and daughter lasted nearly an hour.

The next day Sue was back. This time she talked about a trip she and her mother had taken when she was a teenager. Again, they shared the afternoon without a single outburst or accusation of covert behavior from Helen.

On the last day of Belinda's absence, Ashley took stock of the changes at Sunset Hills, and she was amazed. Helen was slapping and hitting things about half as often as before, and Edith seemed more focused during her visits with Irvel.

The Past-Present strategy was working!

Reaching Irvel was easier than the others, of course, because the place where she lived was obvious. Irvel was stuck back in a time when her Hank was strong enough to fish every day, back when sharing peppermint tea with the girls was the highlight of each afternoon. Weeks ago, Ashley had asked Irvel's niece, an attorney who lived an hour away, to round up as many pictures of Hank as possible. Hank and Irvel, Hank and their children, Hank by himself — it didn't matter so long as Hank was in the photograph.

A box of pictures had arrived in the mail that week, and Ashley had purchased frames for several of them. Earlier that afternoon, while the residents of Sunset Hills napped in their recliners, Ashley hung the photographs on Irvel's bedroom wall — all but one of them.

The missing photo was a close-up of Hank in his twenties, the lazy grin that showed up in every photo stretched across his face. The moment she saw the photo, Ashley had been drawn to it, driven to bring the man's face to life on canvas. Days earlier, she'd taken it home and set it up next to her easel.

The man's portrait had taken up every spare moment since then, and she still had a few days' work to do before she could present it to Irvel. Ashley could hardly wait. But for now the wall held eighteen pictures of Hank — a monument to the man and all he'd meant to Irvel through the years.

Ashley stepped back and studied the images. How much one could learn from photographic art, from the expressions and actions of the people frozen in a single moment of time.

Hank Heidenreich had been tall and handsome in his day, a man whose smile and touch seemed to come easily. The pictures of Hank and Irvel showed his arm slung loosely around her shoulders, his face taken up by a grin that traveled straight up his cheeks to his eyes.

The photos of Irvel were also telling. In Hank's arms she had the look of joy and security and utter peace. Together, their love glowed so brightly that it almost seemed to affect the quality of the picture — as though the photographer had used special lighting.

Ashley stared at the photos a moment longer and let her mind drift. Where was Landon this afternoon? Had he found Jalen? Was he okay after all he must have seen and done at Ground Zero?

God, please help him. Help him find his friend. Help him be safe. Please . . .

She'd kept her promise. Whenever she thought of Landon, she prayed, just as he'd asked her to do.

He was a hero now, of course. The local newspaper had done a spread on how he'd saved the little boy's life back in July and now was one of those digging through the rubble of the World Trade Center. Landon's mother had been quoted in the article saying that hundreds of Bloomington residents had sent letters thanking her son for his heroic efforts. Several had even proposed marriage.

Ashley sighed. She'd called Landon's mother after the article appeared. "How is he?" She had hesitated. "I've been . . . worried about him."

"You mean" — the surprise in his mother's voice caught Ashley off guard — "he hasn't called you?"

"Not yet."

"I'm sorry, Ashley. I would've let you know sooner. He's working every day — sometimes sleeping twelve hours straight before going back to Ground Zero. I'm surprised he hasn't called you."

Deep down, Ashley was surprised too, but she shook it off.

Landon would always be special to her, but clearly he had decided to move on with life. He'd been gone more than two weeks, and there'd been no word from him. If he was getting marriage proposals here in Bloomington, the same was probably true in New York.

Why did that bother her, anyway?

She'd always known she wasn't the right person for Landon Blake. And that was still true, even though she'd told him about Paris. Even though she'd prayed for him and gone to church these past weeks. She enjoyed the music and even Pastor Mark's messages. But she was hardly a woman of faith, hardly suitable for a man as committed to God as Landon was. He needed someone like Kari or Erin.

But if Landon wasn't the right man for her, who was? Who would grace the walls of her final days? The question dangled in the winds of uncertainty as Ashley headed into the kitchen. She unloaded the dishwasher while the women napped, but still she had no answers for herself.

When Irvel woke up, Ashley led her to her bedroom, then stepped back to take in the old woman's surprise.

"My goodness, dear. Hank must have been by while I was asleep." She reached out toward the pictures one at a time, making her way slowly along the collection. "He's certainly a handsome one, isn't he?"

Ashley swallowed back the emotion welling in her throat. "He is, Irvel. Very handsome."

Irvel shook her head and cast a backward glance at Ashley. "Sometimes I think that man spends too much time fishing. I haven't had a day alone with him in . . ." She looked down for a moment, then back at Ashley again. ". . . in a week, at least."

"You like the photos?"

"Like them?" Irvel smiled, and the sparkles in her eyes shone through her cataracts. "Dear" — she lowered her voice — "it makes me feel like he's right here in the room. Like he never went fishing at all."

Ashley felt the warmth of Irvel's smile in the deepest, dark places of her being. This was why she'd taken the job, after all. So the hardened layers of her heart would be chipped away, so she could learn to feel again.

"Come on, Irvel, let's go have a snack." Ashley held out her hand.

Irvel took one last look at the wall of photos and turned toward Ashley. As she did, she tilted her head, her eyes completely void of recognition. "I'm sorry, dear. I don't think I've introduced myself."

Ashley smiled and linked her arm through Irvel's as they left the room. "I'm Ashley. I work here."

Ashley worked a double shift that day, and after the residents were asleep, she pulled out her files and studied one in particular, the file belonging to Bert. A letter from Bert's son had arrived in the mail earlier that day. Ashley hadn't had time to read it until now.

She slid her fingernail beneath the envelope flap and pulled out a page of single-spaced type.

Dear Ms. Baxter,
First let me thank you for making an effort to reach my father. If you feel that knowing more about his past will somehow help him, I'm glad to provide whatever information you need. I support you and whatever you can do with the details I've provided. I've been thinking about the history I gave you earlier, and I forgot something. It may not be important, but I thought you should know.

Ashley felt her heart rate quicken. She needed as many facts about Bert's background as possible. Somewhere there had to be an explanation for his incessant circling. She let her eyes race ahead.

I told you Dad worked with horses, but I didn't tell you how. Dad was a saddler — a saddle maker. He crafted the finest saddles in the region and brought in as much money that way as he did running the dairy farm.

The letter went on to explain that the dairy farm had been in the family for years and practically ran itself. As a young man, Bert had felt little significance in overseeing such a self-sufficient operation. So he'd hired men to keep the farm running and built a shop where he began making saddles.

"Horse people from all over the country used to buy Dad's saddles," the letter continued. "He spent hours every day working the leather, rubbing oil into those saddles until they shone. He was more proud of his saddle making than almost anything else he did."

Ashley's breath caught in her throat. Bert had spent hours every day rubbing oil into saddles?

She pictured Bert the way he looked now, the way he looked every day. That determined, vacant stare — driven to make circles along the edge of his bed all day long.

Suddenly it made sense.

Bert wasn't rubbing out the wrinkles in his comforter. He was rubbing his saddles, trapped in a time when his days held purpose and his actions were appreciated by countless customers.

Ashley tucked the letter inside Bert's file and rested her forehead on her fingertips. She could be wrong about Bert, but there had to be a way to find out. What could she do? Bert wouldn't talk, let alone listen to her. Her knowledge about his saddle making meant nothing if she couldn't somehow use it to reach him.

For fifteen minutes, Ashley sat there searching for a solution. Then it hit her. She knew exactly what to do to bridge Bert's past and present. But it would take a few days. And that meant pulling it off when Belinda was here.

But that shouldn't matter. What Ashley did during her hours as a care worker need not bother Belinda so long as the house rules were followed. And there were no rules forbidding the thing she was about to do.

Besides, who knew what might happen if she was right? Her plan could be life-changing for Bert and the greatest proof of all that Ashley's experiment was working.

Now it was simply a matter of putting it into action.

Chapter Twenty-Four

Landon was beyond exhausted.

After four weeks at Ground Zero, fatigue and soul-numbing weariness were permanent conditions for him and the others. The days of sifting debris and locating bits and pieces of human remains were taking their toll, leaving many of the rescue workers depressed and disoriented, as though time and life and all sense of normalcy had ceased forever.

The rest of America was getting back to life. Stock market reports were leveling off. Businesses had stopped making drastic layoffs. Anthrax, the deadly disease whose spores had been found in political offices and postal centers after the terrorist attacks, wasn't in the news as much anymore. Instead, headlines were filled with the impending war effort — Operation Enduring Freedom. Though eighty thousand airline-industry workers had been laid off after the attacks, people were flying again. For most of America, the nightmare of

September 11 seemed to be lessening.

But at Ground Zero, the task had only begun.

Officials were saying it could take a year before the debris of the twin towers was completely explored and removed from the heart of New York City. The papers reported that ninety thousand tons of debris had been taken from the site in the first eleven days alone. The actual weight of the rubble pile was more than any of them could imagine.

At the same time, rescue workers had recovered bodies or body parts of fewer than three hundred people. And the farther down into the debris they dug, the fewer human remains they found. However many bodies were eventually recovered, the number would clearly fall far short of the thousands missing, those incinerated when the jets hit, or pulverized when the buildings collapsed. The latest reports indicated that more than four thousand people were missing from the World Trade Center — victims from more than sixty countries.

Landon's routine had changed little since his first day at the scene. But in the quiet places of his heart, the subtle differences were enough to alarm him. Or they would have been if he wasn't so worn-out.

He stepped out of the bucket-brigade assembly line and trudged down the block toward Canal Street. Lately he'd been taking his lunches at Nino's, a diner not far from Ground Zero. Since September 12, Nino's had been serving free meals for the rescue workers. Volunteers — many of them women — packed the place. They wore paper hats and aprons and sometimes hung around the tables of firefighters longer than necessary, looking for a way to be useful.

Landon walked inside and waited until his eyes adjusted to the dim lighting. He scanned the room and found a place in the corner. Nodding to a few firefighters along the way, he stopped at a quiet booth and slid in, his legs aching from his morning shift. A buzzing worked its way through his weary body, and he felt nauseous. His forearms dropped like anchors onto the table. He let his head fall forward.

Where are you, God?

The thought hung in the stale air awhile and drifted away. How long had it been since he'd read his Bible or really shared his heart with God? He knew the problem. Working at Ground Zero made him feel isolated, as though even God couldn't understand how he felt.

Landon drew a deep breath and coughed. The temperatures outside were dropping, but his body was hot and sweaty in his uniform. He sat up again, running the jacket sleeve across his brow. His faith was still intact. Nothing could shake that. But in all his life he'd never felt so far away from everything that mattered to him — Ashley, his family, his God. Even his reasons for becoming a firefighter seemed foggy, filtered through the heart-wrenching experience of working at Ground Zero.

A blonde volunteer wearing a tight sweater and bright lipstick brought him a glass of water and set it in front of him. She waited by the table for a moment. "You okay?"

The corners of his mouth lifted mechanically. He wasn't in the mood for conversation. He wanted to eat and get back to work. "Yeah. I'm fine."

Fine? Landon exhaled hard as he watched the volunteer walk away. Nothing could be further from the truth. Desperation penetrated every fiber in his soul because of one very painful truth: They still hadn't found any sign of Jalen.

Landon had been unable to do the one thing he'd come to do — find his friend dead or alive. Instead he'd taken on the role of a machine — a machine that wasn't supposed to notice the broken cell phones and money clips and wedding rings mixed among the chunks of debris in the hundreds of buckets that passed through his hands each day. A machine dedicated to retrieving the dead, nothing more.

The blonde volunteer was back. This time she had a tray with an oversized turkey sandwich and a pile of chocolate-chip cookies. She set them down and slid into the booth across from him. Landon lifted his head and studied her. She was maybe twenty years old, but her eyes looked thirty at least. He picked up the sandwich. "Thanks."

"Sure." She stuck out her chin, her tone gentle. "You don't look fine."

"Yeah, well" — Landon didn't recognize his own voice — "I can't find my friend."

The blonde knew better than to rush into conversation after a line like that. She waited, meeting his gaze head-on. "I'm sorry."

Landon shrugged. "It doesn't matter. He's gone. Like the others."

"He was a fireman?" She crossed her arms.

"Yep." Landon leaned back and laced his fingers behind his head. Volunteers had talked with him before, but none of them had sat down and joined him for lunch. The diversion was almost enjoyable.

"I'm Kaye." She held out her hand.

Landon took it, but only long enough to be polite. He didn't offer his name. "What brings you here?" He stretched out his legs and accidentally brushed hers in the process.

"I worked at the World Trade Center." Her gaze fell briefly to her manicured nails. "I took reservations for the restaurant. You know, the famous one at the top."

Landon took a bite of his sandwich and waited.

"I was supposed to work that day, but my little brother was sick." She helped herself to a sip of Landon's water. "No one I knew made it out."

Sadness came over Landon, and for a long while his eyes held hers. The two of them shared something that everyone at Ground Zero seemed to have in common, something the rest of the world couldn't understand. A pain, a sense of incalculable loss that only those in the middle of it all could completely grasp. "I'm sorry."

She shrugged. "I don't have anywhere to go — no job, you know. So I figured I could volunteer here for a while. At least

I'd be doing something to help."

"I know the feeling."

Landon finished his lunch and offered the young woman a cookie. There was a comfortable quiet between them, as though meaningless conversation was a luxury of the past. Somehow their shared experience made Landon feel connected to her. She was a complete stranger, but she knew what he was going through, what they were all going through.

"Where are you from?" She took another sip of his water.

"Bloomington, Indiana." The young woman across from him was the best thing his eyes had taken in since he'd arrived in New York. What had she said her name was?

"You got a girl back home?"

The question pulled up and parked in the front of his mind. He could picture Ashley, the way she felt in his arms, the way being with her this past summer had almost made him cancel his plans and stay in Bloomington. Why hadn't he called her? Was it because the sound of her voice, one slightest bit of interest from her, would have had him on a plane in an hour?

Landon let his gaze fall to the table. That was exactly why he hadn't called.

And he couldn't go home now, couldn't leave until they'd found Jalen. He pulled himself from the memory and stared at the blonde. She was waiting for an answer. "Sort of."

"I figured." She stood and took off her hat and apron. "Listen, my shift is up. Wanna take a walk?"

It had been half an hour since he left the work line, but Landon wasn't on anyone's schedule except his own. Volunteers were allowed to come and go as they pleased, and none of them needed to be asked to get back to work.

Still, he had to walk back to Ground Zero, didn't he? What would it hurt to walk with this girl, whoever she was? "Sure." He slipped out of the booth, stood, and put his helmet back on.

They stepped outside, and the pungent air made them wince at the same time. "The smell of death." The girl fell in beside him.

"No doubt." In the light of day, Landon could see that she had long legs and a striking figure. Something about her made him feel almost alive for the first time in weeks.

Halfway to the rescue site they found a bench and sat down.

"So . . ." She was wearing old tennis shoes, and she gave him a light kick. "Why'd you become a fireman?"

Landon needed to get back to work. Maybe this was the day. If only they could move a little faster. If only they had more people on the line, they would find Jalen. He brought his thoughts back to the girl's question. "It was in me, something I found out in college."

For reasons Landon couldn't understand, he began to tell her his story, how he'd gone to Texas to study animal science, how he'd planned on coming back to Bloomington and setting up shop as a veterinarian.

"Then I met Jalen." Landon stared across the street at the recovery effort going on in the distance. "It was like finding a lost brother. We were that much alike."

The blonde said nothing but moved a few inches closer. Her eyes never left his face.

Landon told her about how he and Jalen had become volunteer firefighters, and he told her about the house fire that changed his life. "Backup units hadn't made it to the scene, so Jalen and I joined the others looking for victims inside." He sucked in a quick breath. "Jalen found a woman collapsed just outside a bedroom. The room was fully involved — flames everywhere." Landon leaned his head back, seeing the terrifying moment in his mind once more. Then he shifted his attention to look at the blonde beside him. "The woman was half dead, but as Jalen carried her out, she screamed for her baby."

"Her child was still inside?" The eyes of the blonde were wide. She moved even closer to him.

"Yeah, a little girl." Landon stroked his chin and once more gazed straight ahead. "I grabbed a blanket and beat out the flames in the doorway to her room." He shook his head. "It was all I could do to find her crib. I carried her outside to her mother, but it was too late." He turned to the young woman beside him. "The baby was already dead."

"That's awful."

"After that, I knew I couldn't be a veterinarian. It would never be enough to help animals when people like that little girl need my help."

They were quiet for a while, watching the trucks pull away one at a time from the mountain of debris. Then, without saying a word, the blonde slipped her hand into his. "Life is too short."

Shivers of electricity coursed through Landon's body, emanating from the place where the young woman's hand was connected to his. Maybe there was life in him after all. There must be if he could still react this way to the touch of a pretty woman.

What am I doing? The question rattled the windows of his conscience. *I need to get back to work.*

But the moment felt bigger than life, more real than anything else waiting for him outside Ground Zero. He angled his body in the direction of the blonde, and before he could make himself stand and walk away, his arms were around her and they were kissing. Oblivious to everything around him, Landon and the woman kissed for a long moment. Finally she drew back and grinned at him. "You didn't tell me your name."

Her statement was like a splash of cold water. Had he lost his mind? What was he doing sitting on a New York City street bench kissing a stranger? He gently pulled free of her grasp and uttered a nervous laugh. "Landon. Landon Blake." He shook his head. "Sorry. I don't know where that came from."

The girl slid closer to him again. "Don't apologize. I mean, what's life about if you can't share yourself with someone? Especially after" — she nodded toward the debris — "after what happened."

He stared at her. What did she mean by that? He stood and straightened his jacket. "Look, I have to get back to work." He stuffed his hands into his pockets. "Thanks for listening."

Before he could walk away, she handed him a card with her name and phone number. Obviously she'd planned on giving it to him all along. "Call me." She gave him a knowing look. "My family's out of town. I'm alone tonight." The expression on her face held no apologies, no embarrassment. "Maybe if we shared the night, it would be easier to spend another day down here. You know?"

Landon folded the card and tucked it into his pocket. "Thanks. You might be right." He nodded his head once in her direction and set off toward the rescue site. "Nice talking to you."

When he was a block away, he turned around, relieved to find her gone. What was wrong with him? Did he really tell her she might be right — that two strangers spending the night together would somehow cancel out the stench of death at Ground Zero? He headed toward the rescue site, but something was welling inside him, something that made it impossible to get back to work just yet.

He wandered around a corner and up a mound of twisted concrete and steel to the place where the makeshift cross still stood. Dozens of flower bouquets surrounded its base; hundreds of messages had been scrawled on the steel or taped to the beam. Almost always, people were gathered here. But in this moment, midway through the afternoon, Landon found himself alone.

Suddenly the thing that was welling within him forced its way to the surface. A cry came from him, a cry that was too soft to be heard above the heavy machinery but racked his entire body all the same. He fell to his knees and hung his head. "God, what am I doing? I feel like you're so far away from me!"

Then, as though God himself had pulled a plug on his emotions, tears spilled from his eyes. He cried for Jalen and for the workers at the restaurant where the blonde had taken reservations until September 11. He cried for everyone buried beneath the rubble and for the senselessness of how all their lives had come tumbling down with the twin towers.

He could picture his friend Jalen, how he must have looked in the minutes after getting the call to the World Trade Center. His blue eyes would have been serious, heart racing as his hook and ladder made its way to the scene. Jalen would have been one of the first ones up the stairwell, one of the first to reach the victims. He'd probably made it to the top of the tower before the building collapsed. No doubt he'd been helping people down the stairs even as the floor gave way.

"Why, God?" Landon shouted the words and balled his hands into tight fists.

Minutes passed, and suddenly Landon felt a hand on his shoulder. He turned and locked eyes with a kind, black man whose energetic smile was known across the country. The man was an author and speaker, a regular at Promise Keepers and other national conferences. Someone Landon deeply respected.

He blinked to make sure he wasn't seeing things. "What . . . what are you doing here?"

The man knelt beside him. The two of them were still the only people near the cross. "I saw you over here." He gave

Landon a sad smile. "You're a believer, aren't you?"

Landon nodded, speechless.

"What's your name?"

"Landon."

The man reached out his hand and introduced himself — as if that were necessary. "May I pray with you?"

Landon's heart was beating hard. "Sure."

The man took Landon's hand and bowed his head. "Lord, this is a dark time for our nation, but particularly for those who serve, those who honor America with their dedication, sometimes with their lives." He drew a quick breath. "Please comfort Landon, meet him in this place, and remind him of his first love. It's easy to be distracted here among so much death. But please, Lord, restore life to Landon's heart and help him see you, help him feel your touch. Even here at Ground Zero. In Jesus' name, amen."

Before Landon had time to ask questions, the man was gone, off to find another hurting person to pray with. Dumbfounded, Landon stared up at the cross. His heart felt like it had been brought back to life. *God, you heard me. You knew what I needed, and you sent someone I could trust.*

Landon remembered the man's prayer. *"Remind him of his first love. . . . Remind him of his first love."*

That was it, wasn't it? His hours at Ground Zero had been so taken up with death that Landon had forgotten to fill his mind with thoughts of life. Thoughts of God, of his goodness and plans for his people. Every good thing he knew to be true about God, every promise and divine truth, had been covered in ash — all but unrecognizable since he'd arrived in New York City.

Yes, he'd forgotten his first love. Not just God but Ashley as well. Someday when this nightmare was over, he would go back to Bloomington. And when he did, he would find Ashley and convince her beyond any doubt that they belonged together. Whether that was a month or a year from now didn't matter. Time wouldn't change the way he felt about her.

The last thing he did before returning to the line was pull the card from his pocket, the one with the blonde's name and phone number. He ripped it in half and stuffed it deep into the layer of debris near the base of the cross. Then he dusted off his hands and headed back to work.

This time he no longer felt alone. He

could sense the Lord at his side, his presence as real as if the two were walking shoulder to shoulder. He stepped into the line and grabbed hold of his first bucket of rubble, suddenly knowing what he would do that night — if not that night, then sometime soon. He would make the call he should have made a long time ago.

Not to the blonde stranger, but to a girl who was in his blood no matter what life dealt him. A girl he prayed would one day recognize God as her first love also.

That afternoon while he worked, Landon prayed for Ashley as he'd never done before. Constantly and with fervor, hour after hour.

Let her find you, God, please. Meet her where she is and let her know you're real. Nothing I can say or do will ever bring her close to you. But you, God — you can reach her. I know it.

Just before dark, a peace came over Landon, almost as though the Lord had hugged him. Landon wanted to raise a victory fist in the air. The peace could mean only one thing: His prayers had been answered. One day — however far off — Ashley Baxter would give her heart to God.

Whenever that day came, Landon had

no doubt that she would feel as strongly for him as he did for her.

Now it was a matter of surviving until then.

Chapter Twenty-Five

Thanksgiving Day was quieter than usual.

By three o'clock the dinner was ready, and John Baxter called everyone to gather at the table for the blessing. He glanced at the circle of familiar faces and wondered why the atmosphere was so subdued. Certainly Luke's attitude played a part; he'd spent the entire day holed up in his room. It was Erin and Sam's last holiday season before they moved — that must have been on the hearts of some of them.

But most likely his family's mood was a direct reflection of their nation's. In light of September 11, most Americans had a greater sense of appreciation for their faith, their families, their freedom, but also a deep sense of sadness, of mourning. The Baxters were no exception.

The country was at war with Afghanistan, and that, too, made for a more somber atmosphere. Reports were coming in daily about bombing missions and the potential for ground troops to be deployed.

The Baileys down the street had a son serving on the USS *Theodore Roosevelt* in the Arabian Sea. The boy was a friend of Luke's, a fighter pilot. He hadn't had a day's rest since the war began.

Everyone held hands as John surveyed the group. Pastor Mark and his wife, Marilyn, had joined them for the second straight year. Everyone was present except . . .

John stifled an exasperated sigh. "Luke!" His voice carried through the house, and the others turned toward the stairs. "Time to eat."

There was a pause, and then they heard a bedroom door open. "Go ahead. I'm not hungry."

A knot formed in John's stomach. Luke had been hiding in his room lately. His absence made John's few conversations with him tense and brief. John had shared his concerns with Pastor Mark, and now the two men exchanged a knowing glance. Around the table, several others did the same.

Next to John, Elizabeth squeezed his hand and nodded — her way of saying she would make the next attempt. "Luke, come down." Her voice was pleasant but firm. "It's Thanksgiving. We're waiting for you."

Everyone in the circle seemed to hold their collective breath as they heard his bedroom door open again. This time Luke said nothing, just bounded down the stairs. John wasn't surprised that he responded to Elizabeth. For some reason, most of Luke's recent animosity seemed directed at him.

"Sorry." Luke took his place in the circle between Ashley and Cole. His expression was one of bored tolerance, but at least he wasn't pushing the issue.

"Thank you." Elizabeth smiled in his direction, but he only nodded and stared up at the ceiling.

John studied him for a moment. Whatever was wrong with Luke, he hadn't been himself since the terrorist attacks. John wanted to order him to change his attitude, force him to be polite, the way he had when Luke was little. But Luke was older now, and this wasn't the time or place.

The others had their eyes closed and were ready for the prayer. John bowed his head. "Lord, thank you for this meal you've provided. Thank you for the blessing of family and good health, for watching over us this past year. We pray for those struggling with losses this Thanksgiving . . ." Images of Reagan and Landon flashed in John's head, and for a moment he was too choked up to speak. "We remember them now, Lord, and we ask that you remember them also. Comfort them, and comfort those fighting for our freedom overseas. Most of all, Father, we thank you for the gift of living in America. Your goodness surrounds us, and we are grateful beyond words."

The meal was unhurried, punctuated with quiet conversation and occasional bouts of silliness from the children. Erin and Sam announced they'd postponed their move until the summer. Uncertainties at Sam's company had led to layoffs. Though management still wanted him at their Texas location, the arrangements had been delayed. Erin seemed relieved, but she was clearly still concerned about the move.

Ashley gave them an update on the residents at Sunset Hills. "I needed a few things for Bert's room — you know, to make him more comfortable. I found one of them on eBay. It should get here any day."

Kari finished a bite of mashed potatoes. "I love eBay, especially when I'm busy." She looked behind her and checked on Jessie. The baby was sleeping peacefully on a blanket in the family room. "You can find almost anything."

"By the way" — Peter set his fork down and looked at Pastor Mark — "we really enjoyed your message last Sunday. You've got us thinking."

John shot Elizabeth a quick wink. The greatest thing to happen to the Baxters since the terrorist attacks was that Brooke and Peter and even Ashley were attending church. Peter was a private man, an accomplished young doctor with a history of relying on himself. Brooke was private too, for that matter. Only an event as life-changing as what happened September 11 could have moved them to enjoy a Sunday sermon.

"Thanks." Pastor Mark shrugged. "That's my job."

Peter glanced at Brooke and then back to the pastor. "Actually, we'd like to meet with you one evening next week if that works for you."

There was silence around the table, as though none of them knew what to say or how to react to Peter's statement. Then Pastor Mark's smile lit the room. "Sounds good to me. Let's talk about it after dinner."

Next to him, John could feel Elizabeth's joy. How many years had they prayed for

Brooke and Peter, that the two of them might realize life could not be explained by textbooks and scientific knowledge alone?

"Mommy, I'm done." Four-year-old Maddie, who never ate a lot, was squirming in her booster seat. "Can I go play?"

"Yeah!" Cole piped in. "Let's build a Lego fort!"

"Me too!" Little Hailey's eyes grew wide, and she tugged on Brooke's sleeve. "Go play."

Brooke grinned. "Okay. Go ahead."

"By the way" — Pastor Mark's wife looked at Brooke as she helped Hailey down from her seat — "how's Maddie doing? Last I heard, she was still fighting a virus or something?"

Brooke's features hardened some. For all their medical training, neither Brooke nor Peter had been able to explain their daughter's strange fevers. It was a topic Brooke didn't like to talk about. "She's well now." The corners of Brooke's mouth lifted, but the fear in her eyes remained. "We're" — she shot a quick look at Peter — "we're praying for her."

Praying for her? John worked to contain his surprise. It was one thing to see Brooke and Peter interested in church and meeting with Pastor Mark. But to have them talk so openly about praying? John silently thanked God. Quiet or not, this was a Thanksgiving he'd never forget.

The meal continued, but Luke said little. When the conversation turned to the war in Afghanistan, he stopped eating and stared at his plate. He dragged his fork through the sweet potatoes, his mind clearly somewhere else.

"I think they got Osama bin Laden." Sam buttered another roll and looked at the others. "If he's dead in one of those caves, no one will find him for months."

"I don't know." Peter's eyes grew thoughtful. "The man's pretty resourceful."

"Pretty evil, you mean." Kari passed the fruit salad to Elizabeth. "I can't believe he had terrorist camps set up right here in the United States. It's too awful."

Pastor Mark focused on Ashley. "What do you hear from Landon?"

All her life Ashley had worked to be aloof, different from the rest of them. But John knew her too well. The emotions that flashed across her face at the mention of Landon's name told him one thing clearly: She loved Landon Blake. For the first time since the two of them had known each other, she actually loved him.

Ashley drew a quick breath. "He hasn't called." She let her gaze fall to the half-eaten food on her plate for a moment. "I think he's planning to stay there for a while."

"Is he still working at Ground Zero?" Marilyn's question was innocent enough, but John could see by the tilt of Ashley's chin that it was difficult for her to answer.

"His mother says he is. He's . . . he's still looking for his friend Jalen."

"Jalen?" Marilyn paused, her expression curious. "The fireman, right?"

"Right." Tears formed in Ashley's eyes, and she blinked them back. "He was working in one of the twin towers when they collapsed."

With that, Luke set his fork and napkin down and pushed back from the table. "Excuse me." He flashed a practiced smile at the rest of them, turned, and headed up the stairs. "I'll be in my room."

A nervous silence mixed with the warm smells of dinner and hung over the table for a moment. Ashley wiped her mouth. "Luke doesn't like talking about Ground Zero." She shook her head and gave the Atteberrys a sympathetic smile. "It's not your fault. He's just — he hasn't heard

414

from Reagan since she left. The whole thing's been hard on him."

John stared at Ashley. How did she know? Luke hadn't been sharing his feelings with John or Elizabeth, but apparently he had been very open with Ashley. John thought about that for a moment. It was probably a good thing. Though Luke's silence toward him hurt, John couldn't be anything but grateful for the renewed friendship between Luke and Ashley.

"I'm sorry." Marilyn took her husband's hand. "I wasn't thinking."

Pastor Mark raised an eyebrow in Ashley's direction. "I'm leading a group at church for people struggling with what happened September eleventh." He looked at the others. "Lots of folks have questions. The group gives them a chance to talk through their feelings. Luke might be interested."

Ashley took a sip of water and nodded. "I don't think he knows about it."

John let his gaze fall to his plate. Of course Luke didn't know about it. He had been to church just once since the attacks.

"Okay." Ashley took another slice of turkey. "I'll tell him."

Across the table, Erin finished her dinner and crossed her arms. "That was your best turkey yet, Mom." She smiled at Elizabeth.

"Thanks. I used a baking bag this time. I think it's more tender than usual."

This was the part of Thanksgiving John liked most — the easy banter and conversation among those he loved. And Erin was right. Elizabeth had outdone herself this year — maybe because she, too, sensed things were changing. There was no telling how many holidays like this they had left, with everyone together at the table.

"Mom says you still talk to Ryan." Erin looked at Kari. "How's he doing?"

Kari's cheeks reddened at Erin's question. "We talk." She took a sip of water from one of the crystal goblets Elizabeth used for special occasions. "He's good. The team's been up and down this year. It's emotional for all of them — right there in the middle of New York."

"I bet. Tell him we're praying for him."

"I will."

John watched his second and fourth daughters. It was unusual that Erin hadn't talked about this with Kari before, but then they'd both been busy — Erin teaching a new classroom of children, and Kari spending her days with Jessie and driving to Indianapolis for modeling jobs once or twice a week. John wasn't sure Erin knew, but Kari was also doing extra reading and Bible study these days, getting ready for a ministry she hoped to start within the year. Pastor Mark had been meeting with her regularly about the idea.

Nearly everyone was finished eating. John wiped his mouth and folded his napkin on his plate. "It's time for the report."

It was a tradition they were all familiar with. Elizabeth called the older children in from the family room. "Okay . . ." She grinned at the children. "Everybody shares what they're thankful for."

"Can I go first?" Cole practically danced with delight. When John nodded, Cole announced that he was thankful for Legos and turkey. Then Cole named everyone present — "and Landon, because he's brave and he's my friend!"

"Very good, Cole," said Elizabeth. "And Maddie?"

Maddie was not nearly as outgoing as Cole. She thought about her list but finally mentioned her mother and her father and her kitty. Hailey, unsure what was going on, simply followed her sister's lead: "Kitty."

"All right, that's a good start." John

looked around the circle. "Who's next?"

Ashley raised her hand. She sat up straighter in her chair. "I'm thankful for the people at Sunset Hills. They're . . ." She searched for the right words. ". . . they're teaching me about life." She glanced down at Cole and kissed the tip of his nose. "And of course for my precious Cole." She looked around the table, her voice soft, tender, her attitude completely different from a year ago. "And for each of you." She hesitated. "I'm thankful because I feel like painting again and because I'm learning not to be afraid to love."

John was glad it wasn't his turn. He wouldn't have been able to speak if it were. He winked at Ashley and nodded, telling her the only way he could that he was proud of her.

Erin was next. "I'm thankful for my faith and my family, for the children I teach, and for the future God has for me." She didn't look at Sam, and John wondered why. Had she omitted him intentionally? He hoped not.

Sam and Peter were thankful for their families. When they were finished, the group turned their eyes on Brooke and waited. Her eyes glistened with tears. "I'm sorry it had to take a tragedy —" Her voice broke, and she pinched the bridge of her nose, searching for the strength to finish. Peter slipped his arm around her.

She sniffed and shook her head. "This is harder than I thought." She sighed and looked at the others once more. "Ever since September eleventh, life has been different for me. More real, I guess. I'm thankful for the wonder I see in my husband's eyes . . . for the flags flying across America . . . and for the way all of you have welcomed Peter and me at church. Even though we haven't been very supportive in the past." The tears pooled and spilled onto her cheeks. She smiled, though her lower lip and chin quivered. "And I'm thankful for my sweet angel girls. For their health . . ."

Maddie was still standing beside her mother. She lifted a tiny gentle finger and wiped a tear from her mother's face. "Don't cry, Mommy."

"It's okay, baby." Brooke framed Maddie's face with her fingertips. "This is the good kind of crying."

John brought his forearms up on the table and gazed at his oldest child and her daughter. Maddie's unexplained fevers bothered John. *Keep her healthy, please, God.*

Kari's eyes were damp too. She hesitated, waiting while Brooke used her napkin to dab beneath her eyes. Then she listed the things that mattered, the reasons she was thankful — Jessie and her family and faith. "But I'm especially grateful for life, that God has allowed me to find hope and a reason to go on. Even after all that's happened." She bit her lip, and John's heart went out to her.

Only a year ago, Tim had celebrated Thanksgiving with them. How completely life could change in the course of just twelve months. John sighed. No, it could change faster than that. Twenty-four hours were enough to change the course of history. If Americans had learned anything recently, they'd learned that. "Who's next?" he asked.

"Me!" Cole popped up from his chair, and everyone laughed.

"You already went." Elizabeth folded her arms, smiling at him. "Now it's Grandma's turn." She rattled off a list of names — everyone at the table and then some. Pastor Mark and Marilyn did more or less the same. Finally it was John's turn.

"Well, first I'm thankful for God's presence among us and for each of you." He felt his expression grow serious as he surveyed the people around him. "The changes this year have been remarkable. Some deeply painful . . ." He narrowed his eyes in Kari's direction, praying she could feel his love and concern. Then he looked at baby Jessie still asleep in the family room. "Some deeply joyful. We've seen relationships restored and the fires of faith fanned into being. But not without cost." He tightened the hold he had on Elizabeth's hand. Luke's face came to mind.

Then John bowed his head, and around him the others did the same. "God, I pray that you might be merciful to us in the coming year, that you continue to be the heartbeat of our home, the foundation of our family. That the scars from our recent tragedies won't remain forever. But that one day, however far from now, we might look back and be thankful for how you've brought us through."

Ashley crept upstairs after dessert. How strange the role reversal that had taken place between her and Luke since last year. Just twelve months ago Luke was cocky and judgmental, firing derogatory barbs at Ashley whenever he had the chance. He was the family's golden boy, full of laughter and zest for life. But he was also bent on seeing justice served at every turn, determined to do right no matter what errors his sisters might make.

Now, though, Luke had become angry and reclusive. Ever since Reagan left, he seemed to have a vendetta against God and nearly everyone else he cared about. In fact, he didn't seem able to relate to any of the family — except perhaps Ashley.

And as for the changes in her own heart, she knew they were partially due to Landon Blake. By letting her talk about Paris, he'd removed a splinter from her soul. In its absence, the place that had festered and bled and pained her was actually beginning to heal. Now some nights she and Cole would read together before bedtime, and Ashley would feel like shouting out loud over the obstacles she'd overcome this past year. She was learning to live again, learning to love. And every day she felt less afraid of her past, more confident that God did care about her after all.

Now maybe she could help Luke remember some of the same truths.

She knocked on his door and cautiously let herself in. "Hey, can I talk to you?"

He was sitting at his desk, his pen moving steadily across a pad of paper, his backpack slumped on the floor nearby. At the sound of her voice he set his pen down and looked over his shoulder. "Sure. Come on in."

Ashley took a spot at the end of his bed and waited while he swiveled his computer chair around to face her. "Homework?"

Luke glanced at his open notebook. "Yeah. Communications. I've got a project due."

She wrinkled her nose. Hadn't he said something about this assignment before? She and Luke had talked more often in the past two months than they had in years. "The one you're doing with that girl?"

"Lori Callahan. She sits beside me in class."

"I thought you finished that."

"Nope. Professor Hicks made it part of the final."

Ashley was quiet for a moment. She swung her foot and leaned back some. The last thing she wanted was to lecture him — especially after all he'd been through. Besides, she'd had plenty of years of feeling like an outsider, years when a lecture was the last thing *she* would have wanted. Whatever Luke's reasons, Ashley understood some of what he was going through. "You missed dessert."

Luke nodded. "I'll get some later."

"Okay." Ashley cocked her head. "So what's bugging you?"

He clenched his teeth, and Ashley was struck by how handsome her little brother was. Over the last few years, she'd done her best to avoid him. But now that their friendship was restored, it was as if she were seeing him for the first time.

The muscles in his jaw twitched. "All anyone ever wants to talk about is September eleventh." He leaned over and dug his elbows into his thighs. "I'm sick of it, I guess."

She studied him, not wanting to probe too deeply. Her tone was gentle. "Have you heard from Reagan?"

"I stopped calling last week." He linked his fingers together. "It took me that long to realize she wasn't busy or away from the phone or gone somewhere. We're finished." He dropped his gaze. "She doesn't want to talk to me."

Ashley shifted position. Reagan's pain and sorrow were understandable. Her silence was not. Whatever her reason for refusing Luke's calls, there had to be more to it than her father's death. "Maybe something else is wrong."

For a split second Ashley thought she saw a flash of guilt in Luke's eyes, but it was gone before she could be sure. Luke inhaled sharply and lifted his chin. "It's over, Ashley. Everything the two of us shared died right along with her father when that building collapsed." He exhaled through tight lips. "I can't do anything about it."

"Okay." She slid back some and grabbed his pillow, lodging it beneath her elbow as she stretched across his bed. "What else?"

"What else?" He twisted his brow. "Isn't that enough?"

"You know what I mean, Luke." She was careful to keep her tone kind. "You're avoiding practically everyone in the family, like you're mad at them."

Luke stood up and paced to the door and back. "Maybe the whole America thing is getting to me." He stared at her. "I mean, isn't it weird? Everyone's suddenly waving flags and going to church. Because of what? Because terrorists found our weak spot?"

Confusion clouded his features. "If it weren't for the Clinton administration, we could have avoided the whole disaster. They let Osama bin Laden attack us three times and never did anything to stop him. Now we're reaping the results. That's supposed to make me want to wave a flag?"

"I know what you mean." Ashley waited. "At first, I didn't really get the flag thing either." She rolled onto her back and doubled the pillow behind her head. "But now I do. People aren't feeling proud about America's mistakes. It's more like a unity thing. We've been knocked down, but we're Americans. We'll get back up." She paused, her voice still soft. "You know?"

He huffed and dropped back into his chair. "I guess." His eyes grew hard. "Then there's the whole God thing. You know me, Ashley. My faith used to be stronger than . . . than cement. But not anymore." He gazed out his window at the setting sun. "I keep thinking, what's the point?"

Ashley was quiet, giving him the chance to continue.

A single laugh came from his lips. "Since September eleventh, people have been flooding the churches. That's what all the newspapers say, and it's true. Look at you and Brooke and Peter." He motioned in her direction. "Why, Ashley? Why do you go?"

"I don't know, really." She sat up and hugged the pillow to her stomach. "September eleventh made me remember what's important in life. Thousands of people go to work one day, and then, in the space of

426

an hour, they're all snuffed out." She paused. "I guess the people I work with at Sunset Hills have something to do with it too. Every day, sitting there watching television, waiting to die." She shrugged. "Church is the only place I find hope and meaning lately. Where all the senselessness makes a little sense."

He squinted at her. "You mean you buy into the whole God thing now? You believe he's there, watching over us — all that stuff?"

"I don't know what I believe." She reached out and squeezed his sock-covered foot. "I just know that lately I feel better believing that God has a plan, even when things are crazy and out of control."

"So what plan could he have? And what's the point of praying when God — if there is a God — is going to do whatever he wants, anyway?" Luke's voice fell, and he leaned forward, his eyes glistening. "I begged him to let Reagan's father live. But that didn't happen."

Ashley wanted to stop the conversation and hug him, tell him it was okay, that they didn't have to talk about this. But she knew it wasn't okay. And he seemed determined to continue.

"Then I got this communications assignment." He waved at the notebook behind him. "Prove God or disprove him. Back your decision with evidence. I said, 'Okay, fine, God. Now's your chance. You can prove you're real by letting things work out between me and Reagan.' " He tossed his hands in the air. "And what's happened? She won't even take my calls."

Ashley was still thinking about the assignment. "Your communications prof asked you to prove or disprove God?"

"Yeah." Luke crossed his arms, the fight suddenly gone. "He won't actually say it, but he believes the only valid worldview is humanism. You know, belief in reason and the human spirit — people choosing whether to pursue goodness or evil. It makes sense. I mean, people help each other, and the results are obvious — like what's happened since September eleventh. God doesn't help us. We help ourselves!"

Ashley was hardly a Bible scholar, but even she knew a theory like Luke was describing flew in the face of their family's beliefs — the beliefs he himself had clung to before the terrorist attacks. She dug her elbows into the pillow and searched Luke's face. "Which side are you taking?"

Luke was silent. His gaze fell to the floor

again, and something defiant filtered through his expression. "I wasn't sure until Lori talked to me."

"The girl who sits next to you?"

His eyes lifted, and she felt a distance between Luke and her, a distance that hadn't been there a minute ago.

"She's been taking me to these meetings about reason and freethinking. Her father's an attorney for this civil-liberties group in Washington, D.C. He's helping us on the assignment."

This time alarms sounded in Ashley's soul. Something about his references to "freethinking" and "civil liberties" — phrases she had heard before from some of the people at the clubs she used to frequent. "You're trying to disprove God?" Her voice was barely a whisper.

If this had been anyone else, she wouldn't have been concerned. People questioned God, after all. Look how long she herself had questioned him.

But Luke? Their steadfastly conservative brother? No wonder he hadn't been hanging around the family lately. He probably felt like an outcast — the same way she'd felt all those years after returning from Paris. "What . . . what kind of evidence are you finding?"

Another humorless laugh came from him. "The terrorist attacks are a great place to start. What sort of God would allow that to happen?" He leaned back in his chair. "The fact that so few people were found alive in the rubble is more proof. People talk about miracles happening. What miracles? Everything that happened that day was random."

A look that was more sad than angry filled his eyes. "Humanism is the only view that makes sense of what's happening. You know — people giving blood, donating money, supporting the victims, that kind of thing. Stuff God can't take credit for."

Ashley resisted the urge to wince. What had Pastor Mark said last Sunday about the volunteers in New York? "Watching them on TV is like watching Jesus with skin. God's at work all over the city." She thought about telling that to Luke or reminding him of something the pastor had said the week before — that evidence of God *is* all around, as close as the nearest tree or river or mountain.

But she stopped herself. This wasn't the time, and she wasn't sure she was up to the argument. The best she could do now was show him she cared.

When he was finished talking, she

climbed off the bed, walked over to him, and wrapped her arms around his neck. "As hard as everything seems right now, deep inside, you know God's real. And one day everything about him will make sense again. Just like it's starting to make sense for me." She kissed his cheek and shot him a half-grin. "Until then, remember something, will you?"

His expression softened. "What?"

"I love you." She messed up his hair. "And everybody else around here loves you."

"Thanks." He gave her a troubled smile. "I love you too. I wish I wasn't so grouchy."

"It's okay. We all have our seasons."

They were quiet for a bit. "Ashley?" His eyes met hers.

"Yeah?"

"I'm sorry."

"About what?"

"About . . . about the way I treated you the last few years." He hugged her again. "I've been a jerk. Do you forgive me?"

"Sure." A sting of tears flashed in her eyes, and she felt her heart constrict. "I'm just glad things are okay now."

On her way home that night with Cole, Ashley thought about Luke's assignment and the idea of proving God. Crazy, brokenhearted Luke. He was too miserable to see the evidence that existed all around him.

Okay, so maybe she wasn't where she should be with God. After all, she'd started praying again only because Landon had asked her to. And maybe she hadn't figured out exactly what Bible verses to read for any given situation.

But God was real. She had no doubt about that.

Luke's apology played over in her mind. *"Do you forgive me? . . . Do you forgive me?"* After Paris, she had been sure the two of them would never be civil to each other again, let alone find that special something they once shared. But now . . . now they actually loved each other again.

She brushed away two fresh tears as she pulled into her driveway.

If that wasn't evidence God was real, nothing was.

Chapter Twenty-Six

Kari had just laid Jessie down to sleep when the phone rang.

She glanced at her watch. Nine o'clock. Ryan's hour, the same time he always called. And since the attacks on America, he'd called every week. Sometimes twice or three times a week. Kari might have been busy, but she wasn't so busy that she didn't notice a pattern developing.

Not only was Ryan calling more often, but she was starting to count on hearing from him.

She found the cordless phone on an end table in the living room and clicked the Talk button. "Hello?"

"Hey."

"Hi." The sound of Ryan's voice made her feel fifteen again. She was beginning to accept the idea that she could no more stop herself from loving Ryan Taylor than she could stop breathing. The interesting thing was that lately she felt less guilty about it. Maybe that was another sign that she was healing, moving on with life. "How's my favorite football coach?"

"Trapped in the middle of a two-game losing streak." His tone was soft, thoughtful.

"It'll turn around."

"Yeah." Ryan yawned. "I hope so. We have twice as many meetings when we lose."

Kari stretched out on the sofa. It had been months since she'd seen Ryan. But every time they spoke, despite the distance, she could feel him right there, sitting across from her. She closed her eyes and pretended he actually was. "Hey, I meant to ask you last time — have you seen Landon lately?"

"No. The team hasn't been to Ground Zero in a week or so. The schedule has us swamped."

"Are there still lots of volunteers?"

Ryan paused, and she could almost see him gazing out the window of his high-rise apartment, searching for the words to describe what was happening around him. "I've never seen anything like it, Kari."

"The support, you mean?"

"Flags flying everywhere. I mean, you can't look down a single street in New York without seeing dozens of them strung

434

up on buildings, flying from office windows, mounted in planters along the storefronts."

"It's like that here, too. People have flags on their cars, their shirts, their bikes. It's like the whole country woke up and realized what a great place America really is."

"Exactly." Ryan sighed. "I never thought I'd say this, but I feel a connection to the people of New York. After working down at Ground Zero, handing out water to rescue workers, seeing how they rarely take a break . . . I don't know, Kari. It gets in your blood."

Like football, Kari wanted to say. A strange feeling washed over her. This bond with New York was something new, something she didn't share with Ryan. She had always pictured him coming back to Bloomington eventually, but maybe he wouldn't. Her heart sank several inches. Maybe her feelings for Ryan were no more practical now than they'd ever been. "It must be amazing, being right there in the middle of it."

"We feel it every time we fly home after a road game." His tone was thoughtful, deep. "It's almost like we're part of the war, especially here. Just by choosing to fly into New York, we're taking a risk, but we're also making a statement to terrorists: 'Go ahead and try to defeat us. We're still standing. In fact, we're standing closer together than ever before.' "

"I never thought of it that way."

"You will. First time you fly to New York." Ryan hesitated, and his tone lightened. "Hey, that's not a bad idea. What about coming to New York for a game? You could bring Jessie, stay at the hotel near the training complex. Just for a few days, Saturday to Monday — something like that."

Kari imagined such a weekend. Ryan would be absorbed in football meetings, team dinners, and the events of game day. She thought back to Ryan's years as a player and the times she'd been around him then. The wives and girlfriends tended to stay together in a comfortable clique, mostly because the men were too busy to join them. Then there were the groupies, the scantily clad women who waited on the fringe of every dinner or postgame gathering.

Ryan was kind to ask, but where would she and Jessie fit into that picture? "I don't think so." Her voice was tinged with sadness. "Not this season. Jessie's too young and . . . well, I wouldn't know anyone."

He exhaled just loud enough for her to hear. "That's what I thought you'd say."

Kari couldn't tell if Ryan was frustrated or just disappointed. She shifted onto her side and stared across her empty living room. "Are you mad?"

"Of course not." Ryan paused. The line was so quiet she could hear him breathing. "How's Jessie?"

Kari was glad he'd changed topics. "Growing fast."

His voice was softer than before. "I bet."

"Can you believe she's nearly seven months already?"

"Wow." Ryan was quiet for a moment. Was he thinking the same thing she was? That if Jessie was seven months old, it had been that long since they'd seen each other. "Is she sitting up yet?"

"Almost. And she rolls over all the time now."

A subtle beep sounded in Kari's ear. "Is that your other line?"

"Yeah, hold on." When he came back his tone was different, more rushed. "Hey, Kari, I have to take that call. Talk to you later this week, okay?"

"Okay." She struggled to hide her disappointment. "Be safe."

"I will."

Kari felt like someone had thrown a wet rag across her heart. Ryan's phone calls usually lasted half an hour at least. They gave her something to look forward to.

After she hung up, she meandered about the house, then decided to turn in early. Why hadn't Ryan offered to come to Bloomington? Was he so caught up in the experience of coaching and living in New York that the idea of visiting her hadn't even occurred to him?

And where exactly was their long-distance relationship going, anyway? They never discussed their deep feelings, never so much as talked about missing each other, let alone loving each other. Maybe he called her only out of some nostalgic sense of friendship and loyalty. After all, they had chosen to go on with their lives long before Tim was murdered. Maybe Ryan merely felt sorry for her, a single mother, raising Jessie by herself.

What are the plans you have for me, God? When will you let me know?

She slid under the covers and closed her eyes. Of course, the Lord had already showed her part of his plans for her. Pastor Mark had told her she might be ready to start her ministry soon. In the meantime he wanted her to start meeting with an older woman in the church, someone who shared her heart for helping women in pain. The counseling materials he'd given her had helped too. They'd taught her how to remember God's truth about relationships.

"It's all about remembering what's important," Pastor Mark had explained during one of Kari's meetings with him. "You'll help the women remember how to love. That type of memory becomes a model they'll follow as their hearts heal."

Remember God's truth. . . . Remember what's important. . . . Remember how to love.

Remembering was a theme that seemed to run through everything that mattered since the attacks: Landon honoring his friend's memory by sifting through the rubble; Ashley helping her Alzheimer's patients live in a place that held happy memories. Very simply, a healthy soul was one that took time to remember.

But what about her and Ryan? Why was she so anxious for his calls lately? And why did she spend so little time thinking of Tim these days?

Kari shifted to her side and pulled the sheets up close to her chin. Somehow, the events of September 11 had served to distance Kari from the pain of losing Tim.

But maybe that was wrong. Maybe she was still supposed to be honoring Tim's memory, thinking about him every hour.

Say something, Lord. Tell me if my feelings for Ryan are wrong. How can I know what to do when he's so far away? Certainly my healing doesn't dishonor Tim.

My thoughts are not your thoughts, neither are your ways my ways, daughter.

Kari blinked her eyes open.

Was that God speaking to her? Whispering to the secret places of her soul? The words were from Isaiah 55 — part of a verse she'd seen in some of the material she was studying. But were they the Lord's answer for her now? If so, what did the words mean?

Do you have a different *plan for me, God? Something I couldn't imagine?*

Maybe God planned to let Ryan fade from her life, to become a memory instead of a constant presence. That would be different — and definitely something she couldn't imagine.

Kari exhaled hard. That couldn't possibly be God's plan for her, could it?

Then she thought of something that made her eyes open wider. For all she knew, the caller who had broken through her conversation with Ryan might have been a woman, someone he was seeing — maybe someone he was getting serious about.

Kari closed her eyes again. As she tried to fall asleep, questions pelted her like hail. For some reason she was afraid of the answers — because it didn't matter how Ryan felt about her or which Scripture verses flashed in her mind. The cloud of guilt and grief that had hung over her for months was finally dissipating, and in its absence Kari's feelings for Ryan were as clear as the afternoon sun.

She loved him.

Because of that, Ryan's plans really weren't the issue. Since she'd first met him she'd never taken the initiative, never been bold enough to truly declare her feelings for him. But now she was a grown woman, a woman who'd learned much these past months. It was no longer enough to let life happen around her. Not anymore.

She sucked in a slow breath, once more wide awake. It was finally time to act on her feelings.

Ideas swirled through her mind until she formed a plan — a marvelous, daring plan that was completely out of character for her. In fact, she could barely sleep from the sheer exhilaration of what she was about to do.

She'd lost Ryan once before when she'd waited too long, guessing at his feelings. But she'd learned a few things since then, and now she was suddenly sure of this much.

She wasn't going to make the same mistake again.

Chapter Twenty-Seven

Ashley's eBay item arrived on Monday afternoon.

She opened the package and inhaled sharply. It was just what she needed — an old western saddle she'd won by bidding just forty-two dollars. Yes, the left stirrup was missing, but the saddle was large enough for an adult and had beautiful markings etched into the black leather.

Ashley had priced used saddles at local tack shops and been quoted prices as high as five hundred dollars — far above her budget.

This one was perfect. So was the worn old sawhorse she'd picked up at the lumber store. The manager had found it in a storage area and had been happy to get rid of it. He'd given it to her for nothing and suggested eBay for the saddle.

On Tuesday morning, Ashley loaded both items into the back of her car. She left them there when she went in for her shift; the last thing she wanted was for

Belinda to walk in on her as she hauled a saddle and sawhorse to Bert's room. Better to wait until Belinda was busy with paperwork. If Ashley could manage to get the saddle into Bert's room, she'd be home free. Belinda rarely went into Bert's room.

Ashley hated to think what would happen if Belinda did find out about her plan. Already the woman was not happy with Ashley. She was constantly removing the sheet from the bathroom mirror, and when she saw Irvel's wall of photos she'd accused Ashley of having too much time on her hands. She didn't know yet that Sue Brown was pretending to be Helen's friend rather than her daughter. But if Belinda found out, Ashley was certain there'd be trouble. Orchestrating conversations that did not pertain to reality was, in a sense, going against house rules.

"Step too far out of line and you're finished," Belinda had told Ashley recently. "Don't push it. You're not in charge here; I am, and Lu listens to me. Give me one reason, and you're gone."

Ashley didn't want the saddle and sawhorse to be the reason.

She locked the car and went inside. Belinda wasn't there yet, but the woman could show up any minute. Ashley said good-bye to the night-shift care worker, then made breakfast, changed diapers, and helped Irvel and her friends to the table. Once they were seated, Ashley served them each a bowl of hot cereal and a cup of peppermint tea. Then she joined them.

"So" — she looked around the table — "how's everyone today?"

Irvel looked particularly rested, her face relatively smooth and free of the worry lines that she sometimes woke up with. "Hank has been nothing but wonderful to me, dear. It's been a lovely week."

The old woman had such a way of tugging at Ashley's heart. She angled her head, seeing Irvel as she must have been two decades earlier, back when she and Hank had shared the same soul. Of course, now that the old dear woke up to Hank's pictures, she was bound to feel more secure. "That's wonderful, Irvel."

Sunlight streamed through the window despite two inches of rain that had fallen the night before. Irvel smiled at her. "You know, dear, in this light you have the most beautiful hair. Has anyone ever told you that?"

"Not today, Irvel." Ashley remembered that Landon had said that exact thing, teasing her on one of their lazy summer days.

Back before the world was knocked off its axis that September morning.

"Well, it's true." Irvel looked at Edith. "Don't you think so?"

"Yes, I like her hair." Edith looked at Ashley for a moment. "It's a nice shade."

Helen lowered her chin and stared at Ashley over her oatmeal bowl. "With hair like that, it's a good thing you've been checked. Sue was checked, but not during breakfast." She picked up her spoon and took a bite of the hot cereal.

Ashley smothered a smile behind her hands. Back when she first started working at Sunset Hills, Helen would have slammed her fist on the table or slapped her leg for emphasis. Not now. The streak of belligerence that seemed to color her personality had faded considerably. Ashley had to believe this was because of Helen's conversations with her daughter. She had a connection to Sue now, no matter how distant. As a result, life was better for all of them.

"You *have* been checked, haven't you?" Helen raised an eye in Ashley's direction once more. "Spies run the place, you know. There was a fellow on TV the other day

. . . looked wild and crazy. Wacky face." She tapped a finger against her temple. "A big zero up here. He was a spy, I know it. But no one ever checked him."

"Yes, Helen, I've been checked. Just before I came in. I'm not a spy."

"Good." She gave a quick nod. "Is that old lady coming to visit today? The nice one — knows my daughter?"

"I believe she is." Ashley was glad Sue hadn't heard that description of herself — especially coming from her mother.

"She's not a spy." Helen blew on her cereal.

"No, Helen, she's not." Sue came by often now. Every time they were together, Ashley's heart picked up hope. Maybe one day, if the friendship between Sue and Helen continued, Helen might actually accept Sue for who she was — her only daughter.

Irvel set down her spoon and stared at Helen. "I'm Irvel." She held out her hand. "Glad you could join us today."

Helen left Irvel's hand hanging and looked across the table at Edith. "Who are you?"

"Me?" The question seemed to stump Edith for a moment. "Edith . . . I'm Edith." The spoon shook in her hand, her voice uncertain. "That's right, isn't it?"

447

"Yes, Edith." Ashley kept her voice calm and confident. She had noticed that the residents did better when the caretakers didn't react to their questions with sarcasm or exasperation, the way Belinda did on a routine basis.

"Edith's our friend," Irvel said. She patted Edith's hand and looked at Helen with politely raised eyebrows. "And you are . . . ?"

"You know who I am!" Helen lowered her brow. "I make sure people get checked around here."

"This is Helen." Ashley gave Irvel a knowing smile. "She's our friend, too."

"This tea is just wonderful." Irvel pointed to Helen's cup. "You should try it." She glanced at her watch, a delicate old silver bangle she wore night and day. Ashley had a feeling it had been a gift from Hank. Irvel took a slow sip of her tea. "Hank will be here in an hour or two, so drink up, Ingrid. Tea is best when it's hot."

Edith tapped Irvel on the shoulder. "I'm not Ingrid. I'm Edith." She pointed to Ashley. "That girl said so."

Ashley sat back and watched with a mixture of amusement and sadness as the conversation unfolded. They really didn't know. These women lived together, ate every meal together, and spent their days in each other's company. But every morning they had no idea who the people around the table were. Introductions were part of their daily routine.

The disease was that wicked.

And although she'd found a way to stop Edith from screaming, there was nothing Ashley could do to clear the permanent fog that clouded the woman's memory. The research Ashley had read said that helping people live at the point in time where they felt most comfortable sometimes worked to restore memory loss. But not always. And clearly not for Edith.

Irvel shook her head and shot Edith a knowing smile. "I know you're Edith." She pointed to Helen. "I mean her. Ingrid over there. The one that's always checking people."

"My name's Helen." An irritated look filled Helen's eyes, and she looked at Ashley for help. "What's with her?" She pointed at Irvel. "The old bat can't remember anything!"

"Actually, I was thinking we could play a friendly game of bridge until Hank gets here." Irvel glanced at the others. "No wagering, though. Hank says the good Lord looks down on wagering."

"Is this scrambled eggs?" Edith poked her spoon into the oatmeal three times. "It doesn't look like eggs."

Irvel shot a look down the bridge of her delicate nose at the food in Edith's bowl. "Dear . . ." She rolled her eyes in Ashley's direction. "That's not eggs. It's corn cereal. Your mother fixed it for us."

"That's ridiculous." Helen raised her hand but stopped short of slamming it on the table. "My mother makes lasagna. She made it today." Helen peered into the kitchen. "But every time she makes it, someone steals it. Just like Sue. They stole my daughter, too. Things are always getting stolen around here."

Irvel sighed as though it was all she could do to be patient with the women on either side of her. "Not *your* mother, Ingrid. *Edith's* mother. Edith's mother made the corn cereal this morning."

"I'm not Ingrid," Helen growled. "Ingrid's in the other room."

Edith hadn't eaten a bite since she'd asked about the contents of her bowl. Now she mouthed the word *mother,* her eyes wide and fearful. "Mother?" She glanced around. "Mother?"

"Spies." Helen shook her head, disgusted. "It's the spies that steal things."

Here we go. . . . Ashley drew a deep breath. Every now and then a healthy dose of reality was necessary to get the conversation back on track. "Actually, *I* fixed the oatmeal this morning."

Edith stared at her. "You're not my mother."

"No," Irvel cut in. "She's not your mother. But she does have beautiful hair. Don't you think so, girls? I've never seen hair like that before."

Ashley could hardly wait for naptime.

All she could think about was the saddle and sawhorse in the trunk of her car, and the way Bert would react when he saw it. Would he recognize the feel of leather? Be drawn to the smell? Would it take him back the way she hoped it would — back to a time when he was useful and needed? If so, it was possible he might regain some of his communication skills. At least that's what the Past-Present school of research taught.

Despite the reigning confusion, the morning went well. Ashley made sure the sheet was over the bathroom mirror, and Edith seemed completely at ease. Irvel had only to look at her bedroom wall to know Hank was nearby. And Helen had asked again about the "nice old woman" who came to talk about Sue.

Sometime during breakfast, Belinda slunk in through the front door and headed back to the office without saying a word. Ashley was glad. The two of them got along better when they avoided each other.

By ten o'clock, the residents had been bathed and were nestled into their chairs for their morning naps. Laura Jo seemed worse. She'd barely eaten anything for three days, and she slept nearly all the time. Ashley looked in at her and quietly came to her side. "Laura Jo?" Ashley took hold of the woman's water cup and worked the straw between Laura Jo's dry lips. The woman took two slow drinks.

Ashley waited. "Are you okay?"

The woman moaned and rolled her head a few inches toward Ashley. She was shrunken; her bones practically poked through her skin. Last time Ashley had checked the woman's health chart, Laura Jo's weight had dropped below eighty pounds. Her doctor had said it would be only a matter of weeks.

Belinda was already taking applications for her bedroom.

"I'm here, Laura Jo." Ashley took hold of the woman's fingers and ran her thumb over the fine bones along the back of her hand. "If you need anything, let me know."

Laura Jo worked her lips as though she was trying to say something. Finally a single word sounded. "Pray."

Pray? Ashley's nerves jingled like wind chimes. "What's that, Laura Jo? I'm here for you, dear. Whatever you need."

Again the woman worked her mouth. "P-p-pray. Pray."

This time Ashley had no doubt. She swallowed her fear. "You want to pray?"

In a small, barely detectable movement, Laura Jo nodded.

Great. Ashley felt a fine layer of perspiration break out across her brow. She couldn't pray with Laura Jo. She wasn't the right person for the job. It was one thing to pray silently for Landon or talk to God in church. But aloud? For a dying woman? Laura Jo needed someone in good standing with the Lord to say that kind of prayer, someone who would know a Bible verse or two, someone to give her peace in her final moments. "You . . . you want *me* to pray?"

Moving like a Disney mannequin on low batteries, Laura Jo nodded. "Praaaay." She gave Ashley a faint squeeze of her fingers.

Oh, boy. The pounding in Ashley's chest

was so loud she was afraid it would frighten the old woman. *I don't know what to say, God. Help me.*

Remember the days of your youth, daughter. Remember . . .

Ashley jerked back an inch. Remember the days of her youth? Where had that come from?

Laura Jo hadn't said it, and there was no one else in the room.

Besides, the words were silent. Almost as though someone had spoken them directly to her heart.

Then it hit her. Could it be God speaking? Was he asking her to remember her childhood, the way she'd prayed aloud back then?

A memory filled her mind. She and Kari as children, holding hands beside their sick puppy. "God, make Brownie better. Please, God." She'd prayed then, hadn't she? Simple words voicing out loud the request closest to her heart.

But that had been more than a decade ago. Could she do it here? For this dying woman? Ashley did a quiet gulp and opened her mouth. *Help me, God. I don't know what to say.*

Then, as though God himself was providing her a script, the words — almost childlike — began to come. "Lord, help Laura Jo. . . ." Ashley's voice was shaky, nervous. But somehow she found the strength to continue. "Be here, and hold her hand . . . please, God. Make her feel happy inside, and be gentle with her."

Tears blurred the image of the old woman's face, and Ashley blinked, struggling to see. "Pretty soon she'll be . . ." Her voice caught, and she noticed that the wrinkles around Laura Jo's mouth had eased some. The urgency she'd had moments before was gone.

Ashley worked to finish. "Pretty soon she'll be home in your arms." Ashley leaned over and kissed Laura Jo's cold, hollow cheek. "Until then, stay with her, God. Give her your peace, and hold her hand so she's never, ever alone."

Ashley felt herself relax. She'd done it! She drew a slow breath and finished the prayer. "I ask this in Jesus' name. Amen."

She smoothed her fingertips over Laura Jo's brow. "Do you feel better now, honey?"

Laura Jo gave a single nod of her head, and in a few seconds she was snoring.

Ashley realized she'd been holding her breath, and she finally exhaled, trembling at what had just happened. She had actually prayed out loud!

The prayers she'd been saying on Landon's behalf had helped her know it was possible. No matter how bad her past, she could initiate conversation with God. But this? These words had obviously come from God himself. What other explanation was there?

Ashley was still overwhelmed by the incident as she drifted from Laura Jo's room and checked to make sure Belinda was busy in the office. When she heard Belinda talking on the phone, she slipped out the back door and headed for her car. She heaved the saddle from the trunk and carefully removed the sawhorse. It was a bit rickety already, and she didn't want to break it before getting it to Bert's room.

The saddle had to weigh twenty pounds by itself, and Ashley set it on the sawhorse. Then she carried the combination up the walk and inside. She was halfway down the hallway toward Bert's room when Belinda rounded the corner at the other end and stopped short, her eyes wide.

"What . . . are you doing?" She strode the remaining steps that separated them and glared at the saddle and sawhorse. "What is this?"

Think of something, Ashley told herself.

But the only explanation that seemed to make sense was the truth. "Bert was a saddle maker." Ashley set the sawhorse down in the hallway and met Belinda's look head-on. "Did you know that?"

Belinda's hands flew to her hips. "So?" She jerked her head toward the sawhorse and saddle. "What're you doing with that — that *thing* in the house?"

"Well . . ." Ashley kept her voice calm. Maybe if she didn't overreact, Belinda wouldn't either. "I thought I'd set it up in Bert's room. That way he wouldn't have to polish the comforter anymore. He could have a saddle to shine . . . like he used to back when he —"

"A saddle? Are you out of your mind?" Belinda's voice was a study in controlled fury. The woman knew better than to yell and wake a houseful of sleeping Alzheimer's patients. But she was angrier than Ashley had ever seen her.

"It's worth a try." Ashley sighed and leaned on the sawhorse. "What would it hurt?"

Belinda's face was red. "Bert's delusional." She pointed at Ashley. "And so are you." Her gaze fell to the sawhorse again, but this time she kicked it, knocking it on its side and sending the saddle skittering three feet down the hallway.

"Hey, wait a minute!" Ashley reached for the saddle, but Belinda stepped in the way.

"You're fired, Baxter. I've had all I can take." She gestured to the saddle and sawhorse. "Get your things, and get out. I'll call Lu and tell her to cut you your last check. She'll back me up."

Ashley felt the blood drain from her face. "Belinda, I think we should talk about this before —"

Belinda raised a hand, cutting her off. "There's nothing to talk about. Get your things, and go."

For a moment their eyes met, and Ashley knew it was over. There wasn't an ounce of give in Belinda, and talking would do no good. Technically, of course, Belinda didn't have the authority to fire her; that right belonged to Lu. She even thought about going to the office and calling Lu, explaining what had happened. But Lu would be on Belinda's side. Belinda was the faithful manager, Ashley merely the newly hired help. Besides, Belinda had already complained to the owner about Ashley a dozen times; Lu had said so. The woman would have no choice but to side with Belinda.

Ashley picked up the saddle and stared

at her boss. "You're serious, aren't you?"

"You bet I'm serious! You don't just waltz into a place like Sunset Hills and change everything. That's not how it works."

Belinda stepped back and surveyed Ashley.

Something about the look in her eyes seemed familiar to Ashley. Suddenly Ashley recognized the same mixture of anger and arrogance she'd seen in Jean-Claude Pierre the last time they saw each other. "But who will take care —"

"I'll take care of the patients until Krista gets here." Belinda narrowed her eyes. "You have five minutes to pack your things and leave."

Ashley's heart raced as she picked up the saddle and sawhorse and carried both items back to the car. Then she went inside again and gathered her files, the ones she'd made about the residents. She grabbed her purse and coat and found Irvel and Helen and Edith snoring peacefully in their recliners.

Was this really it? She was being forced to leave without even saying good-bye?

In the corner of the room she saw Belinda take up her position, watching her, making sure she did as she was told. Ashley didn't care. There was something she had to do before she could go.

She walked up to Edith and hugged her, tucking her face alongside the old woman's and stroking her wiry white hair. "Good-bye, Edith. May God watch over you."

Then she did the same to Helen and finally, Irvel. "I don't know how, Irvel, but someday I'll see you again." Tears burned a trail down either side of Ashley's face. "You take care of Hank."

When she was finished saying good-bye, she slipped on her coat and took one last look around the room. Then, without turning back, she headed to her car. The cold morning stung at her damp cheeks, and she wiped them with the sleeve of her coat. She glanced at the house once more, climbed into her car, and started the engine.

"God, help me." Now that she'd prayed with Laura Jo, the words came more easily, as though they'd been there all along. Ashley leaned her head on the steering wheel for a moment. "What am I going to do?"

Irvel and Edith and Helen felt like family. How was she supposed to walk out on them now — just when they were starting to make progress? Who would make sure the mirror stayed covered for

Edith? And who would encourage Sue to continue her friendship with Helen? Most of all, who would assure Irvel that Hank was coming back?

It was all so unfair.

The tears came harder as Ashley pulled away. It was just as well that Irvel and her friends were asleep. Her tears would have troubled the poor dears. And what would be the point of that?

After today, they wouldn't remember her anyway.

Chapter Twenty-Eight

The taxi couldn't go fast enough.

Once Kari landed at La Guardia Airport, it was all she could do to bide her time until she could finally see Ryan. The trip was a surprise, something she'd been planning since the last time they spoke.

Kari had checked the Giants' schedule. The team had a bye on December 2. She wasn't sure how much Ryan would be tied up that weekend, but she knew he wasn't leaving the city. He'd told her that much.

It was four-thirty Thursday afternoon, and Kari figured she'd arrive at Ryan's apartment first, take him to dinner, and then find a hotel where she could spend the next few nights.

A quiet chuckle eased from her throat as she gazed out the taxi window at the busy streets. Her parents hadn't believed her when she first brought up the idea.

"Just like that?" Her mother's mouth had hung open. "You're going to New York?"

"Right." Kari had grinned, feeling more alive than she'd felt in weeks. "And I need you to watch Jessie."

"Where" — Kari's father swallowed hard — "where will you stay?"

"Dad!" Kari's face had grown hot. "At a hotel. Of course."

"Your father and I have decided nothing would surprise us at this point, dear."

"Besides, I'm a grown woman. I can go to New York if I want to."

"I know." Her father had stepped closer and kissed her forehead. "Just be careful. It's still . . ."

"Soon?"

"Right." He moved back beside her mother and repeated, "Be careful."

"Dad, I've lived in New York, remember? And I've known Ryan forever." She looked at her mother. "In all my life, I've never acted on my feelings for him. Until now."

Her mother looked alarmed. "What exactly are you planning?"

"A visit." Kari spread her hands in front of her. "Nothing more. Just a way of letting him know he's still in my heart."

"He is, isn't he?" Her father's frown faded.

"Yes." Kari's voice had grown soft. "I

think about him all the time."

"Then go." Her mother smiled, the concern gone from her expression. "If September eleventh taught us anything, it was that life is short. If you care about Ryan, tell him. And let God take it from there."

The taxi was closer now, moving through the heart of the city. Kari peered out the window, mentally comparing what she saw with what she remembered from her modeling days. They passed barricaded streets and boarded-up windows. American flags flew in countless storefronts, along sides of buildings, and from nearly every car and cab in the area. Maybe it was her imagination, but she seemed to see a difference in the eyes of the people teeming along either side of the street. A depth of loss and camaraderie Kari hadn't seen before.

The effect sent a chill down her spine and brought goose bumps to her arms and legs.

"How many more miles?" She leaned forward so the driver could hear her.

"Five or six."

"Thanks." It was then that she noticed two photographs taped to the driver's dashboard. One was of a police officer, the other of a woman in a uniform of some kind. Both looked uncannily like the driver.

Kari hesitated but couldn't help herself. She pointed at the pictures. "Are they family?"

"My son and my sister. Haven't found either of 'em."

"I'm . . . I'm sorry." Kari felt her heart settle several inches deeper in her chest. Why had she asked, anyway? The tragedy that had happened here wasn't merely a spectacle to be gazed at. It was real life, affecting real people — people like this cabdriver, who would never see his loved ones again.

The chill was gone. In its place a sobering reality surrounded her. She'd be more careful with her questions next time.

Her thoughts turned to Ryan once more, and she glanced at her hand. She'd taken her wedding ring off and placed it in a velvet box she kept in the bottom drawer of her bedroom dresser. It was time . . . and one day little Jessie might want it.

Kari glanced at the ticking meter. Five more miles. How would it feel to be with him again? The two of them had gone through so many seasons in life, so many highs and lows. Of course she needed to go to him now. She loved him, and there wasn't a thing she could do about it. Maybe it *was* too early. But every time she prayed about the situation, she came away feeling the same. Now that the fog of Tim's death was beginning to clear, now that she'd spent time healing, now that she'd studied and prayed and searched her heart . . . the truth was both simple and obvious.

Ryan Taylor was everything to her. And she needed to let him know.

The maze of streets seemed to go on forever, but finally the driver pulled up outside an apartment complex. A doorman stood guard at the front.

"This is it." The driver nodded to the meter. "I prefer cash if you got it."

Kari doled out the amount along with a healthy tip. "I hope they find them. Your son and your sister."

The man nodded but said nothing. As Kari climbed out and grabbed her bag, she saw him wipe a tear. She stood next to her suitcase on the curb and watched the taxi pull away. *Help him, God. Bring him peace, please.*

There was no still small voice above the roar of the city. But God had heard her — that was the important thing. And she'd learned something from the cabdriver: being in New York City was going to be harder than she'd thought.

She turned to the doorman. "I'm here to see a friend of mine."

"His name?" The man's posture was stiff, but there was compassion in his tone.

"Ryan Taylor."

"Is he expecting you?"

"No." Butterflies swarmed in Kari's gut. "Can I go up anyway?"

The man showed a hint of a smile. "I need to ring him first." He turned to a panel of buttons and picked up a telephone receiver. Kari couldn't hear any part of the conversation.

After a few seconds, the man turned to her. "Go ahead." He told her the apartment number and turned a key that opened a door to the lobby.

Kari wheeled her bag through the double doors and toward the bank of elevators. Suddenly she felt nervous, the same old doubts crowding back into her mind. What if he wasn't glad to see her? What if his feelings for her had changed months ago, back when she had been so desperate to work things out with Tim? Maybe he would think her presumptuous for showing up unannounced.

No, that wasn't possible. He'd asked her to come, after all. And now she was here.

The elevator rode smoothly to the

twelfth floor. Her knees knocked as she made her way down the hallway to the appropriate apartment. For the briefest moment she thought about turning back. When it came to Ryan, she'd never done anything this crazy before.

She knocked on the door. It was too late to turn back now.

The door opened, and there he was. Ryan Taylor, his eyes wide, mouth open. Every one of Kari's doubts dissipated like fog on a summer day. "Kari . . . I thought . . . when the doorman said a woman was . . . I mean, I figured it was a mistake. Where — how did you . . . ?"

"Ryan." She let go of her bag and moved into his arms, savoring the feel of his body against hers, breathing in the reality of him. "I can't believe I'm here." Her voice fell to a whisper, choked by the joy of seeing him again, of being with him. "I couldn't stay away another minute."

He held her tight. "You came." The words were drenched in longing, the same longing she'd heard so often in his voice when they'd spoken on the phone, even when she'd done everything in her power not to think of him. The moment he spoke the words, she knew.

He had not moved on with life. It was

the sort of detail she couldn't possibly have known without being here, seeing him in person, feeling his arms around her.

No matter that nearly seven months had passed since they'd been together or that the weekend would end soon enough. The feeling was the same as it had been the first time he held her. The same as it had always been, with one difference.

This time it was stronger.

Ryan couldn't stop looking at her, glancing over his shoulder as they made their way through the city that evening and found a restaurant. She was really here! And what did it mean — the fact that she'd come? So far — other than the hug they'd shared when she first arrived — she'd given him no reason to think her visit was for anything other than because he'd invited her.

They were halfway through dinner when Kari pulled out a photo of Jessie. There was no question about it. The baby bore an uncanny resemblance to Kari.

"Wow." Ryan's mouth hung open for a minute. "She's perfect." He took the picture carefully, studying it. "I can't believe how much she's grown."

Kari beamed. "I can't believe I'm here. I

haven't been away from her for more than a few hours — until now." She took the photo back from Ryan. "I miss her."

"Me too." His voice was low and thick, strained with emotion. It didn't matter that he hadn't seen little Jessie since she was born, had held her only during those first days of her life. The child had worked her way into his heart without his even knowing it. Ryan lifted his face to Kari. Their eyes met and held. "But I've missed you more."

Ryan slid his hand across the table and linked fingers with her. He saw questions in her eyes, but nothing that told him to let go. She clasped her hand around his. "I had to come, Ryan. I . . . I couldn't stay away."

"It's not the same as talking on the phone, is it?"

Ryan felt a rush he couldn't explain, like a tidal wave of love and joy and happiness. Here, in this single moment, all was right with the world.

But how was he going to say good-bye in three days?

The visit was going faster than Kari wanted.

It was their second day together, and

they were back at his apartment. Ryan sat on the sofa, his long legs stretched out in front of him. He'd poured two glasses of water and was waiting for her. The television was off.

It occurred to Kari that they needed to be careful. She was so glad to see him that until now she hadn't thought about what it would mean to be alone with him. After all, the last several times they'd been together, the idea of anything happening between them had been unthinkable. First she'd been trying to save her marriage — and even then they'd barely resisted temptation. Then she'd been a grieving widow still recovering from the birth of her child.

But now . . . now she was none of those things.

She sat beside him and turned so she could see his face. Just looking at him made her feel alive again, whole, the way she hadn't felt in longer than she could remember. Still, there were things she wasn't sure of.

Neither of them had said anything about their feelings for each other — not since Ryan left for New York. That was understandable, considering the events of the past year.

But now, had enough time passed? Kari

didn't know. She was sure about only one thing: Now that she was here with Ryan, she didn't ever want to leave him again.

She drew a slow breath. "I still can't believe I'm here."

He raised a single finger and traced it along her brow, his eyes never leaving hers. "Ever notice" — this time Ryan's voice was utterly bare, all the polite pretense stripped away — "how shallow our phone calls are?" He paused, his eyes as deep as the ocean. "We talk about everything but us."

"I was just thinking that."

"So why do we do it?"

"What's there to say?" Kari curled her feet up beside her. She was grateful this conversation wasn't taking place over the phone. They couldn't have talked about this without seeing each other's eyes, reading each other's feelings. "You live here; I'm there."

Ryan sat back and breathed out slowly. "Forget about that for a minute. It's been almost a year since Tim died, and you've never . . ." He stopped and let his head fall back against his beige leather sofa.

"Never what?"

He hung his head, and suddenly she wished she could make this easier on him.

But even now, all they had was borrowed. In another day she'd go back to Bloomington, and they'd be no closer to the relationship they'd both always wanted.

She touched his shoulder. "Ryan?"

"I'm sorry." He moaned and lifted his head. "Never mind."

"No, come on. What were you going to say?"

"It's just . . . I miss you all the time." She could almost see him grasping for words. "Something about that makes me feel guilty. Like I shouldn't even tell you."

"Because Tim died, you mean?" Her tone was quiet, encouraging him to bare his heart — something he hadn't done since their day on Lake Monroe more than a year ago.

"Maybe. I mean, it *must* be that." He hesitated and locked eyes with her again. "You're still getting over his loss, and here I am thinking about myself, my feelings for you." His voice dropped a notch. "Kari, if you only knew."

She rubbed his shoulder. "Would it help if I told you I'm at peace about Tim?"

"At peace?"

"Yes." Kari leaned closer, her voice soft. "Tim wouldn't have wanted me to spend the rest of my life in grief."

"Why . . . ?" His eyes searched hers, and she saw a flame of hope ignite there. "Why didn't you tell me sooner?"

"I think I just figured it out myself. And then . . . well, I didn't think it was fair." Her voice was pinched, strained from the emotion choking her throat. "I didn't want to presume anything."

He looked away and laughed. Not a sarcastic laugh, but the kind that sang with relief. His eyes met hers again. "Are you serious?"

She nodded and felt a sheepish grin creep up the sides of her face. "Completely serious."

"Kari girl." He took her face in his hands and spoke straight to her soul. "Only God could have taken me to a place where my heart didn't long for you and miss you every day, every hour."

Another, quieter laugh came from him. "Why do you think I call so often? Why do you think I asked you to come?"

Kari shrugged. Ryan's hands felt wonderful on her face. They made it hard for her to concentrate. "Because you felt sorry for me?"

"Sorry for you?" Disbelief filled Ryan's expression. "I would have called you every night, but I was trying to give you space.

Give you time. Feel *sorry* for you?"

Kari felt as if she were floating. All these months she had wondered about Ryan, what his feelings were, and whether they would ever again share a night like this, a night in which they could be honest with each other. The way they'd been that night at Lake Monroe.

And now here they were.

Kari felt her smile fade. For another twenty-four hours, anyway. After that, then what?

He seemed to sense her questions. He skimmed his thumbs beneath her eyes and along her cheekbones. "Don't worry about tomorrow, Kari. God will take care of that." She covered his hands with her own and let her forehead fall against his. Ryan's voice dropped to a whisper. "The important thing is that after tonight we never have to wonder how we feel about each other."

Ryan was right. Kari lifted her head and searched his eyes. "We don't, do we?"

"No." He shook his head. "Never again."

From the moment she walked into Ryan's apartment the day before, Kari had wanted to kiss him. Now the feeling was more than she could resist. She felt him draw closer, and he brushed his mouth against her neck, her cheek, her ear. Her eyes closed as he whispered against her face in a voice she'd memorized back when she was a teenager. "I love you, Kari. I'll always love you. Believe me, okay?"

She nodded, her cheek touching his. "I love you, too."

Slowly, in a dance that had been planned before time began, their lips found each other. For the first time since his football injury, the moment was neither hurried nor bathed in guilt. This was the passionate kiss of two people who had spent a lifetime longing for each other.

A kiss that said more about the way they felt now than any words ever could.

Kari had already checked out of her hotel and had her suitcase by the door. The cab would be there in five minutes, and she and Ryan stood in a private area of the lobby, inches apart, trying to find the easiest way to say good-bye. Tears welled up in Kari's eyes before she said a word.

What was keeping her in Bloomington, anyway? Why didn't she go home, grab Jessie, and get on the next plane back to New York? She could stay here as long as he had a job with the Giants. With her contacts, she could probably even get some catalog work.

But that wouldn't be right. Ryan would be busy, and she had no support here — no pastor helping her work through her past, no fledgling ideas about a ministry with hurting women. No family. No one to baby-sit Jessie. New York City — even the kinder, gentler New York that had emerged after September 11 — was no place for a single mother with a new baby. Her heart would always be with Ryan. But for now, at least, Bloomington was her home.

That didn't make leaving him any easier.

She let herself fall against him and rested her head on his chest. "I wish I didn't have to go." Her arms came up around his neck, and she held him, remembering a dozen other times when she'd said good-bye to him.

"Then stay." He slid his hands around her and latched his fingers near the small of her back.

"I can't."

He studied her face. "I know."

They were quiet for a moment, gazing into each other's eyes. "If I look at you long enough, maybe I can keep a part of you here with me."

They shared a long kiss, but in the end they said very little. What was there to say? They couldn't talk about the next time they'd be together or make promises of seeing each other soon. There was no telling when the next time would be.

The only sure thing was how they felt about each other. And for now that would have to be enough.

Ryan walked her outside and waited until the taxi appeared. Then he hugged her once more. "Take care of my little girl."

Kari nodded, dabbing at the wetness on her cheeks. "Bye." Ryan set her suitcase in the trunk, and she climbed inside the cab. Their eyes held long after the door was closed, until the driver pulled away and turned a corner.

Only then did Kari let the tears come freely. A deep, agonizing sorrow welled within her and came out as the simplest prayer Kari had ever uttered.

Please, God, let us be together one day. Please.

The pain of watching Kari leave was so strong, Ryan felt it with each minute that passed. By the time he got back to his apartment, he was tempted to call the Giants' front office and tell them to find someone else. He was going back to Bloomington.

But that wasn't his style. He needed to honor his commitments — the way his father had taught him.

No, he couldn't leave New York now. He owed it to the team to stay and finish the season. After that, though, he and Kari would have some serious possibilities to discuss.

He was fairly sure the Giants would extend his contract another year. If not, he could find a position with another NFL team. But where would that leave him and Kari? Would she marry him and move to New York? Would she want to follow him across the country while he worked his way into a head coaching position? Was that what the Lord wanted for both of them?

He sighed. There were too many unknowns. At this point there was only one thing Ryan was certain about. Kari had been away from him for less than an hour, and already he couldn't wait to see her again. He poured himself a glass of milk and settled into the sofa — the same spot where he'd sat the day before and kissed her. She would be arriving at La Guardia soon.

He pictured her, a beautiful brunette turning heads as she made her way through the airport, and a twinge of anxiety sliced at his heart. He'd never worried much about flying, even the first few weeks after September 11, when the whole country seemed to fear the skies. But now he felt compelled to pray for the safety of the plane Kari was about to board.

Because after finding her again, he couldn't bear to lose her now.

Chapter Twenty-Nine

The numb feeling was creeping back.

Landon needed a break from Ground Zero, needed to take a day and sit in the local chapel and weep over all he'd heard and seen and smelled these past two months. But still he kept working.

He'd worked through Thanksgiving and barely taken time to eat a cold turkey sandwich put together by some volunteers. Since that strange afternoon a month ago, he'd stayed away from Nino's. He wasn't at Ground Zero to socialize or commiserate with other hurting folks. He was here to find Jalen.

When it became clear his friend was dead, Landon moved into Jalen's two-bedroom apartment. He and Jalen's parents boxed his clothes and belongings, and afterward it seemed only right that Landon stay there. After all, they'd been planning to share the place.

Staying in Jalen's apartment kept Landon focused, but he spent as little time there as possible. Every hour was a reminder that the job he'd come to do wasn't finished yet. It wouldn't be until he found Jalen.

Now it was Monday afternoon, Landon's eighty-second straight day of sifting through rubble, clearing bucket after bucket of dusty human remains and other debris from the place where the World Trade Center once stood. Sometimes he slept a dozen hours straight before finding the strength to come back. But he always came. Day after day since the moment he'd arrived in New York.

A bucket went by, and then another, and another. Landon's hands were numb from the sameness of the job. They were still finding body parts fairly often, but it had been a long time since they'd found a firefighter.

It was two in the afternoon, and Landon figured he'd work until dark. He did that most nights, and sometimes he stayed later, working with the night crew. He had nothing waiting for him back at the apartment except a telephone. And he couldn't bring himself to call Ashley. Hearing her voice would only make him want to get on the next flight home, forget he'd ever spent a single day in the nightmare that was Ground Zero.

Another bucket went by. And another.

Then from the front of the line, the lead workers waved their hands, and one of them called out, "I've got a fireman."

Landon's insides reacted the same way they always did when he heard those words. His stomach fell to his knees, and images of Jalen flashed in his mind — times when the two of them had run together on those early Texas mornings or shared volunteer time at the station. He could almost see Jalen — smiling, waving to him, telling him to hurry up and get to the East Coast.

Landon swallowed as something he'd told Ashley echoed in his mind once more: *"Fighting fires in Bloomington is a pastime. In New York it's a passion."*

The captain at the front of the line knew about Landon's friendship with Jalen. If they found his body, the man had promised to let Landon know immediately. The endless parade of buckets had stopped, and several rescue workers were trying to remove the latest body from the rubble. Landon could see a firefighter's boots and jacket.

Landon held his breath while the captain tramped down the pile of debris and headed in his direction. A slow breath escaped through Landon's teeth. It couldn't be, could it? After all this time? And with so many firefighters still missing? Had they actually found Jalen?

The captain slowed as he approached, and his eyes met Landon's. "Blake?"

Landon struggled to find his voice. "Yes, sir?"

The man's eyes fell for a moment and then lifted to Landon's. "We've found your friend. I thought you'd like to help us up front."

Landon's head began to spin. His mouth was suddenly dry, his movements slow and deliberate as he passed his bucket to the man next to him and stepped out of line. "Yes, sir. Thank you."

The others tried not to stare as Landon fell in behind the captain and headed up the hill toward the front of the line. Halfway there, Landon caught a look from the old retired fire captain, the one still looking for both of his sons. Their eyes held for a moment; then the older man looked away.

Landon kept walking, staring at the circle of firemen ahead of him and the outline of a body in their midst. He had dreaded this moment since he arrived in New York, dreaded it and longed for it. It wasn't right that Jalen's remains stay buried beneath cement and twisted steel. But at the same time Landon feared what they might find. A partial body? A skeleton? It was bad enough to see mutilated strangers removed from the rubble.

But Jalen?

A knot of sorrow lodged in his throat, and Landon gulped it back. He moved into the circle surrounding Jalen's body. The sight of his friend — lifeless, mangled, forever still — knocked the wind from Landon. His knees buckled. "Dear God, no . . ."

A fireman nearby put his hand on Landon's shoulder, steadying him. Landon leaned into it, drawing the strength to stand. A surge of nausea rose within him, and he put the back of his hand to his mouth, determined to handle the moment in a way that would've made Jalen proud.

His friend had been one of the lucky ones. His body was intact, protected like several of the others because of his fire gear. Jalen's face was partially decomposed and marked by the tons of debris that had covered it. But he was recognizable, if only by the gold name tag still pinned to his jacket. It was scratched but legible. *Lieutenant Jalen Hale.*

Landon reached down and touched the toe of Jalen's boot as a mountain of anger rose within him. How dare those terrorists do this to his friend? How dare they cost the world someone as good as Jalen?

He drew a tired breath and let the anger fade. In its place an overwhelming sadness began to build. *It's okay, buddy. We got you out. You can rest now.*

Landon let go of Jalen's boot and moved closer, adjusting his friend's helmet so it fit firmly on his head. *I should've been with you, buddy. Maybe then we would've survived this thing together.* Landon hung his head and struggled to breathe. *Why didn't you get out of there before it fell, Jalen? Why?*

There was a stir of motion behind him, and Landon turned around. The morgue workers had arrived. He sucked in a quick breath and straightened himself. He hadn't been there on September 11 to help Jalen out of the building before it collapsed, but he could help now. He joined the others and maneuvered Jalen's body onto a bag laid out across a stretcher. Gently Landon took Jalen's lifeless hands and, one at a time, crossed them respectfully over his still chest.

One of the workers zipped the bag as the

captain handed Landon an American flag. "You do the honors, Blake."

"Yes, sir." Landon took the flag and stared at the red, white, and blue. His entire body shook. *You did us all proud, Jalen. This country will never forget you. I'll never forget you.*

A wave of dizziness swept over him, and he shook it off. How was it possible that the bag before him held the friend he'd laughed with so often, planned with and schemed with? That face of his, so full of life, would never smile again. Landon wanted to drop to the ground and weep, but he couldn't. A hundred pairs of eyes were on him, and there was still one thing left to do.

The chaplain wasn't around, but that didn't matter. Landon took his helmet off, clutched the flag to his chest, and bowed his head. Out of the corner of his eye he saw the others down the line do the same.

"God, we give you our brother Jalen. He's . . ." Landon's voice cracked, but he refused to give in to the riptide of emotion tearing at him. "He's your man now, God. Make him a captain, and give him one of your best stations up there, okay?" He sniffed hard, forcing himself to be strong. "And let him know we love him."

Landon lifted his head and stared at the dark, zippered bag on the stretcher. Moving with great care and respect, he draped the flag over his friend's covered body.

It was time to carry Jalen out.

"You okay, Blake?" The captain laid a hand on his shoulder.

Landon cleared his throat. "Fine, sir." He anchored one side of the stretcher. "Let's go."

Several firefighters joined him, and together they carried Jalen's body down the pile of debris, a hundred yards away to the refrigerated truck.

A county official led them inside and to the left. "Thank you." He nodded at Landon and the others. "We'll take it from here."

They passed the stretcher to four morgue workers, who disappeared with it around a makeshift partition. The other firefighters turned to leave, but Landon stayed. The county official was waiting, but for a moment Landon couldn't find the words. He swallowed hard and shook his head, pointing in the direction they'd taken Jalen.

"He . . . he was my friend." Landon pressed his lips together to stop them from trembling. "Take care of him for me, okay?"

Protocol would require the county official to agree and nothing more. But this was Ground Zero. There, in the refrigerated makeshift morgue, the graying man crooked an arm around Landon's neck, pulling him close. "I'm sorry, son." His voice was thick. "I'm so sorry."

The tears came then, and Landon could do nothing to stop them. "Jalen . . ." He bent his knees and squatted down, unable to see. "Jalen loved fighting fires here."

Although he'd worked at Ground Zero for over two months and had seen the county official nearly every day, Landon didn't know the man's name. But the official gripped Landon's shoulder and allowed him to cry, allowed him to weep and groan and grieve Jalen's loss the way he hadn't been able to do since first seeing the attacks on television.

Because Jalen's death had never been real until now.

Two minutes passed, and Landon couldn't get a grip. He felt buried beneath the death and destruction and loss the same way Jalen had been buried beneath the twin towers. It wasn't right! So many firefighters, all driven to save lives, all rushing up the stairs into a death trap. Why hadn't someone stopped them?

How would he tell Jalen's mother? What details would she want to know? And what about all the others still waiting to find a friend or family member? What about the retired fire captain still working the line, still waiting for his reckoning moment?

Landon wanted to struggle to his feet, but he couldn't. He didn't want to return to the pile again; he wanted to walk to the back of the truck, find Jalen's body, and sit by him for a while. They needed more time together, time to talk. Time for Landon to apologize for taking so long to get him out. Time to tell him about what had happened and how the country was responding.

The sobs shook his body until he felt another hand on his shoulder. "Blake . . ."

He turned and saw the captain, the same one who had led him to the front of the line when they first realized the body was Jalen's. "Y-y-yes, sir."

"When's the last time you had a day off?" The man's tone was gentle, almost fatherly. Landon guessed this wasn't the first time he'd seen one of his own break down since September 11.

"Well, sir . . ." Landon's knees shook as he stood up. He pinched the bridge of his nose and squeezed his eyes shut for a moment, trying to clear the tears enough to see. "I haven't had a day, sir."

The captain's eyebrows lifted. "Not a single day? Not since you got here?"

Two quick, silent sobs racked Landon's shoulders. "No, sir. I . . . I wanted to find Jalen, sir."

"Look, Blake" — the captain took hold of Landon's upper arm — "you need to go home."

"Home, sir?" Landon blinked. His head was spinning . . . any minute he was going to pass out. "I work *here* now, sir."

"I realize that. But you won't be of any use to us if you don't take care of yourself."

Landon waited, still longing to be with his friend one last time.

"We have a lot of shortages in the department, as you know." The captain's voice was firm but compassionate. "I need men like you manning a station, not sifting through rubble."

He paused, his gaze direct. "Go home, Blake. Take a few days. Then come back and report for duty at headquarters. Your one-year contract will begin December tenth, and it will begin in the firehouse. You've done more than your share here at Ground Zero."

Landon had no idea how he made it

back to the apartment that afternoon. But somehow he found a way to contact Jalen's parents and his own, and book a flight back to Indiana. He'd done what he set out to do. He'd found Jalen and helped remove him from the rubble.

In the process he'd said good-bye to one of his closest friends.

Now it was time to spend a few days with the other.

Chapter Thirty

Ashley was in no hurry to get another job until after Christmas.

She still had a little of the accident settlement money left, and besides, she and Cole were having a wonderful time together. They took trips to the library and read a dozen Dr. Seuss books — Cole's favorite. Evenings were spent watching *Dumbo* or *The Lion King* and eating Ashley's homemade oatmeal cookies.

"You're my best friend, Mommy. You know that?" Cole wrapped his grubby arms around her one morning after breakfast. "Plus you're the bestest reader in the whole world."

Ashley wished there was a way to thank Irvel and Helen and Edith. In a few short months they'd taught her more about love and life and making memories than she'd learned in all her years.

She had lived in fear and shame far too long — but no more. Her past mistakes were not Cole's fault, and she could do nothing about them now. Cole would be young only once, after all. And these times with Cole were what she wanted to remember when she was old.

When guilt about her days in Paris or her missed opportunities with her son tried to sink its claws into her, she would shake it off even before a few minutes went by. Then she'd call for her son. "Come here, buddy. Mommy needs you."

She'd hug him or kiss him or read to him.

A week after Ashley lost her job, her mother gave her a teasing complaint. "What happened to my boy? He hasn't spent the night here in forever."

"I'm making up for lost time, Mom." Ashley stooped down, kissed Cole on the nose, and laughed as he playfully wiped it away. "As much as possible, I want him with me."

Now it was nearly two weeks since she'd been fired, and that afternoon, Ashley had given in and let her mother take Cole for a few hours. She wasn't far away. In fact, she was just out front, fifty yards from her parents' front door. She had decided to create a painting of the Baxter house, the way it looked in early winter, bathed in the waning afternoon sunlight.

Bundled in an oversized parka, she sat in front of her easel and studied the sun rays as they hit the north side of the house where the dormers stood out. The image captured her so completely, she barely heard a car pull into the driveway behind her.

Must be Dad.

But the car didn't continue down the drive, and the fact that it was even there quickly slipped Ashley's mind. The temperature was dropping, and her fingers were stiff. She pressed the bristles into the pale gold color she had mixed and gently splayed them against the side of the palette, separating the fine hairs. She was running out of daylight, but she wanted to finish blocking in the sky before the sun set.

Once more she stared at the house. In this light it looked almost as though God himself were shining a lantern on the Baxter home. It was that effect she wanted to capture in her painting.

With featherlight strokes she added a shimmer of light to the left side of her canvas. She was about to dip her brush again when she felt someone come up behind her and take hold of her shoulders.

Before she could turn around, she knew

it was Landon. His touch sent chills down her spine despite her heavy parka, chills that had nothing to do with the dropping temperature. But how could it be? She hadn't heard from him since he left for New York.

She spun around, and there he was. "Landon." She wanted to ask him a hundred questions, but only one mattered. Had he found Jalen? She couldn't voice the question. Instead she soaked in the sight of him and saw a canyon of pain in his eyes.

Something in his expression told her his time in New York had changed him. He smiled at her, but his eyes didn't sparkle the way they once had. She wanted to hug away the hurt, to hold him in her arms until he was okay again.

Dropping her brush, she nearly knocked over her easel as she stood up and slipped her arms around him. He still hadn't said a word, and she wondered if something else was wrong. Maybe there'd been another tragedy.

"Landon?" She pulled back and studied his face. She still couldn't ask about Jalen. "Are you okay?"

He lowered his chin, his eyes unblinking. "We found him."

His words hit her like so many bricks.

"Oh, Landon . . . I'm sorry."

"I . . ." He shook his head, struggling. On top of every other emotion battling for position in his eyes, Landon was clearly exhausted. Like the other workers at Ground Zero, he probably hadn't taken a day off in weeks. Maybe months. No wonder he hadn't called her. Whatever hours he'd kept in New York, the task had taken its toll on him.

His voice was barely audible over the icy afternoon breeze. "I guess I always thought there was a chance. As long as we didn't find his body, then maybe . . ." Landon shrugged. "Maybe he'd gotten out somehow. Maybe he was wandering the city with amnesia or trapped somewhere in an underground pit with a miracle supply of food and water."

Ashley nodded and exhaled hard, sharing his sense of defeat. What could she say? She hadn't known Jalen, but she had seen the light in Landon's face when he talked about their times together in Texas, seen the pictures of the two of them when she'd been in Landon's house. It was hard to imagine the smiling young man . . . dead.

"I prayed for you. Like I said I would."

"I know. I can tell." He searched her eyes. "You have no idea how good it is to see you." He slid his arms around her waist and drew her closer, burying his face in the shoulder of her parka. "There was so much death, Ashley. It felt like . . . hell — the way I picture hell being."

She loosened the hold she had on his neck and ran her fingers along his shoulders. "But you're alive, Landon. You're here, and you're alive."

"Seeing Jalen like that, lifting his body from that awful pile of debris and silt . . ." His voice choked. "Hardest thing I've ever done, Ash." He studied her face. "Apart from leaving you."

There it was. The truth about how he felt. Even if he hadn't called, he'd been thinking about her the same way she was thinking of him. Ashley knew what was coming, but she couldn't believe it. Couldn't believe he was here in her arms again.

"Landon." The months faded like so many hours, and their lips met in a desperate kiss that was part sorrow, part grief. Part uncertain passion. When they pulled away, tears stained both their faces. "I missed you."

"Me, too. Every hour, Ashley." Their eyes held a moment longer; then Landon sucked in a deep breath and tried to smile.

"Let's get your stuff inside." He helped gather her paints and fold her easel. "You have no idea how good this air smells."

For the first time there was the hint of life in his eyes. Ashley took it as a good sign. Maybe after they spent time together, he'd be able to move on, despite the awful things he'd seen. Maybe his eyes would once more reflect everything good and right and loyal within him.

The way they had before he went to New York.

Side by side they carried her things to the house. They had barely gotten through the door when Cole spotted them. "Hey, you're back!" Ashley watched her son hurl himself into Landon's muscled arms and throw his little-boy hands around his neck.

Landon squeezed him for a long while. "That's the best hug I've had in weeks, buddy." He winked at Ashley over Cole's shoulder. "I missed you."

"Yeah, me too." Cole's voice brimmed with barely contained excitement. "After you went away, I didn't watch *any* baseball games! Just football." Cole framed Landon's face with his hands. "And Mommy doesn't wrestle very good."

"No." Landon slipped Cole back to the

floor but held tight to his hand. "Girls aren't very good wrestlers." He dropped down to Cole's level. "But your mom's not bad. I definitely think you should keep her."

Ashley's parents welcomed Landon as though he were their own son. He stayed for dinner, and throughout the evening Ashley couldn't take her eyes off him. Her heart jumped around within her like she was some crazy, lovesick teenager. After dinner they ate the banana bread her mother and Cole had made, and then, sometime around eight o'clock, they headed back to Ashley's house.

Cole fell asleep on the way, and Landon carried him into the house and gently laid him in bed. Finally they were alone, and Ashley took her place on the sofa. Landon lit the fireplace and then moved to join her. But he stopped when he saw one of her paintings on the opposite wall behind the sofa. He studied it for a moment the way he always did when he took in her work, his eyes narrow, thoughtful.

"That's beautiful."

She smiled. "Thanks."

"You're good, Ashley." He cast her a serious look. "People would line up for the chance to buy these."

Ryan Taylor had said the same thing a year ago when he'd come to her house after their day together at the mall. Ashley remembered being flattered that he'd even noticed her work. But the praise sounded different coming from Landon — more . . . meaningful. Maybe it was because Landon cared about her heart. When he looked at her artwork, he didn't see colors and shading and depictions of light.

He saw her.

Landon made a slow circle of the room, studying each painting. He stopped at her most recent piece — one of Cole on the backyard swing.

"Ash, that's gorgeous. You captured him perfectly." Landon moved closer and studied the detail. He gave a soft chuckle and shook his head. "I love that boy." He glanced at her, making a fist and pressing it to the place above his heart. "Now that he's in here, I can't get him out."

"He loves you too." A sadness swelled within her. What a price little Cole had paid for her own stubborn behavior. If only she'd seen Landon for who he was years ago, when she first came back from Paris. If she had, she doubted he'd be interested in moving to New York City. He'd be here with her and Cole.

The three of them might even be a family.

She pushed the thought away. There was no going back now. Landon had other plans, other commitments. He must have. Otherwise he would have found time to call her from New York — at least once in a while. Yes, he'd kissed her a few hours ago, but there was no way to know what he'd meant by it. And she was too afraid of his answer to ask him.

After a while he returned to the sofa and sat beside her. He shifted, settling back into the cushion as his eyes found hers. "It feels so good to be here."

"It's weird." She stretched out beside him, her legs adjacent to his. "You and Ryan Taylor both out there in New York, and Kari and I still here. Kari flew out to see him last week. Ryan isn't sure if he'll stay in New York next year. He has to finish the season first."

"Yeah, I saw him down at Ground Zero once. He and a few players were helping with water."

The question she'd been afraid to ask dangled in the warm light of the crackling fire. Finally Ashley had no choice but to voice it. "You're going back, aren't you?"

A sigh eased through his lips, and he

cocked his head, his eyes begging her to understand. "Yes."

She wasn't surprised, but that didn't make his answer any easier. Why had he come home, then? Was she merely a diversion, a way to refuel after too much time on the front lines? His life, his career — all of it was in New York now. And there was no telling whether he would ever move back to Bloomington again.

For a moment a wild notion flashed in her mind. She could move to New York City. Take Cole and start life over on the East Coast. That way she and Landon could be together as often as they pleased, and maybe one day . . .

The idea fell flat. Who was she kidding? Paris had left her hating big-city life. New York would be loud and hectic, and it would kill her creativity. Painting would be impossible, and besides, she could hardly take Cole away from the family support she had in Bloomington.

His eyes were still locked on hers. She struggled to find her voice. "When do you go?"

"The end of the week."

She crossed her arms and pressed them into her stomach. Anything to ease the knot that had formed there — a knot of hopelessness and despair mixed with the absolute certainty of something she hadn't fully realized until earlier that afternoon.

She wasn't falling in love with Landon Blake. She was already there.

But it didn't matter; it was too late now. Landon was moving on, and there was nothing she could do about it, nothing she could say to make him change his mind. Nothing she *would* say even if she could. Because working in New York City was something Landon clearly wanted, and it would be wrong to stand in his way. She'd had her chance, and she'd blown it.

"Then what?" She kept her tone even, not wanting to make him feel guilty for his decision.

"I take Jalen's place at the station."

"Jalen's place?" She was awed at the thought. The two of them were supposed to work together. But now, with Jalen gone, the experience would be completely different. Every call, every fire, Landon would feel Jalen with him, feel as though he were fulfilling Jalen's passion. She understood why he wanted to go back. But still . . .

"Why . . . why'd you come home?"

Landon took her hands in his. "The captain said I needed time away." He hesitated. "I'll begin a one-year contract when I get back."

Ashley swallowed her disappointment, but her mind was reeling. It didn't make sense. If he was going back, if he was still taking the job even after all that had happened, then why was he here now? He could have gone to his parents' house and called her once before his flight back to New York. Instead, he'd found her the moment he got home. Did he still have romantic feelings for her, or had he finally accepted her as "just a friend"? The way she once wanted to think about him?

Landon lifted her hands and held them to his face. "You're cold."

Ashley felt herself blush. Her hands always got cold when she was nervous. "Cold hands, warm heart, I guess."

"You don't need cold hands to prove that, Ashley." He shot a look at her nearest paintings again. "Look at your work." His eyes softened, and his expression grew thoughtful. "You can't fake that kind of warmth. And you can't put it on canvas if it isn't in you."

He lowered her hands but still kept hold of them. "You didn't tell me you'd lost your job."

Ashley bit her lip and shook her head.

Her father had mentioned it over dinner, probably assuming Landon already knew. Landon had missed much about her life, her heart, while he was away. Most of the time she had doubted he was coming back — at least not for a long time. "You" — her voice was barely a whisper — "you never called."

"No." Again his eyes searched hers. "I couldn't."

"You *couldn't?*" Her voice rose and a splash of anger colored her words. It was unavoidable. Her frustration ran deep, as though it had been silently building in the basement of her heart for weeks. "Every day I wondered how you were, whether you'd found Jalen." Her tone became more sad than angry. "One call, Landon? You couldn't make one single phone call?"

He didn't react, but his expression was more intense than she'd ever seen it. "I couldn't because I knew what would happen."

"What?" Ashley shook her head, trying to make sense of his answer. "What would've happened if you called, Landon?"

His head fell back a bit, and he stared at a spot on the wall behind her, his eyes distant. "It was so awful, Ashley. Death . . .

grief . . . devastation in every direction, filling every breath." A horrible pain, raw and haunting, filled his features as his gaze met hers again. "Don't you see? The sound of your voice would've put me over the edge and sent me running home, desperate for the next plane out of New York." He squinted, his eyes watery. "I couldn't do that to Jalen."

His explanation cut Ashley to the core. How shortsighted she'd been to mistake his silence for anything but what it had been — a driven, single-minded determination to find his friend. "I'm sorry, Landon. I didn't think —"

"Don't." He lifted one of his hands from hers and brought a finger to her lips. "You don't owe me an apology. I should've called you." He leaned forward and gave her a tender kiss on the forehead. "I wanted to. I just couldn't." He dropped back to his spot. "Understand?"

"Of course." His answer made his silence clear, but it didn't answer the bigger question. Why was he going back? It was a question she wasn't ready to ask, so she bit the inside of her lip and waited for him to talk.

"Okay." Landon drew a slow breath. "Tell me about your job. What happened?"

Ashley took a moment to mentally switch gears. "Belinda. She didn't like me from the beginning."

Ashley told him about her Internet discoveries, how she'd tried to reach the residents at Sunset Hills with methods that Belinda and Lu considered controversial. Ashley let her gaze fall to her lap. "Maybe it *is* better to keep them grounded in the present." She lifted her eyes to his. "But you should have seen them, Landon; it was amazing. Edith stopped screaming. Helen was almost normal. Irvel wasn't worried about whether Hank was late." She raised one shoulder. "It seemed good to me."

For a long while Ashley sat there looking at Landon, studying his face. Ever since the day she met him, Ashley had worried that he was too simple, too conservative, that life with him would be predictable and routine. But now she wondered where she'd gotten that idea. And there was something else — a quiet depth to him that she hadn't noticed before. A depth that was intensely attractive.

He released one of her hands and pushed a wisp of hair off her forehead. "You miss them."

"Yes." Tears stung at her eyes before she could stop them. "Especially Irvel."

"What you did was right, Ashley. I agree with that pastor you read about. Memories are from God." He cupped the side of her face and pulled her close until their lips came together. Their kiss was tentative this time, as though they both had questions. When he pulled back, his eyes caught hers, and she felt a piercing bit of the hurt that was to come. The hurt of telling Landon good-bye after being in his arms again, after knowing for sure that her heart would never love another man the way she loved him.

"Sometimes . . ." His tone was low and spoke volumes about his feelings for her. Their faces were inches apart, and the glow from the fire shone in his eyes. "Sometimes memories are all we have. All that keep us going."

"What memories kept you going?" She kissed him again. "At Ground Zero?"

This time he brought his other hand up and worked his fingers into her hair. "Memories . . ." He moved his lips over hers. ". . . of this." His fingers trembled against her face. "After I left, I sometimes wondered if the summer really happened. Or if it was all just a dream."

"I thought . . ." She swallowed, searching for the courage to continue. "I thought after I told you about Paris — your feelings for me would change."

He kissed her chin and the tip of her nose, and finally her lips again. "I'm here, aren't I?"

Their arms came around each other, and they kissed the way Ashley had wanted to since the moment she saw him again. With each minute, the passion between them built until there was no question that the ground they were treading was dangerous. She pulled away first, breathless. Before she could change her mind, she stood and stretched, raising her hands over her head. "Okay." She exhaled hard. "I think we need a break."

Landon gave the seat beside him a pat. "Come on, Ashley." His voice was heavy with desire. "We're okay."

She shook her head and waved a finger at him. "We're *not* okay." The last thing she wanted was to lose control and to share a moment with him that they'd spend a year regretting. If that happened, he'd leave in a few days feeling he owed her something. And she couldn't have that.

No; if Landon wanted to fight fires in New York, he should go and do so without any obligations back in Bloomington. That way, if he ever came back, if by some miracle they found each other again, their love would be for all the right reasons.

"Besides . . ." She held out her hand and helped him to his feet. "I don't think Pastor Mark would approve."

Immediately Landon's desire faded first into confusion and then into utter disbelief. "Pastor Mark?" Landon couldn't have looked more surprised if she'd announced she was becoming a nun.

"Yes. I don't think he'd approve." Ashley stifled a giggle and flopped back onto the far corner of the sofa. Her recent church attendance was one more thing Landon had missed.

He leaned against the opposite sofa arm and stared at her. "You've been talking to Pastor Mark?" His eyes were wide, unblinking. "What else haven't you told me?"

She gave him a sheepish grin. "A lot."

"Okay." He anchored his elbows on his upper legs, his eyes shining with anticipation. "So tell me about Pastor Mark."

"It's not that big a deal." Ashley pulled her knees to her chin, her eyes fixed on his. "After September eleventh, I started going to church with my family." She shrugged. "It just seemed like the right thing to do." A nervous laugh slipped out. "Me . . . Ashley Baxter . . . at church every Sunday.

Can you believe it?"

"Ashley . . ." His mouth hung open. "That's amazing."

"What?" His reaction made her suddenly uncomfortable. "So I went to church. Is it that shocking?"

"No, it's just . . ." He stopped himself and shook his head. "Never mind." He shot her a smile. "That's great, Ash. Really."

There was something he wasn't saying, but she didn't feel like pushing the issue. What if he wanted to know specific details about her and God? Even after praying that day with Laura Jo, Ashley wasn't sure exactly where she stood. She hadn't started reading her Bible or anything like that. And she didn't want to disappoint Landon by saying so.

She volleyed a smile back at him. "I thought I would just go that one time — right after you left. Everything about life seemed so sad and crazy after the attacks. But at church that Sunday — I don't know, I had this sense of peace." Her smile faded. "You know?"

"Definitely." His expression reflected a joy she hadn't seen before. Ashley couldn't quite define it, but it was there. Whatever the reason, she was glad. It felt wonderful to see him happy. It made him look more like himself, less like the battle-scarred warrior she'd welcomed home earlier that day.

They settled back onto the sofa and watched a comedy on TV, avoiding the kisses that had nearly gotten them into trouble before. Much too quickly the evening was over, and Landon left to spend the night at his parents' house.

The days after that sped by in a blur of lunches with Cole and walks together in the cold winter air, games of catch, and on their last day together, a series of footraces in front of Ashley's house. For the most part, Cole was the winner.

"You're the champion of the world, buddy." Landon raised Cole's hand in the air and paraded him around the yard as though he'd just won the Olympics.

Cole grinned big and pumped his fist. Then he threw his arms around Landon's neck and said something that made Ashley's heart catch. "I wish you could stay for always, Landon. . . ."

"Me too." Landon tousled his hair and picked him up off the ground.

"Can me and Mommy go with you when you leave?"

"Not this time, buddy." Landon hugged

Cole close and set him down again.

There was no missing the fact that Landon and Cole shared something special. Yes, Cole had always enjoyed his time with Ashley's father. But in all ways that mattered, Landon was the young father figure Cole had never known.

The afternoon passed, and Ashley tried not to think about it too much. But that night, the images of the two of them together made it impossible for her to sleep.

What if Landon never came back? What if he lost interest in her or fell in love with someone else? What if he became someone different after a year in New York — someone who couldn't be bothered with a difficult woman and her fatherless son?

Whatever the future held, Ashley was certain of this much. It would yield no easy answers.

And after Landon left, the questions would only get harder.

Chapter Thirty-One

Sunday afternoon came too quickly.

After church, Ashley brought Cole and Landon back to her house and fixed them grilled-cheese sandwiches and tomato soup. Then, when it was almost time for Landon to leave, he stooped down to Cole's level and hugged him close. "You take care of your mom now, you hear?"

Cole lowered his chin and lifted his eyes. His lower lip quivered, and Ashley knew he was doing his best not to cry. "I will." He coughed twice. "Are you comin' back?"

It was the question Ashley had been afraid to ask since Landon returned. She held her breath and waited.

Landon messed his fingers through Cole's hair and didn't look in her direction. "I'd like to." He braced his hands on Cole's shoulders. "Some things God doesn't tell us until it's time. Okay?"

Cole managed a brave smile. "Okay."

Until it's time? Landon's words rang out again in Ashley's mind. What was that supposed to mean? She drew in a quick breath and made a point to ask Landon later.

"Now, how 'bout you run outside and play while I say good-bye to your mommy. All right?"

Cole nodded but stayed where he was, anchored in Landon's arms. Then he hugged him once more, burying his face near Landon's muscled shoulder. "I love you."

Landon's eyes glistened, and he didn't speak for several seconds. "I love you too, Cole. Stay close to Jesus."

Cole nodded, then pulled away. He grabbed his coat and mittens, and in a flash he was in the backyard, leaving Landon and Ashley alone.

Landon said nothing, just held out his arms and waited while she crossed the room and came into his embrace.

"I'm such an idiot." She let her head fall against his chest.

With gentle hands he stroked her hair and massaged his fingers into the base of her neck. "That's a funny way to say good-bye."

She lifted her eyes, aching from the mistakes she'd made in the past and the toll they were taking on her now. "How come I didn't see it?"

Landon waited, his face patient, kind.

"You were everything I could have wanted, Landon. Even back then, before Paris." She uttered a sound that was something like a laugh, but without the humor. "You know what I used to think?"

He twisted his face and stared at the ceiling as though he were trying to solve the world's most difficult riddle. "Not a clue. Besides, my dad taught me never to guess what women are thinking." A smile filled out the area beneath his cheekbones.

She relaxed a bit, caught off guard by his playfulness. "I thought you were too safe."

He took a step backward and pointed to himself, his eyes wide.

"I know, I know." Ashley waved her hand. "I've had time to think about it since you left. You're not safe; you're crazy."

She held up a finger. "First, you switch from future veterinarian to firefighter." Her second finger came up. "Then, you risk your life to save a little boy." She raised her third finger. "Finally, on little more than a whim, you decide to up and go to New York."

Her hand fell to her side. "Of course, then there's Jalen." She felt the silliness fade from her expression. "What kind of man stays at a place like Ground Zero for that many weeks looking for his dead friend? Breathing who knows what and wearing out his hands and . . . and his heart into a tattered mess?"

She linked her fingers at the back of his neck. "I was an idiot, Landon. I never even knew you."

"You forgot something." He nuzzled his face against hers.

"What?"

"The first crazy thing I ever did was fall in love with *you*."

She thought about that for a while. He was right. She was hardly the conventional catch in high school. Oh, she'd been a cheerleader for a while — a very short while — as her parents and her sisters expected. But after that she had hung out with a retrohippie group and worn strange clothes and stranger hair.

Meanwhile, Landon was quietly charming, conservative, liked by everyone at Clear Creek High School. He could have gone out with any girl. But instead he pursued her and her alone, even when she would barely give him the time of day. There was nothing safe about that.

"See?" She gave herself a light smack on the forehead. "I should have known it then."

"It's okay, Ash." He was serious again.

"All that's behind us."

"It's not okay." She pushed away from him, hovering precariously between playfulness and despair. "It's too late. I figured it out too late."

"What did you figure out too late?" He caught her hands and brought them around his waist.

She sighed, and the frustration in her felt like it was leaking straight from her soul. Her eyes caught his, and she felt the burn of tears. There was a thickness in her throat when she tried to speak. "That I . . . I love you, Landon. I *do* love you." The tears spilled onto her face, but she did nothing to stop them. "I love you the way you always wanted, and now it's too late."

"Because I'm leaving?" He searched her eyes, and with a gentle touch of his thumb he wiped her tears.

"Because everything's different now." Her voice was a notch louder than before, almost shrill, and suddenly Ashley recognized something she hadn't before. She was afraid — afraid of what might happen if Landon spent a year fighting fires in New York City. She swallowed hard and ordered herself to be calm. Her voice was barely more than a whisper when she spoke again. "Look what happened to

Jalen. That could've been you, Landon. Don't you think I realize that? If you hadn't been hurt in that apartment fire here, you'd have been right there beside him."

"Oh, Ashley, honey." He held her until her body stopped shaking. When she was somewhat calmer, he took her face between his hands and pulled back just far enough so he could see her eyes. "Remember when you told me you were going to church? I acted kind of funny, and you thought it was because I was shocked that you'd gone? Remember?"

Ashley nodded.

"I was going to tell you something, but" — he glanced around the room as though he were looking for the right words — "it didn't seem like the right time."

"What?" She sniffed, savoring the way his hands felt against her face, memorizing the smell of his cologne, the sound of his voice.

His eyes locked onto hers and he looked straight into the most private places of her heart. "I prayed you'd go. When I was at Ground Zero one day, I felt like I was falling apart. Like I was becoming someone else." He blinked twice. "A man prayed with me, and after that I felt strong again. And right there, kneeling in the rubble of the twin towers, I prayed for you, Ashley. And I knew . . . I knew that somehow God would lead you back to him. I knew because I heard his answer."

She felt goose bumps rise along her neck and spine. "You prayed I'd go to church?"

"No." He gave her a gentle smile. "I prayed you'd fall in love with God. With everything about him, Ashley. His truth, his church . . . his plan for your life."

For an instant, the old feelings flashed in her mind, and she had the urge to argue or run. God's truth? His plan for her life? It all sounded a little too church-ladyish. But there was that deep joy in Landon's eyes again, a ray of light that told her he was talking about something more than women's groups and Sunday potlucks. "Do you think . . . do you think that's happening to me?"

Landon nodded. "I do."

A sob caught in Ashley's throat, and she laughed. "Really?"

"Really."

"I kind of wondered about God." This was the conversation she'd wanted to have with him for the past three days. Now they were out of time, so she did her best to sum up her feelings. "I kept thinking church was nice and all. But God — he was sort of scary. How could he be interested in me after all I'd done?" She lowered her chin, still horrified by the memories of her past. "I'm still not good enough for God. I wouldn't blame him if he didn't want me now."

Landon stroked her head and drew her near once more. "None of us is good enough."

"You are." She muttered the words against his chest. They were so close that she could feel his heartbeat.

"No, Ash." He pulled back and peered at her. This time his eyes held the faintest trace of guilt. In the distant places of her mind, she wondered what he'd done that could possibly make him feel guilty. All Landon had ever done was think of others. But he shook his head. "No one is good enough. Not me or you or anyone else."

Memories of her childhood flashed in Ashley's mind, and she could hear her father saying the same thing a dozen years ago. *"We all need a Savior. No one can get to heaven by being good."*

They dropped their hands to their sides, and he wove his fingers between hers. She held on, dreading the fact that any minute she'd have to let go. She let her gaze fall to her feet. If Landon was right, if her father was right, then how did she move on from here?

"What am I supposed to do, then?"

"It depends on what you want." His eyes held hers.

Everything around her faded except the sound of his voice.

"Do you want a friendship with God, Ashley?"

If he had asked her about becoming a Christian, she would have hesitated. The word *Christian* was so vague it was almost meaningless. Her father called himself a Christian, but then so did the girls at church who had shunned her when she came home from Paris pregnant and alone.

But a friendship with God? It sounded too good to be true. She gave a slow nod of her head. "I'd like that. If he would want me."

"He wants you." Landon's voice dropped to a choked whisper. "All you have to do is ask." He hesitated. "You know?"

"You mean pray?" Her heart was beating harder than before. She could hear the anxiety in her tone. "Now?"

"Not now." Landon gave her a half-smile. "Later, when you're alone with God. When the timing's right."

Relief flooded her soul.

All her life she'd avoided a moment like this. People had tried to get her to pray before. She had seen people go through some kind of practiced prayer thing — the sinner's prayer or something like that. But it had always seemed forced and unnatural. If she was going to ask the Lord to be her friend, ask him to forgive her, she didn't want to do it here with Landon. Not that he would ever try to force her, but this type of prayer was something that would have to take place between her and the Lord alone.

Landon looked at his watch. "I've gotta go."

"I know." The pain was so real, Ashley could barely breathe. "Pray for me, okay?"

"Always." He leaned into her and kissed her once more, a long kiss that would have to be enough for now. Maybe forever. He hugged her. "I meant what I told Cole. I'll call, and when my year's up I'll —"

She shook her head. "No, Landon. No promises. It's like you said. Some things God doesn't tell us until it's time."

His breath warmed the side of her face. "When did you get to be so smart?"

She angled her head, ignoring the fresh tears that pooled in her eyes. "I have this amazing friend praying for me."

He kissed her forehead. "Good-bye, Ashley."

"Good-bye."

She watched him go, felt her heart grow heavier with each yard that came between them. But not until he was gone did she shut the door and fall to her knees. An ocean of tears had been building within her since the moment he'd told her his plans. Not just because he was leaving, but because he might never come back.

The sound of the patio door opening made her sit back on her heels and cover her eyes. Cole rounded the corner and stared at her. "Mommy, what's the matter? Are you sick?"

Two quick sobs shook Ashley's shoulders. "No, I'm . . . I'm just sad."

"I know what to do." Cole was at her side in a flash. "Grandma says you're supposed to pray when you feel sad." He slipped an arm around her neck and pressed his face against hers. "You want me to pray, Mommy?"

Ashley sniffed. "Yes, honey. Pray . . . pray that Mommy will know for sure that God loves her."

Cole squeezed his eyes shut and, in beautiful childlike sentences, he did just that.

★ ★ ★

The answer to Cole's prayer came first thing in the morning.

Before Ashley was even awake, Lu from Sunset Hills called.

"Hello?" Ashley crooked her arm across her eyes. She had a headache from crying so much the day before.

"Ashley, I hate to wake you, but something's happened here. Something bad."

Ashley sat up in bed, her heart pounding. "Is it Irvel?"

There was silence on the other end.

Ashley had to remind herself to breathe. She was completely awake now, adrenaline coursing through her like a drug. "Lu, tell me. What's wrong?"

"It's a long story," Lu sighed. "I fired Belinda this morning. You're the only person who can do the job, Ashley. Please come back to Sunset Hills."

Ashley's mind raced. What had Belinda done? She forced herself to concentrate on Lu's offer. "I . . . I don't want to be a bookkeeper, Lu."

"I'll hire someone else to do the books." Lu sounded like she was ready to cry. "The residents here were different around you, happier. Nothing's been the same since you left. Please, Ashley. Come back.

Whatever you were doing, do it again — and train the staff to do the same thing." She grabbed a quick breath. "Will you, Ashley? Please?"

Elation replaced every frightening thought Ashley had. Joy filled her heart, and she struggled to find her voice. She was going back! She would see Irvel again and hear about Hank. She would add to the wall of photos and cover the mirror for Edith and bring back the saddle and sawhorse. Tears spilled onto her cheeks as a peal of wonderful laughter slipped from her throat. "When do I start?"

They worked out the details, and Ashley promised to be there first thing in the morning. That way she could spend one more day with Cole before returning to Sunset Hills. Lu had assured her she could still be finished by three, so she and Cole would have afternoons and weekends together.

After she hung up, Ashley stared at the ceiling in awe. It was the perfect arrangement.

She dried her cheeks, and then it hit her. Cole's prayer! Her son had prayed that she would know for sure God loved her. Ashley let her mouth hang open, amazed. She still hadn't prayed the way she knew she should. And yet here God was, answering her prayers and the prayers of her little boy, just hours after they'd been uttered.

It was only then that she buried her face in her pillow and really began to talk to God. She begged his forgiveness for a lifetime of bad choices, and she asked him to be her friend, her Savior — then and always. After that, she told him every other thing that was on her heart. Thirty minutes later she stood up and stared out the window.

She was a new person; she could feel it. God's mercy and grace flooded her, consumed her as they never had before. God loved her! He loved her, and nothing would ever change that.

Not because she was good or because she had finally prayed.

But simply because she was his.

Chapter Thirty-Two

Kari was finding ways to keep busy.

Pastor Mark had arranged for her to meet with Martha Oglesby, one of the older women at church, a woman who shared Kari's vision of helping others who might be suffering in their marriages. Twice a week they got together to talk and pray and work through the types of issues Kari might be dealing with once she began such a ministry. Between that and taking care of Jessie, there were whole hours every day when she could avoid thinking about Ryan Taylor.

The nights were something altogether different.

Whatever the future might hold for the two of them, right now God had them apart for a reason. And until they could be together, they each had a job to do.

Ryan's was to honor his contract.

And hers was to honor God with the work he'd given her.

"I don't know what tomorrow holds, sweetheart," her mother had told her the last time they talked about Ryan. "But I have a feeling that somehow it involves Ryan Taylor."

Her mother's words played lightly on her heart as she made her way toward the church office that Monday afternoon. She rounded a corner and headed through the sanctuary toward Pastor Mark's office. He had called earlier and asked her to come by. "There's something I'd like to discuss with you."

She entered the pastor's office and found him on the phone. She took her familiar spot on the sofa across from his desk and waited. After a few seconds he hung up and gave her his usual greeting: "Hello, Kari. How's your family?"

She smiled and gave a light shrug. "Good, I guess. Ashley got her job back. Erin and Sam seem to be doing pretty well. She's glad they haven't moved."

The pastor nodded. "And I've been meeting with Brooke and Peter. They're not quite to the point of committing, but they're interested. It's exciting to see how far they've come." Pastor Mark's smile faded. "I haven't seen Luke."

A heaviness settled over Kari. "He's struggling." She folded her hands. "I've talked with Mom and Dad, and they think it's a phase — something he has to work through. But I'm worried." She hesitated. "His faith took a real hit after September eleventh."

"I'm sorry." Pastor Mark sighed, his eyes still on Kari. "I'm praying for him. Have your dad keep me posted."

"I will."

The pastor hesitated and settled back into his chair. "Well, Kari. Martha thinks you might be ready."

"Ready?"

"To meet with someone else, someone who's having difficulties." He wheeled his office chair around, dug through his file drawer, and pulled out a sheet of paper. "I have someone in mind."

The sadness over Luke dimmed, and a surge of excitement welled within her. Of course, Kari had thought herself ready months ago. But if Martha thought so, maybe she really was. "What's her situation?"

"I talked to her on the phone." Pastor Mark studied the paper. It was covered with half a page of handwritten notes. "She called last week, and from what I gather she's young, no children. Struggling in her marriage. She said she's planning to leave her husband in the next few months. She needs complete confidentiality."

"Does she know me?"

"I didn't mention your name." The pastor looked up from the notes. "And she didn't give me hers. She was very timid on the phone, worried that someone might find out." His eyes fell to the notes again. "I told her we had a woman here at church who might be able to meet with her, maybe listen and pray with her. I promised that no one would ever have to know her name or that she was meeting with anyone."

"What did she say?"

"It wasn't the answer she was looking for." Pastor Mark gave Kari a sad smile. "I think she's pretty set on a divorce."

Kari's heart broke for the woman. Marriage could be so difficult, especially with all the pressures that came from daily life. Yet, if she and Tim had worked through their problems and found unity and love again, so could this woman — whoever she was.

"What are her reasons?"

Pastor Mark lifted the paper so he could see it better. "There's no affair, at least not at this point. Apparently the woman has a male friend at work who listens to her, but she says he's not the problem."

"What is?"

"Looks like the trouble started when her husband got a job transfer out of state. They're supposed to move this summer. The woman told me she's already decided to stay here. But I think she's struggling with that. She's been a believer all her life. Her family won't understand. That kind of thing."

Kari leaned forward and stared at Pastor Mark.

The description almost sounded like Erin — except Erin hadn't been confiding in any coworker, and she certainly hadn't made plans to divorce Sam and stay in Bloomington. Kari felt a splash of relief as she worked through the details in her mind. No, the woman must be someone else. "How'd you leave it with her?"

"She agreed to meet with you as long as no one else at church finds out. To tell you the truth, I think she's looking for a way to ease her guilt. If she meets with you, at least she can say she tried. I think she's hoping you'll come alongside her, pat her head, and tell her it's okay to break up her marriage."

"Exactly what I won't tell her." Kari gave Pastor Mark a sad smile.

"Do you think you're ready?"

Kari's heart swelled with the thought of

using her past, her pain, to help someone else. "I do."

"Okay then. When can you meet with her?"

"I'll call her this week and set it up."

Pastor Mark scribbled something on a piece of notepaper and handed it to Kari. "Here's her number. She didn't leave a name."

Kari took it, and as she looked at the seven digits, her eyes grew wide. She felt the blood drain from her face, and her heart skittered into an unrecognizable pattern.

It wasn't possible.

Why hadn't she said anything to Kari? And how would she react when she found out Kari was the person she was going to meet with? None of it seemed even remotely possible. When had she decided to leave her husband, and why hadn't she told anyone else? And what about this male friend? Who was he?

Kari had no answers, no facts to go on except one — the one very undeniable truth that she held in her trembling hands.

The phone number on the slip of paper did not belong to a stranger.

It belonged to her sister Erin.

Chapter Thirty-Three

Irvel's bruises were enough to make Ashley sick.

The old woman lay in bed moaning, her withered arms discolored with patches of deep purple and blue, streaked with lines of blood red. Her head rolled from side to side, her eyes wide and fearful. There was a strong odor in the room, as though Irvel hadn't bathed in days. Not only that, but her hair was separated in oily sections, matted to her head. She looked like she'd aged ten years in two weeks.

Ashley barely recognized her.

"Irvel?" She crept into her room Tuesday morning, her stomach in knots. What in the world had happened to her? She went to Irvel's bedside and took the old woman's hand. "Hello, Irvel, how are you?"

Irvel stopped moaning and turned her eyes to Ashley. There was a moment when she looked like she might scream. But instead, her lids lowered, and she smacked

535

her lips. Then she began singing. "Great is Thy faithfulness, O God my Father. . . . Great is Thy faithfulness . . . O God my Father. . . . Great is Thy . . ." The words were rusty and fast, and she spouted them over and over, completely out of tune.

They sounded like they were coming from a crazy person.

She's acting like Laura Jo! How could this happen? Anger built up in Ashley, but she contained herself. Irvel didn't need her outrage; she needed her sympathy. And her help.

"Irvel, it's Ashley. I've been gone awhile, but I'm back." Ashley's voice cracked, and she blinked back tears. "How are you, Irvel?"

"Where's Hank?" Her words were dry and pasty, and her eyes darted from Ashley to other spots around the room. Irvel let out a loud moan. "I can't find Hank."

As confused as Irvel had always been, she'd never acted delusional, the way a person with more advanced Alzheimer's might. But now . . . were pain pills making her act this way, or had something snapped inside her? Maybe she had a fever. . . .

Ashley lifted her other hand to Irvel's forehead, but the movement made Irvel cower deeper into her pillow. "Don't hurt me!" she shouted. She winced, closing her eyes and waving her hands in Ashley's direction.

Immediately Ashley withdrew. "It's okay, Irvel. It's okay."

What had Belinda done? Irvel had never acted this way before. Ashley clutched at her waist, willing away the growing nausea. "I'm sorry, Irvel. I won't hurt you. You're safe now."

"The Lord is my shepherd; I shall not want. He maketh me to lie down in green pastures; he leadeth me beside the still waters. He restoreth my soul. . . ."

Tears filled Irvel's eyes as the Twenty-third Psalm tumbled from her lips. When she'd recited it twice through, her voice fell to a little-girl whimper. "I want Hank."

"Hank's all right, Irvel." Once more Ashley struggled to keep the anger from her tone. It was crucial that Irvel hear only kindness. Whatever had happened, she'd obviously been terrorized enough. "Everything's okay."

"I'm in trouble." Her moaning stopped suddenly, and Irvel attempted to focus on Ashley. "Hank's looking for me. He wants to help."

With all her heart, Ashley wanted only to

cradle Irvel in her arms and rock away the pain, assure her that she and Hank would be together soon and that no one would ever hurt her again. But she couldn't even do that. Right now Irvel was too frightened to be touched at all.

"You're okay now. It's all right."

Irvel narrowed her eyes once more and held Ashley's gaze longer than before. "You know Hank?"

Ashley lifted her gaze to the photos still hanging on the wall. And to the portrait she'd painted of the man. "Yes, Irvel." A sad smile tugged at the corners of her mouth. "I know Hank."

"I thought so." Like a summer breeze, peace blew across the old woman's wrinkled features. For the first time that morning, Irvel looked more the way Ashley remembered. "Is he coming by this afternoon?"

"Did he tell you he was coming by?" Ashley kept her voice as unthreatening as possible.

"Yes." Irvel smacked her lips again, and for a moment her eyes darted about. Then they found Ashley's once more, almost as though a battle were going on in Irvel's mind — a battle for her sanity. "He said he was coming."

"Hank's never let you down before, has he?"

"Never."

"Well, then." Ashley rubbed her thumb gently down the length of Irvel's bony fingers. "I'm sure he won't let you down now."

"Yes." As though someone had flipped a switch, the oppression seemed to lift from Irvel. Her countenance grew pleasant and confident, almost the way it had been before. "Of course." She smiled and nodded, her body visibly more relaxed. "Why didn't I think of that?" She looked at Ashley. "I don't believe we've met, dear. My name is Irvel."

"Hi, Irvel." Ashley fought another wave of tears. "I'm Ashley. I think we're going to get you a bath and wash your hair. Get you cleaned up."

Light flashed in Irvel's eyes, and her smile crept higher up her face. "Hank would like that."

"I'm sure he would." Ashley gave Irvel's hand a gentle pat. They'd talked long enough. Irvel needed her rest. "Then maybe later we can have tea."

"Peppermint tea?" Irvel's eyes grew wide.

"Exactly."

"Oh, my dear." Irvel brought her other hand across her body and clasped it over Ashley's. "That would be lovely. How did you know? Peppermint is my favorite."

It was seven-fifteen, and Ashley was supposed to meet with Lu in five minutes. "Tell you what, Irvel. It's still pretty early. You get some rest, and we'll start our day in about an hour."

"All right." Irvel's eyelids opened and shut a few slow times, and she yawned. "You know, dear . . ." She lifted her bruised arm and gestured in Ashley's direction. ". . . you have the most beautiful hair. Just beautiful. Has anyone ever told you that?"

The story came out the moment Ashley was alone with Lu.

"Have you seen her?" Ashley was on her feet, pacing across the small office, her eyes locked on Lu. "The police need to be called about this."

"I've called them." Lu's voice was calm and somewhat defeated. "I took pictures. The police are talking to Belinda today. Her attorney is claiming it was an accident — that Irvel fell and that's what caused the bruises."

"I saw finger marks up and down her arms, for heaven's sake." Ashley had to work to keep her voice in check. "The woman should be in jail."

Lu drew a long breath and stared at a document on her desk. "With Alzheimer's patients it's often their word against a caregiver's. Since the patients have a tendency to fall or act out, most of the time it's difficult to prove abuse." Lu gave a weak shrug. "Besides, elderly people bruise very easily. A single fall can leave a person Irvel's age black-and-blue over half her body."

"So what's going to happen?"

"If the police don't have enough evidence, they'll drop the case."

Ashley clenched her jaw and groaned. "How'd you find out?"

"I wouldn't have if it weren't for Krista. She worked the morning shift that day, but she left for a doctor's appointment. She got back quicker than she expected. When she walked in, she found Irvel on the floor and Belinda standing over her, shouting at her."

Lu rested her forearms on the desk. "Krista said Irvel had been more restless than usual that morning. Talking constantly about Hank, that type of thing.

Krista didn't know how to handle her."

Ashley felt her heart sink. "So Krista left for her appointment, and Belinda took over. Is that it?"

Lu nodded. "Apparently Belinda was in a foul mood. Several times — even before Krista left — Belinda yelled at Irvel and ordered her to stop talking about Hank. That afternoon, Irvel refused to sit in her recliner. Instead, she shuffled back and forth from the window to the door, watching for Hank. Several times she tried to leave through the front door. When Krista left, she warned Belinda that Irvel might try to escape."

Lu hung her head for a moment. When she looked up, there was anger in her eyes. "Belinda laughed and told Krista, 'Not on my shift, she won't.' " Lu hesitated. "From there it's pretty easy to piece together what happened."

"You think Irvel tried to leave?"

"If she wanted to see Hank bad enough, yes."

Ashley closed her eyes and pictured what might have happened. Poor Irvel would have been desperate to find Hank. Each time she tried to leave, Belinda must have grabbed her by the arm and forced her into her chair. Eventually, Belinda probably became crazy with frustration. That last time, she must have grabbed Irvel and threw her to the floor.

"At any rate, that's where Irvel was when Krista returned." Lu was clearly devastated by the details of the story. Telling it appeared to have sapped her strength. "By that time, Irvel was writhing on the floor in pain, and her arms were already discoloring. Krista heard Belinda say, 'Serves you right, you crazy old bird. You better get to your chair and stay there. You try to leave again, and next time it'll be worse.' "

Ashley was horrified. If Belinda had been there, she would have gladly pulled the woman's hair out and thrown her through the window. "What happened then?"

"Let's just say Belinda was very surprised to see Krista. She stumbled over her words and finally explained that Irvel had fallen." Lu exhaled hard. "Krista had the good sense to find a private phone and call me with the story. I called the police and met them in the living room fifteen minutes later. A doctor was here within the hour."

Ashley shook her head, her fists tight. "I barely recognized Irvel this morning."

"The doctor says her wounds are mostly superficial."

"Right." Ashley huffed. "Did you see the fear in her eyes? She's afraid of her own shadow."

"I know."

There wasn't much else either of them could say about the incident. Lu went over the details of Ashley's new job title and pay increase. She had hired a bookkeeper who would begin the following Monday. Until then, Lu would stay each day and run the office.

By eight-thirty, Ashley and Lu were finished talking, and Ashley set about making breakfast. Edith and Helen joined her at the table and introduced themselves. Before the meal was over, Ashley remembered the bathroom mirror. She slipped away, covered it with a sheet, and returned to the table.

Ashley spent the next two hours bathing Irvel and the others and making sure everyone had tea. Then, when the residents were all napping, Ashley went out to her car and brought in the saddle and sawhorse. At lunchtime she lugged them down the hallway into Bert's room. He was nibbling crackers and sipping soup from a small bowl, and he looked up when she entered.

"Hi, Bert." Ashley slid the sawhorse

across the room and positioned it near the foot of his bed. "I've got something for you."

Bert said nothing and directed his attention back to the soup.

Ashley took hold of the saddle and swung it over the sawhorse. Then she reached into a bag and pulled out an oilcloth. She sat on the edge of Bert's bed and waited for him to finish eating. Every day for the past two weeks she'd regretted not being able to carry out this plan. Now that she was here, no one could stop her.

Ashley couldn't wait.

Finally, Bert finished and pushed his tray aside. As he struggled to his feet, Ashley came alongside him. "Look, Bert. I brought you a saddle. I wondered if you could shine it for me."

Bert stared at the floor and resisted some. But after a moment, he allowed Ashley to lead him to the sawhorse. She positioned him directly in front of it, facing the saddle. Then she tucked the oilcloth into his hand, lifted it, and set it squarely in the middle of the saddle. "There, Bert. You can shine it now."

All the time she'd worked with Bert, he'd never expressed any emotion whatsoever. Not anger or sorrow or loneliness. Nothing. Now, as Bert felt the oilcloth connect with the saddle, he stood utterly still. Ashley took a step back, staring at Bert's hand, holding her breath while she waited to see what he would do next. She half expected him to sidestep the sawhorse and return to the edges of his bed, where he'd been making circles as long as anyone could remember.

But he didn't move.

He fixed his gaze on the saddle, and then it happened. He began to rub small, tender circles up and down the length of it. After a few seconds, his other hand came up and gripped the saddle. His fingers moved over the worn leather in a practiced manner, as though they were coming to life after years of being dormant.

Ashley could barely keep quiet. Bert understood what the object was! He recognized the feel of the saddle beneath his hands. With each passing minute, his shoulders grew straighter and his movements less trancelike, more purposeful.

She was still staring at the saddle, watching Bert's hands as they rubbed circles on the leather, when Ashley saw a tiny water drop hit the surface. Then another. What was this?

She shot a look up at Bert's face. Only

then did she understand exactly how much Bert had needed a saddle. His eyes told Ashley everything she needed to know.

Because now, as he rubbed a saddle for the first time in decades, Bert was doing something Ashley had never seen him do before.

He was crying.

Chapter Thirty-Four

Ryan Taylor had made his decision.

Now he stood in the middle of the Giants' practice field and stared at the stadium's lighted American flag billowing at one end. It was twenty-two degrees that night, and the skies were clear. Still, the winter wind cut at Ryan, and he wrapped his parka more tightly around his neck and face.

What a ride it had been, coaching in the NFL — minicamps and summer camps, the preseason and every hard-fought game since then, the emotional jolt of being so close to Ground Zero after September 11, then a disappointing season that had left them a dismal seven and nine in league.

Ryan studied the flag. No matter what the record showed, the New York Giants were winners. And so were their fans — the people of New York City. Long after wins and losses were forgotten, the tragedy of September 11 and its horrifying impact on the people of this town would resonate deep in Ryan's heart. He would never again look at an American flag without seeing the tattered one that had been pulled from the rubble of the twin towers, never hear mention of the terrorist attacks without picturing the way those flaming buildings looked through the window of his own apartment.

In fact, even as late as three weeks ago, when the Giants were on a winning streak, Ryan had spent hours wondering how he could convince Kari to move to New York and tag along behind him while he coached.

He had kept his thoughts to himself whenever he and Kari talked, careful not to bring up the subject. What could he say when most of the time he'd been too confused about the future even to guess at what he wanted to do?

I love Kari, God. He would pray the same way several times each day. *Show me what I'm supposed to do. Tell me where you want me and whether the timing's right for us.*

In the end, the decision had been made for him. Ryan smiled and dug his hands deeper into his pockets. Not by the coaching staff — although it appeared that way — but by God himself. The Lord had peered into his heart and known there was only one way Ryan Taylor could be happy.

Even now Ryan was certain that what happened at the end of the season had been a direct answer to his prayers.

"We'll be making some coaching changes." That was how the Giants' head coach had put it to him.

Ryan had understood what the man was saying. Because of his constant praying, he hadn't been angry or disappointed. The turnover rate was higher in professional coaching than in just about any other field. It was the nature of the job — win or else. After the Giants' losing season, coaching changes were inevitable, as were the offers from other teams. The moment Ryan was officially released from his contract with the Giants, half a dozen other teams had wanted to interview him. Denver, Oakland, Detroit, Chicago — for a week after the season ended, the list had seemed to grow each day.

Now it was mid-January, and Ryan had spoken with owners from every team that called. But only this afternoon had he made the decision to contact each of them with his answer.

Ryan sucked in a breath of freezing air and took one last look. Then he headed out the side entrance to his car and home to an apartment, where he planned to spend the evening packing.

After a year in the NFL, Ryan Taylor was walking away.

Not to a position with another team. Not to a spot in the analysts' booth for one of the networks — another offer that had come his way last week.

But to Bloomington, Indiana, and to a woman who'd captured his heart when he was barely more than a boy.

Kari opened her door and smiled at the familiar young woman on her front step. "Hi, Erin. Come in."

At first, Erin had been terrified to learn that the person she'd be studying with was her very own sister. But Kari had promised her anonymity — the same as if they hadn't known each other. Now, several weeks since they'd begun meeting together, they were finally getting to the heart of the issues.

The problem wasn't surprising. Erin didn't want to move away. She didn't trust Sam or love him enough to follow him to Texas. And when she and Kari first began meeting, she had no plans to change her opinion.

They had spoken about Erin's male friend, and Kari had convinced her sister that such a relationship could only get her in trouble. After that, she had finally given Erin an assignment.

"I want you to remember why you fell in love with Sam." Kari had handed Erin a booklet. "There are some examples in here, but let's go over some simple things you can do."

Kari explained that Erin could read cards and letters Sam had written her back in their dating days or watch their wedding video. Photographs could help her remember special times when love was new. Then, when the memories were fresh, Erin could write a list of things she'd appreciated about Sam back then.

"Remembering why you fell in love with your husband is like training your heart to look for those same qualities in him now."

Erin's response was fairly typical. "What if he's changed?"

Kari smiled. She'd felt the same way back when she and Tim were in counseling. "Believe me" — Kari patted her sister's hand — "those things you liked about Sam are still there. Even if you have to look harder to find them."

"Then what?"

"Honor him . . . compliment him. Build him up so he knows you still love him."

Erin had been skeptical at first. But now, as she stood on the step, a rare smile lit her face. Before she even came in, she opened her arms and hugged Kari close. "Thank you so much, Kari."

Kari felt her heartbeat quicken. She pulled back and searched Erin's eyes. "Thank you for what?"

"It worked!" Erin moved into Kari's living room, pulling Kari behind her. "It was the best week we've had in years."

"You mean because you remembered why you loved him?"

"Yes! I thought it was crazy — outdated, one-sided, whatever. It didn't make any sense to me at all. But nothing else was working, so I figured I'd give it a shot. Two days later, Sam and I went a whole evening without fighting. He became a completely different person. Kari, I'm serious. Whatever else you have to say, I'm ready to listen."

Kari couldn't contain her joy. She giggled, grabbing Erin's hands and squeezing them. "You know why, don't you?"

"I don't know why. I just know it works." Erin blinked back tears.

"Because it's from God." Kari breathed a silent prayer, thanking God for Erin's breakthrough. "God wants us to remember our first love — both with him and with our spouse. When we remember that way, we're better able to honor the person we're unhappy with. After that, everything else falls into place."

Kari opened her Bible and spread it out on her lap. "Today we'll go a little deeper. . . ."

Kari shivered as she walked out of church that Sunday morning.

It had been a moving sermon. Pastor Mark had encouraged the congregation to examine their lives and then move forward. "Aim for the high road, the place where God wants you," he'd told them. "And don't let anything get in your way."

No regrets, he'd said. Make the most of every opportunity so that when life was over, that one statement would be true.

During the message, Kari had glanced down the row at Ashley. Her younger sister was nodding and taking careful notes. Was it possible that just a year ago Ashley would have laughed at the thought of even going to church? Yet here she was, growing in her faith — sold-out to Christ.

Kari's study with her sister Erin had continued, and although Erin and Sam still had their differences, their marriage grew stronger every week. Erin had confided to Kari that she was pretty sure she would be moving to Texas with her husband when the time came.

Brooke and Peter continued to attend church — though Maddie had been sick again lately, and they'd missed some Sundays. Still, the impact of September 11 remained with them, convincing them they needed God.

All the Baxters were where they should be. Everyone except Luke.

Kari remembered the look on her father's face when she'd asked him earlier that morning if Luke might be coming. Cole was going to sing a solo in church with the kids' choir, and Ashley had invited Luke.

"I don't think so." Her father's eyes were heavy with pain. "He told Ashley he didn't think it would be appropriate."

How had her brother's views become so twisted? Kari didn't know, but she would make a point to call Luke that week and talk with him. Maybe if she reminded him that he was loved and prayed for . . .

She reached her car and shifted Jessie to her opposite hip so she could use the keys. Her daughter was eight months old now and jabbering constantly. Although the rest of her life still hung in an uncertain balance, Kari was deeply grateful for her little girl. She opened the back door and buckled Jessie into her car seat. Then she pulled a bottle from her bag and handed it to her.

"There you go, sweetie. We'll be home in a few minutes, and you can take a nap."

Kari moved to the driver's door but stopped short. An envelope was pinned beneath her wipers.

Strange, Kari thought. She glanced at the other cars around her. Hers was the only one with something on the windshield. The envelope was damp, so she opened it slowly, careful not to rip the letter inside.

The moment she unfolded the paper, her heart skipped a beat. The handwriting was Ryan's. But Ryan was in New York. In fact, he'd been so busy with meetings he hadn't called her for several days.

Her eyes scanned the short note:

Dear Kari,
Meet me at Lake Monroe in an hour.
I'll be at our spot waiting for you.

There was no name, no signature, nothing but the handwriting to convince her that the note was from Ryan. Kari stared at the words again — the way the circles didn't quite come together and the loops looked almost like straight lines. It was his, wasn't it? Could it have been someone else's?

No, it wasn't possible.

Ryan was the only person she knew who wrote like that.

Kari was still studying the note, trying to figure out what to make of it, when she felt a tap on her shoulder. She jumped and turned around. "Dad!" She was breathless. "You scared me."

Her father's eyes held a twinkle. "Sorry." He grinned. "Your mother and I were just wondering if we could watch Jessie this afternoon." He cooed at the baby. "We, uh, thought you might need the help."

Kari clutched the note but let her hand drop to her side. "Help for what?"

"Oh, you know," her mother's voice teased, "in case you need a few hours to yourself this afternoon."

John nodded. "To hang out at the lake or something."

At the lake? Kari looked at the note in her hand once more. "Wait a minute! You guys know about this?"

"Hmm." Her father's eyes grew wide with mock innocence. "My goodness, what's that?"

Kari's mom grinned. "Looks like a note!" Her parents nudged each other. "Wonder who could have left it on your car?"

Kari grabbed her mother's arm. "Mom, if you've seen Ryan, you have to tell me. Come on! I need to know."

Her dad shrugged. "All I know is a little bird . . ." He looked at her mother again.

"A big bird, actually."

John nodded. "Okay, a big bird told us you might need help with Jessie this afternoon. Something about a visit to Lake Monroe — wasn't that it?"

"Yes, I think so." Her mom pointed to Kari's car. "How about you follow us back to our house, get Jessie comfortable in her crib, and find an extra coat and some gloves."

"You really aren't going to tell me, are you?"

"Nope." Her father made a zipping motion across his lips. "We're really not."

Kari laughed. There was no point pushing the matter. She did as her parents said, followed them back to their house, and changed into something warm to wear. When Jessie was down for her nap, she set out for Lake Monroe. The whole time, her heart soared with happiness. The note had to be from Ryan. Somehow he'd already talked to her parents and arranged for them to watch Jessie. But why the mystery? And why Lake Monroe, when they could have visited just as easily at her parents' house?

She pulled into the parking lot exactly one hour after finding the note and peered down toward the edge of the water. There — sitting atop a frozen picnic table — was Ryan. She would have recognized his profile, his build, a hundred yards away.

The moment he heard her car, he turned and grinned. It was him! He had come and turned a cold, wintry Sunday into the warmest day in weeks. With careful steps she made her way down the slick bank. He stood and waited, his eyes fixed on hers.

When she was only a few feet away, she stopped and studied him.

"I see you got my note."

"I did." She took another step toward him. "You didn't tell me you were coming."

He held out his hands, and she came to him willingly, unable to wait another minute to be in his arms, to feel his warmth against her. "You're really here. I can't believe it, Ryan. I knew it was your writing, but still . . ." She snuggled her face against his shoulder. "I thought it might be weeks before you could get away."

"Well . . ." He drew back, and their eyes met and held. "I had this question I couldn't ask you on the phone." His eyes shone with a love so real and true it warmed Kari to the deepest places in her heart. "I figured the only way to ask it was to come here and do it in person."

Kari's heart skipped a beat. She knew he'd been released by New York, but so far he hadn't decided about the other teams. Had he made his decision? Was he moving to another state — maybe farther away than before? She blinked twice, her voice barely audible over the winter wind coming off the lake. "What question?"

Ryan gripped her jacket and eased her closer, kissing her long and slow. "The question I've wanted to ask you all my life."

His grin faded, and a hint of tears glazed the surface of his eyes. Slowly he dropped one knee onto the damp shore and reached for her left hand.

"Ryan!" Shock danced across her heart. Was this . . . ? Could it be . . . ?

"I spoke to your parents earlier today, and they gave me their blessing."

"Their blessing?" Her head was spinning, but she willed herself to concentrate.

"Kari, all my life I've been telling you good-bye, seeking after things I thought would make me complete. . . ." He paused, his words slow and deliberate as he struggled to keep a grip on his emotions. It had taken them so long to reach this point. She tightened her hold on his hand and loved him with her eyes. "When the only time I'm ever whole is when I'm with you."

He looked straight to her soul. "You complete me, Kari. You always will."

He opened his right hand, and there in his palm was a diamond solitaire. Not large or too flashy. But just right. Never breaking eye contact, he slipped the ring on her finger. "Marry me, Kari girl. Live with me here in Bloomington. Let me be a father to Jessie and whatever other children the Lord might bless us with. Please, Kari. There's nothing in my life I want more."

The tears came unbidden, streaking down her face and past the raised corners of her mouth. She dropped to her knees in front of him and circled her arms around his neck. "I've dreamed about this since I was a girl. Are you really here?"

"I'm here, Kari. I don't ever want to leave you again."

She leaned back and searched his eyes. "What about your coaching? I won't stand in your way, Ryan. If that's what you want, I'm willing to talk about it."

He shook his head. Never in her life had she seen him more certain. "What I want is right here with you and Jessie. I'm not interested in traveling the country and giving my life to football. I want you, Kari. Only you."

She laughed through her tears. The wetness of the ground was working its way through her jeans, making her knees cold, but it didn't matter. She could stay this way in Ryan's arms forever.

She held her left hand out and stared at the ring. "It's beautiful, Ryan. How long have you been planning this?"

He hesitated, waiting until her eyes caught his again. "Since I was fourteen."

"I love you, Ryan Taylor." She kissed him, wiping her tears against his cheek.

"There's just one problem." Ryan sounded serious.

Kari held her breath and looked at him. *No, God, please . . . no problems. Not now.* "What?"

"You haven't answered my question."

She could feel the grin spread across her face. With an awkward motion, she stood up and helped him to his feet. Then she took hold of his hands and looked into his eyes one more time. "Yes, Ryan Taylor, I'll marry you." She leaned her head back and shouted toward heaven. "Yes! A hundred times yes!"

He pulled her to him and touched the sides of her face with his fingertips. "I love you, Kari. I hope you never get tired of hearing it — because this time I'm not going anywhere. Not ever."

Was she dreaming? None of it felt real yet, and she giggled as she hugged Ryan again. "I can't wait to tell Mom and Dad."

"There's one thing I want to do first."

Kari angled her head, waiting for Ryan to explain.

"Pray with me, Kari. Please."

He took her hands in his and bowed his head. Together they thanked God for his sovereignty and for his divine timing, for his gift of love, and for his leading in their relationship.

Then they thanked him for removing one word from their vocabulary forever — a word that had haunted them as far back as they could remember.

The word *good-bye*.

Chapter Thirty-Five

Luke Baxter felt like a different person altogether.

He and Lori Callahan had gotten an A on their assignment. With very little effort, really, they had successfully — at least by Professor Hicks's standards — argued that God did not exist.

Privately, Luke thought the assignment results seemed a bit flat and manipulated. After all, there wasn't a concrete way to prove or disprove God's existence. But in the process of doing the assignment, something life-changing had happened to Luke. He had discovered the power of humanism — the worldview Professor Hicks swore by.

The only surprise was that he hadn't discovered it before. The basic ideas of humanism were everywhere these days, weren't they? Print advertisements for the Winter Olympics touted "Celebrate Humanity," and a newly formed coalition had begun running commercials encouraging people to fight terrorism by going to work and getting involved and continuing the quest for education. "Fight Terrorism," the ads instructed America. "Live brave."

And that was what mattered, wasn't it, in light of September 11 and the continuing threats from terrorists? That people supported each other and lived bravely together? It was all about people, not God.

Luke and Lori had discussed this topic at length, often at her parents' house with her father present.

"Religion is dangerous," her father had said on several occasions. "People don't need a crock full of traditions and old wives' tales." He would smile that serious smile of his. "They need tangible answers and faith in the one thing they can count on — the basic goodness of humanity. Especially at times like this."

Lori's father had been thrilled when he found out that Luke had an interest in law. "A boy like you — bright, intelligent — that's exactly what we need to keep all the crazy right-wingers from eroding our constitutional rights."

The idea sounded appealing to Luke and, not long after the semester ended, he made his decision. He would study law and become the same kind of attorney as Lori's dad. By now — the middle of January — he was spending more time with Lori and her family than he was with his own.

It was only a natural progression of events, of course, that he should be gone more often from his parents' house. After all, neither of them seemed interested in debating with him the reality of God. Certainly they wouldn't consider his point of view valid. How could they? None of them saw the burgeoning movement of humanism as a viable alternative to mainline Christianity. Not yet, anyway.

In addition to being stubborn, his family — in fact, most of his sisters — were outspokenly disappointed in the things he said and the company he kept. "You're breaking Dad's heart," Kari had told him last week. "At least talk to him, hear him out. This is all about losing Reagan, Luke — don't you see that? Dad can pray with you, show you some Bible verses, help you understand what's going on."

Show him some Bible verses? Couldn't Kari see he was past that now? Luke had always gotten along with Kari, but with statements like that, she'd crossed a line. "You know what's wrong with you?" he shouted at her as he left the room that day. "You think every problem can be solved with a prayer and a Bible verse."

He stopped at the foot of the stairs and uttered a single laugh. "Look at the people buried beneath the World Trade Center, Kari. Lotta good prayer and a Bible verse did them!"

She'd started to say something, but he hadn't wanted to hear it. How come it had taken the terrorist attacks to make him see how closed-minded his family was?

Out of the entire family, in fact, only Ashley seemed to understand what was going on with Luke. Or at least, she didn't tell him he was ruining his life like the others did.

"I love you, Luke," she'd told him a dozen times since the attacks. "Whatever you believe, whatever you do with your life . . . I'll always love you." She would hug him or kiss his cheek. "I missed out on too many years of loving you to ever let that happen again."

Ashley was treating him the way he should have treated her all those years after she came home from Paris. But then he was a different person back then — as judgmental and narrow in his thinking as the rest of them. Of course, Ashley had no idea how much they actually had in common. He hadn't told anyone about

567

what happened between Reagan and him the night before her father was killed.

It wasn't something he planned to share. Not ever.

Not because he thought what he and Reagan did was wrong — he was past that now. It just wasn't anybody's business.

When he thought about it, Ashley's acceptance of him was further proof that the human spirit was the greatest force of all. God wasn't what motivated Ashley to extend love and friendship to Luke. It was her innate sense of personal kindness and love — the very attributes that were so obviously at work in the United States since the attacks.

Sure, in the past he would have credited God and faith and answered prayer for the changes in his sister. But how could he hold on to those childish beliefs when they hadn't proved the least bit reliable? If God was real and prayer worked, then it would work every time, wouldn't it?

The way he saw it these days, Christians had a way of celebrating what seemed like miraculous answers to prayer and sweeping under the rug the times when prayer didn't make a difference. So even the most devout believers seemed to carry some type of doubt about God. How could he put his trust in a higher power who wasn't consistent?

Not that it had been easy to leave behind a lifetime of training. Every now and then he'd dismiss God and prayer and faithfulness, and the strangest whisper would seem to blow across his heart:

I have loved you with an everlasting love, my son. Return to me.

Luke had no intention of returning. He chalked up the strange murmuring to an overactive imagination and a lifetime of conditioning. As the weeks went by, the whispers had grown quieter, until now they were barely noticeable.

"It's like you were brainwashed," Lori said one night when he told her about the imperceptible voice and the message it brought. "I can't believe you swallowed that stuff all your life."

The thing with Lori was sort of weird. He wasn't exactly attracted to her, although he had no doubt about her feelings for him. Way back on the third night of meeting to do their communications report, she had asked him to sleep with her. He'd politely turned her down, explaining that he was still in love with Reagan. But the truth was, he'd never dated a girl so direct before. To him, it was like playing a

game of basketball without an opponent —
no challenge, no mystery whatsoever.

Still, the more time he spent with Lori,
the more fun they had together. She might
not be the type of girl he could see himself
marrying one day, but her intellect was exciting. It had brought him to another level
of thinking. And she wasn't bad-looking,
with her clear green eyes and her cloud of
dark curls. One of these days, they were
bound to cross the line from friendship to
dating. Already they'd kissed a few times,
and Luke could see things getting more serious between them.

And why not?

He was a free man, after all. His relationship with Reagan was history. He called
her only once in a while anymore, in-
tending to wish her well and offer his sympathy about her father. But she still had
not accepted even one of his phone calls.

All of it — Luke's decision to embrace
humanism, his idea of becoming a civil-liberties attorney, and his growing friendship
with Lori and her family — had made such
an impact on Luke that he had spoken to
his father early this week and asked if they
could have an evening to talk.

"Definitely. What night works for you?"

Luke hated the way his father had

looked relieved by the question. *He thinks I'm going to go back to the way I was. Well, he'll know the truth soon enough.*

They'd decided on Thursday night, and Luke expected the discussion would go well. His dad would be disappointed with Luke's decision, of course. But still, he was a good man, one of the best Luke had ever known.

Despite his determination to cling to an irrational faith, the heart of humanism beat strongly in John Baxter.

Luke could only hope that heart would be evident on Thursday night.

John Baxter was worried about his only son.

The rate at which Luke was slipping from them was no longer something John could reason away. He and Elizabeth had watched him turn into a reclusive, critical young man whose faith had all but disappeared. They had talked at length about the decisions Luke was making and the influence Lori Callahan seemed to have on him.

When they weren't talking about Luke, they were praying. Every night and each morning, they asked God to get Luke's attention and snap him back to the only reality he'd ever known — the reality of faith and the certainty that life came from a God who did care and did love him, regardless of the heartaches that came with living.

On Thursday, the day he'd agreed to meet with Luke, John not only prayed every chance he had, but he fasted as well. Fasting wasn't something he did often, and never did he share the fact with anyone except Elizabeth. But that day, he felt it was necessary.

On the way home from his office he prayed again. *Be with us tonight as we talk. Let peace and love prevail. Speak your words through my lips. Please, Father. Don't let my only son get away. I couldn't bear it.*

The answer that John heard now, deep in his soul, was the same he'd heard all day.

The thief comes only to steal and kill and destroy; I have come that they may have life, and have it to the full.

It was a Scripture verse John and Luke had memorized together when Luke was just eight years old. Back then it had opened the door to Luke's blossoming understanding of all the goodness God had in store for those who followed him. Now it reminded John that Luke's struggles would not be happening except for one thing:

The enemy was at work.

What *had* happened? Luke had been the strongest one, the golden boy destined to live a life of faith. But hadn't he shown signs all along that his faith wasn't what it should be? What about the way he'd reacted to Ashley's situation? And Kari's? Somehow, during his teenage years, he'd become rigid and legalistic, forgetting the power of grace and forgiveness.

John wondered why he hadn't talked to Luke back then, when he'd first noticed those changes.

He had no answers for that, any more than he fully understood what was happening to Luke now. But this he knew: No matter how bad the situation looked, God would win in the end. His purposes would prevail. John only hoped that one day soon Luke would remember the truths he'd known and believed as a young boy, the very truths he was running so hard from these days.

That night, when dinner was finished, Luke came home and found John in the family room. John tried to read him, but it was impossible. Luke seemed stiff, his face tense and anxious. "Can we talk now?"

"Sure." John smiled. The last thing he wanted was to come across as suspicious.

If Luke wanted to talk, he needed a good listener, and John intended to be just that.

They made their way upstairs to John's home office. John shut the door and took a seat opposite Luke. He looked at him, hoping his expression was kind. "May I say something before we begin?"

"Sure." Luke made brief eye contact with John and then dropped his gaze to the floor.

"I'm proud of you for wanting to talk." John clasped his hands and leaned forward. "I know you're going through a hard time." He gave his son a lopsided grin. "It means a lot that you asked for this meeting."

Luke licked his lips and shifted. "Okay."

"So . . ." John leaned back. "What would you like to talk about?"

Luke lifted his eyes. "I want to move out."

John's stomach turned. There was no anger in Luke's voice, just determination — frightening, unbending determination. *Help me here, God. Help me.* Luke's mind had obviously been made up long before this discussion.

John drew a slow breath. "Okay, that's understandable. You're old enough to get a place of your own."

Luke raised an eyebrow, as though

John's answer surprised him. "I've also made some career plans."

Calm. Be calm. "I'm listening."

"I want to be a civil-liberties attorney. It's something Lori's dad told me about." Luke's voice had an edge to it. "Make sure human freedoms aren't trampled by narrow, closed-minded, special-interest groups."

John's lungs deflated like leftover party balloons. He could guess what "narrow, closed-minded, special-interest groups" Lori's father had in mind. "As your father, I will respect whatever decisions you make, Luke. I'll never love you less or hold it against you if you choose that type of career." He anchored his elbows on his knees and brought his face closer to Luke's. "But I can't let you tell me that without sharing something with you."

"What?" There was defiance in Luke's tone, and John feared the direction the conversation might go.

"It's a verse that's been playing over in my mind all day while I prayed for you." John hesitated. "It's from John 10:10. Jesus is talking, and he tells us, 'The thief comes only to steal and kill and destroy; I have come that they may have life, and have it to the full.' "

Luke stared at him, his expression stony. "That's all you have to say?" His voice was louder than before. "I tell you I'm moving out and pursuing a career as a civil-liberties attorney, and you quote me some Bible verse?"

Panic worked its way through John's veins. Who was this young man across from him? And what had happened to the golden boy who'd loved God? The one who had been troubled by his sisters' poor choices? The one who had been determined to do things God's way, no matter the cost? "It's the verse you and I memorized when you were a young boy, Luke. I thought you'd remember."

Luke stood and stared down at him. "I'm not a young boy anymore, Dad. I'm a grown man, and I have my own ways of understanding what's happened in our country this past year." He clenched his fists. "Don't you get that?"

"Yes, I get it." John remained in his seat, his voice as steady as it had been when they first began speaking. "I'm only trying to help you, son."

"I don't need help!" Luke brushed his fingers through his hair and glanced up at the ceiling. His anger was palpable, like a physical shield around him. "I have a right to my viewpoint without your trying to 'help' me . . . or change me back to how I used to be."

"Lower your voice." John finally let his own frustration show. "You will always be entitled to your opinion. But you will not speak to me in that tone of voice. Do you understand?"

Luke uttered a short laugh and shook his head. "You know, Dad, I really thought you were enough of a man that we could have this conversation without your turning it into a lecture. Or bringing God into it."

"Well, then." John's voice was back to normal, but his heart was breaking. "I guess you don't know me very well. God isn't something I bring into a conversation. God is my life. When I talk to my son, a little bit of God is bound to ooze out."

"And that's why I'm leaving tonight." Luke headed for the door.

"Luke, think about what you're saying." John stood and reached his hand toward his son. "If you don't want me to share Bible verses, I won't. There's no reason for you to run off like this." John held his breath and grabbed at the last straw. "Think of how your mother will feel."

Luke rolled his eyes. "She won't miss

me. She's already told me how she feels about Lori. The two of you don't agree with anything I'm doing these days." He opened the door. "I'll spend the next few weeks with a friend of Lori's. My things'll be out by the first of the month."

Three hours later Luke was gone.

John tried to replay the familiar Scripture verse in his mind while Elizabeth wept in his arms in the quiet of their bedroom. Where was the encouragement, the hope about the future, the reassurance that with God's help, somehow Luke would one day come to his senses?

John had no answers for himself. All that played over and over in his mind was the first part of the verse: *"The thief comes only to steal and kill and destroy."* It was *that* part that shook him to the core, that had never in his life seemed more true. The part that kept him up all night, praying desperately for the safety of his only son.

That God would save Luke before any of those things actually happened.

His family would be furious with him. But then that was nothing new.

Luke stood at the window of the apartment he now shared with Lori Callahan off campus. His other plans for an apartment had fallen through sometime after Christmas. Lori's father had already rented this place for her. So when she suggested he move in, too, Luke couldn't think of a single reason why not.

Kari and Ryan had asked everyone to gather at their parents' house tonight for some kind of dinner party. It didn't take a genius to figure out what the big deal was. They were obviously going to announce their engagement. Kari had made a point of calling the day before to see if he was coming.

"Probably," he'd told her.

"Please, Luke. This means a lot to Ryan and me. He really wants you there."

Luke had stifled a sigh. "I'll try. I have a lot of homework."

"Try hard."

Luke couldn't relate. There had been nothing upbeat about his life since the terrorist attacks. There were a few bright spots, yes, but mostly his days were an empty, meaningless vacuum. And maybe that's all life had been before September 11 too. People were born. They died. In between, they did their best to make money and help as many people as they could.

That was it. No God, no heaven, no eternity to look forward to.

But that wasn't how his sisters saw it, and they never let him forget that fact. Luke felt a tension in his shoulders as he stared into the dark night. He had nothing against Kari or any of his other sisters. But they didn't understand him. All of them except Ashley were constantly trying to change him — sharing Scriptures, offering to pray, telling him he was going through a phase or that he was depressed.

Lori came up behind him and massaged the muscles at the base of his neck. "You look tense."

"I am." He didn't turn around. He was living with Lori now, doing everything that went along with that. It was an agreeable arrangement, but it wasn't love.

"Because of your family?" Lori ran her fingernails lightly down his sides. She lifted his white T-shirt and left a trail of kisses between his shoulder blades.

He grew still beneath her touch, not wanting her advances. "I guess."

"Go, then." She let his shirt fall back into place and came up alongside him. "If you want to be there, go. Your father won't fight with you tonight. Not if it's some big announcement for Kari and Ryan."

Luke shook his head. "I don't want to be there. I just feel bad, that's all."

Lori studied him for a moment. "Let me know if I can help." She walked away and headed down the hallway toward their room.

The emptiness in Luke's heart swelled until he wasn't sure he could take it anymore. Why was he even here? What was he doing living with a girl he didn't love — a girl that sometimes he could barely stand? And what was his family doing at the Baxter house without him? Had they all written him off? Or were they holding hands around the dinner table, praying he'd come to his senses?

Why was the emptiness getting to him tonight? Normally it didn't bother him; it was part of his life now. To believe there was no God was to believe there was no meaning in anything.

Work, relationships, children — all of it was meaningless. An ever-changing process that led nowhere.

He closed his eyes and let his head fall against the cold window. Last week's snow had already melted across much of Bloomington, but winter was just getting under way.

Suddenly, Luke remembered last spring, when he and Reagan played softball, watched hoops on television, and read the Bible together.

How could he have been so gullible? Reagan had never loved him. If she had, she wouldn't have disappeared so completely after one little mistake.

Looking back, it didn't even seem that bad. They'd slipped up — once. But was that any reason for her to cut him off completely? Since September 11, she still had never once taken his calls or responded to his messages.

No, it was clear to Luke now that Reagan had never really loved him. It was God she loved. And now that same God was exacting of her a terrible penance for one little slip.

She could have at least spoken to him, told him how she was handling the loss of her father. But instead she'd cut him out of her life. And if losing Reagan was the price he had to pay for breaking the rules that awful Monday night, then the whole faith thing was a game. One Luke didn't want to play anymore. Not now. Not ever.

He opened his eyes and stared across the darkened landscape once more. It was over — everything about life as he'd once known it. But no matter how hard he tried, he couldn't keep his mind from dwelling on the same two questions that had plagued him ever since he moved in with Lori.

Where was Reagan now?

And did she ever — on a cold winter night — find herself pressed against a dark window thinking about him?

Chapter Thirty-Six

The idea came to Ashley almost as soon as she started back at Sunset Hills.

Family Day, she called it. A Saturday afternoon when all the relatives would be welcome to visit at the same time. Sunset Hills would provide dinner, and Ashley's new philosophy on Alzheimer's care could be showcased.

Already the improvements in the residents had been so dramatic, even Lu had taken to studying the Past-Present ideas.

"You're right," she told Ashley one afternoon after looking up research cases on the Internet. "I've talked to the owners of other adult care homes. Improvements can be drastic when you help Alzheimer's patients live where they can best remember."

"It's hard to argue with the results." Ashley had beamed at Lu.

"I'd like you to continue training the entire staff to handle the patients the way you do."

It was Lu's last comment that convinced

584

Ashley to create Family Day. She found Lu a few days later. "Once the staff understands, let's have an open house for family members. That way they'll see for themselves how this approach works."

Lu grinned. "I can hardly wait."

Family Day was set for Saturday, January 19, and Ashley was surprised at the response. At least one relative for each of the residents planned to attend. Best of all, Bert's son from Wisconsin was coming. Ashley had called to tell him something dramatic had happened with his father.

"That's okay, Ms. Baxter." Bert's son had sounded tired. "You don't have to lie to get us to come. It's been awhile since I've seen Dad, so I'll be there. I'm not expecting miracles."

Ashley couldn't wait to see the man's face when he realized he was wrong.

Family Day dawned sunny despite the cold temperatures. Helen's daughter was the first to arrive. The two had continued their conversations about "Sue" several times each week, and not once had Sue let on that she was anything but a visiting stranger. Ashley wasn't sure, but she sensed a breakthrough was coming.

That day Sue and Helen sat together in her room sharing stories about Sue, as usual. Ashley checked in on them now and then, and at ten o'clock she brought the women each a cup of tea. They seemed lost in conversation, so Ashley crept back toward the door and watched.

"After the spies took my Sue" — Helen pointed to her dresser drawer — "she still lived in here."

Sue glanced at Ashley, and the women exchanged a knowing look. This was the first time Helen had trusted Sue enough to talk about her drawer of photographs. Sue quickly returned her attention to her mother. "Is that right?"

Helen's face grew noticeably softer. "Wanna see?"

Sue took her mother's hand. "That would be wonderful."

Slowly, Helen went to the dresser, opened the drawer, and pulled out the framed picture she'd shown Ashley months ago. "This" — her voice broke — "this is my Sue."

"She's very pretty, Helen. Just like I remember her back when she was younger."

Helen clutched the photograph to her chest. "When she was . . . younger?"

They were treading dangerous ground. Ashley closed her eyes and prayed that Helen wouldn't become combative.

Sue cast a gentle look at her mother. "I knew Sue very well. That's how she looked when she was a girl."

For a long while Helen stared at Sue, almost as though she were seeing her for the first time. Slowly, tentatively, she drew the photograph away from her chest and held it out so the image of the young Sue was positioned just below the face of the older Sue.

Ashley watched, mesmerized. *Please, God, let her understand just this once. For Sue, Lord . . . please.*

Helen looked from Sue to the photograph and back again. "You know, you sort of have Sue's eyes."

It was at this point that Helen was most likely to snap. Ashley could picture her ordering Sue from her room, accusing her of being a spy, and stealing Sue's eyes, insisting she had somehow hidden Sue from her.

Ashley bit her lip and waited. *Please, God.*

At first, Sue said nothing. She reached for the photo and held it up beside her face so Helen could clearly see both images. "Yes. I looked just like Sue when I was younger."

A wetness gathered in Helen's eyes.

"You . . . you did?"

"I did." Sue kept the photograph adjacent to her face. She obviously wanted her mother to see the resemblance — a resemblance that even thirty years couldn't hide. Sue's voice was the softest caress. "Same eyes . . . same face. Same everything."

Helen leaned forward and peered at Sue the way she might if Sue were standing in the middle of a dense bank of fog. She squinted, and her soft, wrinkled chin began to quiver. Then she lifted one trembling hand toward Sue's face and brushed back a lock of her daughter's graying hair. "Sue?"

Tears filled Sue's eyes, and a sob slipped from her throat before she could recover. "Yes, Mama, it's me. Sue."

"My Sue?"

Ashley felt tears slipping down her own cheeks as she watched the scene unfold. It was a miracle, a moment stolen from yesterday. With Alzheimer's there was no telling if they would share a time like this again. Every day brought with it a new set of challenges. But here, now, Sue was being given a gift that few children of Alzheimer's patients ever get.

The chance to watch her mother remember — even if just this once.

Sue set the photograph down and leaned into her mother's arms as though she were thirteen again. "I'm here, Mama."

Helen began to cry. "Sue!" She stroked her back and nuzzled her face against her daughter's. "I thought . . . I thought I'd never see you again."

"I know, Mama." Sue's tears streamed down her face, but her voice was clear, and a smile punctuated her sobs. "I know."

"Someone took you away from me." Helen sniffed twice and ran her fingers over Sue's hair.

"No, Mama, I'm here. I'll never leave you."

Helen buried her head in her daughter's shoulder. "I missed you, honey. I never stopped missing you."

Ashley took a step back toward the hallway. It was a bridge. That was the benefit of allowing Alzheimer's patients to live in their memories, in the past, where they were comfortable. Sometimes, during moments like this, the memories were strong enough to span the gap between yesterday and today. Strong enough, in this case, to allow a mother and daughter the chance to love the way they hadn't in years.

Lu walked by and paused, glancing over Ashley's shoulder. She leaned close and whispered, "What's happening?"

Ashley wiped her tears and smiled, keeping her voice low enough that it didn't interrupt the conversation between the two women. "Helen remembered her. It's the first time in years."

"That's impossible." Lu stared at the two women and then back at Ashley. "I think we'll change your title from manager to miracle worker."

Ashley grinned. "That's not my title." She pointed upward. "It's his." Lu wasn't a Christian believer, but Ashley had a feeling she would be one day.

"Well." Lu stared at Sue and Helen, and shook her head. "I'd say he's doing a pretty good job."

Bert's son and his family arrived just after lunch.

This was the moment Ashley had been looking forward to since she gave Bert his saddle. The changes in Bert had been dramatic and ongoing. Ashley even planned to write about them in a paper and submit them to several of the groups she had found on Web sites. Her experience would be further proof that allowing Alzheimer's patients their memories was a good thing.

Ashley met the man, his wife, and their two daughters at the door and welcomed them. When they were seated, Ashley smiled at them. "I'll go get your father."

Bert's son exchanged an odd look with his wife, and Ashley knew what they were thinking. How would Ashley get Bert out of his room? The old man hated leaving the place and was always withdrawn and difficult when he was brought into the commons.

Ashley giggled to herself and hummed as she made her way to Bert's room. He was polishing his saddle the same way he did every afternoon at this time.

"Hi, Bert." She stopped in the doorway and grinned at him. "How are you?"

He turned and smiled at her. His movements were still slower than they might have been, but there was life in his eyes, and his voice was laced with awareness. "Got me a saddle."

"I see that." Ashley held out her hand. "Your son's here to see you, Bert. I told him I'd get you."

Bert's hand stopped in midstroke. "My . . . my son?"

"Yes. It's Family Day. Your son and his family are here."

"David?"

Ashley wanted to shout out loud. Bert remembered!

The changes in Bert had happened quickly after he'd gotten the saddle. First he began making eye contact, and then he started talking. But he'd never showed any awareness that he even had a son — until now.

"Yes, David Riley. Your son."

"Lives down the road . . . old dairy farm."

"That's right." Smiling, Ashley reached her hand out a bit farther. "Come say hello to them."

Bert's eyebrows lowered, and he nodded his head slowly and seriously. "Believe I will." He set the oilcloth carefully on top of the saddle and took small, hesitant steps in Ashley's direction. When he was almost there, he took her hand and let her lead him from the room.

David stood when Ashley and Bert entered the room. There was silence for a moment, and then David took a step forward. "Hello, Dad. It's me, David." The man was a younger version of Bert — tall and proud, with muscled shoulders and calloused palms. He made his way across the room and held out his hand.

Ashley stepped back as Bert took his

son's fingers and held tightly to them. "Hi."

Across the room, David's wife let her lower jaw hang open, her eyes wide. Quietly she whispered, "How in the world . . . ?"

David cleared his throat. "Do you know who I am, Dad?"

Bert narrowed his eyes and grinned at David, their two hands still joined. "You're my boy. Chip off the old block."

David shot a look of shock and gratitude over his shoulder at Ashley. Then he pulled his father into an embrace and held him that way for a long time. "I've missed you, Dad. You don't know how much I've missed you." He pulled back and sniffed, clearly trying to control his emotion. "How . . . how are you?"

Bert stood there a bit awkwardly and patted David on the back. "Got me a saddle."

Ashley covered her mouth with the back of her hand, not wanting her own feelings to interrupt the moment. *God, you are so good! Thank you for this.* She swallowed, trying to find her voice. "Your dad's been talking a lot these past weeks, haven't you, Bert?"

He looked at her, and a childlike smile lifted the corners of his mouth. "Got me a saddle."

Ashley directed the two men to sit on the sofa while Lu went through the house and summoned the others — Irvel with both her grandson and her niece; Edith and two granddaughters; Helen, clutching tightly to her daughter, Sue; and Laura Jo's son, who had flown in from California for the first time in more than a year. When they were all gathered, Lu explained that the philosophy at Sunset Hills had changed quite a bit over the past six months. "We invited you here today because our new manager has found research that proves how crucial it is for Alzheimer's patients to be allowed to live in their memories. If the time they remember best is ten years ago or twenty, then we allow them the luxury of living there. Ashley Baxter, our manager, will tell you more."

Ashley had no intention of going into great detail about Alzheimer's research with the residents seated around the room, but she felt there was no harm talking in general terms. Ashley explained the differing schools of thought when it came to Alzheimer's patients. "Let's say you spend your life as a beauty queen. Once Alzheimer's strikes, you might believe you're still thirty-five and stunningly beautiful."

Ashley smiled in Edith's direction. The

woman was staring at her hands, snuggled between her granddaughters. The conversation did not mean a thing to her. Although she had been more at peace since she'd stopped seeing her own reflection, she was as lost as ever — maybe even worse than before.

Ashley continued. "And let's say every time you walk into a bathroom, you scream because you think a witch is after you."

Ashley paused and looked around the room. "The old school of thought teaches caregivers to force an Alzheimer's patient to recognize current reality or be sedated. So the care worker would insist that there is no witch, that you are simply looking in a mirror. And if you kept screaming, the worker would simply give you enough drugs to knock you out."

She looked back at Edith. "In this house we've decided to try a different approach. Instead of forcing our residents to acknowledge current reality, we've decided to let them live in whatever era of their memory makes them happiest.

"In the case of our screaming resident, for instance — and yes, this is a real example — we simply covered the bathroom mirror, and the screaming stopped. The reason? Our patient hadn't been seeing a witch. She'd been seeing her own reflection." Ashley could hear the compassion in her voice. "A reflection she no longer recognized because she was living decades in the past. Back when she didn't look the way she does now." Ashley smiled at Edith's granddaughters. "Ultimately, our patient is calmer and happier."

Ashley continued, sharing examples without alerting the residents that they were being talked about. Afterward she fielded questions from several of the family members but heard none of the negative responses Belinda had warned her about. The improvements in the residents were too convincing. Now the family members wanted only to know how they could cooperate with what was obviously already working.

Ashley encouraged the family members to stay for the turkey buffet later that afternoon and to visit as long as they were able. Then she made the rounds, spending time with each of the residents and their various relatives.

Irvel had recovered fully from her encounter with Belinda. Her bruises had faded and she was her amicable, social self. She still received weekly visits from her niece, and together they still recited the

Twenty-third Psalm and finished their visit singing "Great Is Thy Faithfulness."

The fact that Irvel's grandson had come today was especially wonderful. Irvel didn't recognize him exactly, but she enjoyed his company and was in fine form with all the visitors that filled the house.

"It's a perfect day for a party," Irvel was saying as Ashley entered her room.

Her grandson smiled. "Perfect." He was a young musician who lived two hours away. He didn't visit often, but when he did, Ashley had the sense that he cared deeply for his grandmother.

Irvel spotted Ashley, and her eyes lit up. "Hello, dear. I don't believe we've met. I'm Irvel."

"Hi, Irvel." Ashley patted the woman's hand. "I see you have your grandson here."

"My grandson?" Irvel looked startled for a moment. Then her eyes found her grandson's, and she grinned. "Oh, him. He's a handsome one, isn't he? Not like my Hank, but handsome all the same." She glanced at Ashley again. "Hank's here, isn't he?"

Hank's image smiled at Ashley from the painting she'd hung above Irvel's bed. "I believe he is."

Irvel settled deeper into her chair. "Isn't that wonderful? Such a good man."

"Yes, he is." Ashley took a step back. "I'll be out with the others if either of you needs anything."

Irvel smiled at her and then tapped her grandson's knee. She looked at him, her face knotted curiously. "Excuse me, what did you say your name was? Grant something?"

"Grandson." The young man gave Irvel's hand a tender pat. "I'm your grandson."

"That's right, Grant's son. I keep forgetting." Irvel nodded for a moment. Then she turned and pointed at Ashley. "Doesn't she have the most beautiful hair?"

Irvel's grandson blushed a bit. He was a shy type, probably not used to being put on the spot. "Yes, Grandma. She's very pretty."

The afternoon wore on, and Ashley made her way to Laura Jo's room. The scene there was more somber than in the other rooms, and Ashley's heart hurt for the aging man sitting at his mother's side.

He was a business executive with numerous responsibilities on the West Coast, yet he'd chosen this time to respond to Ashley's invitation and come see his mother. He gave Ashley a weak smile when she entered the room. "It won't be long."

Ashley nodded. The man was right. They'd been expecting Laura Jo to die for weeks now, but she was holding on. Maybe for this — the chance to be with her son one last time. Ashley thought it was possible. No matter that Laura Jo hadn't been out of bed in years. She still responded — faintly — when Ashley prayed with her, and now, with her son at her side, she seemed more peaceful than ever.

Ashley patted the man's shoulder. "It was good of you to come."

He stared at his mother and smoothed his hand across her brow. "I love her. She was a wonderful woman all my life. Strong, driven, determined to raise us right." He cast Ashley a backward glance. "She loved God very much."

"She still does." Ashley felt her heart constrict as she looked at Laura Jo, withered and shrunken, struggling for every breath.

The man looked at his watch. "I have a plane to catch late this evening in Indianapolis. I should probably get going."

Ashley nodded. "I'll leave the two of you alone so you can say good-bye."

The unspoken message was clear. This wasn't any old good-bye. It was probably the last time this man would see his mother alive. Ashley blinked back tears as she made her way into the kitchen. Ten minutes later the man found her, his eyes red and swollen. He handed Ashley a business card with several phone numbers. "Call me, will you? When it's time. I know you have most of this in your files, but you might not have my cell number. I want to make sure . . ."

Ashley promised and thanked the man again.

He met her eyes and held them. "Thank you, Ms. Baxter. I wouldn't have come if you hadn't called. Being here with her was a very great gift."

The day finally wound to an end. One by one the visitors left. The night care worker arrived, and Ashley drove to pick up Cole at her parents' house.

"How 'bout a dinner date with Mom?" She gave him a playful poke in the ribs.

"Really?" Cole hooted. "You mean like a Happy Meal?"

"Of course!"

They drove to their favorite restaurant, and after they sat down with their food, Ashley listened as he shared a dozen stories from his day.

The whole while she couldn't help but

remember Laura Jo and her son. Would there come a time when she might look into Cole's eyes and not know him? a time when she would be dying and Cole would leave his busy life to come to her side? Ashley couldn't imagine either scenario; yet working at Sunset Hills had taught her it could easily happen one day.

The phone call came long after she'd gotten home and put Cole to bed. It was Lu, and Ashley knew something was wrong the moment she heard her voice.

"What happened?" Ashley leaned against her kitchen counter and waited.

"It's Laura Jo. She passed away an hour ago."

For an instant there was a sinking feeling, as though the wind had been knocked from her. Then just as quickly Ashley felt a surge of joy. "She'll never be confined to a bed again."

"No. She's free."

Ashley told Lu where to find the card with the cell-phone number for Laura Jo's son. "He's probably halfway to L.A. by now, but he's expecting this. I'm sure he'll come back to help with the details."

When they hung up, Ashley made her way across the dining room and stared at her painting of Cole on the swing. Life was so short, so transient. Here today, making memories and keeping schedules . . . and then tomorrow, making plans for a funeral service.

Something about Laura Jo's death made her long for Landon even more than usual. His year in New York had just begun, and already it felt as though he'd fallen off the face of the earth. He hadn't called, but that didn't surprise her. He had much to learn in New York and a schedule that would keep him almost constantly on the run.

Ashley headed into the living room and flipped through a scrapbook she kept on her coffee table. Halfway through she found the picture she was looking for. It was of Landon in his uniform, holding a beaming Cole on his hip. Ashley had taken the photo one day late last summer just after Landon had started back to work. Before September 11. She and Cole had stopped by the fire station for a visit, and she'd taken her camera along.

Now she looked closely into the photo, staring at Landon's eyes. Even in the snapshot, she could see they were deep and full of goodness. Were those the eyes that would haunt her when she was old?

Her gaze moved onto Cole, her precious sunbeam. How happy he looked in

Landon's arms, how natural and right. Would the three of them ever be together?

Be with them both, God. Watch over Landon in New York. Keep your hand on my Cole as he grows. And if it's your will, please bring us back together again someday.

It was late, but there was only one thing Ashley wanted to do, one thing that could allow her to vent the feelings welling within her. She crossed over to her studio, pulled out her paints, and propped up the picture of Landon and Cole beside the easel where she could see it. Then she began to paint, creating an image of the two people she loved most with emotions that lay deeper than the Grand Canyon. With each stroke, she felt herself painting their faces across the canvas of her soul, where she could see them even decades from now.

One day — no matter what happened between them in the future — she would give this piece to Landon. She would let him know it was her best painting ever, the work she was born to create.

Not because she'd grown as an artist, but because Landon had led her back to God. And God, in all his grace and mercy, had done two very miraculous things with the events of the past year.

He'd taught her the importance of having something to remember, a saddle to shine. Then he'd done something she hadn't thought possible.

He had taught her to love again.

Those of you who journeyed with us through book one, *Redemption*, know how this series got its start. When Gary Smalley contacted me about writing fiction with him, I was thrilled.

When he said, "Think series," I went blank.

For weeks I prayed about the series idea, asking God to show me a group of plots that would best exemplify the kind of love taught and talked about by Gary Smalley and the staff at the Smalley Relationship Center.

Ideas would come, but they seemed too small for something as big and life-changing as the dream Gary and I had come to share.

Then one day I was on a flight home from Colorado Springs when God literally gave me the Redemption series — titles, plots, characters, themes, story lines. All of it poured out onto my notebook while goose bumps flashed up and down my spine.

The basic heart and direction of the series remain true to that early vision. However, as the Baxter family has come to life on the pages of these books, their problems have changed and adapted to fit their personalities, and certainly to fit the landscape of events happening around them.

We finished writing *Redemption* just about the time terrorists attacked American soil on September 11. Originally, that first book would have covered a time span that included that infamous day. Very quickly, the editors at Tyndale came together and agreed to make a change. Instead of ending in the spring of 2002, *Redemption* would end in the spring of 2001. And that set up the rich blend of tragedies and conflicts you just read about in book two, *Remember*.

What a privilege it was to write about a time that touched us all so deeply. The stories of loss and desperation that came from those events will forever be with all of us who witnessed them. Like you, I will always see the events of September 11 as clearly as I did that morning when I watched them unfold from my living-room sofa. What happened that day changed us all. It seems only right that it changed the Baxter family as well.

After Gary spent time helping people at Ground Zero, his insights and experiences opened many possibilities for our novel. Experiences with the people, places, sights, sounds, and smells of the cleanup effort in New York City. And insights into what it means to remember the important things in life.

I pray you saw the beauty of remembering at work as Kari worked through her grief and waited for God to lead her forward. Memories played a significant role in Ashley's treatment of the Alzheimer's patients and in Landon's search for his missing friend. Something beautiful and rare happens when we allow memories of days gone by to teach us lessons for today.

I hope you will take from the pages of this book one of Gary Smalley's teachings: the importance of remembering. Tuck it into your back pocket, and use it sometime soon in your own life. Certainly it will be a theme you see again as the Redemption series continues.

Some of the mysteries laid out in the first book have been solved now. You know that Kari and Ryan will marry soon and that Erin is open to working on her marriage. But what about Luke and Reagan? And what about Ashley and Landon? Will Landon ever move back to Bloomington? Will Brooke and Peter finally figure out what's been troubling their small daughter or openly embrace their rekindled beliefs?

The Baxters are people like any of us. They live by faith, but they also stumble, and sometimes they stumble hard. As I mentioned before, the Redemption series will read like many of my other novels. The characters will be flawed and their problems the same kinds you and I face, despite our belief in God. The difference is this: Although each book will stand alone as a novel to be read and enjoyed unto itself, the whole story will not be finished until the end.

Until the final book, *Reunion*.

Normally I do not leave my readers wondering what happened to the characters in a particular book. But in the case of the Redemption series there will always be some questions left unanswered, some issues unresolved until the very end. I wish I could tell you now what will become of John and Elizabeth, Kari and Ryan, Ashley and Cole, Brooke and Peter, Erin and Sam — and what will happen to Landon Blake.

But I can't.

The books that lie ahead are written on the pages of Gary's heart and mine, but they have yet to be typed across the pages of my computer screen. As they emerge, we will bring them to you.

My prayer and Gary's is that you continue to enjoy this series, and in the process that you gain a deeper understanding of what L-O-V-E really means (Listen, Offer yourself, Value and honor, and Embrace). Perhaps in riding out the next few years with the Baxters, you'll find yourself expressing that new understanding in your own relationships.

And maybe, just maybe, the Redemption series will help change the way you live together, the way you love.

I leave you with the message of *Remember:* We must remember how to love, remember what's important, and remember God's truth as it applies to our relationships. Will we make mistakes? Of course. But if you're one who's messed up a relationship, you've come to the right place.

This series is about redemption. God's redemption. The Bible says that accepting God's gift of redemption is the first step to real love. And real love is what the Redemption series is all about.

If you need to know more about the redemption God has for you, I urge you to contact a local Bible-believing church and talk to a minister — someone like Pastor Mark at Clear Creek Community Church. Then make a decision to accept God's offer of redemption while his salvation can still deeply affect your life.

Don't wait. The truth is, we may not have much time to make things right. If we ignore God's offer of redemption here and now, tomorrow we might find that it's too late. The best time to say yes to God is always today.

Thank you for traveling the pages of *Remember* with us. I hope you'll pass this book on to someone else. Then keep your eyes open for the next book in the series. The answers to some of your questions are just ahead in *Return,* book three of the Redemption series. In the meantime, may this find you walking close to God, enjoying the journey of life, and celebrating his gift of redemption.

As always, I'd love to hear from you. Please contact me at my Web site: www.KarenKingsbury.com, or write me at my e-mail address: rtnbykk@aol.com.

Blessings to you and yours, humbly,
Karen Kingsbury

A Word From Gary Smalley

Remembering is not something God takes lightly, and for obvious reasons. The very core of operating as a Christian is to "remember your first love" — God Almighty — and to remember what's important according to God's truth. If we don't remember these things, we leave ourselves open to the top two most destructive forces at work in relationships today: pride and fear. These attitudes and emotions destroy bonds of trust, intimacy, and love, and they fly in the face of all the Lord has for us in our relationships.

Still, there are times when we are either too busy to remember or too jaded to believe in the past. The following is a brief list of six practical ways you can incorporate the ability to remember into your relationships today.

SIX WAYS TO REMEMBER

1. *Remember the important things in life.* The more time passes, the busier we get. Isn't that true? Our list of bills and expenses and unfinished projects grows longer with each year. Make a point of having "remember days," either alone or with someone you love. This may be a spouse or a parent, a sibling or a child — even a friend. Take a walk or a drive, plan a quiet hour over coffee, and reflect on the essentials, the things that are truly necessary for your relationship to work. During this time, make a list, and take a hard look at it. How much time do you spend each day on things that don't even make the list?

2. *Remember your shared faith.* We often begin our relationships in a flurry of promises — of shared prayer time, church attendance, and Bible study. Walk back through your past, and see if this was the case with the person you love. If so, are you still sharing your beliefs this way? God wants us to remember our first love — both in our relationship with him and in our relationships with each other. In both cases, the bond that builds lasting rela-

tionships is none other than Jesus Christ.

3. *Remember how your relationship started.* Think back to the time when your relationship first began. Look at photos or videotapes of your early days together. Whether this is a marriage or a relationship with a parent or child, your decision to walk down memory lane and admire the foundation of your love will always be an important one.

4. *Remember what you first liked about that person.* Take an hour or an afternoon, and write a list of the character traits, personality quirks, and attributes that helped build your relationship with this person. Perhaps these are details that still apply. Or maybe the busyness of life and the burden of various troubles have buried the traits you liked most in the person you love. Examine the list closely. Are you still looking for these things in that person?

5. *Remember the good times you shared together.* Photographs and scrapbooks have a way of triggering a series of memories. Force yourself to think back on the happy times together. Again, this might be the time you and your five-year-old took walks each evening. Or it

might be the time you and your partner first began to date. Either way, make a list of how the two of you interacted during a time when things between you were at their best. These remembered thoughts will go a long way toward replacing the sometimes troubled thoughts of that same relationship today.

6. *Remember lessons from your past.* If you've walked as a believer for very long, you know that troubles have a way of coming and going. Jesus told us that in this world we would have trouble, but not to worry: He's already overcome the world (John 16:33, my paraphrase). Obviously, remembering that single bit of truth will go a long way toward helping you let go of today's troubles. In addition, though, remember the way God has delivered you from your past troubles. He who was faithful to do that will also be faithful to deliver you through whatever relationship troubles you might currently be experiencing.

Remember shows the importance of working on our relationships through the use of our memories — not just in our marriages but also in the special bonds we share with our children and parents, our siblings and friends.

If you or someone you love needs counseling or other resources to improve a key relationship, I urge you to contact us at:

The Smalley Relationship Center
1482 Lakeshore Drive
Branson, MO 65616

Phone: (800) 84-TODAY (848-6329)
FAX: (417) 336-3515
E-mail: family@smalleyonline.com
Web site: www.smalleyonline.com

DISCUSSION QUESTIONS

Use these questions for individual reflection or for discussion with a book club or other small group. They will help you not only understand some of the issues in *Remember* but also integrate some of the book's messages into your own relationships.

1. Before September 11, in what way did Landon Blake's memories play a part in his decision to take a job in New York City? Explain.
2. As helpful as remembering can be,

painful memories can actually stand in the way of healthy relationships. How was this the case in Ashley Baxter's relationship with Landon? with her family?

3. Explain Ashley's goal in taking a job at Sunset Hills Adult Care Home.

4. How did Kari's memory play a part in her healing after the death of her husband? In what way do you think remembering may have helped Ryan Taylor during this time?

5. After working at Sunset Hills for several weeks, Ashley began to discover something about the memories of the Alzheimer's patients she worked with. What did she discover?

6. Describe the Past-Present ideas Ashley found on the Internet. How did this help her make the residents at Sunset Hills calmer and happier?

7. How did Ashley's work at Sunset Hills affect her personal life? What did it make her feel about her own memories?

8. When Ashley shares the painful memories of her time in Paris, what does Landon remind her? How does this, in turn, change Ashley's life?

9. After September 11, when Landon

goes to New York to work at Ground Zero, what do you think drove him to work nearly eighty straight days?

10. How does Kari use the importance of remembering to help Erin in her marriage?

11. What can you learn from the happy memories in your life when it comes to your relationships? What can you learn from the darker memories?

12. Throughout the Scriptures God asks his people to remember certain things. Why do you think remembering is so important to God? How would your faith grow if you were to remember in the ways suggested in the passages below?

"And remember these instructions when the Lord brings you into the land he swore to give your ancestors long ago, the land where the Canaanites are now living." (Exodus 13:11, NLT)

"Remember your Creator now while you are young." (Ecclesiastes 12:6, NLT)

"Remember what I told you: I am going away, but I will come back to you again." (John 14:28, NLT)

"You should remember the words

of the Lord Jesus . . ." (Acts 20:35, NLT).

13. Describe a relationship you would like to see improved. What are the problems, the conflicts? How would your ability to remember possibly improve that relationship? Detail a plan based on the suggestions in the previous section.

14. Purchase a "memory journal" — any lined notebook will do. Jot down important memories from your past and the lessons you learned — or can still learn — from them.

15. What role did forgiveness play in Ashley's relationships to Landon? God? herself? Luke? Kari?

16. In what ways would you find freedom and peace if you were to seek forgiveness from God and others? In what ways would you experience freedom and peace if you were to extend forgiveness to others — including yourself?

17. How did the redemption theme — the overall theme of the series — reveal itself in this book? In whose lives did you see redemption at work?

18. In what ways does your life need redemption? How will you find it?

19. Whose relationships were marked by honor? In what specific ways did the
20. characters show honor?

How are you currently showing honor in your relationships? How would you like to grow in that area? How will you accomplish that?